The Shield of Masl

Also published by New Guild

S.O.S. - Men Against the Sea
Elvis in Wonderland
Privy to the Mayor's Council/The Helper
(a two-story anthology)
Melody for Lizzie
Rainy Days and Mondays
Charlatan
A Child of Silence
Attack and Sink
The Fourth Service

Dedication

I have written this book with many spirits from the 'Land of Shadow' peering over my shoulder:

Mashona, who kept me 'within his armpit' while I was a child;

my 'brothers-in-arms', Taffy, Spud and Indabushe, who lie buried in the soil of a foreign country; and

Numbela, who also died before her time.

'Ngibongile kakhulu – I have praised you greatly.

'Ngiyanibonga futhi ngitusa enithe nangenzela khona –
I praise you all and applaud you for what you have done for me.

'Salani kahle!' – Remain gently.

THE SHIELD OF
MASHONA

Bill Russell

NEW
GUILD

A New Guild Book

Published by New Era Writer's Guild (UK) Ltd
5 Cogdean Walk, Corfe Mullen
Wimborne Minster, Dorset BH21 3XB

PO Box 11476
Bloubergrant 7443, South African
Tel: (+21) 557 6281
Fax (+21) 557 0704

PO Box 100 806
North Shore Mail Centre
Auckland 10, New Zealand
Tel/Fax: (+9) 443 8069

British Library Cataloguing in Publication Data. A catalogue record for
this book is available from the British Libary

ISBN 1 899694 25 0

This book was designed and produced by
Crispin Goodall Design Ltd
463 Ashley Road
Poole, Dorset BH14 OAX

Printed the United Kingdom by Warwick Printing Company Ltd

Any reference to persons living or dead is purely coincidental.

Forward

People may have forgotten – or were never told – about the heroic involvement of an army of South African volunteers who fought many desperate battles in the forefront of the Allied Forces during World War II.

They played a decisive role in forcing the vastly superior Italian army to abandon its African Empire and in thwarting Field Marshal Rommel's armoured columns from capturing the Suez Canal and throttling Great Britain's sea supply routes.

They fought and died at the tip of the Allied British 8th and American 5th Armies in the fanatically contested advance up the length of Italy, opposed by elite units of the German army. The regiment in which the author served won no less than 12 Battle Honours during that campaign and it suffered the appalling loss of 145 men killed in action and 15 who died of disease – of those who survived, many were wounded, some of them twice or even three times.

> They shall not grow old,
> As we who are left grow old.
> Age shall not weary them,
> Nor the years condemn.
> At the going down of the sun,
> And in the morning,
> We will remember them.

Prayer of the Memorable Order of Tin Hats

Author's Acknowledgement

Without the unstinting support of Alannah Evans and the innovative enterprise of New Guild, this book would still be lying in the box in which it lay for 20 years.

Chapter 1

It was the witchdoctor's interpretation of his disturbing dream that had brought old Mashona to the home of his young Lord Mabonca – Hamish MacTavish.

He had dreamed of war as he so often did nowadays. In his dream he stood in the forefront of the battle, adorned with the regalia of as illustrious a regiment as any that had ever come from the wild hills of Zululand. The dream itself was simple enough. Amidst the clang and thrust of blades and the roars and grunts of sweating fighters, he had covered the back of his comrade with his wide oxhide shield.

But then the dream confused him. Standing among the corpses when the battle was done, he saw that the comrade his shield had covered was an infant. A white infant. And the only white boy-child he knew of, but had not yet seen, was the newborn son of his Lord Mabonca – Hamish MacTavish.

For the fee of an unblemished white goat, Maseko the witchdoctor had divined from the scattered bones and charms the meaning of the dream that had perplexed him.

He, Mashona the Bankrupt, son of Nongwazi, had been charged by the "amadlozi", the spirits of the Zulu ancestors, to cover the white child with his shield. The infant itself was to give him a sign if it was, in fact, the child of his dream.

His thoughts were interrupted by the child's mother who came into the kitchen to greet him. Although he returned the greetings and answered the polite questions of his Lady Uvemvane – Marion MacTavish – his mind was still fixed on her infant son.

He drew the corner of his faded red calico loincloth modestly between his legs and squatted beside the wood stove. The mist had chilled him and the fire-warmed bricks were comforting against the age-wrinkled skin of his naked back.

To gain a moment to compose himself, he withdrew the brass cartridge containing his snuff from the slit in the lobe of his ear. Pouring a little mound of bitter aloe onto the heel of his hand and closing each nostril in turn with the pressure of a finger, he snuffled noisily. He wiped the rheum from his nose with his hand and rubbed his hand on his thatch of ochre-stained hair.

He glanced furtively at the baby son of his Lord Mabonca, cradled in the arms of the Lady Uvemvane, then his eyes slid away from the child. It was unseemly for a man to look upon an infant so young, for, until the two teeth of the child had appeared in the gums of the lower jaw, a child was considered an intimate part of the woman who had borne him. Nor, until the teeth appeared, could a child be considered a person.

His head nodded agreement with his thoughts, for little doubt remained in his mind. Though he had only studied the infant hurriedly, he felt it was definitely the one he had seen in his dream and he wondered how one so young would be able to give him any sign of recognition.

A shudder of shock passed through Mashona's gaunt body. He had not noticed the child move in its mother's arms, yet its eyes were fixed on him and it almost seemed as if the child knew his thoughts. Was it possible for an infant to understand there was a bond between them? Could an infant also have a vision?

The child looked away from him as if aware that it was unseemly for any man to acknowledge its existence before the sprouting of the teeth. Mashona's eyes were drawn to the window the infant was staring at with such concentration and again he felt a shock of surprise. There was a fly on the window. One single fly. And this child of his vision had not only seen the fly, he was watching it intently.

"By our sister! This is an omen," he breathed to himself. If ever a man needed confirmation from the spirits, surely this was it? No ordinary infant could possibly notice any creature as small as a fly on a windowpane across the width of a room. Yet this child was watching the fly as a scout watches the movements of the enemy. Excitement tingled in the old warrior's blood.

Only the eyes of the child moved, while its hands and entire body were motionless. Its eyes turned away from the window and looked again into his for a fleeting moment, before looking back at the fly on the windowpane.

"Habe!" Mashona's fingers covered his gaping lips. This was indeed an omen. The spirit of the child had warned it that it was being watched, even as it watched the fly. Here was a wonder! The spirit of this infant had told it to turn and lead his own eyes to see that which it was watching. This little one of his dream was aware of the tie which the spirits of the ancestors had created between them.

Even in its infancy this child knew that he, Mashona the Bankrupt, son of Nongwazi, had been instructed by the amadlozi to cover its back. So be it! The purpose of the vision which had bewildered him was now clear in his mind. Who better than he, himself, could the spirits have found to hold this son of his Lord Mabonca MacTavish safely within his armpit.

He would instruct this child in the arts of war and he would nurture the gifts of observance the spirits had bestowed upon the child, and the child's cunning would grow to exceed that of all his enemies. He,

Mashona the Bankrupt, would hold his shield over the back of this favoured child in the future battles which the spirits could foresee.

The old warrior rose to go. He was in a hurry to leave the presence of the child which custom would not allow him to look at. He raised his open right hand above his ear in salute to the Lady Uvemvane. There was a gleam of purpose in his fierce old eyes.

He would return when the teeth of the child stood up from the gums like the tusks of a young bull hippopotamus. Then the child would no longer be considered an intimate part of his mother and he would be able to 'see' him and name him according to custom.

Hidden by the mist, he turned at the gateway to face the house. He balanced his wide-bladed stabbing spear in his right hand. In his left hand he held his tall war shield and a throwing javelin. Lifting his shield above his head, he saluted the house that contained the child which had been entrusted to him by the amadlozi. Then he turned and strode away into the swirling mist, no longer feeling the nip of the cold.

Mashona paused at the corner of the house. For a few moments he stood watching his Lady, Uvemvane MacTavish, and the child of his vision. She was watering a border of flowers while a cloud of butterflies sipped the wet blossoms. The child, which custom had forbidden him to visit until he had cut his first teeth, sat on the lawn beside her.

The child sat strangely motionless as he watched the butterflies and Mashona noticed that he was not merely looking at the butterflies. He was watching one particular yellow butterfly. The old warrior stalked across the lawn to see what had captured the child's interest. His bare feet made no sound on the soft grass as he moved silently forward to see if there was something about the butterfly the child was studying which set it apart from the others.

As he approached, the butterfly fluttered higher and disappeared over the top of the hedge. The child watched it go and then turned his head suddenly, as though he had known all along that Mashona was there behind him. His sudden movement unbalanced him but for an instant the two little teeth showed in his smile before he toppled over on the grass.

Mashona knew the infant could not have heard his footfall on the soft grass, nor could it have smelt his body smell, for the breeze was from the child towards himself. Yet the spirits had warned the child of his approach. The child had known that he was there behind him! Mashona was excited. If there had ever been any doubt concerning the name which he and his counsellors had decided to give this child, its actions had removed that doubt.

Mashona was smiling with satisfaction when Marion MacTavish put down her hose and turned to right her baby son. She was surprised to see Mashona standing there and felt a chill of apprehension to see him dressed for war.

He carried his black oxhide shield and wore a black necklace made from a cow's tail around his neck. His upper arms and lower legs were adorned with the tail brushes of black cows, and on his head a bunch of long black tail feathers from Sakabula widow finches wafted in the light breeze.

He raised his shield and spears in salute. "Chieftainess Uvemvane, I, Mashona the Bankrupt, son of Nongwazi, have come to see your child. I have come to greet the little warrior who has shown his teeth to the people."

Marion scooped her little Peter into her arms and held him possessively to her bosom as though to protect him from some unknown danger. She was aware of the significance of Mashona's visit and why he was dressed for war.

Though she was borne of a Scottish father and a Scottish mother, at heart Marion MacTavish was as much a Zulu as the gaunt old warrior who was some forty years older than herself. Both she and Mashona had grown up in the heartland of the Zulu people and their earliest days were steeped in Zulu lore. The seal of their friendship was their common bondage as exiles in this land of the Swazis, and her ability to speak fluent Zulu.

She had left Zululand because of her marriage to Hamish MacTavish. Mashona had fled to Swaziland as a fugitive from the retribution of his King, Cetshwayo. In the after-battle purification ceremony of the 'wiping of the axe', Mashona and the sweetheart of his youth, Mbaiyita, had lost their caution and indulged in full intercourse, where only the 'coming on the thighs' was permitted. And from that brief, exquisite 'wiping of the axe', Mbaiyita, favoured daughter of the Zulu King, had conceived.

Marion understood that Mashona's announcement that he had come to 'see' her child meant that her infant son was no longer exclusively hers. Now that his two teeth were in his mouth, he could be seen by the people and Mashona had come to name him as an individual person. And it was the thought of the naming that frightened her. Instinctively, she recoiled from the knowledge that somehow, in the naming, her child was about to be taken away from her.

To Marion it seemed as if she no longer existed. She could see that Mashona's attention was fixed on her child. He held up his war shield and his wide-bladed stabbing spear in salute to her son.

"I see you, little Chief. Son of the Lord Mabonca, Grandson of Mabobmo MacTavish. I see you!" Mashona greeted the child. "Mashona the Bankrupt, Son of Nongwazi, greets Isinkwe. Isinkwe, I have praised you," he said.

Hugging her little son, Marrion had a hollow feeling that in some way Mashona's greetings had taken him from her arms.

Posturing before the child, Mashona commenced stamping his feet in an old man's imitation of the wild war dance – the 'giya' of a warrior. He hissed through his teeth and stamped towards the child, the cow-tail fringes on his legs whipping up and down as he advanced. The broad blade of his stabbing spear, the Seeker, jabbed left and right into the imaginary enemies of the child Peter, whom he had named Isinkwe.

Marion clutched Peter tightly and turned away from the old warrior. "No! Father Mashona, stop it! You will frighten the child out of his wits."

Mashona halted and leaned grinning on his shield, panting a little from the exertion of his war dance. "The teeth of the child shine, Uvemvane! He is unafraid. He laughs! Observe, Uvemvane! The young warrior has no fear of the old warrior who salutes him. He is unafraid of the fate for which the spirits of the amadlozi have fashioned him." His voice rang with approval.

"Fear not, Uvemvane. This one was born favoured by the spirits who were themselves warriors before they departed into the land of shadow. In the armies of his King, the brother warriors of this Isinkwe will praise him. His name will be shouted with honour around the cooking fires, when the warriors gather to eat the meat of the cattle of those they have vanquished.

"Have no fear, Chieftainess Uvemvane. The amadlozi have appointed me to keep this child within my armpit, while he learns and grows up to fulfil his destiny as the eyes of the armies of his King. He will be the scout of scouts." Mashona peered left and right with widely dilated eyes, miming the questing eyes of a scout.

To Marion, the thought of another war was preposterous. There could be no more wars, she assured herself. Only four years had passed since the end of "the war to end all wars". Germany had been convincingly defeated and the whole world was at peace.

She felt a little silly about being afraid of the prophecies of her old friend, Mashona, and smiled at him uncertainly. There could be no harm in indulging the old warrior a little, knowing that in his care, nothing could ever harm her child.

"Father Mashona can teach my son," she held Peter up so Mashona could see him properly, "but there can be no more wars, my Father. My child will grow in peace!" She said the words more to convince herself than to convince the old warrior.

Mashona's eyes hardened, and he shook his head. "There can be no peace, Uvemvane! The elders of our people advised King George to destroy the Germans utterly. They counselled the King of the English to burn down all the kraals of the Germans.

"They advised King George to kill every man and boy of them and to fill the bellies of every woman with the sons of Englishmen, as we ourselves would have done. But subjects do not question the decisions of kings. I tell you, Uvemvane, that even now, there is a new generation of young German warriors weaned from their mothers' breasts and the milk that nurtured them was bitter with the taste of revenge."

Marion hugged Peter to her bosom and stepped back involuntarily from the ferocity in Mashona's eyes.

"Have no fear, Uvemvane! While I live, I will prepare him for the battles he will fight. And when my spirit has gone to abide with the amadlozi in the land of shadow, it will be ever near to guard over this little one.

"This has been foreordained, Uvemvane! It was manifested to me in a vision. Where the footsteps of this young warrior lead, my spirit will follow and he will walk in the shadow of my shield."

Mashona stepped towards Marion and held his shield up over Peter's head as though to protect him from a shower of spears. The sour smell of the old warrior's sweat and that of his rawhide shield comforted her strangely. They were the never-to-be-forgotten smells of her own happy childhood, sheltered among the Zulu people whom she had loved.

"'Yebo'! Yes, Isinkwe! Little chief! Young warrior of the King. You will defeat the Germans again, as your father did before you. But when you fight them, the fight will be more difficult, because the Germans will not risk a second defeat. They will not make war until they are certain of victory. But I will instruct you how to fight them, even as the amadlozi have willed it."

He laid his shield on the grass at his feet and placed his spears beside it, then held his arms out for the child. Little white arms reached out and Peter passed from the fragrance of his mother into the sweat and fat-anointed embrace of the old warrior.

Peter looked past the red mottled scar of the old bayonet wound puckering the side of Mashona's face, from that bloody battle in the night at Rorke's Drift, forty-three years previously. The gold-brown eyes of the infant looked through the dark eyes of the man and contemplated the soul within him. And in the soul of the man the child found what he wanted and he leaned forward and hugged the old man's scarred face.

Then he leaned back and, still gazing into Mashona's eyes, his hand reached for the cartridge snuff container in the slit in Mashona's ear lobe.

"Behold Uvemvane, the choice of your son!" Mashona's voice was hushed with awe. "The prettiness of the beads that adorn my neck are not to his liking. See! His hands reach for the things which are of men, who themselves are warriors." He turned his head to bring his ear lobe within reach of the child's groping fingers and winced as the child tugged sharply.

"Father Mashona, you have praised my son with the name Isinkwe. Could it be that my Father means isinkwe, the little bush-baby?" She was perplexed and hurt. Of all the praise names Mashona and his counsellors could have chosen, they had named her only son after one of the least significant of all creatures.

Mashona ignored her interruption and continued as though she had not spoken. "The eyes of this child are large and round and it has been observed when the evening comes and the sun has gone, that the black pupils of his eyes grow until none of the brown iris can be seen. It is thus too with the bush-baby that sees in the dark."

Marion craned forward to examine her son's eyes as though she had never noticed them before.

"Uvemvane, it has also been observed that this child does not cry in the darkness until he feels the warmth of the arms that lift him up to comfort him. His cries stop when he sees his mother in the doorway of the room. Is it not so?"

Marion nodded her head. What Mashona said was true. No matter how quietly she came to him in the dark, Peter always stopped crying when she entered his room. He seemed to sense her presence. The notion that he could see her had never occurred to her.

Peter's gaze was still fixed on Mashona's eyes. The chubby hand still held the cartridge case in the lobe of Mashona's ear. "Observe how still the child is as he watches me, Uvemvane. Like the bush-baby, his body is all eyes. He does not look to direct his fingers to the bullet in my ear, because his eyes have told his hands where to find the bullet. Behold! The eyes of the child do not blink while he watches." A gratified smile deepened the creases in Mashona's face.

"It is not only with his eyes that this little Isinkwe watches. He watches with his whole body. While his eyes watch, his ears watch too. He is aware of the smell of the things around him and of the sounds they make. He is aware of the feel of the thing in his hand. I tell you, Uvemvane, there can be no doubt of the intentions of the spirits, when they chose this one for a scout, and heaped upon him all their gifts."

Mashona's conviction filled Marion with a sense of awe. She had the ridiculous feeling that the child she was watching belonged to somebody else and she was seeing him for the first time.

"Uvemvane, this child is aware of everything surrounding that which he is watching. He is also aware of the eyes that watch him, even though they be behind him. By our sister! Uvemvane, this one is as watchful as the bush-baby. He will see what others fail to see and he will

13

hear when others hear nothing.

"This one is like the isinkwe, hidden in the leaves of a tree. He cannot be seen himself, but he is aware of every other creature moving in the darkness on the forest floor beneath him. He will hear them and he will see them and he will smell them. And while he sleeps his spirit will warn him of their presence.

"These are the gifts of the spirits, Uvemvane. It remains only for me to instruct him in the use of them, and to cover his back, so the gifts of the spirits are not wasted on one who is dead."

Marion began to speak, but Mashona's uplifted hand cautioned her to silence.

"Watch, Uvemvane, Isinkwe's hand has learned the feel of the bullet and he will now wish to know the taste of it." Withdrawing the bullet from the lobe of his ear and wiping it with the corner of his loincloth, Mashona held it up for Peter to take. The child took the bullet unerringly, without moving his gaze from Mashona's eyes.

He lifted the cartridge case to his mouth and a trickle of saliva dribbled down his chin. Marion took a handkerchief from her sleeve to wipe it away.

"Let it be, Uvemvane. The mouth of a teething child must run with saliva to keep the gums soft for the sprouting of the teeth, even as the rain softens the soil for the sprouting of seeds. Cubs of lions temper their teeth on the bones they chew, for their teeth are their weapons. This one chews a bullet. So be it, his choice is the choice of a warrior."

Marion's heart rebelled. Little bush-baby indeed! Her son would grow tall like his father. "Father Mashona is mistaken." Her voice was defiant. "When my child has grown to manhood he will be renamed, because a big man who is named after such a small animal will bring scorn on those who named him."

"Chieftainess, there can be no mistake. This child has been studied by the women who have visited the household of Uvemvane. In the fondling of this child they have examined every bone in his body. He is not like the puppy of a big dog with loose skin and over-large feet." He held Peter up for her to have a good look.

"The skin of Isinkwe fits his body. His hands and his feet are also in accordance with his size. His wrists and his ankles are neat and strong. There is no part of this child that will grow large and clumsy." He spoke with the patient tone of an adult explaining something to an uncomprehending child.

"The wisdom of the spirits is very great, Uvemvane. They would not bestow upon the scout of their own choosing the body of an ox. This one will not grow to be a buffalo. By our sister, Uvemvane, this little 'inxele' will be a neat man."

"Inxele!" the word exploded from Marion's lips. She stared at

Mashona aghast. "Inxele! Is my Father saying that my child is left-hand-ed?" Her voice was horrified. She stared at the saliva-slimed little left hand holding the cartridge case to his mouth.

Mashona looked at her surprised. "Does Uvemvane tell me she does not know her child is left-handed?"

"He is only a baby!" Marion protested, "how can anybody say at this age, if a child is left-handed or right-handed?" She reached out to take Peter away from him, but the old man half turned from her and seat-ed the child on his shield on the grass.

Peter fingered the short hairs on the oxhide shield and looked up at Mashona with a two-toothed smile of delight. Mashona held a cau-tioning hand up towards Marion, his attention riveted on the child. Peter leaned forward and beat the shield with his open hands.

"Observe, Uvemvane," Mashona whispered. "The left hand is quick-er than the right." Peter stopped beating the shield. He reached for the broad-bladed Seeker lying on the grass beside the shield. He reached with his left hand. Mashona shouted with delight. "The war-rior reaches for the stabbing spear. Umhlolo! It is an omen! When he is grown to be a man, this one will choose to fight his enemies at close quarters. Watch, Uvemvane! He now wishes to test the weight and the balance of the Seeker."

Like an eagle snatching a hare, Marion scooped Peter up and hugged him protectively. "He will not be a warrior!" Her voice was defi-ant. "He is not left-handed! He is not a little isinkwe that can see in the dark! He will grow big! He is not a dwarf!"

The look of horror on Mashona's face cut off her indignant words. He covered his bowed head to ward off evil. "Hau! Hau! Hau! Hau! – Maye babo! Maye babo!" he wailed in anguish. His arms pressed down on his bowed head and he crouched as if in pain. "Dwarf? – Umvevane! – No one spoke of any dwarf!"

"Do not say the word! Oh my Father! – Oh my Mother! Uvemvane, we did not speak of any such calamity!" He rose and his patting hands fluttered reassuringly over the child. "Chieftainess, this child of your womb is no dwarf! His body is without fault. His bones are correct. He will grow perfectly, Uvemvane! It is only that the spirits of past warriors have fashioned him to their purpose." Stooping, he picked up his two spears and held out the Seeker for Marion to see.

"Consider, Uvemvane, the fashioning of this spear. It is for close fighting, my Chieftainess. It is short. It is strong. And the blade is wide, to make a river for the blood of its enemies to gush forth and bring death swiftly." He spoke in shocked, hurried tones, then he dropped the Seeker and held out the slender throwing javelin. "Behold the Falcon, Uvemvane. It has been fashioned long and slender for a dif-ferent purpose. It must streak through the air to stoop as the falcon stoops, into the uncovered backs of those who flee from the blade of the Seeker.

"Each to its own purpose, Uvemvane. Even so with this child. The spirits would not choose an elephant for a scout, when they could choose the eyes and the stealth of a bush-baby." He put the spear down and raised his open hands, pleading for her understanding.

"The left-handedness too, is of their choosing. It is not uncommon among people, nor is it uncommon among animals. In every herd of elephants there is always one whose left tusk is blunt and worn from use, and even so among other wild creatures and cattle also.

"A child who is born left-handed is fortunate, Uvemvane. He can be taught to be ambidextrous unlike one who is born right-handed – he remains right-handed and his left hand remains stupid until the day of his death.

"I knew a man well, who was left-handed. He was my comrade in the battles of my youth. He too was neat of body. A great fighter, Uvemvane!" His words tripped over one another in his hurry to mollify her. "At the instant of striking, he would change hands with his stabbing spear, and where his enemy parried a thrust from the right, that thrust came from the left. Many men stood in the instant of death, with that left thrust spear stuck through their ribs and a look of surprise in their dying eyes.

"Uvemvane must not coddle this child. He must run naked like the children of my own people. Then, when he is grown, the skin of his body will be as the skin of Uvemvane's face, which feels neither heat nor cold, for it has never worn clothing. Then, when he goes out against the enemies of the King and finds no shelter from either rain or sun, he will not suffer as the others who have grown up with clothing to cover them."

Mashona's parting salute was directed more at the child than at the child's mother. He feared her unexpected resistance to his intentions. So be it! His duty was clear enough. One did not weigh the purpose of the spirits against the whims of a woman, even if that woman was the mother of his ward.

Chapter 2

Marion's eyes were etched with worry as she watched the gaunt old warrior stride purposefully into the distance. For a long while she stood quite still. A thoughtful frown creased her forehead.

Yes, she mused, it was uncanny how the old Zulus chose a name for a person. At least now she understood why Mashona's wives had visited so often and taken such an interest in Peter. They had been sent by Mashona to examine every single detail about her infant son.

The Zulus of her childhood had named her Uvemvane when she was small. Uvemvane, the butterfly. Somehow, by the time she had cut her own two teeth they had divined the love of flowers that would develop in her as she grew older.

They chose the inevitable name. They had named her husband Mabonca, a person who is carefully groomed. And so he grew up to be. Not only groomed in appearance, but meticulous in mind and in everything he did. Even to the point of intolerance of those whose behaviour did not conform with the standards he expected of them.

She marvelled at their ability to choose names when the children were so young. Yet they were never wrong. Each child grew and developed to suit the name of its infancy. The name they gave a child was the exposed gem when the dross of characteristic complexities had been winnowed away. It was the nucleus of the child's psyche. One did not think of a person in any particular way until one heard the Zulu name which had been given. Then suddenly one became startlingly aware of the individuality of that person.

And now, Isinkwe. The bush-baby. Marion nodded her head thoughtfully. Her mind was full of speculation. From this moment her child would be known as Isinkwe, throughout the land. He would be called Isinkwe by his playmates, for everybody spoke the language of the land.

Long after Mashona had disappeared behind the distant trees she stared after him with a dawning sense of expectancy. She stood as still as the child in her arms, sharply aware of her surroundings. This was a new sensation which excited her senses.

Her mind identified the different small sounds she could hear. She picked out the different scents wafting to her nostrils. A flying grasshopper whirred past her and, with her new awareness, she followed its flight to where it alighted in the grass. Every object she could see was crisply defined and it seemed as though Mashona's words had lifted a veil from her mind. Even her thoughts had a new clarity.

She squeezed Peter into the hollow of her shoulder. His body yielded but his neck craned upwards so he could see over her shoulder. She turned her head to discover what had captured his interest and she saw his round-eyed gaze was fixed on a thrush which had alighted at the edge of the lawn, where it worried at a runner of grass sheltering the grasshopper she had heard alighting.

She held the child away from her shoulder but his eyes remained fixed on the bird. His body was rigid with concentration and the little hand resting on her arm was motionless. He was totally absorbed in the drama he was watching. Every fibre in his small body was concentrated on the efforts of the thrush to dislodge the grasshopper. The bird tugged aside the runner of grass and its beak stabbed forward like Mashona's Seeker, to pluck the grasshopper from its hiding place. The orange membranes beneath the grasshopper's wings fluttered on either side of the bird's beak as it flew up into the foliage of the plum tree.

Marion felt Peter's tremor of excitement. He remained motionless and only his eyes moved. They followed the bird's flight to the spot where it had disappeared into the foliage and remained fixed on that spot. For several moments she watched his unblinking eyes. Sunlight gave them depth. She noticed that the pupils, contracted by the glare, still seemed larger than they should have been. As she turned to get the sun out of his eyes, he turned too. Not for one second did his gaze move from the spot where the bird had flown into the canopy of the tree.

"Isinkwe, my little son," she whispered, "I thought I knew every pore of your body. Why had I not noticed before?" She walked back to the house pensively. It seemed to her that this child in her arms was not the same child she had lifted up so proudly to greet Mashona such a short while ago. Isinkwe! Had the name changed her child in some magical way? Or had the signs always been there and she had not seen them? It seemed to her an age had passed and something new had come into her life.

She stopped at the door of the house. The child was still staring at the plum tree. Then his head turned quickly and the brown eyes that looked at her sparkled with the joy of a secret shared, and he smiled at her. Her breath caught in her throat. So it was true! All along, her little Isinkwe had been aware that she was watching him.

"Uvemvane, I did not name this child. Every child manifests its own name," Mashona had said. "I only proclaimed his name." Yes, my old Zulu friend, Mashona, you were right! You were very, very right! Isinkwe, the bush-baby! Observant, efficient little hunter.

Dew drops on the leaves of the fruit trees sparkled in the flat rays of the rising sun. Marion felt a little guilty about having such a small child out in the garden so early in the morning, but this was the best time to catch cutworms killing off her young vegetable plants. Besides, she was worried. She had not spoken to Hamish about Mashona's visit of the previous afternoon. She needed to have her child to herself for a while longer to study him more closely. She also felt a bit guilty about the way she had treated Mashona. Perhaps it wouldn't do any harm if she did allow him to "keep Isinkwe in his armpit" for a while. At least Peter would be safe under Mashona's watchful eye, even if he was far too young to understand any of the things the old man wanted to teach him.

Preoccupied with her thoughts as she examined the young plants for signs of wilting, she was unaware of Mashona's approach. The child beside her sensed his presence. He turned his head and looked up at Mashona, but it was a fleeting glance because he was intent on watching what his mother was doing. Mashona watched the child without moving. His eyes showed the satisfaction he felt at having failed to approach the infant unnoticed, and he knew he had named him well.

Marion bent over a wilted plant. Beside the base of the stem there was a little round hole in the soil, indicating the presence of a cutworm. She lifted the plant out with her trowel and placed it in the pathway between the beds. Carefully spreading the soil clinging to the roots of the plant, she exposed the charcoal grey body of a curled up cutworm.

She looked up at Peter to show him the cutworm and was startled to see Mashona standing behind him. It also surprised her that Peter had already noticed the curled up worm. He was leaning forward, watching it intently, his little body as rigid as the body of a pointer dog over a covey of partridges. Mashona placed his fingers over his lips to indicate silence and while the child watched the worm they watched the child.

After a few moments the worm felt safe enough to move. It uncurled from its death sham and began to hump across the ground towards the cover of the plants. Peter's head jerked up. He smiled a two-toothed smile at his mother, then he turned his head to include Mashona. It was a smile acknowledging the fact that the three of them together had witnessed something unique, a silent appreciation of the comradeship they had shared in the successful hunt for the worm.

Mashona shook his head in wonder. "Uvemvane, this child is but an infant, yet the spirit within him is the spirit of some great hunter. I say it is the spirit of a great hunter, because only the wisest hunters are aware they too are being watched, while they watch that which they hunt."

Lifting Peter up in his sinewy arms, he said: "Come, Isinkwe, my child. This garden of your mother, the Lady Uvemvane, contains many things to see and to learn from. There are creatures which are hunted and there are those which hunt them. Together we will study their ways and from them we will learn wisdom. We will observe their cunning and their caution, which reward them with food, and their moments of carelessness, which reward them with death."

During the weeks that followed, Marion's heart warmed to the joy that lit up Peter's eyes whenever he saw Mashona approaching and the way in which he lifted his arms for the old warrior to take him. She worried a little about what Hamish would say if he knew of the growing bond between them. She guessed he would disapprove, because it was contrary to his own staid conventionalism. Hamish had not been named Mabonca for nothing. She consoled herself with the knowledge that her child was completely safe while he was with Mashona and that nothing dare harm him, because the watchful old Zulu was always armed and alert.

By the time Peter was two, Marion had become increasingly anxious about the lack of any suitable child to be a companion for him. Then one morning Mashona arrived holding the hand of a shy, brown-skinned boy, about five years older than Peter. Marion was struck by the lightness of the child's brown skin and by his bright, intelligent eyes.

"This child is my grandson, Uvemvane. His name is Indabushe, the lynx. Like the lynx, Indabushe is stealthy and unobtrusive. And as the eyes of a lynx search in the darkness of the night for food, the eyes in the mind of this child search for wisdom.

"Uvemvane, it is not good that Isinkwe should grow up without an older companion. Every young child needs an older child to help him and to teach him and to care for him. Therefore I have brought Indabushe."

Marion liked the look of the child, but she wondered what Hamish would say about this little lynx being his son's companion. Mashona misinterpreted the reason for the doubt in her eyes and he spoke quickly to dispel her misgivings.

"Have no fear, Uvemvane. I have given much thought to this matter of a companion for your son. His other Grandfather was John Dunn, the Scotsman, friend and confidant of the great King, Cetshwayo. His mother is a daughter of my household. He has the same Scottish blood as our Lord Mabonca, and through him, his son, Isinkwe. It is good that these two children of the same blood should grow together.

"Though Indabushe is a child of my household, Isinkwe is a child of my heart, and the chosen one of the amadlozi. I will train Indabushe to cover Isinkwe's back, in preparation for the time when I must depart to the land of shadow."

Indabushe and Peter became bosom friends. From the first day of their meeting until the day they were parted twelve years later to attend their respective schools they were brothers, constantly under the watchful eye of Mashona. In all matters, Indabushe, as the older brother, was held answerable for the well-being of the younger brother who was entrusted to his care.

Mashona taught them together and as a teacher he had no peer. Unable either to read or to write, he used the world around him to illustrate the lessons which he taught the two boys. The insects and the birds in the garden were the medium for his teachings, and every lesson he taught them underlined the rules of survival. In a hundred different ways he taught Isinkwe and Indabushe the danger that threatened every hunter, that of being hunted himself while concentrating on his own intended victim.

In the dawn of each day the two boys had to examine the garden and from insignificant marks on dew-wet leaves and tiny tracks on the ground, he taught them to read the saga of the night. And always, while they were examining anything, they had to keep checking that nothing was observing them.

Time passed and Peter learned to walk sturdily between Mashona and Indabushe, watchful and alert. He learned to be careful where he placed his feet and to tread soundlessly. Mashona taught them to avoid leaving clearly defined footprints which a tracker could follow. Peter watched Indabushe and copied the movements of the older boy.

From time to time Hamish remonstrated with Marion about the barbaric way their son was being reared. Marion managed to placate him with assurances that Peter was coming to no harm. He was happy and healthy, and thanks to Mashona's vigilance, he was safe from snakes and from eating poisonous seeds and berries.

Peter and Indabushe crouched side by side watching the spider's web. They were hidden behind a bush with only their eyes showing. From his hiding place beside them, Mashona took dead flies from the palm of his hand and flicked them, one by one, onto the trembling threads of the web. "Watch carefully," he whispered.

At first the spider acted with extreme caution as it stalked across its web to secure a fly. They watched without moving as fly after fly arrived on the web and the spider became greedy and lost its initial caution. After a while it began to scuttle heedlessly to and fro across its web to secure each newly arrived fly.

"The spider has grown careless," Mashona whispered. "It no longer pauses to see whether it, in turn, is being watched by enemies."

A wasp which neither of the boys had seen, arrived seemingly from nowhere. It grappled with the spider and dropped with it from the web to the ground. On the ground the wasp stung the spider then gripped it with its legs and flew away, dodging low among the grass stems, lest it too became the victim of a watchful bird.

Mashona stood up and, stamping his feet and posturing with the Seeker, he stabbed it into the spider's web. "This is what happens to those who grow careless," he said, stabbing the web again to emphasize his words.

He concluded the lesson as he concluded every lesson, by recounting every consideration of the entire drama, reminding them of how they had enticed the spider to its doom. He also reminded them of every detail of the precautions the three of them had taken to watch the drama unfold without their own presence being detected by the luckless spider.

Then followed the more serious part of the lesson he had been leading up to with his demonstration of the spider and the flies. He took Peter and Indabushe to the little model battlefield which he had set out for them. Grains of brown sorghum seeds represented the enemy, tiny conical pods from a eucalyptus tree were the warriors of their own army, while a handful of maize seeds made out a herd of cattle.

"Little warriors, let us now say that spider was not a spider at all. Let us say the spider was a regiment of enemies which our King had sent us to destroy. Those enemies were numerous, more so than ourselves, and therefore stronger. So we had to devise some way of dividing the enemy army, before we would be able to destroy it." He peered closely at each boy in turn, to satisfy himself he had their undivided attention.

"We would not be able to entice that army to divide its strength with a handful of dead flies, as we enticed the spider, would we?" The round-eyed boys shook their heads, wondering what was coming next. "We learned from the spider that an army of enemies can be enticed to lose their vigilance by their greed. And an army which is not vigilant soon gets eaten up. Is that not so?"

"Siyavuma!" – we agree – the boys chorused.

"If you were that army and you woke up in the morning and there, before your eyes, was a multitude of fat cattle, you would be tempted to attack the herders and capture those cattle for your king. Remember, we are no longer talking of spiders, we are talking about men and men are far cleverer than spiders."

"Siyavuma!" the boys agreed again.

"Therefore we would have to offer them something even more tempting. We could have a hundred women following the cattle and each women would carry a grain basket on her head. Each woman would have a baby tied to her back and a rolled-up sleeping mat on top of the grain basket. That would interest the enemy, would it not?"

"Siyavuma, Baba! We agree, Father."

"We would have only fifty warriors guarding the cattle and the women. And when our warriors with the cattle saw the army of their enemies, they would desert the women and the cattle and run away over the crest of the hill. The undefended cattle and the women would then be easy to capture." He raised his eyebrows at them in query and they quickly nodded their heads.

"The enemy would send a strong force to capture the cattle and the women. They would not all go, because they would fear a trap of some sort. But they would send a big enough force of warriors to destroy any trap that might be waiting for them.

"Observe! This, my young warriors, is the first part of our trap! We have succeeded in splitting what was a very strong enemy force into two groups." Mashona gathered half the sorghum seeds which were the enemy and dribbled them in a column racing to capture the women and the cattle, across the shallow "river" which he had drawn in the sand with his finger. He pointed to two concentrations of eucalyptus seed cones on either side of the racing enemy.

"Here we have two groups of our own warriors hidden in the reeds along the river. They attack the centre of the enemy column which is running across the river and they split the enemy column in the middle. The front half turns back to assist the back half. They do not see our warriors, who are disguised as women, throw down the empty baskets from their heads, drop the bundles of leaves which are the babies on their backs, and pluck their stabbing spears from their rolled-up sleeping mats." He held up his hand to stop the boys fidgeting with excitement.

"Nor do they see another strong force of our warriors emerge from where they were concealed amongst the cattle. They are crouching behind their oxhide shields, calling as calves call to their mothers and answering one another as cows answer their calves when they call. Habe!" The boys jumped at Mashona's ejaculation of surprise.

"The remaining half of the enemy army which has stayed behind is unable to help its brothers, because they themselves are threatened by attack from another body of our men who have crept up behind them in the night!"

Mashona reached out and scattered the enemy from the battlefield with a sweep of his hand. "We enticed the spider. The spider forgot to look behind him. The wasp attacked and the spider is no more.

"Likewise, we enticed a strong enemy. We divided his force, then we attacked his divided forces and divided them again. Then, like the wasp, we attacked him from behind. No matter which way he turned, he would have spears stabbing into his back. I swear by our sister, that because of our cunning, we ate the enemy up, piece by piece."

He nodded affirmation at the boys and they nodded their agreement back at him. They waited silently while Mashona deliberately withdrew his cartridge case of snuff from the slit in the lobe of his ear and decanted a little of the brown powder onto the heel of his hand. His eyes moved searchingly from one boy to the other and the boys felt uncomfortable. There was something they had forgotten. They looked at each other and then back at the old warrior.

Mashona lowered his voice to a whisper. He waved his extended index finger in the air above his head. "If that enemy had had one scout, just one scout, we would not have been able to destroy their warriors, because victory always goes to the one who can surprise the other."

Mashona glared accusingly at Isinkwe and Indabushe and the two boys looked uneasily over their shoulders. "Yes!" The word exploded from Mashona's lips. "We three were so interested in watching a battle, we also forgot to post a scout to cover our backs. So now we are also dead. He rose stiffly and stalked to the hedge. He moved the toppled wheelbarrow away and exposed his grass-stuffed greatcoat, which lay like a concealed enemy, with a broad-bladed stabbing spear beside its empty sleeve.

"You, Isinkwe, would not listen! Three times while I spoke of the battle, I saw your eyes drawn to this wheelbarrow. The spirits were warning you, but you would not listen.

"Though the voice of the spirits is but a whisper, it will be there to warn you all your life, so you must be listening for it at all times. Now, because you would not obey that whispering voice of the spirits, we have all been killed."

Mashona crouched with the two boys among the flowering shrubs in Marion's garden. Their eyes were fixed on the white-breasted shrike, perched on the top of the telephone pole. Every now and then Mashona's scarred face would twitch in a tight smile of satisfaction as he noticed Peter move very cautiously to check that they in turn were not being watched from behind.

They waited for the bird to spot one of the many cutworms they had dug up before the sun rose. The movement of a worm attracted the bird's attention. Swooping down from its perch in a smooth dive, the bird landed next to the worm. It snatched the worm up in its hooked beak and glanced around apprehensively.

"The bird is careful," Mashona's whispered words were almost inaudible, "it watches for cats and snakes." The bird flew up to its perch and turned its head from side to side. It ate the worm and sailed down for another. Then it saw the movement of the cluster of worms

24

which Mashona had stupified by shaking them in his cupped hands before placing them under an overhanging cabbage leaf. As the bird swooped and alighted beside the worms, Mashona touched Peter's arm with the tips of his fingers. The moment of crisis was very close. The fierce old warrior's eyes were fixed on the bird, willing it to do what he expected it to do. "Observe carefully, my little warriors!"

The shrike did not look around before it picked up a worm. It had had enough to eat, so it flew to the lemon tree and impaled the worm on a long thorn, then it flew down again immediately and took a second one, then a third and a fourth. It impaled each one on a thorn in a hurried manner, before diving for the next.

Mashona's fingers fastened onto Peter's arm. "The bird has grown careless!" he hissed through his teeth.

There were only a few worms left when the hurrying bird flew towards the lemon tree to impale another victim. Then suddenly, out of the blazing eye of the rising sun, a diving sparrowhawk streaked over the garden. There was a small thud and a puff of white breast feathers as the sparrowhawk skimmed low over the hedge with the dying shrike clutched in its talons.

Though Mashona stage-managed each lesson in a way that gripped the interest of his young pupils, every lesson bore the same message. "When you are in a war, my young warriors, you must keep watchful and live, or become careless and die. Especially 'you', Isinkwe, for you will be the eyes and ears of the army of your King. You will be the one who is out in front. The amadlozi have ordained it!"

As Peter grew in size and strength, Mashona's classroom expanded beyond the hedge which enclosed the spacious garden of his Lady Uvemvane. It expanded to the open countryside surrounding the garden, to the tall grass of the veld where partridges reared their chicks. It stretched to include tangled thickets where birds made their nests and field mice cleared little roads to scuttle along, in search of grass seeds and other morsels of food.

Here the lessons that Mashona taught the boys expanded also. They learned to watch and wait for hours on end to observe and familiarize themselves with the repetitive habits of every creature. Then he taught them how to set the right kind of snares to capture the creatures they had studied so carefully.

They caught pigeons and francolins and field mice, to add relish to the stodgy maize porridge which was the staple fare of Mashona's household. After every successful hunt, Mashona explained to the youngsters how and why the actions of their victim had made it possible for it to be caught. He explained what their quarry should have done to avoid capture and the precautions the three of them had taken to outsmart their quarry and any possible enemy who might have been watching them while they hunted.

He reminded them of how they had avoided using the same approach route to their traps when they checked them; he taught them never to leave by the same route they had used to get to a place and thereby to avoid a possible ambush on their way back; he reminded them of how they had used slanting sunlight to dazzle their quarry – and shade to hide themselves.

He reminded them of how they had used the wind to mask their body scent; how they had taken advantage of the movements of wind-blown grass and bushes to cover their own movements; how they had avoided breaking tall grass stems and zig-zagged their way through dew-drenched grass to avoid leaving a path which others might see and follow. He reminded them of how they had carefully searched the countryside before they made their first move.

Marion had come to her son's rescue on many occasions, but as time went by she had to agree with her husband that the boy really should be exposed to a more conventional education. She had hoped vaguely that somehow the problem would sort itself out, but had failed to appreciate how strongly Hamish felt about the matter.

In the meantime, Mashona expanded his classroom again, to the rushing streams and the wild hills of tumbled granite surrounding the village of Mbabane; to the heather- and bracken-choked glens, where they hunted hares and an occasional small buck.

Knowing it would all soon end, Marion kept many bits of information from Hamish, to enable Peter to enjoy what freedom he still had left. She did not worry about the boy's welfare. Many an evening after a day out in the veld he had no appetite for his supper, but she kept this information to herself. She knew he had feasted on wild fruits and edible plants or that he and Indabushe and Mashona had shared a roasted guineafowl, or a fire-grilled hare.

In the evenings when he returned home, his clothes were as neat and tidy as they had been when the boys had left in the morning. From this and the evenly tanned skin on his body, she also knew that out in the veld her son ran as naked as the native children, regardless of the weather.

Like the native boys, her son learned the art of the throwing-stick to bring down birds and running hares. Mashona also taught the two boys the craft of using a stabbing spear, with small spears he had fashioned for them. Mashona's battle scars bore testimony to his first-hand knowledge that the rifle was infinitely superior to the spear on the battlefield, but he insisted that the expertise of Zulu spearmen was superior to the clumsy parries and thrusts of bayonets wielded by British Infantrymen. He taught the boys every trick he knew.

He pestered Hamish into buying a small pellet gun for Peter and when Hamish reluctantly bought the gun, Mashona cajoled the police officer, who had also fought in many battles and who was a lonely man, to instruct Peter in the use of the gun. The childless police officer soon warmed to his task of tutoring a boy as naturally talented as his new pupil.

Then the time came for Peter to go to school and he hated it. He regarded it as a punishment. It was not only the restrictions of the classroom he detested, he hated being parted from Indabushe for the best part of every day.

The last hour of each school day was the worst hour of the day for both boys. Peter fretted for the freedom of the open veld and Indabushe fretted to glean a few grains of learning from the school lessons Peter had been taught in class.

Indabushe was always anxious to open Peter's school case and apply his keen mind to the problems of Peter's homework. He absorbed more from the homework than Peter absorbed from a full period in the classroom, and it was only with Indabushe's help that Peter mastered enough of his homework to satisfy Marion, so she would allow them to go and play in the veld.

It was also only with Indabushe's assistance that Peter managed to scrape a pass from one standard to the next. Yet he was never unpopular at school. He responded in a friendly manner to the other children's approaches, but he would allow none of the intimacy which he shared with Indabushe.

None of them suspected that Hamish's conventional mind had finally filled with outrage at what he considered to be the uncultured and unacceptable rearing of his son. He first noticed it in Peter's speech. The boy appeared to be unnecessarily slow in answering questions. Then Hamish was horrified when he discovered that Peter's mental tardiness was due to a problem of comprehension. He had to translate his father's questions into Zulu in his mind and then translate his thoughts back into English again before he could respond.

Even Mashona, for all his vigilance, did not detect the imminent danger stalking the three of them. Hamish's anger dropped onto them like an undetected leopard pouncing from a tree onto the back of a grazing buck. The surprise of his attack was complete and devastating and it brought the joys of their wilderness world crashing about their ears.

Despite Marion's tears and intercessions, Hamish had made up his mind that the only place for their son was the regimented environment of boarding school. In Peter's own interest he wanted him removed from the well-intentioned but undesirably pervasive influence of any derelict Zulu warrior, or his uneducated, coloured grand-children. Hamish also flatly refused to be moved by any of Mashona's impassioned pleas that Peter be permitted to remain at the village school and not be banished to a school in far-away Durban.

Mashone tried hard to dissuade Mabonca from sending the boy away. In Durban there would be no Indabushe to help Isinkwe with his homework – this would incur the wrath of the teachers and they would beat Isinkwe severely; when Isinkwe's heart was heavy and he, Mashona the Bankrupt, was not there to comfort him, his child, Isinkwe, would surely pine away and die; who would care for Isinkwe in Durban? They would not feed him at that far-away school – he would die of starvation; he was too young to be sent away from his home. Who would look after the boy when he was desperately sick with the fever for which that Durban place was notorious? Was the Lord Mabonca not aware that Durban was a place crawling with deadly black mambas? Who would comfort the child as he lay dying from the bite of one of those lethal snakes?

Mashona pleaded for the child to remain in Mbabane, where nothing could harm him. Had not he, Mashona the Bankrupt, son of Nongwazi, faithfully held his shield over the son of the Lord Mabonca and protected him from all harm, since the day of his teething? Did his Lord Mabonca consider that he, Mashona, was no longer capable of holding the boy safely within his armpit?

However, Hamish was adamant. His son's lack of progress at the local school was disgraceful. He was learning nothing at all and the only answer to the problem was the disciplined system of a good boarding school. Peter was thirteen and on the brink of adolescence. It was time he was brought up as an Englishman. It was also time Mashona saw to it that his own grandson, Indabushe, was sent off to the mission school at Manzini.

Marion tried to soften the blow to the old warrior by reminding him, through her own tears, that the ordeal of boarding school was similar to the initiation he himself had gone through before he became a man. And Mashona's eyes filled with tears, because for the first time ever, the Lady Uvemvane was lying to him. Even the police officer he had consulted had told him that the period of boarding school to which Isinkwe was being sent could not be less than five years, where-as the period of initiation of a Zulu boy was counted in weeks.

Mashona would not be consoled. They were taking the very meaning of his life away from him. His life had become worthless. The task with which the amadlozi had entrusted him was being torn from him as ruthlessly as a calf is torn from its mother's body by a prowling hyena as she lies down to give birth.

Mashona became deeply depressed. Indabushe had already left and soon, soon, Isinkwe too would be gone. In a matter of weeks he aged visibly. His shoulders slumped and his springing stride became the hesitant tread of an old man.

During the last week before Peter left for boarding school a soggy mist shrouded the village of Mbabane. In the stillness of sleepless nights Peter listened to drops of water dripping from the leaves of the fruit trees and plunking metallically in the downpipes of the mist-shrouded house.

Mashona kept to his hut as pneumonia had congested his lungs. At times when Peter sat beside him he feared the old man was dead. He lay still on his grass sleeping mat under a threadbare blanket on the smoothed cow-dung floor, with his head propped up on a carved wooden pillow.

Each time Peter leaned forward to make sure Mashona was still breathing, the seamed and scarred old face creased deeper in a weak smile. "Have no fear, Isinkwe my son. A faithful dog does not die at the feet of its master. It takes the offence of its death out into the veld where it will cause no reproach," the wheezing voice whispered.

"Push the wood closer into the heart of the fire. The cold aches in my bones." Peter leaned forward and did as he was asked. He blew into the embers until a small flame popped over the ends of the smouldering faggots and wavered beneath the rising thread of smoke.

Peter came to visit Mashona for the last time to say goodbye, as he was leaving for boarding school early the next morning. Hamish was taking him by car up the mountain road to catch the Durban train at Breyten station, on the Transvaal highveld.

He ducked under the brush of 'intelezi' leaves the women had tied over the low doorway to ward off evil spirits. Crawling through the hut entrance, Peter found that Mashona had risen from his sleeping mat. The hut was smoky from the medicinal herbs the old man was burning on the small fire beside which he squatted. The pungent smoke opened the congested passages to his lungs and eased his laboured breathing. A small flame on the end of a cord stuck into a condensed milk tin of paraffin lit the hut with a soft yellow light.

Peter greeted Mashona and squatted opposite him with the glowing embers of the fire between them. A bundle of dried, narrow, grey 'imphepo' leaves lay next to the fire. As Mashona placed a sprig of the herb on the embers, the furry grey leaves darkened and curled, releasing a strong smell of camphor. It made Peter's eyes smart a little, but it dried up a sniffle in his nose from the damp and cold of the mist. It also cleared the old man's chest. When he spoke, his voice was stronger than it had been for the past week. It almost seemed as if he had recovered from the pneumonia which had prostrated him.

Mashona searched Peter's eyes. "Isinkwe, son of Mabonca," he said with only a slight wheeze in his voice, "in the morning of tomorrow, you and I will reach the fork in the pathway of our lives. It is good that the spirits permitted us to walk together for so long." He stopped for a while, remembering the things they had done together.

"Side by side we drank the pleasant waters of many streams and we were refreshed. In the steep places among the rocks when the sun was hot and we were weary, we found numbela trees heavy with fruit, which we ate to revive our spirits. You walked safely in the shadow of my shield and the point of the Seeker went before you. You found shelter within my armpit.

"Now you are no longer a little boy. You must walk the path alone, according to the will of the spirits." For a few moments he fussed with his snuff container. He sniffed a little of the brown powder and a fit of coughing convulsed his emaciated frame.

"Trust no one to walk with you. Their eyes will not see the lurking dangers which your eyes will see. So go your way alone, Isinkwe, and go without fear." He stopped talking to take a few deep breaths.

"You have been gifted with powers other men lack. Choose two good men to cover your back in the battles which lie ahead of you, and when they can no longer cover your back, my own spirit will hold a shield above you. For surely my spirit will search for your footprints on the path you will tread, and it will follow where you have gone."

He paused to regain his breath and to wipe rheum from his eyes with the heel of his hand. "Soon," he continued, "the signs of manhood will manifest themselves in your body. The nipples on your chest will harden and hurt. Your testicles will descend and hang like the testicles of a man and the spear of your manhood will rise up to salute the maidens you will meet along the path.

"At times your voice will squeak like the voice of a girl. When you do not expect it, your voice will boom with the power of a man. At times you will be ashamed and confused. Do not hide from these things, Isinkwe, my son. This is the time of testing which the spirits visit on every boy.

"Some stand up to this test and emerge as men. Others succumb. Though they grow to look like men, their spirits have wilted and they fear the things which are of men." He reached across the smouldering fire through the tendrils of herbal smoke and rested his fleshless fingers on Peter's knee.

"I know in my heart you are not as they are. You will not fear to stand alone as a man. You will not be one who needs others close to you so that you can feed on the courage of their presence when you face the enemies of your King."

Mashona's old wives were in their own huts. The old warrior and

Peter were alone in the great hut. Mashona spoke of many things as though the spell of his words would entangle the boy and keep him with him. It was getting late, and when Peter leaned forward to rise to his feet Mashona stayed him with a raised hand.

"Bide a while, my son. The time has not yet come for me to say `go gently'. This I will do tomorrow at the showing of the sun. For friends do not part in the darkness of the night. I will be there to place your feet upon the beginning of your journey on the long, long path you will have to follow all the days of your life.

"On that path you must walk in front and let the others follow. A cunning enemy will permit a scout to pass through the ambush, so they can eat up the others who come on carelessly behind. Remember, the snake that is disturbed by the feet of the one who walks in front will be ready to strike the one who follows.

"Do not proceed like a buck which will leap forward when it is startled and can therefore be caught by the neck in the noose that has been set for it. Watch and think before you move. Study the object of your hunt before you hunt it – especially when those to be hunted are men, who themselves are warriors and also skilled in the art of hunting men."

Mashona stood up stiffly and stretched the aches from his cramped limbs. He fell into a fit of coughing and gasping for air. Peter held him until he had recovered and was able to speak again. "Your father's household will be waiting for your return," Mashona wheezed. "I will prepare you now for the path that awaits your feet."

Mashona freed himself from Peter's supporting arms and took a brush of fresh fronds of flowering 'intelezi' leaves from a peg in the thatch side of the hut. He dipped the green brush into a gourd and, as he circled Peter, flicked a fine spray of herb-perfumed droplets over him.

"Go now, Isinkwe, child of my heart. Your spirit has been purified. I will come to you in the morning. Go now. Go gently!"

"Stay gently, my Father." Peter's eyes smarted with tears. A painful lump ached in his throat. "Stay gently, Baba!"

That night Peter slept badly. His mind would not rest. In the small dark hours of the new day a freezing wind began to blow. It rattled the corrugated iron sheets of the roof and stripped the mist off the land.

In the morning there was no sign of Mashona. The biting dawn wind crawled up the sleeves and under the skirts of the warm winter coat Peter wore. It nipped at his fingers and nose and numbed his stamping feet. He felt sick with apprehension. His mind was filled with the sight of Mashona as he had seen him the previous night, coughing and choking and gasping for breath. He felt torn in two. He could not leave without saying goodbye to Mashona, nor would the train in Breyten wait for him if he did.

Hamish MacTavish eventually lost patience. "We cannot wait any longer, Peter, we must go!" His voice was sharp with impatience. "Perhaps the old man has decided to wait for us where our road joins the main road to the Transvaal. That's the nearest point from where he lives. He's in no condition to face up to such a long walk in this filthy weather, but that old man is a big enough damned fool to try it." Hamish shook his head. "Poor old chap," he relented, "he is devoted to you, Peter, with the kind of devotion only a Zulu warrior understands. If he is not at the junction, he must be too sick to move. I'll visit his kraal tonight when we get back and say your farewells for you."

Well-known and once dearly loved landmarks of his early childhood slid achingly past the breath-misted windows of the car as it gathered speed. Peter watched dumbly. The old landmarks had lost their enchantment. Somehow the magic had been torn away from the passing countryside he had roamed as a little boy between Mashona and Indabushe.

The junction was empty. Mashona was not there. Peter's disbelieving eyes searched frantically across the empty landscape. "I'm sorry, Peter. He hasn't come." Hamish's voice killed the last faint spark of hope. "Close your window now, we're all freezing."

Kent's Rock, a bleak and bare dome of granite, grey as the gloom of the morning, flashed past. It was the last possible point at which Mashona could have met the car, unless he had walked throughout the freezing night to the steeply climbing road up Mtonjaneni mountain. Marion put her arm around his shoulders. She sensed how he was feeling.

Hamish changed into low gear to start the long winding climb up to the border post at Oshoek and the corrugated miles rattled away under the labouring car. Halfway up that endless climb, a monolith of granite towered beside the road, from the top of which a scout would be able to watch the road for miles in either direction.

A scarecrow figure rose up on the very top of the rock. A skin-wrapped crone stood up at his side to support him, while a second frail woman helped him to hold his shield against the tug of the wind worrying at the flapping skirts of his tattered greatcoat.

"Mashona!"

The whispered word sounded like a prayer in the closed warmth of the car.

Mashona brushed his helping wives aside and tottered to the edge of the rock, raising his shield and the Seeker in salute to his Lord Mabonca's car, which skidded to a stop on the gravel road below him. In the car Marion leaned back in her seat with her eyes tightly closed, the tears squeezing through her lashes and streaming down her cheeks.

Hamish had to get out to close the back door Peter had left swinging in the wind when he leaped out of the car before it had stopped. He watched his son bound up the slope of the rock to where Mashona stood waiting for him.

On the summit of the rock Mashona faced Peter. His skin was grey with exhaustion. His Adam's apple bobbed in his throat and he swallowed and gulped before his words of greeting would come out. Tears dripped from his old eyes.

"I see you, Father," Peter whispered brokenly. "I see you! I praise you, my Father, and I praise the Mothers who accompany my Father." He dashed the tears from his eyes with the back of his hand. "I see you, but I must hurry and go. The train will not wait and the time was eaten up while we waited for you. You have been praised, my Father. I praise you greatly. Stay gently .. Stay gently, .. 'Sala kahle'!"

Marion watched through tear-blurred eyes as her young son and the old warrior, silhouetted against the cold winter sky on the top of the rock, shook hands in the traditional way: palms together; palms gripping each other's thumbs; then palms clasped together again. Then, in a most untraditional way, Mashona's arms encircled her son and held him to his chest.

Her breath caught in a sob. High on the rock she saw the great black war shield covering her son as it had covered him since infancy and through all the days of his childhood. "Umhlolo!" she whispered reverently. "It's an omen!" Her mind unconsciously phrased the thought in the Zulu idiom.

Peter hid himself in the school library to nurse his harrowing hurt, clutching the crumpled letter from his mother telling him Mashona had died. Mercifully Marion did not detail how, on their return journey in the late afternoon, they had found Mashona's shivering and exhausted wives lamenting pitifully beside the emaciated corpse of the old warrior who had collapsed and died at the foot of the rock.

Peter hid the misery constricting his soul during the first months of boarding school. He kept to himself as much as possible in the bustling, prescribed environment. He yearned for the close companionship he had had with Indabushe and for his lost freedom in the tumbled hills of Swaziland. In his mind he relived the times he had loved, like the excitement of watching his whirring throwing-stick intercepting the flight of a francolin. Memories of hunts with Mashona on carefree days drenched in sunlight filled his mind and he could feel again the stiff fronds of bracken scratching his bare legs as he ran headlong in pursuit of a hare. He longed for his home, shrouded in the silent mist.

But mostly he yearned for Mashona. His heart felt numb when he thought of him. He felt in some incomprehensible way that the old man who had never let him down while he lived, had let him down by dying.

Peter had never thought of living without Mashona, even though the old warrior had often spoken about the time when he would have to depart to dwell in the land of shadow. He had not made it sound like dying. And in any case, Mashona had promised him that his spirit would always be with him. Then suddenly he was gone. He was dead! And all that was left was the aching emptiness in the place in his heart, which Mashona had always filled.

Peter erected a secret memorial in his mind to Mashona and to the memory of the brotherhood he had shared with Indabushe. As an expression of remembrance, he diligently practised and developed new skills based on the lessons Mashona had taught them when they were all together. He excelled at shooting and fencing and boxing. He walked with the silence and balance of a cat and he avoided the rowdy company of the other boys, who admired him, feared him, and left him to himself.

And in his mind he called himself Isinkwe, because this was the name Mashona had given him.

It was Peter's fifth year at boarding school. He was eighteen. Because of his inability to apply himself to his school work, he had to be kept back at the end of his first year, in standard six. He was only due to write his matriculation examination at the end of the following year, when he was nineteen.

On a sweltering Sunday morning he was jammed among the throng of boys in the school library to listen to the British Prime Minister's formal declaration of war against Germany. Eager boys roared their approval and slapped each other's backs and shouted their hopes that the war would not end before they had finished their schooling. On the bronze plaque on the War Memorial the names of the ex-students who had fallen in the 1914-1918 Great War took on a new meaning and a host of young eyes read those names and silently pledged revenge.

In the new term of 1940, instructors from the Royal Durban Light Infantry commenced training the boys in the arts of warfare. Peter was in his element. He was appointed senior student officer of the school's Cadet Battalion and he threw himself wholeheartedly into the training programme.

There were no more school holidays in the hills of Swaziland, as he spent every spare moment on the shooting range or at cadet training camps. He received his instructions to report to the headquarters of the Swaziland Pioneer Corps directly he finished with his schooling, and because of his school cadet achievements and his fluency in the Swazi language, he was to receive an immediate commission.

Hamish was delighted that Peter was to enter the war as a commissioned officer and that his son would be posted to a labour battalion and would therefore not have his life exposed to danger. Because he himself had endured several months in the trenches in the previous war, he was more than pleased that his son would not have to do the same.

Peter kept his peace. He had plans of his own.

Chapter 3

A speeding jeep skidded to a stop in a cloud of dust. In the sky above, the leading German Stuka bomber turned on to the tip of its right wing and plummeted in a vertical dive onto the shallow dugouts the men were digging. A big man wearing the two pips and crown of a Colonel bounded from the jeep and dived into the half-dug trench beside Peter.

Peter looked up and saw the outline of the wings and the fuselage and the motors of the leading bomber. This was it! He could see no other part of the aircraft's body. It was going to be a direct hit, or a very near miss.

A stick of bombs fell free from the screaming bomber and the desert around him geysered sand fountains from machine-gun bullets. "Duck Colonel!" he said tersely to the stranger beside him, "this one's ours." He covered his ears with his hands and pressed his face to the ground.

A sharp crack sounded beside him, followed immediately by another, which was drowned in a series of thundering explosions that evacuated their lungs and made the ground jump, showering them with a hailstorm of gravel and sand. Again he heard the sharp crack. He turned his head and saw it was the Colonel beside him, lying on his back, firing carefully aimed shots with his pistol at the next diving bomber. He grabbed the Colonel's extended arm to pull it down into the trench before it got blown off, but the Colonel jerked his arm free.

Shock waves of sound smashed against Peter's ears and flying stones and shrapnel howled past inches above his head. Another avalanche of gravel cascaded onto them. The Colonel swore and turned onto his stomach, firing at the back of the bomber as it checked its dive with lowered flaps and levelled out to start climbing.

The ground still bucked and shuddered from exploding bombs, and machine-gun bullets stitched seams across the ground with the sound of ripping canvas. Acrid fumes burned his throat. Beside him, the Colonel shook the empty cases from the cylinder of his pistol, reloaded hurriedly and carried on firing. In the trench next to them, the Thompson sub-machine-carbine of the Colonel's driver chattered bursts of automatic fire at the rear of the plane. The last of the Stuka bombers slowed as it lifted its nose. Its engine roared with power as it climbed steeply behind the others, and Peter and the Colonel stood up in the trench.

Peter searched the sky to make sure there were no other planes around. Beside him the Colonel again reloaded his pistol with impatiently jabbing fingers. Peter bundled up his shirt and used it to brush sand and chips of stone from his hair and his sun-browned body. He picked up his shovel to carry on digging.

"Where's your rifle?" the Colonel barked at him.

He looked up into the Colonel's smouldering eyes. "It's in my dugout, Sir." He stood smartly to attention.

"Are you telling me you've got more than one dugout?" The Colonel's voice was tinged with fury. "Where's Battalion HQ?" Peter pointed in the direction of Battalion Headquarters and, ignoring the Colonel, he resumed his digging as the Colonel strode purposefully across the desert in the direction Peter had indicated.

"That's the Colonel."

Peter looked up at the man who had spoken. It was the Colonel's driver. He was busy thumbing bullets into the empty drum magazine of his tommy-gun, which he held clamped under his left arm. "Are you new in the regiment?" he asked, watching the Colonel marching away.

"Ja!" Peter replied tersely, still smarting at the Colonel's implied slur.

"He's the hell in with you guys for not shooting back at those German bombers", the man said. "Just wait until he gets hold of that 2IC of his. He never liked the bastard anyway. He'll chew his bloody balls off!

"You don't know the Colonel," the man's dark eyes challenged Peter. "I tell you, man, he's the best bloody officer in the South African army. You'll bloody soon find out what kind of a fighter he is! But you'll learn for yourself when he's finished chewing the balls off the 2IC.

"The name's Dolf. Dolf Hanekom." The man transferred a handful of bullets to his left hand and reached out to shake hands, by way of introducing himself.

"I'm Peter MacTavish."

"Pleased to meet you, Peter, but you must excuse me. I must go," he added hurriedly and grinned, "I don't want to miss hearing what the Colonel's got to say to the 2IC." His grin widened as he turned away and ran to catch up with the Colonel.

Peter stopped digging and looked up as the stacatto notes of a bugle rang out across the desert and men froze to identify the call. The urgent short notes of the General Alarm jarred their ears. In the act of throwing a heap of gravel from the trench, Peter dropped his shovel and raced towards the dugout. Everywhere men sprinted to their dugouts for their weapons and equipment, wondering what it was that threatened them.

The German General Rommel and his Afrika Korps were supposed to be 200 miles away to the west, at Agheila, licking their wounds and patching their battle-damaged tanks. Had they broken out once more and outflanked the units at the front? Was it tanks, or motorised infantry, that were about to sweep into the Stormberg Regiment's positions? Peter anxiously scanned the empty desert horizon as he ran.

Inside the dugout he shrugged his shoulders into the straps of his webbing equipment and snapped shut the buckle of his belt. He pressed two clips of ammunition down into the magazine of his rifle and checked that the rim of each round lay correctly in front of the round beneath it. His eyes searched the desert again as he slid a round into the breech, closed the bolt and hooked the safety catch back with his index finger.

"Prime grenades!" Corporal Wolmarans handed out grenades and primers. While the men arranged themselves for all-round defence, Peter primed six grenades in between frequently scanning his surroundings for clouds of dust rising from racing German tanks.

Jannie Muller rearranged the bipod and rested his shoulder against the butt plate to check the lie of the Bren gun for comfort. Beside him, Lance Corporal Willem de Beer and Boet Botha stacked spare magazines on a nearby groundsheet for rapid loading. Boet Botha laid the spare barrel beside the gun with his towel over it to keep the sand out. The bustle of preparation subsided and the men waited in silence.

Again the notes of the bugle sounded: "Fall in `A' .. Fall in `B' .. Fall in every Companeee!"

"Now what the hell's going on? Move boys! On Parade!" Corporal Karel Wolmarans led the Section at the double to the edge of the parade ground.

"Markers!" The Regimental Sergeant Major was in a hurry. The big Colonel was pacing impatiently to and fro behind him. The officers formed up quickly at the right rear of the parade and stood dead still.

"Markers outwards turn quick march!" The next command thundered out before the markers had taken up their dressing. "Getton parade!" The men stepped off smartly and double-quick marched into their platoons.

"Close order! Flanks close in on the centre, without interval .. Move!" The order came before the previous one had been fully carried out. The Colonel's driver rolled an empty petrol drum to the front of the parade ground and upended it. The Colonel gripped the driver's shoulder for support and jumped up onto the drum. The RSM marched up and halted. He saluted the Colonel. "Parade present, Sir!" he reported.

"Thank you, RSM!" The Colonel's voice was as big as his body. The RSM marched briskly to the right flank of the battalion.

"Battalion!" The parade braced their shoulders. The RSM about-turned. He saluted to the front and stood at ease.

"Fall in, the Officers!" The Colonel impatiently punched the palm of his left hand with a closed fist while the officers stepped it out to their positions in front of their Companies or their Platoons. Peter glanced around the sky with troubled eyes. His straining ears listened for the distinctive throbbing beat of German bomber engines. The bunched Battalion was a prime target.

"He must be bloody mad," Sybrant Bekker whispered out of the side of his mouth. "One bomber now, and the whole Battalion's fucked."

"Quiet, in the centre rank!" Sergeant Koen Swartz's cross voice was strongly accented. His family in South-West Africa was German speaking. The athletic-looking Padre took up his place in front of the petrol drum the Colonel was standing on. He nodded towards the RSM.

"Battalion! .. Battalion 'shun! Standat ease! Remove headgear!" The Padre laid his helmet at his feet. He needed both hands to prevent the wind from blowing over the pages of his Bible.

"We will draw inspiration from the reading of the Holy Scripture", the Padre said, "about a resolute people who faced up to what we are facing up to today. I read from the book of Nehemiah. Chapter 4 verses 14 to 21:

"And I looked, and rose up, and said to the nobles, and to the rulers, and to the people, be not ye afraid of them: remember the Lord, which is great and terrible, and fight for your bretheren, your sons, your daughters, your wives and your houses."

Peter guessed the Colonel had told the Padre to read this particular text. He felt it was aimed at himself for not having his rifle with him while he was digging. He also felt it was unfair because he was not the only one.

"And it came to pass, when our enemies heard that it was known unto us, and God had brought their counsel to nought, that we returned all of us to the wall, every one to his work.

"And it came to pass that from that time forth, that the half of my servants wrought in the work, and the other half of them held both the spears, the shields, and the bows, and the habergeons; and the rulers were all behind the house of Judah.

"They which builded on the wall, and they that bare burdens, with those that laded, (every one) with one of his hands wrought in the work, and with the other hand held a weapon."

"Good for them," Sybrand muttered, "they were just bloody lucky that bombers hadn't been invented in those days."

"For the builders, every one had his sword girded by his side, and so builded. And he that sounded the trumpet was by me.

"And I said unto the nobles, and to the rulers, and to the rest of the people, the work is great and large, and we are separated upon the wall, one far from another."

"That old bugger must have been the Colonel's grandfather," a voice whispered.

"In what place therefore ye hear the sound of the trumpet, resort ye thither unto us: our God shall fight for us. So we laboured in the work: and half of them held the spears from the rising of the morning till the stars appeared."

The Padre half turned his back into the wind and closed his Bible carefully. For a full minute there was silence, while the lesson from the scriptures sank in. Then the Padre's voice spoke quietly. "Let us pray together .. Our Father who art in Heaven..."

The Padre ended the prayer. He saluted the Colonel and took up his place behind the petrol drum rostrum.

"Pay attention!" The Colonel's voice thundered across the desert. "I would like to say to you men that I'm delighted to rejoin you on the threshold of this Regiment's baptism by fire. But I'm not! At this moment I'm ashamed to have my name linked to this Stormberg Regiment."

Men raised their eyebrows and glanced at one another, wondering what the Colonel was getting at.

"For two years we have trained and waited for this opportunity to get to grips with the enemies of our land. You men volunteered to leave your homes to fight the Germans, as your fathers did before you. You volunteered to fight! Yet today when the enemy showed himself, you cowered in your funk holes like a colony of meercats when an eagle flies past. Since you arrived here a week ago, four men have been killed and twelve wounded. And what have you done to avenge them? Nothing! Not a single thing except dig holes to hide your weapons in and other holes to hide yourselves in!"

"No! No! Wait a bit, Colonel!" Several men spoke out crossly in protest and Peter wondered at such unchecked breech of discipline. From his experience of school cadets he was shocked to hear ordinary riflemen voice their disagreement with anybody as senior as a Colonel.

"Nobody ever won any war with a spade!" the Colonel shouted the men down. "The Germans will not surrender because you men can dig holes faster than they can. You weren't given weapons for the purpose of hiding them in holes! Your weapons were issued to you to be used to defeat the enemy!"

"No! What the hell, Colonel! Must we try to bayonet their bloody bombers? Where are the anti-aircraft guns we're supposed to have?" The man, Sybrant Bekker, seemed to have no respect for the authority of senior officers.

"QUIET!" The RSM's shout cracked like a whiplash to quell the indignant clamour from the ranks as voices shouted to be given anti-aircraft guns.

"Are you men telling me you are going to skulk in you funk holes and wait for anti-aircraft guns to come and win this war for you? No, men! Right here and now, we'll decide whether we're going to fight the enemy with what we've got, or whether we're going to disband this Regiment and go back to our homes, and hand in weapons that have only shot at targets."

"Colonel!" the men shouted indignantly, "give us the guns and we'll fight! We're not afraid of the Germans. Just give us the guns and we'll show you what we can do."

"The Colonel must have got sand or something in his brains, he's gone bloody mad," Sybrant said loudly for all to hear.

Colonel Hamman held up his hands and the clamour stopped. The men had always known him to be a fair man and they gave him a chance to speak.

"Your anti-aircraft guns were on their way. They were due to arrive here tonight. But I have sent Major Oberholster to stop those guns! I don't want them! They can rust in the desert until I send for them. And I won't send for them until I'm satisfied that this Stormberg Regiment deserves to be assisted by those guns!"

"What's happened to the Colonel? Sounds like he's off his rocker!"

"No anti-aircraft guns in the world," the Colonel continued, while he smashed his right fist against the palm of his left hand to emphasize his words, "were designed to win a war. Only infantry can win or lose a war! No battle has ever been won in the history of this world, until the infantry were standing guard over the land they had captured or defended, and denied that land to the enemy! No battle was ever lost, until the last infantryman laid down his weapons or ran away!"

"If he doesn't give us those guns we'd better start running too!" Sybrant's voice muttered again, and a few men sniggered at the remark.

"Infantry might call on the assistance of the Air Force, the Navy or the Artillery," the Colonel shouted. "They may need help from tanks or armoured cars. They may even ask for help from anti-aircraft guns. But none of these things can do the job of winning the war for them."

"We're not going to win it without those guns, that's for bloody certain," another voice called out.

Colonel Hamman ignored the voice. "South Africans are known as the finest riflemen in the world," the Colonel continued. "You men are going to prove that this is still true. You are the sons of proud fighting fathers. Don't disgrace them." He held up his hand to quell the growl of protest from the ranks.

"Ja, Colonel," a man shouted, "our fathers never had Stukas bombing the shit out of them every day, and fuck-all to shoot back with."

"Listen, men!" the Colonel's voice rose to a roar, and the noise stopped. "You were born with rifles in your hands. The enemy weren't. You have good rifles and the RSM has promised me he will keep you supplied with all the ammunition you'll ever need, to keep the standard of your shooting in top form."

"No! Bugger it," Sybrant spoke out, "when did he last try to shoot a tank or a bomber with a bloody rifle?"

"QUIET!" The Company Sergeant Major barked. "Sergeant Swartz, that Sybrant Bekker in your Platoon, who's been doing all the talking. Kick his arse!"

"You all heard the lesson the Padre read us today," Colonel Hamman continued, "about a brave people who lived the best part of two and a half thousand years ago. They had a wall to build and they carried on building it, right under the noses of their enemies. The difference was, those fine people built with one hand while their other hand held a sword. We're going to do the same."

He glared at the men challengingly, punching the palm of his left hand with his right fist. "Those Old Testament guys didn't hide their weapons in holes while they did what they had to do. And you're not going to do it again either. This is the sort of thing that destroys the fighting spirit of what could be a splendid regiment. I'm afraid I had to accept the resignation of the Officer responsible. He's already on his way to GHQ, in Cairo."

Peter thought of Mashona. The old warrior would have raised his shield in salute to the words of this fighting Colonel. His presence felt so real that Peter wondered if he was the only one who could hear the sibilance of the Zulu battle hiss through Mashona's teeth.

"From this moment on, none of you will move one inch without a loaded rifle in your hands. You will eat with your loaded rifles beside you. You will sleep with your rifles beside you. When you go to relieve yourselves you will squat with your rifles beside you. You will get so used to the feel of your rifles that you will pick them up in the morning before you remember to put your trousers on.

"Listen to me, men," he punched his palm rapidly, "things are bad in the world. I've just come from General's Order Group in Cairo. Europe is a smouldering ruin. From the Gulf of Finland in the North," he pointed dramatically to the North, "to the Black Sea in the South," his arm described an arc of 180 degrees, "the armies and the civilian populations of Russia have their backs to the wall and German bayonets at their throats. Thousands die of starvation every day in their beleaguered cities. Most of them children. But the people fight on, despite the savagery of the German attackers, which defies description."

The man behind Peter started to whisper something but Sergeant Swartz's voice cut him short. "You! Sybrant Bekker! Report to me after the parade, in battledress, greatcoat and full kit. We'll see after a couple of hours pack-drill if you'll still have any breath left to talk crap."

"Losses at sea of sailors, ships, and of vital supplies for the Allies, due to German U-boat and air attacks, have reached crisis point for Britain," the Colonel shouted. "The Germans have a stranglehold on Norway in the north right through to Crete, here in the Mediterranean Sea. They've already got the Rumanian oil fields."

"Right here, Rommel is going to do his damnedest to pull off a South hook, to outflank our defensive line at Gazala and capture the Suez Canal. He will then rush eastwards and grab the oil fields of Iran. There he'll meet up with a pincer movement of Germans from the north. If we let this happen we'll have lost the war, and that will be the end of civilization and freedom."

He paused and his eyes swept across the assembled men. "Boys," he said in a confiding tone, "if we lose this war, I've got a feeling the Germans won't forgive us in a hurry – especially men like myself and more than half of you guys with German names."

His voice rose to thunder again. "It's no good us shouting for guns to help us. Those guns are needed more urgently elsewhere. The Far East is now on fire. The Japanese are sweeping away everything that stands in their path. Their barbarity is worse than that of the Germans. We have just been told they recently captured 65 Australian nurses and killed them all with machine-gun fire."

He pointed to the north again. "Thirteen days ago, at 3 o'clock in the morning, in a howling blizzard, Russian infantry mounted a surprise attack on the SS Death's Head Division, north of Novogrod. They picked the toughest target they could find, under the worst possible conditions. They were driven off, but not until they had knocked the hell out of Germany's most elite troops.

"Any time you guys consider you are having a hard time, think of the guts of those Russian infantrymen.

"Here in the desert it's our job to stop Rommel before he gets to the Suez Canal. Reinforcements of troops and supplies of war materials that were earmarked for us have been redirected to the Far East and other places, where the threat is greater than it is here. So, men, we will get on with it and do what we have to do with whatever we've got." He pounded the palm of his hand again for a few moments while he stood thinking about something.

"Tomorrow there will be no more digging." He seemed to have made up his mind about whatever it was that had worried him. "Digging will only continue if you can satisfy me you men have got enough of your fathers' guts, to stand up and fight. If you haven't, I'll ask General Auchinleck to take back our rifles and convert us into a Labour Battalion.

"If you don't want that, then tomorrow we will spend the whole day fighting with bayonets, because that's what this Regiment is going to do when we've fired our last bullet at the enemy. The more you sweat now, the less you'll bleed later. The next time the bombers come, we will show them we're here to fight. Every man in this Regiment will give them a go, including the cooks!"

"Parade!"

Every man braced up at the RSM's command. "You have all finished talking shit. You will now listen carefully to what the Colonel has to say."

The Colonel nodded his thanks to the RSM. He pulled a notebook from his pocket and had a brief look at the notes he had made. "In this Regiment we have forty Bren guns," he said. "Each of these guns is capable of firing one magazine of ammunition at the rate of 450 rounds a minute."

Keyed up with suppressed excitement, Peter listened to the Colonel's words as he used to listen to Mashona outlining a plan to defeat an imaginary enemy.

"I know you can't keep up this rate of fire, but the figure of 450 rounds still holds good if every Bren gun empties one magazine at each diving bomber, then changes magazines and empties the new magazine up the bombers tail feathers as he pulls out of his dive.

"According to my arithmetic, this means the Bren guns alone can fire 300 rounds a second at each aircraft." The men stood stock still, listening intently. Apart from the odd pot shot at enemy planes, none of them had ever thought of concentrating small-arms fire at them.

Peter could see the Colonel's plan taking shape and he had to force himself to stand still. He felt the old thrills he had felt as a child, listening to Mashona, with Indabushe fidgeting with anticipation beside him.

The Colonel referred to his notes again. "Between the section leaders and the drivers, we have 50 Thompson sub-machine carbines. Each of these guns can fire at the rate of 600 rounds per minute, which gives us another 500 rounds a second". He glanced down at the notebook.

"We have 368 rifles, and every rifleman in this Regiment is capable of firing one aimed round every three seconds. This gives us 7,360 aimed rounds per minute, which is 122 shots per second.

"The officers and sergeant majors can help with their pistols and add another 15 rounds a second to our fire power. If I've done my sums correctly, we are capable of sending up 937 rounds of aimed small-arms fire per second at any aircraft that wants to try us, and that is one hell of a smack of fire power. Most of you men are damned good shots and I tell you, I'd hate to be on the receiving end of what you are going to give the next lot of dive bombers that visit us."

Peter felt like cheering the Colonel. Mashona's plans had been aimed at imaginary enemies. Now the enemy was real.

"We are not going to lie in our funk holes and pop off odd shots at them. As each bomber tips on to its wing to start its dive, every man in this Regiment is going to add his contribution to the almost solid pillar of bullets that is going to rip through that bomber. By the time its bombs fall free the plane will be going too fast to shoot at with any hope of success, so we'll go for the next one.

"One thing to remember! Once a bomber starts his vertical dive, he can't change his direction. If you can only see the silhouette of the front of his bomber, then the bombs he drops and the fire from his machine-guns are either going to hit you or be very, very close. This is the time to duck! But if you can see any part of the fuselage at all, that bomber is going to miss you and there's nothing the pilot can do about it. So don't be shy about showing a bit of yourself, while you give him everything you've got.

"Then," the Colonel held up his extended index finger, "when he drops his flaps to start climbing after his dive, his ground speed slows to something like 45 miles an hour. That's the moment to hit him up the backside with everything we have that will shoot."

All around him, Peter saw men nudging one another and grinning. They were as eager as he was, to try out the Colonel's plan.

"Don't worry if no aeroplanes fall out of the sky." The Colonel continued "Those things are tough. But rest assured you will cause them a lot of serious damage. Your bullets will weaken propellers and struts and reinforcing members. You will break controlling cables or at least weaken them, so they'll snap as soon as they are under strain. You'll rupture hydraulic oil pipes and short out electrical circuits. You'll scare the daylights out of the pilots and they'll be damn lucky if they aren't spouting blood like watering-cans by the time they've pulled out of their dive.

"Many of those planes won't make it back to their bases, because their pilots will die on the way. Some planes with structural damage will limp behind their returning squadrons and get shot down like lame ducks by the anti-aircraft guns of our forward units. Or by patrolling fighters. And some of them will crash-land in the desert, when their last drop of petrol has leaked out of bullet-riddled fuel tanks."

Men shuffled their feet and waved clenched fists in front of them, and every man on the parade was smiling as widely as Peter with excited approval.

Colonel Hamman raised his voice above the buzz of elation. "And I can promise you guys not one of those planes will be able to refuel, rearm and return to bomb us or anybody else, before it has been thoroughly inspected and repaired by overworked mechanics. And those mechanics simply won't have the time to attend to them quickly, because of the multiple damage your bullets would have done to so many of them.

"Let's say we miss half our shots, or even three quarters. We will still be hitting each bomber with 1 500 bullets every six seconds when he starts his dive. And with more than double that, when he starts to climb after his dive. At a quarter of our potential efficiency, that plane will be hit by something like 4 000 bullets. Let's be conservative and halve the hit rate and then halve it again. We will still rake him with 1 000 hits before he can get away from us.

"How would any of you men like to be strapped into a seat inside a little thin-skinned aeroplane that is hit by 1 000 bullets?

"This Stormberg Regiment has no fighting history. You are going to make that history. The watchword of this Regiment from this moment on, is "Attack". Whether it be aircraft, or tanks, or infantry, or whatever the enemy sends against us, we will hit the nearest ones with a jet of small-arms fire that will send him reeling.

"Some of us will die before our fight is finished..."

The exuberant men stood still suddenly, sobered by the Colonel's chilling words. Their smiles faded and they listened unmoving. But the eyes which were fixed on their Colonel, showed no sign of fear. Every man in the Stormberg Regiment stood ready to pay whatever price was asked of him, in defence of his beliefs.

"Some of us will be wounded. But those who live will return to our Fatherland, with the triumphant banner of a proud regiment flying above their heads."

The Colonel turned and called to the Padre. "Padre, pray for us! Pray to Almighty God to give us the steadfast courage to carry out the task that is assigned to us, whatever it may be. This is our offering for our land and our people. Pray to God, Padre, that it is acceptable."

While the Padre prayed, Peter noticed some of the men glancing up at the sky. He saw no fear in their searching eyes. They wanted the bombers to come. They wanted to show Colonel Hamman they were every bit as worthy as their fathers and grandfathers had been.

Peter smeared the sweat from his eyes with the back of his forearm. His bare chest heaved with laboured breaths. A few dull red patches on his ribs showed where the scabbard of his opponent's bayonet had penetrated his guard and struck home. He and Koos Retief leaned gasping on their rifles, grinning breathlessly at each other.

"I'm buggered," Koos panted, "you got me ten times for every time I got you. I've been doing this every day for two years, and you tell me this is the first time you've ever used a bayonet? Your eye is good and you're too quick for me." All around them pairs of men were duelling, or resting briefly to get their breath back. All of them were grinning.

From time to time their eyes roamed the sky for approaching bombers.

Colonel Hamman and his officers and non-commissioned officers were also stripped to the waist and wet with sweat. They mingled with the struggling men, helping, advising and demonstrating. "No! Not like that," Colonel Hamman roared at one man who was not using his weight to help drive home a thrust. "Don't poke your bayonet at your enemy. Clip the butt of the rifle to your hip with your elbow and throw your whole body forward when you lunge.

"Go for the throat. You'll never stick that bayonet through a wet greatcoat and the tunic that's underneath it when it's raining. Use a short jab. Six inches of steel in the throat is all you need to take the fight out of him.

"Don't poke at him with your arms only. It's too easy for him to knock your bayonet aside. Leap forward with your feet. Here! I'll show you." He demonstrated several lunges for the man's benefit. "Corporal van der Post," he shouted at the hard-worked Section Leader, "give this man a bit of extra attention. He needs help.

"Come on you two. What are you grinning at? You're the new English-speaking man in the Regiment, aren't you? Can you speak Afrikaans?"

"Yes, Sir," Peter jumped to attention.

"You were the man without a rifle yesterday?"

Peter nodded in shame. "None of us had rifles, Sir, we were on digging fatigue."

"Alright, man. Don't feel bad about it. All that's changed now. On guard! Let's see if you know how to handle that rifle you've got."

Peter realised he would never be able to parry the thrust of a man as big and as powerful as Colonel Hamman. When the Colonel lunged, Peter struck his bayonet against the side of the Colonel's bayonet and used it as a push-off point, to leap aside out of harm's way. He drove the butt plate of his rifle at the Colonel's face. The Colonel swung his head to one side and struck Peter's rifle butt smartly away.

"Very good, very good!" He grunted and leaped back and raised his rifle to ward off a down chop. He sprang back again and half turned to avoid the toe of the butt of Peter's rifle streaking to bash his testicles.

Then Peter was under his guard and closed in chest to chest, before the Colonel could regain his balance. Peter dropped the butt of his rifle to the ground between his feet and grasped the muzzle cap with both hands. As Colonel Hamman jumped backwards, Peter sprang towards him and jerked his bayonet up sharply against the under side of the Colonel's jaw.

Colonel Hamman caught him in a bear hug. "OK .. OK .. OK!! I'm dead! You can stop now," he laughed. "Where the hell did you learn to handle a bayonet like that?"

"From an old Zulu warrior, Colonel, he taught me with a stabbing spear".

"Right! What's your name?"

"Peter MacTavish, Sir."

"MacTavish! You speak like a Pom. Are you from overseas?"

"No, Sir. My father's in the Colonial Service. I was born in Swaziland."

"How old are you, MacTavish?"

"Nineteen, Sir. I turn twenty in April."

Colonel Hamman appraised him silently for a moment. He liked what he saw. About five foot six, he mused. Wide shoulders. Narrow hips. Athletic. Strong. Compact. Neat. As poised as a leopard. Penetrating eyes. "MacTavish, aren't I correct in thinking you're supposed to be in the British Army's Pioneer Corps?"

"Well .. er .. Yes, Sir." He decided the best approach in dealing with a man like Colonel Hamman, was to talk straight. "I was supposed to take a Commission with the Swaziland Pioneer Corps, Sir, but they are a non-combatant Corps. Sir, I was sort of brought up to fight, by an old Zulu, so I wanted to join a fighting regiment."

"MacTavish, we all saw that your old Zulu made a damned good job of teaching you how to fight. But why did you choose a regiment that's mostly Afrikaans-speaking and all the men in the regiment are quite a few years older than you are? And how the hell did you manage to get into this Regiment in the first place, without me knowing about it?"

"I came straight from school, Sir. I saw this Regiment marching to the troop ship in Durban, so I just sort of marched along with them, Sir. I said I'd been robbed and my kit and my papers had been stolen. Sir, your 2IC told me to stick around until you rejoined the Regiment and you would decide what you would do with me."

"What do you want to do, MacTavish? Do you want to go back to the British, or do you want to stay with us?"

"I want to stay, Sir!"

"Then you stay! If the Brits come looking for you I'll make sure they don't find you. If a man goes out of his way to join a fighting regiment, I believe that man deserves a bit of help. I'm glad to have a young man with your spirit." Colonel Hamman shook hands in a friendly way. "Go around and help the men who are not doing too well. Teach them your fancy footwork and that dirty little up-thrust of yours that damn nearly made me bite my tongue off."

Peter heard, or rather, felt the faint throbbing of aircraft engines in the distance. His shout of warning was a shout of challenge. The outlying picket also heard them and his short warning blasts on his whistle prickled the men's nerves with excitement. They scattered and ran, rifles in hand, for their trenches.

The leading Stuka canted on to the end of its wing while six hundred and fifty pairs of eyes watched it eagerly. Peter's finger held the first pressure on the trigger of his rifle, then squeezed. Six hundred and fifty weapons fired at the same time. He reloaded and fired five times in rapid succession. His rifle kicked like a mule. There was no give in the ground behind his shoulder blade to cushion the shock of each kick. He watched for the bombs to detach themselves from the body of the plummeting Stuka, but no bombs appeared. The bomber did not pull out of its dive. It came screaming down and crashed nose first into the ground and exploded deafeningly in an eruption of flame and flying debris.

A roar rose from the half-dug trenches. The following two Stukas pulled out of their dives to avoid the blast. They did not release their bombs. Tracer bullets streaked threads of fire into their bodies and all around them, like attacking swarms of iridescent bees. The other seven bombers dived one after the other through a wall of bullets.

They dropped their bombs and lowered their flaps to pull out of their dives, and as each plane lifted its nose to climb, a fiery trail of tracer bullets followed it. One of them faltered in its flight as though its pilot had pulled back the controls in mortal agony. It hung vertically in the sky for a bullet-riddled second, then it slipped sideways and spiralled into the earth.

A third bomber failed to climb. It flew away low over the desert, streaming a faint trail of smoke behind it, until it was out of sight.

Wildly yelling men bounded from their trenches and cavorted jubilantly, waving their rifles above their heads. Colonel Hamman pranced around holding his clenched fists high in the air. He tried to shout something, but his voice was drowned by the ecstatic cheers of the men.

There had been one casualty. Kobus Mostert had been killed by machine-gun fire from one of the bombers. He had died with an empty cartridge case in the chamber of his rifle and eight empty cases lying beside him.

He had died fighting. He had not died cowering in his trench and his comrades buried him with honour. The rifles that fired the three volleys as the blanket-wrapped body was lowered into its desert grave were immediately reloaded, ready to avenge his death.

"Greater love hath no man than this, that a man lay down his life for his friends. We will remember him!" The Padre's words were proudly spoken.

Many months had passed, and Major Jonker sat with Captain Steyn and the three Platoon Commanders in Company Order Group. "Jack," Major Jonker leaned towards Lieutenant Ingle, "there's one more thing to discuss before we dismiss. The Colonel's given me a letter he thinks will interest you. Apparently he's had a signal from GHQ ordering him to start training us for warfare in Europe. Mountain fighting, street fighting, etcetera. One of the things we are going to need, which we couldn't use in this flat desert terrain, is snipers." He took a letter from his clipboard and laid it face down on the table in front of him.

"He thinks this might be the answer to your problem child. It's from a Captain Van der Walt. He's started a school for snipers at Helwan and he's looking for volunteers."

"Do you mean MacTavish, Major? He's not really a problem. It's just that I feel the boy is talented and we're not making the best use of his potential. He doesn't want promotion and I can't offer it to him again. He doesn't like mixing very much; he prefers keeping to himself. MacTavish is a bloody good soldier and I'm sorry he's not interested in assuming leadership. He seems to be saving himself up for something, yet every job I give him, he does quickly and properly.

"If he's a bit of a misfit, it's probably because he was educated at a better school than the rest of the men. The depression didn't affect his father like it affected the farmers. He would make a damned good scout, but we don't have any mustering for scouts."

"Your MacTavish, Jack, is one of the best shots in the Battalion, and from what you've told me I think he's better suited to this highly specialised role than anybody else I can think of. There's only one snag I can see. This Captain Van der Walt has stressed the fact that he doesn't want anybody under the age of thirty-five. He only wants steady, mature men, who have outgrown the impetuous age. How old is MacTavish, Jack?"

"Twenty, Major."

"Only twenty? I thought he was older. Anyway, we'll send him if he wants to volunteer. Sniping is a deadly job and Van der Walt will only accept volunteers. The Colonel says he'll give MacTavish a letter explaining why he thinks your boy's age should be overlooked. That is, if you feel you can spare him?"

Lieutenant Ingle nodded. "I don't want to lose a damn good man, Major, but I do believe he will be more use to us as a sniper than as a rifleman."

"Read the letter for yourself, Jack, then you can supply me with MacTavish's details. The Captain writes that out of every sixty men he gets, he's going to fail forty. Apparently it's a hell of a stiff course. We've been warned that the expected injury rate could be as high as twenty per cent.

Chapter 4

"No! .. No! .. Bugger this for a joke!" Captain Van der Walt glared at Peter as he jumped down from the truck that had brought him. The Captain was a tall, slightly stooped, falcon of a man, with a shock of unkempt grey hair and piercing black eyes. His shirt was threadbare and bleached almost white by the sun. "No! .. Fuck it! .. No! I told them to send me men. This is not a bloody kindergarten!

"What the hell did they send you for?" he raged, glaring into Peter's face. "Don't those bloody fools realise even the toughest men get broken on this course?"

Peter swallowed hard and saluted, staring straight ahead at the tall captain's unshaven chin. He handed Captain Van der Walt the letter from Colonel Hamman, feeling ill at ease, as he saw that he was years younger than the older men who stood around grinning at him, and he had a hollow feeling in his stomach. They would send him away. He was too young. The war would be in the history books by the time he was old enough to be a sniper.

"I was trained to be a sniper, Captain," he blurted desperately. He remained standing at attention and felt a flush of blood surge up his neck to his face.

Captain Van der Walt folded the letter and slid it into the pocket of his shirt. His black eyes stared into Peter's. "Who trained you?" he barked.

"An old Zulu warrior, Captain. He taught me everything he knew, when I was a small child."

A powerful man, mahogany brown from the sun and as hard as biltong, clapped his huge hand down on Peter's shoulder. He wore faded sergeant's stripes on the short sleeve of his shirt.

"You s-still are a s-small child sonny," the Sergeant stuttered, "what's your p-praise name?"

Peter whirled to face the Sergeant, smiling widely with unexpected pleasure. The Sergeant had addressed him in Zulu. He noticed the Sergeant's eyes blinked rapidly and there was a gleam of challenge in them. "Isinkwe, Sergeant."

"So you are a little b-bush-baby, are you?" He examined Peter with rapidly blinking, penetrating eyes. He was searching for the reason why this young soldier had been named "Isinkwe". He understood the matter of naming and noticed Peter's balance; his cat-like poise and watchful eyes.

The Sergeant grinned at Captain Van der Walt. He had not removed his hand from Peter's shoulder. "I've g-got a feeling, Henty, this little b-bugger'll make the grade." His eyes blinked in time with his stuttering. "G-give him the prisoner t-treatment and let's s-see what happens."

There was a look of confidence in Sergeant Brown's eyes. For a few moments Captain Van der Walt stared at him thoughtfully. He and Sergeant Brown had hunted together in South West Africa before the war and he knew the Sergeant wasn't given to flights of fancy, nor did he act on impulse.

Still watching Sergeant Brown with speculative eyes, Captain Van der Walt drew his pistol from its holster. He emptied the cartridges from the cylinder into his hand and checked that the weapon was safe. Handing the cartridges to the Sergeant, he cocked the pistol and gave it to Peter. Then he turned around to face the other way and spoke without turning his head. "Sonny boy, I'm your prisoner. Stick that pistol into my back and march me away."

Peter did not know what to expect. He balanced his weight on the balls of his feet, ready for instant action, and behind the Captain's back he changed the pistol quickly from his right hand to his left.

He stuck the rigidly extended index finger of his right hand against the Captain's back, held the cocked pistol against his left shoulder and stretched his body as far away from the Captain as he could get. He leaped back as he sensed the beginning of the Captain's lightning spin. The Captain's forearm struck his wrist and hurled his right hand into the air. No man on earth could have pulled a trigger quickly enough to shoot him when he ducked and turned.

In an unchecked flow of movement, the Captain chopped the inside of Peter's right elbow with the bone-hard edge of his hand. Twisting Peter's arm painfully, he flipped him onto his back on the burning desert sand. The Captain froze and stared down at him in disbelief.

The rock-steady muzzle of the pistol, drawn back against Peter's shoulder, pointed straight at the centre of his chest. For a moment they stared into each other's eyes. Neither of them moved. The knuckle of Peter's trigger finger whitened and the hammer of the pistol dropped with a flat click, loud in the breathless hush.

"You should know the Z-Zulus don't call anybody Isinkwe for f-fuck all, Henty." Sergeant Brown's voice broke the spell of silence. He reached down a big hand and pulled Peter onto his feet as though he weighed nothing.

A grin spread across the Captain's face. "Nobody's ever caught me out before. Maybe the Sergeant's right. I'll take you son, but don't cry if I break you."

Smiles faded from the watching faces when Captain Van der Walt turned to look at the men. "This course is bloody tough," he said to them. "It's got to be. Sniping is a hard and dangerous job. You'll have to lie dead still all day under a blistering sun, or freezing rain, watching the enemy. If you move you're a dead duck. By the time I've finished with you, you'll be able to lie still while ants are chewing your balls off. You will learn the kind of muscle control that will enable you to hold back a sneeze, while a fly crawls up one nostril and out of the other one."

A man's laugh died on his lips when the Captain turned his head to look at him with eyes, Peter thought, that were as deadly as those of a black mamba.

"This includes all of you." His black eyes moved slowly from man to man. "If you're ever taken prisoner, you might get one chance in a million of escaping. Germans don't like snipers any more than we do. I'm either going to break every bone in your bodies, or else I'm going to teach you how to exploit that very rare chance of escaping. The moves I will teach you are all crippling or killing and a bit difficult to practise without annihilating all your friends."

He stalked as soundlessly as a prowling leopard along the semicircle of men facing him, while his eyes bored into those of each man he passed.

"I'm going to teach you men how to fight with a knife. If you don't learn fast enough, you are going to get that knife stuck into you. I'm going to teach you how to tackle armed men and kill them with your bare hands. I'm going to teach you the most lethal tricks ever devised by those deadly little yellow bastards living in the Far East. I'll teach you how to kill, using almost every part of your body as a weapon."

His measured voice chilled the listening men. "You're going to learn to take hardship and physical torture in your stride. There are sixty of you men here now, but by the end of the first week there'll be only forty left. Ten of you will have run away and ten will be in hospital. At the end of eight weeks there will be only twenty left, and another twenty in hospital."

At the slightest movement from any man, the Captain whirled and faced the culprit, half crouched as though about to spring at him. He seemed to have eyes in the back of his head.

"Those surviving twenty men will have passed through the hell of physical endurance tests, shooting tests, navigation, compass and map-reading, examinations on field craft and concealment and camouflage, and tests in enemy recognition, so you will know which man to shoot and which ones to leave alone.

"Then for the final two weeks you will practise and repractise every bloody thing we've taught you. When I've finished with you, you will be the toughest, most deadly bastards on earth. Almost as tough as my instructors. You'll be able to operate efficiently and independently, even after days and nights without food or sleep. Then you will graduate as snipers – NOT sharpshooters! Any bloody fool who can shoot straight can be a sharpshooter. But a sniper is something very special. He is a highly trained professional."

Peter's shoulders twitched with a spasm of excitement. This was what old Mashona had trained him for. He felt Mashona's presence behind him and the old man's touch of reassurance. It was a small movement but the Captain had seen it. His head swung with the reflex of a wild animal and his unblinking eyes stared at Peter for a silent moment.

"Even this hidebound Army," he continued, ignoring the interruption, "recognises the unique value of snipers and accords them certain privileges. A sniper carries no rank because he doesn't command any troops. He takes his orders from only one man, and that man is the Colonel of his Regiment. Not even your RSM can tell you what to do. If the King himself tries to give you an order, you can tell him to kiss your arse.

"The Army decided to be big-hearted towards its snipers, because the top boys know what kind of hell you've been through to qualify. They also know snipers will get a sniper's reward. And that reward is death!

"A sniper is most likely to get blown to hell by a mortar bomb. I told you a little earlier, Germans don't like our snipers any more than we like theirs. If they get a feeling there's a sniper around, they'll blast apart every possible hiding-place in the countryside, until they get him.

"Statistics show the average life expectancy of a sniper in action is six hours. Hundreds of snipers have died to provide the statisticians with enough figures to arrive at that average. So now you know what you can expect. When you are not in action, you can do whatever you like. Nobody can make you do anything you don't want to do. But I warn you, don't sit on your arses and get soft.

"Practise your trigger pull on a tennis ball, to keep your hands supple and strong. Keep your body fit with exercises and do the same with your mind, so you will be able to switch off and not even hear the explosions of the mortar bombs that are probing for you. These are the sort of things that can get you a bonus of living for a half hour or so longer."

He stopped prowling and faced the men in silence, while his eyes moved again from man to man. "I'm going to turn my back on you. I've kept one truck waiting. If anybody wants to climb onto that truck and go back to his unit, I won't look around to see who it is. Any one of you is free to leave now and return to your unit if you've decided sniping is not for you. I have explained this to your Commanding Officers. The only men I want on this course are the suckers who are willing to sign their own death warrants.

"Right! Close your eyes and keep them closed until I tell you to open them. Those who wish to leave may do so privately."

Peter screwed his eyes closed. He could feel his heart pounding and he tingled with excitement. He would stay. It was unthinkable he should leave just because of what the Captain had said. Signing your own death warrant was just the Captain's way of saying things to frighten off those who didn't understand what sniping was all about. The Captain wouldn't frighten him into leaving. Death was not for him. Death was for those who failed to absorb every detail of every lesson they were about to be taught.

"Let your spirit help me, Baba Mashona," he breathed. "This was what you wanted for me since I was a baby in the arms of my mother, Uvemvane. I will go without fear because I know that I walk in the shadow of your shield."

Peter felt himself cringe with shame for what he considered the weak-spirited desertion of those who were leaving before the training had started. He listened to the sound of boots whispering in the sand and grating on pebbles. He heard kitbags fall with a thump in the back of a truck. He counted four of them. A rifle fell with a clatter onto the steel floor.

"Sergeant," he whispered, to cover his embarrassment.

"What is it?" Sergeant Brown spoke beside him. "If you want to b-bugger off you d-don't have to ask anybody."

"No! No," he said hurriedly. He felt hurt that the Sergeant could think such a thing of him. "No, Sergeant, I just wanted to ask you what your praise name was."

"Cimela. W-why do you ask?"

"We both understand what lies behind a naming, Sergeant. Cimela! The one who extinguishes," he said quietly as though to himself. "Cimela. The one who turns out a light, or puts out a fire, or switches off." He waited in silence for the Sergeant to reply.

"They named me C-Cimela, because my eyes b-blink rapidly. T-they must have known then t-that I would stutter when I learned to t-talk."

A truck engine revved, gears grated in the unsynchromeshed gearbox, and the truck pulled away clattering and clanging. Peter tried to rid his mind of the sound of the departing truck and with it, the last chance he might have had to leave with them. But his mind was drawn by the feeling of eyes boring into him. He kept his own eyes closed waiting for the Captain's permission to open them.

"Cimela can also mean the one who extinguishes life," he whispered. The Sergeant beside him said nothing. "Or a killer!" He forgot about waiting for the Captain. He opened his eyes and looked directly into the gold-eyed stare of Sergeant Brown. For a moment their eyes locked and Peter noticed the Sergeant's eyes were no longer blinking.

"ukuCima! To kill," Peter murmured to himself. "Or to extinguish life." He didn't realise he had spoken the disturbing words of his thoughts.

"You know your Z-Zulu, Isinkwe," Sergeant Cimela Brown smiled. It was a hard, dangerous smile. Peter felt the hairs rise on the back of his neck. He unconsciously shifted his weight to balance on the balls of his feet in case he might have to move fast. But the Sergeant's eyes softened. He blinked rapidly and lines of cynical mirth deepened at the sides of his smile.

"You c-can't fool those old Zulus, c-can you? When they s-see those first t-teeth appear they already know what the c-child will be like when he grows to be a m-man."

"Right!" The Captain's bark drew everybody's attention. "You can look around now. Pay attention! First of all I want you to meet your instructors. They're the toughest bunch of bastards I could find in the whole army. I'm not asking you to love them. I doubt whether their own mothers would be prepared to go as far as that. But I advise you to listen to them if you want to carry on living.

"I'll start with myself. My name is Henty van der Walt. I was a sniper in the last war. I must have been a bloody good one too because I lasted for two years in the front line. I made one mistake and I was bloody lucky to get away with a bullet through my shoulder and another one through the cheeks of my arse. I should have got killed. No other sniper I ever heard of was lucky enough to survive the consequences of a mistake." His words removed the smiles from the faces of his audience.

"There's no rank on this course, or in the profession of sniping. The sergeants are sergeants because they're instructors. As for me, you can call me Captain, or you can call me Henty, or you can call me the biggest bloody shithouse you've ever seen. It makes no difference to me.

"I'm not here to acknowledge your salutes. My job is to turn you men into the most deadly killers in the army. In war this is necessary. I want to make you as efficient as possible for two reasons."

He resumed his silent-footed prowl that reminded Peter of a caged animal.

"The first reason is to equip you to inflict the most telling damage on the enemy. You will do this by systematically removing the finest fighting leaders and artillery observers they can put into the field against us. The second reason is to make you so tough and so bloody expert, that you will live through the hell your job will subject you to and survive to tell your stories to your sons. If you are lucky enough, you might be able to bullshit one of God's Angels into marrying you and turning you back into human beings, if you manage to survive this war."

He stopped prowling to challenge his listeners with his eyes. Crouched over like a lion about to spring, he stared from man to man.

"I'm going to teach you everything I learned as a sniper, plus a hell of a lot I've thought about during the last twenty-four years of earning my living by hunting big game in South West Africa, Bechuanaland Protectorate, Angola and the Belgian Congo."

During the ensuing few moments of silence his bead-black eyes flickered over his future pupils. They seemed to linger doubtfully for an instant on Peter, whose youthful appearance contrasted sharply with the weathered features of the older men around him.

"To assist me, I have here," he pointed to the first of the sun-shrivelled, bearded men who stood in a ragged line nearby, "Sergeant Bokkie van As. Professional safari hunter, Mozambique, plus twelve years of undetected poaching in the Kruger National Park and in Southern Rhodesia."

His hand pointed to the next man. "Sergeant Attie Oelofse. Kenya, Congo, Tanganyika, Uganda. The Police of all four of those countries are still looking for him. Successful poaching has made Attie a wealthy man."

The listening men looked at Sergeant Oelofse. They were not sure whether the Captain was joking or not. Some smiled while others watched with expressionless faces, waiting for a cue from him. But he carried on with an impassive look.

He indicated the next instructor. A sharp-featured Bushman of a man. "Sergeant Shorty Charnaud. Northern Rhodesia, Ruanda, Congo, Tanganyika, Kenya. You name it, he's hunted there. Shorty can steal the tusks out of the Chief of Police's tame elephant from inside its stable, without waking the dogs. Shorty's speciality – swamps, rivers and crocodiles. If any of you men have anything of value, either give it to Shorty now, to save him the trouble of stealing it later, or have it locked up for safe keeping."

Shorty smiled a ferrety smile at the Captain. One of the men guffawed and grins spread across the faces of others.

"You might think I'm joking, but I'm not." There was no smile on the Captain's face. "I chose these instructors for their ability as snipers. Not for any endearing qualities they may have hidden somewhere inside them. But listen to them and live, or ignore what they teach and die. It's up to you." He turned to the last instructor and Peter sensed a change in the Captain's feelings.

"This big guy is Sergeant Cimela Brown. I warn you all now, don't try anything with this man. Cimela was the best anti-poaching game ranger Rhodesia ever had. He was forced to leave the Game Department after his sixth appearance in court to answer charges of homicide, for killing poachers with his bare hands. Ex game ranger, Zululand. Expert hunter, especially of men. Safari guide. North Western Cape, South West Africa, Angola, Northern Rhodesia, Bechuanaland Protectorate. Very good with a knife. Make damned sure you don't get on the wrong side of him. We have hunted together from time to time and I tell you, I know him well.

"Cimela hates all poachers and that includes my three other Sergeants here. Especially Attie Oelofse, the rich one. The only reason Cimela hasn't murdered them yet, is because I need them to train you bastards. If ever he meets them in the bush after the war he will kill them, and they understand this very clearly."

A few of the new men smiled a little uncertainly and shuffled their feet. There were no doubts in Peter's mind. Somebody like Mashona had named the big man after he had cut his first teeth and he knew that what the Captain had said was a plain statement of fact.

"The reason they made me a Captain was to give me the authority to control men like these." He turned away from his instructors and stalked silently to and fro as though deep in thought and Peter noticed his indrawn lips were set in an uncompromising line.

"These instructors are all expert shots. For the first couple of weeks they will fire very close warning shots at you, and towards the end of the course they will shoot at any part of you they see sticking out.

"You are all well-trained and battle-experienced men. If you weren't, you wouldn't be here." He glanced again dubiously at Peter. Sergeant Cimela Brown reached out his big hand and rested it on Peter's shoulder and he pulled Peter towards him. It was a possessive, protective gesture. "You can l-leave this one to me, H-Henty," he said.

"There'll be other instructors," Captain Van der Walt continued. "Instructors in camouflage and concealment; artillery observer instructors; navigation instructors; unarmed combat instructors; and there'll be Intelligence men who will tell you what to look for and things to recognise. You'll be taught by engineers about mines and booby traps. Mortar fundis will teach you how to call down accurate mortar fire to destroy German snipers, observation posts, lookouts, etc, or how to call down a curtain of smoke bombs to help you take up a position – or get out of one in a hurry.

"These men are all experts in their various fields. They will not come here. You will be taken to them where they've got all their props and gadgets prepared for you." He stopped in mid-stride and faced the new snipers, leaning towards them to add emphasis to what he was about to tell them.

"Listen to me, men," he commanded. "There's no use for snipers here in the desert because the kind of war we are fighting is too mobile. But when we get into Europe and the slogging fighting starts, you men will be in great demand. Before your regiments dare advance, your Commanding Officers will have to know what lies ahead of them and you'll be the ones they'll send to find out.

"The Germans will know damned well you'll be watching them. They will expect you to hide yourselves in a reasonably bomb- and bullet-proof position. They'll have their mortars ranged on every likely looking spot and machine-guns on standby to cut you down if you try to run for it.

"They know you'll have to get to your chosen position in the dark and either the approaches to it, or the spot itself, will be mined or booby trapped, or both. They are retreating and they know they will never have to cross that terrain again, so they'll cover the traps they've set for you very professionally. They've got all the time in the world to do it. You'll be their public enemy number one and they'll spare no efforts to get you. And they won't give a damn for the children who get blown to bits when they play there after the fighting's moved on."

Still bending slightly forward and with his fingers hooked like the claws of an animal of prey, he walked along the line looking intently into the eyes of each man as he passed him.

"We have prepared similar situations for you to train and learn in." His tone was emotionless. "We have set explosive devices to make your training as realistic as possible. We obviously don't want any of you killed on this course, so we've reduced the charges in the booby traps we've set for you to drive home lessons of observation and anticipation. There is just enough explosive left to blow off a finger or break an ankle if you step on one of them, or to blast enough sand and grit into your eyes to blind you.

"This might seem like a waste of good men to some of you, but you must remember, the Germans simply can't have you lying around watching them. They're a very determined people and bloody good at their job.

"To win, we've got to be just that much better. My task is to produce quality and not quantity from this course. If any man gets seriously injured, his misfortune will be a better example to the others than any amount of teaching. Try to think of it that way."

Judging by the expressionless faces around him, Peter decided most of them disliked the idea as much as he did. He wanted to be a sniper. He didn't want to be maimed learning to be one.

"I know every one of you is a crack shot. You have all been taught to aim one inch below an enemy's navel, allowing a six-inch error in every direction from your point of aim. You've been taught not to kill a single bloody German, but to wound the bastard. This will immediately put him out of action and also the two guys nearest him, who will stop shooting at you to help him. You've been taught to shoot at his belt buckle, because even if you miss it, you'll bugger up his spine or his hip joints or his pelvis, pancreas, intestines, spleen, kidneys, or even the lower lobes of his lungs." He glared at each man in turn, to confirm that this was what they'd been taught. Some of the men nodded and others grunted their affirmation.

"Right," he continued. "You were taught that these are all permanently disabling shots which will overtax doctors, nurses, hospitals and rehabilitation centres, and use up enormous amounts of scarce drugs and other costly medical supplies. Those droves of crippled guys will also play up hell with enemy morale.

"Get all they taught you right out of your heads! It might be bloody good tactical shooting in battle, but it doesn't apply to snipers! Your targets will be artillery observers, snipers, leaders and individuals who are causing our side the most misery. These bastards have got to be killed!

"You aim at the centre of his chest, halfway between his bottom ribs and his collar bones. Your bullet has got to hit within a circle of five inches across, so you never shoot from further than three hundred yards. This is a heart, nerve, blood vessel shot. It will crash through the man's breastbone and drive splinters of bone, muscle tissue, arteries and veins right through his heart, upper lungs and spinal column. It'll hit him with such force it'll bowl him over and he'll never be able to tell anybody where the shot came from. And nobody else will be able to tell from the position he is lying in where the shot came from either. It's a killing shot."

He lifted his right hand and waved a pointing finger emphatically with flicks of his wrist.

"Never, under any circumstances, try for a head shot. The brain is a hell of a small and tricky target, particularly when it's partly protected by a steel helmet, which might deflect your bullet. There's also a danger that, as you squeeze the trigger, the bastard might turn his head suddenly to look at something.

"It takes the human brain one tenth of a second to register and react to something seen. In that time a man's head could have nodded twice or turned through the best part of a semicircle before your bullet reaches him. Unless you kill your man instantly, he might just be able to tell the others where your bullet came from.

"In any one day you fire only one shot. For the rest of that day a thousand pairs of eyes will be looking for you. If you fire again from the same position, it'll be the last shot you'll ever fire. Within minutes mortar bombs will turn you into mincemeat.

"I'm not going to ask you men to listen to me, but I warn you that while you lie dying you'll be bloody sorry that you didn't. Sharpshooters shoot from the top of trees and tall buildings and other bloody silly places they can't get away from when the mortars start searching for them. Snipers never fire from any position that isn't bulletproof and hasn't got a reasonably safe escape route. You men are too valuable to get yourselves killed out of sheer stupidity. Stick strictly to the tips we give you and with a hell of a lot of luck, you might just be able to keep alive until the enemy finally surrenders."

Peter looked around him with searching swings of his head. His face showed surprise and expectancy. A tiny cloud crossed the face of the sun for a moment and he distinctly smelt untanned leather. It was the smell he had known so well as a child. It was the smell of Mashona's shield. The sour odour of sweat which he also smelt could have come from the men who stood around.

"I wish you all good luck." The Captain's tone was sincere. He noticed Peter glance up at the sky and look around and sniff the air. "What's wrong with you, little Isinkwe? Can you smell the Germans already?"

"No, Captain. I smelt leather!"

Captain Van der Walt shook his head sadly and turned to Cimela Brown. "It looks like your little bush-baby's fucked in the head before he's even started," he said.

"Right, men! Fall in, in one line, shoulder to shoulder." He turned to face the Sergeants. "Cimela, you take the number ones. Attie, the number twos. Shorty, the number threes. Bokkie, you take the fours."

"From the right .. In fours .. Number! One .. Two .. Three .. Four .. One .. Two .. Three .. Four .." Peter was a number three but Sergeant Cimela Brown walked towards the standing line and took a handful of Peter's shirt and pulled him from the rank of men. "You c-come with me, Isinkwe," he growled.

"Henty, I'm t-taking this little b-bush-baby into my squad. If I don't k-kill the little prick, I'm g-going to make him into the b-best sniper of the whole l-lot of them."

Peter had dug himself in halfway down the stark, eroded wall of the wadi. The bank was almost precipitous. It dropped away from in front of him to a wide, flat valley of sand. He had selected his position a few days previously with the greatest care. Under cover of darkness he took soil from the spot and wet it from his water bottle and stained the net that was to cover him the exact colour of the surrounding soil.

It was a good position. It commanded a wide field of fire and it was bulletproof. It had a reasonable line of retreat down an eroded fissure in the face of the wadi, a yard away from where he lay, as invisible as a desert lizard against the desert background. But he knew that somewhere, Cimela was searching for him and the thought niggled in his mind. He would know soon enough when Cimela had found his hiding place. The bullet burn across his right shoulder blade still stung when he moved his right arm. He had learned his lesson and Cimela would never find him again.

Nobody must know where he was hiding. Please God, not Cimela! And not the men he would be watching as soon as the sun rose and they started their work.

His skin prickled and he experienced a creepy feeling that Mashona was near him, warning him of danger. He tried to picture the old man, hoping he would remember the most important things he had taught him about hiding while watching an enemy and he remembered the straw-filled greatcoat warrior that Mashona had hidden behind the wheelbarrow. There was nothing he could think of that he hadn't taken into consideration. But instead of an image of Mashona, it was an image of Cimela that crowded his thoughts and goose-pimpled his skin.

He had survived his first six weeks of torture and learning and he didn't want to fail the course now. The desert sun had burned him as brown as the weathered stones lying along the foot of the wadi wall below him. He knew what it was like to lie still for endless hours and suffer cramps, hunger, thirst, gut-wrenching anxiety and all the other torments of body and mind.

He wondered at times whether it was because of their unendurable sufferings that snipers gave away their positions and got themselves killed, just to end it all. If he died, death would relieve him of Cimela's scathing criticisms that made him cringe with mortification. Nor would there be any more of Cimela's "t-tongue lashings", which hurt more than the physical agonies.

A hundred feet below him a squad of men halted in the early morning sunlight to begin their tasks for the day. There were a hundred and three of them. He recounted them carefully. The senior man was a Captain of Engineers. He was assisted by three sergeants and ten corporals.

Under cover of darkness he would have to make his way back past their sentries, under the very real threat of getting shot, and provide Cimela with a comprehensive written report of their activities. Cimela would want to know every single detail, including their ranks and attitudes. Cimela would also want to know which one of them he had decided to shoot and why he had selected that particular individual.

Peter watched and thought and ached. Cimela would want to know how the men handled their weapons. Were they instinctively familiar with them or were they careless? The lessons he had learned and the tips he had gleaned buzzed like flies in his mind. And over and above every other consideration, his subconscious mind crawled with the feeling that Mashona was trying to warn him of something.

He hadn't had that feeling the day before. It had started nagging him since a pebble had rolled down the wall of the wadi while he was about to get into his slit trench, long before the sun rose. His nerves were strung like the strings of a fiddle as he waited for the shock of Cimela's bullet. Imagining the nerve-jarring crack and the scorch of pain, he tried to sink lower into his shallow trench.

He wondered if his net was covering him properly? Had he concealed every scrap of the darker soil he had excavated? Was the colour of his net really a perfect match for the surrounding soil? Did the ends of the dark line he had made across his net meet exactly with the dark stripe in the wadi face across which he lay?

These were things he had been unable to check in the dark. The magnification of the field-glasses made it feel as though his eyeballs were being drawn from their sockets. And all the time, with increasing certainty, he knew that Cimela was watching him.

The sun beat down relentlessly. At eleven o'clock he sucked a little tepid water from his water bottle through the thin rubber tube, without moving his head or his arms. He had not forgotten to open his fly and leave his penis hanging over the little hole he had excavated beneath his body, so he could urinate without moving. He urinated a few drops into the hole and he wondered how his body could possibly manufacture sufficient water to pass even a few drops, while the sun sucked the moisture through his pores.

His skin crawled with the certainty that very soon Cimela would spring his trap. He could feel his unseen presence. He knew Cimela was watching him as a mongoose watches a snake and the feeling was so real, he became obsessed with the belief that if he stretched out his hand he would be able to touch him.

The knowledge that not even a lizard could stalk him without him seeing it, gave him no comfort. There was not an inch of cover Cimela could use to creep up on him without showing himself. Painfully slowly, he eased forward in his slit trench to make certain.

The lower face of the wadi was bare. Cimela was not down there. Fraction by fraction he turned his body so he could examine the rugged wadi bank above his position. On a tiny ledge, thirty feet above him, he saw a desert shrew cleaning its face with its paws, so Cimela was not up there either.

The absurd notion that Cimela had crept into his trench beside him pushed all other thoughts out of his mind. He put down his field-glasses and stretched his arm backwards to make quite sure Cimela hadn't wriggled into the three inch gap, like a snake.

The faint crunch of disturbed gravel and the sound of a loud fart flushed his heart with adrenaline. He threw aside his net to launch himself into the erosion fissure that was his escape route, but Cimela's iron hand clamped around his ankle and jerked him back. He had anticipated Peter's reaction and he pounced onto him from his own slit trench, a yard behind and a yard to the left of Peter's trench.

Peter fell onto his back with Cimela on top of him. He could not fight because his arms were restricted in the narrow trench. Cimela's knee pressed agonisingly into his groin and his iron fingers gripped Peter's ears to give his thumbs purchase to press Peter's eyeballs back into his skull.

The pain of Cimela's knee in his groin and the pressure of the thumbs threatening to burst his eyeballs made him want to vomit. Cimela changed his grip. He grabbed a handful of Peter's hair and pulled his head back and Peter felt a bite of pain as he grabbed at the blade of Cimela's knife pricking his throat.

"Don't damage your t-trigger finger, you bloody fool. Lie still, my little b-bush-baby. A man can't f-fight so good when he's blind and he can't f-fight at all when his balls are squashed or his throat is c-cut, either." Cimela did not relax his hold nor did he relieve the pressure of the knife that felt as though it was about to burst through the skin of Peter's throat and plunge into his windpipe. "Clever little b-bastard, aren't you? It took me the whole f-fucking day yesterday to f-find you. That f-false trail you laid had me f-fooled completely. I bloody nearly put a shot into that d-dummy you rigged up for me to f-find.

"Lie still, f-fuck you! Suffer now rather than die later.

"You made two f-fuck-ups that would have cost you your life. Your n-net was too smooth. The texture didn't exactly m-match the background. Texture is the ability of a surface to retain s-shadow, remember? If you had tied a f-few more little knots in your net you would have made it look r-rougher, and I wouldn't have found you in a m-million years.

"The second and biggest f-fuck-up you m-made was not trusting your wonderfully developed s-sixth s-sense. I w-watched it working on you for bloody hours before you f-finally pulled your finger out and decided to dive for safety. I let you s-sweat to teach you to trust that f-feeling you get. Move immediately! Don't just lie there with your f-finger up your arse, waiting to get shot."

Cimela pushed his knife into its sheath. He stood up and pulled Peter onto his feet. "Once I knew where you w-were, it was simple. There was only one way you could be w-watching and that was away from the w-wadi. I came in the night while you were writing your report and m-made my place a little way behind you where you would n-never dream of expecting me to be. I t-tied a piece of cotton around a small stone and w-waited for you. When you came to take up your position I p-pulled the cotton and made the stone rattle down the wadi. The n-noise distracted you and made you look away from where

I was l-lying, right behind you.

"Ch-cheer up, Isinkwe. You were bloody good. Remember that the element of surprise always g-gives the attacker the advantage. Your sixth sense put you on the defensive. In b-battle the advantage will be in your f-favour and you will shoot the shit out of the Germans before they know w-what's hit them."

Peter smouldered with resentment, pain and humiliation. "Why couldn't you just tell me what I did wrong?" His voice was dangerously edged. "Why the hell did you have to half kill me first, when you had the bloody advantage, like you said you had?"

Cimela smiled one of his rare, disarming smiles. "I wanted to get my own back on you for m-making me suffer so long. You see, I had to teach you to recognise that wonderful s-sixth sense the good Lord gave you. So I had to wait while it w-worked on your nerves for a few hours, without you knowing where I was. Trouble was, I had to wait so long, you m-made me bottle up a b-block buster of a fart, until I was afraid it would either b-blast the ring out of my arsehole, or else you'd smell my breath b-before you got the m-message."

Despite his pain, Peter laughed aloud. Cimela was not the kind of man he could ever hate. But he promised himself his day would come.

Captain Henty Van der Walt pressed his clenched fists down onto the tabletop. "There's one more thing I want you to bear in mind, young man," his voice was tight with impatience. Dozens of men he knew would give their right hands to become instructors at his school of sniping. He would try once more, but there was no way he would kiss the little bush-baby's arse to get him to join them.

"None of us have been able to make you see the light. This is the third course we've run and I've no hesitation in telling you, you've proved yourself to be the best sniper we've produced. Cimela has given you a harder time than he has ever given anybody in all his life. He did this to prove to me you were a natural, even if you are too young."

He leaned forward and fixed Peter with his black-eyed stare. "I put each of the Instructors out against you and you outsmarted every one of them. I tried you out for myself and you made me look like a monkey. Then I put you out against each of the Instructors and you nailed every one of them."

Peter smiled to himself at the memory. He'd got his own back alright, but it had been touch and go. The only thing that had saved him was flicking Cimela's knife out of its sheath and throwing it away before Cimela could get at it.

"Little bastard f-fucking near killed me." Cimela gingerly touched the padded elastoplast patch covering the knife prick over his jugular vein. "He t-took me from behind like an eagle taking a dassie off a rock. Little shithouse made me listen to a f-fucking lecture, with his knife stuck halfway into my neck."

Captain Van der Walt continued. "I put it to you for the last time, Isinkwe. As a Sergeant Instructor in this school, you will be doing your country a far greater service than you could ever do as a battalion sniper. Cimela has told me of your childhood and the kind of training you were given by some old Zulu warrior. You've showed us all what a fine grounding that was.

"Cimela swears you keep the spirit of the old bugger with you to look after you. The two of us have lived all our lives in the bush with people like your old Zulu, and we've seen too much to mock at these sort of things we Europeans don't really understand. I could do with somebody like him to cover my back at times. If he doesn't cover your back, you're going to get yourself killed. Of that I'm bloody certain. And all Cimela's hard work will be wasted.

"Before you decide you want to go back to your Regiment, there are a couple of things I want you to think about. I'm perfectly certain no German sniper will ever outsmart you. But unfortunately I'm just as certain your efforts to help win this war as a sniper will never be of any use, because you're going to get yourself killed."

He bashed both fists down on the tabletop in anger. "Listen to me, damn you! It won't be your fault that will get you killed. It's your age. I have a very good reason for not wanting any men on this course younger than thirty five. Look at it this way.

"An older sniper will know his job and do his job. He might be called on to lead others into a position to do their job, because he's the only guy with the savvy to get them there. Then, no matter how dangerous the job is for them, and no matter how much he could help them if he stayed with them, he would pull out and report back as he was told to do, so that he is again available to do what nobody else can do!"

The Captain shook his head with frustration. "You won't do that. I'll bet anybody a pound to a pinch of shit, you'll stay and join in the fight and get yourself written off. Look at us guys," he waved his arm in a circle, to encompass his immediate surroundings, "I'm a bloody good sniper myself. So is Cimela. So is Bokkie. So is Attie. So is Shorty. But we are a hell of a lot more use training a couple of hundred other snipers, than we would be if we did the shooting ourselves. Bugger it all man! Can't you see why it's important to keep you here as a bloody good instructor rather than let you go and commit suicide simply because you're too fucking young to be a sniper?"

Peter started to speak but the Captain cut him short.

"Shut up," he barked, "I'm doing the talking! A sniper's job is to select the right man and to kill him. Then he must get himself out so he is available for whatever else his expertise is needed. He might be needed to observe what nobody else is capable of observing, and live long enough to get that information back to the guys who need it.

"That is one side of the story. The other side is that your nature would make you a bloody fine instructor, but a piss poor sniper. You're not a killer! Every one of the instructors agrees you lack this instinct, and they should know because they're killers themselves."

Cimela snorted like a startled wildebeest. "Just listen who's talking!" He turned to Peter before the Captain could say any more. "You remember when you f-first arrived here, Isinkwe," he grabbed Peter's shoulder and shook him and let go hurriedly when he remembered what had happened the last time he tried to grab him.

"We agreed nobody can ever fool those old Z-Zulus when it comes to naming a child. When your first teeth showed, that old Z-Zulu of yours knew bloody well you were not a k-killer. That's why he named you Isinkwe. B-bush-babies aren't killers either. There'a hell of a lot of other n-names he could have chosen, instead of Isinkwe."

"Thanks, Captain," Peter's voice was sincere. "And thanks to you too, Cimela, but I'm going back to my Regiment." Nothing they could say would deflate his self-confidence. He had visualised the scene a hundred times during his hours of watching and waiting. He would rest the tip of his foresight on the top button of the enemy's tunic, instead of on his belt buckle. The rifle would kick and he would follow the flight of his bullet into that tunic. When it struck, the tail-heavy bullet would flip over and rip sideways through the enemy's heart. It would be as simple as that.

"I've made up my mind. Mashona trained me for scouting and you trained me for sniping. So that's what I'll do. He promised he would return from the land of shadow to cover my back, so I'll just have to rely on him when things go wrong."

Captain Van der Walt glanced at his watch. "All right," he growled, "bugger off and get yourself killed, if that's what you want. Anyway, it's time for the Intelligence boffins to give you another session of brain-washing, to make you mad enough to want to kill every German you see."

"The only thing that's going to make this b-bush-baby want to kill anybody, is when something breaks his bloody heart or b-blows his balls off with a m-mortar bomb," Cimela added, shaking his head regretfully. He had grown attached to Peter and he didn't want to part with him.

The Intelligence Major looked out of place in battledress. "My God." His words were strongly accented in what sounded to Peter like German. He adjusted his metal-framed spectacles and pointed his beak of a nose at each man as he counted, "there's only eighteen of you left. I'm afraid Captain Van der Walt is going to have to lower his exacting standards," he said. "He'll have to push batches of men through his courses a lot quicker, if we're going to meet the demand for the snipers we'll need in Europe.

"Anyway! Let's get on with it! I've got a lot of slides to show you, so I'll have to keep the lead story as short as I can. The slides will explain themselves. I'm afraid the quality of some of them is not too good, because you must understand they were made from photographs smuggled out of Europe, mostly from Germany and Poland, by resistance agents, at enormous risk. Anybody caught with these sort of pictures would be shot – if they were lucky. Or else tortured to death."

He readjusted his spectacles and cleared his throat again. "For more than a year, Military Intelligence has been receiving reports of wholesale genocide of European, Balkan and Russian Jews. For a long time they were unable to accept the stark truth of what was happening, nor could they believe the reported inhuman brutality with which these atrocities were being carried out. But the testimony of the growing trickle of refugees who have succeeded in escaping from Europe, can no longer be refuted.

"At first their evidence was too ghastly for civilized minds to comprehend. No normal being could accept the truth that any nation, even one as intellectually barbaric as the Germans, could inflict such cruelty on other humans."

Peter wondered what was coming next. He glanced briefly at Shalom Jacobson, whom he knew was Jewish. Then he shuffled into a more comfortable position on the backless bench he shared with the other snipers, to listen to what the Major had to say.

"Intelligence checked and cross-checked the validity of as much of the unbelievable information as they could. Unfortunately this could not be done quickly, and while they wasted time checking, millions, I repeat, 'millions' of civilians who were innocent of any crimes, were being systematically rounded up and annihilated.

"Without the slightest compassion, troopers of the German SS are forcibly parting grandmothers from grandfathers, wives from husbands and children from their parents. They herd their victims into scientifically constructed buildings and exterminate them with poison gas".

He paused for a few moments while the snipers looked at one another uneasily. His glasses seemed to be worrying him. He took them off and bowed his head over them, while hazy mental pictures of the holocaust formed in the minds of the listening men. The Major wiped his glasses thoughtfully with his handkerchief while he stared at the rectangle of light in the doorway.

"I am now with Military Intelligence," he said. "A short time ago we received authenticated reports that the concrete floors of some of these extermination chambers have to be re-laid at regular intervals. The concrete is torn up by the clawing fingernails of the suffocating Jewish inmates in their death throes. This could well be true of many other such places we don't know about yet.

"To the Jews, unswerving belief in their God, Jehovah, and the sanctity of the family unit, are the keystones of their very existence. They are an industrious people. Their practical application of mutual help has often brought them more prosperity than members of the host nations among whom they've lived. It has also brought them jealousy, envy and hatred."

He paused and fiddled with his spectacles while the snipers waited expectantly. He coughed nervously and looked up, as though surprised to find himself facing an audience.

"I want you men," he continued, "to understand what the Germans are doing to Jewish civilians and how brutally they are doing it, so as snipers you will want to kill them whenever you get the chance. If you don't hate them and you kill them simply because you've been especially trained to do so, you will be as morally sterile as they are."

He shook the phantoms impatiently from his mind. "I don't know how much more of this I can stand," he spoke as though to himself, "but I must get on with it." He stalked to the door of the Nissen hut and switched off the lights. The room was dark. Draped blankets covered the windows and it was stifling hot. He stumbled over his feet and groped his way back to the table.

A switch clicked and a brilliant white screen leaped at the men from the darkness. Click. Peter jolted upright on his seat. The dreadfulness of the scene that sprang to petrified life on the screen slapped his sensibilities and he stared at it in horror. A completely naked and exquisitely appealing girl, with tear-streaked cheeks and her mouth open, was frozen in the square of projected light. The girl was in the act of collapsing. She had soiled herself.

German soldiers stood around her in various poses of battering her with their rifles. One smirking soldier had the muzzle of his rifle poked into the nest of dark curly hairs between the girl's legs.

"The bloody bastards!" Shalom Jacobson had risen into a half crouch as the words hissed through his clenched teeth.

"Crime: being Jewish." The Major's voice was chillingly unemotional. "Sentence: to serve in an army whore-house until she becomes infected with VD, or goes insane, or until she gets too thin and lethargic to give the troops an enjoyable screw – ten to twenty men a day. Then to the gas chambers."

Despite the heat, Peter felt a shiver of revulsion contract his stomach. He leaned forward and stared at the screen as fascinated as a rabbit staring at a python. The girl was beautiful and he wondered how anything human could treat her so brutally. Her look of stark horror made him want to rush to help her. Unconsciously his hand dropped to the knuckleduster-handled sniper's knife strapped to the outside of his left calf. The Major's hate-hardened voice penetrated his thoughts of revenge.

"This girl is somebody's daughter. Somebody's sister. Somebody's sweetheart. She comes from a loving home where she was cherished. Look how her well-washed hair shines. She was probably gently brought up. If the Germans win the war, this could be your younger sister we are looking at. We .. ah .. er .. This picture was taken from the body of a German soldier who we .. er .. who some partisans executed for murdering a young Polish girl .. After he had raped her."

The men sitting on the backless benches moved their heads to release their tension and leaned forward with their hands on their knees, waiting. Their faces were hard with revulsion.

Click. The tortured girl vanished. A picture of a railway platform took her place. It was crowded with naked people of both sexes and all ages. Uniformed German guards were herding them into cattle trucks with kicks and blows of rifle butts. In the foreground a wrinkled, naked grandmother clasped a bare, crying baby to her pendulous bosom for warmth. Her other arm was around the shoulders of a plumpish, younger woman. Her daughter perhaps. Mother of the child. Beside them a naked old man stood looking up to Heaven with his toothless mouth open in a cry for deliverance to his great God, Jehovah.

"Crime: .." the Major's clipped voice cut across their shocked senses, "being Jewish. Sentence: extermination in the gas chambers. You will see from the pinched nipples on the breasts of the women and the shrivelled penes of the males, that it is bitterly cold. The soldiers are wearing greatcoats. Notice the absence of wedding rings on fingers or bracelets or chains or earrings or watches. The Germans have ripped them off for loot. After these people have been gassed, the gold fillings will be broken out of their teeth. Their clothes have already been taken to be shredded and processed into clothing for the so-called Master Race."

Click. A lively scene fraught with dread sprang onto the screen. Open cattle trucks crowded with excited children waving happily to their parents, who were clinging to each other in an agony of heartbreak.

"These happy children are being taken out to the countryside for a picnic. On their way to the picnic they will be given chocolates their parents have provided. The chocolates are impregnated with cyanide. Those grieving parents have sent their children out to die quickly from the deadly poison, to save them the excruciating trauma of lingering deaths at the hands of the Germans."

"Oh God, oh God!" Shalom moaned.

Click. Bodies of dead and dying, lying in heaps and rows, and strewn over the steps of another railway station. Blood in pools. Blood in the gutters. A terrified young boy with a shattered hip – smashed by a bullet from the machine-gun at the end of the platform – trying to drag himself to safety. An SS soldier was striding towards him with his fixed bayonet poised to lunge.

"The bastards .. The fucking bastards!" Shalom's voice was choked. He tugged a length of crumpled toilet paper from his pocket to wipe his eyes. A hand beside him reached over for a piece of the paper.

"Machine-gunned Polish Jews and Jewish sympathisers, reluctant to board the trucks 'en route' to the gas chambers. The boy is fortunate. A moment after the searing agony of that bayonet piercing his chest, he will convulse into a state of terminal shock. Even if he lingers on for a few minutes, his body will be traumatized beyond the experience of pain."

Peter touched his lips with the tip of his tongue. His mouth was as dry as ash. He swallowed hard. The picture stayed frozen on the screen while the Major stood watching Shalom.

"What's your first name, Jacobson?" the Major asked.

"Shalom, Major." His voice was choked with emotion.

Peter turned to look at him. He felt a surge of sympathy for him. He had never thought of Shalom as anything other than a good sniper. He was as hard as nails physically and when he was cross his black eyes looked as deadly as Captain Van der Walt's.

"Where was your father from, Shalom?" The Major removed his spectacles and peered short-sightedly at him.

"Lithuania, Major. He's old now. He's a tailor in Johannesburg."

"Tell me, Shalom, have you still got relatives in Lithuania?"

"I don't know, Major. We were a big family. I remember having cousins at Vilnyus, Kaunas, Ukmerge and in the country between those places."

"And now, Shalom?"

"They used to write to us. Three years ago their letters stopped coming. Some nights I heard my mother crying for them."

The men sat unmoving as they listened. Until a few moments ago, Peter had simply regarded them as snipers. It seemed strange that they also came from individual families, the same as he did.

"As a sniper, you'll get the opportunity to avenge them," the Major said.

"Yes, Major. Both me and Gordon." He indicated the fair-haired, hazel-eyed man on the other side of him. Peter turned his head so he could see Gordon's face in the light reflected from the screen. He certainly didn't look like a Jew.

The Major combed his fingers through his thinning hair. "With a name like Gordon, I took you for a Scot."

"Major, my name is Maich. Maich Gordon." A ghost of a smile touched Gordon's lips. He glanced at the faces of the other snipers. "There were Gordons in Israel a hell of a long time before there were Gordons in Scotland," he remarked. "And Jewish snipers are nothing new either, even if they did use bows and arrows. Our fighting history was ancient long before the days of Joshua."

"Did you also have family in Europe, Maich?"

"I had family there, Major. I don't know if any of them are alive now."

The Major's shoulders sagged tiredly. "What can I say?" He sighed and looked hopelessly at Maich Gordon. "Only we can understand", he spoke quietly. "You see, I'm Jewish myself."

He turned to face the horror, pictured on the screen. "I took this picture," he said. "I dressed myself up in German uniform so I could move around freely. I had to get this picture out. I had to show the civilized world what was happening to us Jews. I had to get it out and I was past caring if I got caught and killed in the attempt. So many had died already. My wife .. my baby .. one more wouldn't make any difference.

"I got away from Poland through Yugoslavia, Bulgaria and Turkey. I stole a fishing boat in Gelibolu and sailed it via Rhodes, to Alexandria, to bring this picture to the Allies." He shook his head and smiled a wry smile. "I needn't have bothered," he said. "The Allies already knew from thousands of pictures of atrocities they had taken from German soldiers."

The room was deathly silent as the snipers listened to the sadness in his voice. He slowly replaced his spectacles and moved his finger towards the control switch.

Click. The terrified boy and the bayonet he was frantically crawling away from, flashed from the screen. Naked scarecrows, starved into apparent sexlessness, took its place. Hundreds of them. Some standing, some squatting and others lying in slush beside a deep trench, half filled with dead and dying scarecrows like themselves. Soldiers stood around shooting at them.

"Crime: being Jewish, or political dissenters, or humanitarian sympathisers. Sentence: hard labour, until starvation emaciates them beyond their capability to perform. Then to be shot like dogs." The Major's stick pointed to a ghoul-like spectre. "This person, or living skeleton, you can't tell if it's a man or a woman, is voluntarily plunging into the pit to join the dead and the dying." The stick moved a little. "This one is crawling to the edge of the pit to slide down into it. He/She is probably too weak to stand."

Click. A scarecrow of a naked woman holding a dead, starved infant in her arms. This time it was the Major who turned away to wipe his eyes. Peter wondered if he was remembering his dead wife and their baby.

"A Jewish Mother!" The Major's voice croaked.

Click .. Click .. Click .. Click. Horror after unspeakable horror!

Beside Peter, Shalom Jacobson and Maich Gordon wiped tears from their eyes. The others faced the screen with faces like rock. A Jewish Mother. The beautiful girl with the rifle barrel between her legs.

He thought of his own mother, Uvemvane, the butterfly, and his eyes hardened. A pain ached in his heart. No German was ever going to get at her, even if he had to murder every one of them in cold blood, to keep them away from Swaziland. So Cimela had told the Captain he wasn't a killer. He'd soon show them how wrong they were.

He was glad to leave the room and walk out into the hot afternoon sunshine. He was unaware that he was flexing his hands and wiggling his fingers to keep them supple for the final infinitesimal squeeze on the trigger of his sniper's rifle. His mind was filled with a vision of uniformed Germans as he would see them through the sights, aligned on the top button of each one's tunic.

Chapter 5

Peter jumped down into the entrance of the dugout he shared with Spud Mahoney and Taffy Rees. He felt happier than he had felt for a long time. After six months of instructing the newcomers to the Regiment, they were back in action where they could do something about getting the war finished. At last they were out of the desert. That campaign was over. Caught between the converging armies of General Montgomery and General Eisenhower, the trapped German forces had fought on with fanatical courage and had dragged the campaign out for many more months than had been anticipated.

The air smelt of the wild flowers and scrub oak, which covered the foothills and choked the valleys. This Southern part of Italy reminded him of Swaziland, with its tumbling streams and ferny clefts. He looked around at the litter of shell-shattered rocks. In a minute or two the Jerries would start shelling again.

"Come inside!" Taffy's voice was edged with anxiety.

Peter twisted past the end of the sandbag shrapnel wall and ducked under the thick, earth-packed roof of the dugout.

"Just in time," Taffy said. "The stonk will begin any second now. I was starting to shit myself in case you didn't make it."

"Come in, me bhoy," Spud said in his broad Irish brogue, "come in and join us. We'll have a mug of coffee, then while Jerry shells us for the next twenty minutes, we can discuss the enthralling subject of copulation."

Peter smiled at Spud. The three of them had been buddies for eight months. "Is there anything else you ever discuss?" he laughed.

"Well now, `course there is, but somehow that subject keeps on creeping back in again. After a loiftime o' chastity in that bloody desert, this beautiful land of Italy is teemin' with pretty girls, and all their men are alanguishin' behind barbed wire in prisoner o' war camps. But we won't be after havin' the Colleens, Peter me bhoy. They're not for the loiks o' us infantry. Whoile we're doing the foightin', and gettin' the shit shot out of us, 'tis the back-line boys that'll be aliftin' the Colleens' skirts."

Taffy changed the subject. "It's bloody strange that the Jerries stick to regular times to shell us. You'd think they'd vary it a bit so they could pin us into our dugouts and make life more bloody miserable for us."

"`Tis the workin's o' the Teutonic mind, Taffy me bhoy. When a Kraut is told what to do and how to do it, he just says, `Jawohl!' and he does it. And he does it well. And those dumb bastards will carry on doin it until they're told to stop. Even if their shelling is like clockwork, you've got to admit it's bloody accurate. If you turned their guns around and told them to carry on, they'd say `Jawohl!' again. Then at exactly ten in the morning and four in the afternoon, they'd be after shooting the shit out of their own cooks and supporting troops."

Yes, Peter thought to himself, it was good to have these two for mates. They had been posted to the Regiment with the "Avenge Tobruk" boys. They had signed the New Oath and stepped into the places of the others who had refused to sign. They fitted in well, even if Spud was fifteen years older than Taffy and himself. Spud was a seasoned fighting man. He had fought in the Spanish Civil War and in Palestine, and he'd also served in the Royal Navy. Taffy had joined the army straight from school.

For six months Peter had trained the two of them as his backup team. They had to help him prepare dummy positions to draw fire and give away the enemy's own position. Each one of them had a radio to contact Big Dries Maritz if ever he needed mortar fire to blow up an enemy, or to drop smoke bombs to cover his own movements. They were always full of nonsense, but he knew he could rely on them to carry out their part of any task they were given. He knew they would rather die than let him down.

The first salvo of German shells arrived in a chorus of banshee wails. Peter checked his watch, it was exactly four o'clock. The ground jarred and trembled with shock waves of explosions, and shrapnel screamed through the air. Then a tremendous blast rocked the side of the hill.

"What the hell..?" Taffy's eyebrows shot up in query. "Sounds like they hit our ammo dump." Voices shouted outside. "They've hit something else too. Sounds like somebody got hurt." A shell exploded close to their dugout and loose soil trickled through the packed poles of the roof onto Spud's blankets.

His eyes blazed. "One o' these days I'm going to catch meself a Jerry and tie the bastard up outside and leave him there while we get shelled. If the bastard's still alive when the shelling stops, he can sweep the dugout and shake the sand out o' my bloody blankets."

The shelling stopped and men's shouts sounded unusually loud in the sudden silence. They scrambled out of the dugout. A mushroom of black smoke hung over the bottom end of the valley they called Hoves Dump, where the ammunition had been stored. But all that was left there were the smoking hulks of five trucks. Peter ran through the settling dust among broken boulders towards the smoking ruins of the stretcher-bearer's dugout, which had also been hit. Further along the hillside the Doctor and Colonel Hamman bounded towards the dugout from the direction of Battalion Headquarters. All four of the coloured stretcher-bearers were dead. Peter helped remove pieces of brown-skinned bodies from the shambles.

"Direct hit!" The Medic Sergeant shook his head and picked up an arm that still wore a khaki sleeve with the two chevrons of a corporal stitched to the material. "He was a good bloke," he said sadly.

"Armour-piercing high explosive! That shell first penetrated the covering of the dugout and then exploded inside." Colonel Hamman's face was as hard as the rock he stood on. After a few moments he looked up and stared at the jagged peak of the mountain which the Germans held on the other side of the wide valley. To the right stood the shattered monastery, perched on a lonely hilltop. Peter followed the direction of his gaze.

Over a low saddle linking two hills above where they stood, Peter could clearly see the peak of the German-held mountain, lit by the afternoon sun. He knew that somewhere within the triangular wedge of the mountain there must be an artillery observation post which directed Jerry's fire so accurately. He turned and looked down to the shambles where the ammunition had been stored.

He looked back at the Germans' peak. Yes! They would have seen the ammo trucks pull in and off-load. It would be easy for them to watch from up there with powerful field-glasses. He would go down to the dump and check the angle. Then he would take sightings from the outside limits of the accurate shelling and work out on the map the most likely position of their observation post.

He felt the pull of eyes and turned quickly to see the Colonel watching him. Colonel Hamman smiled grimly at him in acknowledgement of the mutual trend of their thoughts. The Colonel nodded his head shortly.

"So you've noticed it too, have you, MacTavish? When the smoke clears and they can see us, they'll be delighted with the results of their afternoon shoot. The Canadians we've just taken over from dug themselves in well and allowed themselves to get shelled every day for months. They told me they also noticed what you've just spotted. They had the face of that mountain bombed by the Air Force and they also had it shelled several times by the Artillery."

"And from the ground, Colonel?"

The Colonel shook his head. "Negative," he said. "They sent in three patrols and none of them came back. From across the river to the foot of that range of mountains the valley is thick with well-protected machine-gun and mortar positions. The enemy defensive line stretches for miles. The whole length of the valley is lousy with listening posts and wire entanglements and booby-trapped minefields. They've got snipers out there too, taking pot shots at everything that moves on our side of the river. Patrols can't even pick up their dead, it's too bloody dangerous, and the whole valley's littered with rotting bodies. There's no chance of outflanking them either."

"If I was a German Artillery spotter, Sir, with all the time in the world to prepare my observation post, I would have blasted a cave for myself into the bottom of that cliff face. I would have built a reinforced concrete wall over the mouth of my cave, with an overlapping opening to get into it, and a small slit through which to observe. The only way to get me out of it would be to push a couple of hand-grenades through the observation slit.

"Colonel, I could do that. After my grenades had killed the Jerries inside the cave, I would blast away the concrete wall. Then if I lit a flare where the wall used to be, to mark the spot, it would give us a point to aim at, and we could keep one gun on stand-by to put a shell into the hole every six hours or so. That would stop them ever using that position again."

Colonel Hamman watched Peter thoughtfully as he outlined his plan to wipe out the German post.

"Sir, when I've found exactly where their observation post is, I'll take Spud Mahoney and Taffy Reese and we'll put it out of action permanently. I'll need another man to help carry enough demolition charges to blow an access hole through the wall with a hefty cone charge, and have enough left over to blow the whole wall away as well."

Colonel Hamman shook his head. "This is not your kind of work, MacTavish. Find the place for me by all means. If we still think we can do it, you'll have the job of getting a demolition patrol of Engineers to the place, and safely out again. I know you have all the experience to do a job like this, but the successful blowing of the wall is a job for expert engineers and not for expert snipers.

"Right now I've got something else for you to do that is in your line of business. The Canadian's OC told me that from the top of the ridge above us there's a good view of a shelled farmhouse, occupied by a German listening post. It's well protected with wire and mines so we can't get in to wipe out the occupants. They're so well dug in we can't blast them out with artillery either."

Peter's eyes watched the Colonel intently as he spoke.

"They've got so cocky, that one of them comes out of the house every day and bathes himself at the horse trough in the yard. He knows he can be seen by anybody on the ridge, and to show what he thinks of us, when he's finished bathing he bends over and shows our side his bare arse. He offers himself as a trap for anybody who has the guts to try to shoot him. It seems to me," the Colonel smiled briefly, "that bare arse would make a very tempting target for a sniper to see if he could score a bull's eye.

"The Canadians lost two snipers trying to get him. The Jerries've got the range to those rocks on the ridge measured to the nearest inch.

Anybody who tries to shoot from up there collects a salvo of mortar bombs right in his back pocket." He stopped speaking and his eyes hardened. "I want those Jerries to learn, as of now, that they've got South African Infantry against them, and we aren't here to play games. We're going to start off by showing them we're here to fight. From this moment on, they're going to learn if any one of them shows any part of himself to the Stormbergs, it's going to get shot off."

The Doctor came up to Colonel Hamman. His jersey was smeared with blood. "The radio operator has been in touch with A Echelon," he said, "they're sending four replacement medics tonight. One of them is a Corporal. He's a damned good man. He's a fourth year medical student, studying under a friend of mine."

Before dawn Peter hid himself on the ridge and waited for daylight. He wore an extra long-peaked cap Spud had made for him, to shade the lenses and prevent sunlight reflecting from his binoculars. He had painted the underside of the binoculars light grey and whitened his face and throat to neutralize the tell-tale black shadow cast by the peak. A small twig fastened diagonally between the lenses would break the symmetrical outline of his face.

Peter lay without moving and searched the hillside for the best place from which to shoot. The hours dragged by and he had to fight the impulse to slap at the persistent flies that tormented him. He ached with the need to stretch himself and to roll his head to ease the tense muscles in his neck, but each time the urge to do so became unbearable, he felt the presence of old Mashona beside him, cautioning him to lie still. He finally decided on a spot some two hundred yards from the occupied farmhouse. There were two football-sized boulders about nine inches apart, twenty paces down the slope from a jumble of big rocks. It was dangerously close, but from there he would have an unobstructed view of the horse trough beside the farmhouse.

Once he had fired, if the Germans decided he might be hiding among the bigger rocks and blasted them with mortar fire, he would be reasonably safe. The shrapnel, rock fragments and the blast itself would fly harmlessly over his head. And those bigger rocks were too well embedded into the hillside to be uprooted and roll down on him.

The two small exposed boulders were too insignificant to arouse any suspicion. They would afford him complete concealment if he dug himself in behind them and covered himself and the boulders with his net. They were bulletproof and offered him a line of escape along a little gully that fed a trickle of seepage water into a natural storm-drain down a fold in the hillside, which would not be visible from the farmhouse. He realised the Germans would not have overlooked that storm-drain.

They would be able to drop mortar bombs directly into it, all along its length right up to the crest, if they thought his shot had come from there.

He imagined the scene from the German point of view, as though he were an observer in the farmhouse. After re-assessing every inch of the ground, he was satisfied that those little boulders were the last place he would ever expect any sniper to use. If he were an observer, bored from weeks of fruitless watching, the unexpected shot would prompt him to search the rocks on the crest, until he realised it had come from closer. By then he would be confused and would direct his search to every bit of obvious cover behind and above where he intended lying.

"Clever little b-bastard, aren't you, Isinkwe," he thought, warming to the thought of Cimela Brown's cynical approval.

Yes. Even if he did have to make a run for it, the gully would protect him from machine-gun fire. And, with a bit of luck, he might be able to make it over the ridge before the mortars could be brought to bear on him.

Exfoliation had caused a crack in the rock on the left, which had weathered into a black line. He would have to mark a black line on his net and be careful to arrange it precisely over the crack. In the afternoon he waited for the German to go through his accustomed bathing routine, but the wind was too cold and the man postponed his bath. Peter reassured himself his man would come the following day. He would be twice as dirty and he would bathe, cold or no cold.

After dark he tensed and relaxed the muscles of each limb in turn so he would be able to move away without any stiffness cramping him. Then he picked his way soundlessly down the slope to his chosen spot. He was too close to the farmhouse to risk digging with his entrenching tool for fear of striking it against buried stones, so he used his small wooden trowel to scrape out a hollow to lie in, behind and between the boulders.

On his way back to the Swartberg's position for food, rest and to make his preparations, he collected lichen from some rocks for staining his net the exact colour of his chosen boulders.

Peter returned before it got light and in the pre-dawn darkness arranged himself so he would not have to shoot with the afternoon sun reflecting from the upper guard of his rifle into his eyes. He leaned a small rock against a tuft of tall grass to cant it over, so it would cast its afternoon shadow over the blade foresight of the rifle. He wanted shade over the end of his rifle to prevent apparent distortion, caused by one side of the sight being lit with sunlight, while the other side was in shadow.

He had decided to shoot over open sights as the range was short and he mistrusted the 7x magnification telescopic sight. It was too powerful. It multiplied his own movements seven times, even his pulse beat, which caused the point of the unnecessarily thick aiming post to bounce around the target. It was also notoriously sensitive and one could never be certain whether or not the recoil from the last sighting shot had kicked the `scope out of zero.

He laid a flat slab of stone directly beneath where the muzzle of his rifle would be, to prevent the muzzle blast from kicking up a tell-tale pall of dust when he fired, then fitted himself into his firing position to check it for comfort. The hollows he had scooped for his feet were correct and the pads of rotting grass he had placed in the hollows for the pressure points of his hips, elbows, knees and forearms were correct. The hole underneath his open fly was in the right position. His water bottle with the drinking tube was easily accessible. Peter's forehead wrinkled with concentration as he focused his brain on each small detail in turn, until he was satisfied that everything was perfect.

At the first glimmer of daylight he spread his net over the boulders with the black stripe directly covering the crack in the rock. It was unlikely that anybody would ever notice that the two small boulders had grown together during the night. But to be quite certain, he planted a slender sheaf of grass stems and angled them across the net-covered gap above the barrel of his rifle. To prevent them from wilting, he watered them and then weighted the edges of the net down with stones. Satisfied with his arrangements, he crawled into his nest and wriggled until his position was as comfortable as he could make it.

When the apricot blush of dawn warmed with the first golden tint of approaching sunrise, Peter ate a large chunk of dark chocolate and washed it down with a pint of water from his spare water bottle. He carefully adjusted the peak of his felt cap to keep his whitened face in shadow and, for later in the day, to keep the afternoon sun out of his eyes. Then he allowed himself in one final wriggle and settled down to wait.

From time to time during the dragging hours of the morning, he tensed and relaxed every muscle in his body to keep his blood circulating and to prevent cramp. To avoid becoming drowsy, he exercised his mind with appraisals of everything he had been taught by both Mashona and Cimela, and rehearsed his aim at the centre of the top button of an enemy tunic, ready for what he had to do when the time came. Several times he caught glimpses of movement through the shell holes and paneless windows in the farmhouse. The Germans had not been shot at during the winter months and they'd grown a bit careless. The old remembered warnings of Mashona about the rewards of carelessness brought a fleeting smile to his lips.

He remembered the days of his childhood when he and Indabushe had watched their intended victims with Mashona beside them, as still as a carving from a block of ebony. He asked Mashona, with barely moving lips, to cover him with his shield. Occasionally he saw the flash of sunlight on lenses scanning the crest of the ridge above him, and he looked down and closed his eyes. "A man gets a f-feeling when he's being watched.. He gets r-restless." He remembered Cimela's words and avoided looking at the places where he had seen the sparkle of light. With almost imperceptible movements, he kept his finger caressing the curve of the trigger.

One of the occupants of the house was suffering from diarrhoea. Four times during the morning Peter watched him run towards a cluster of bush-tangled boulders behind the house, where a mound of subsoil indicated the excavation of a latrine pit, and he smiled sardonically to himself at the thought that if the others knew he was watching them, they would all be suffering from diarrhoea!

Along the skyline on the opposite side of the valley, through the nine-inch gap between his own boulders, he had a good view of the mountain where the Germans had their artillery observation post. Later in the day the sun shone directly onto the band of cliffs along the mountain tops which he could see clearly through the peep-hole in his net. In the centre of the valley a serpentine hedge of dark vegetation marked the course of the Rapido River.

Dividing the cliff face into squares, he searched each square yard by yard. He also searched the valley for natural features, such as small folds in the ground, which a patrol might be able to use for cover to stalk the mountain. He noticed five patches of unmatching discoloration where excavated soil from listening posts or mortar pits had not been expertly camouflaged. While he watched, intermittent gunfire rolled like distant thunder across the sweep of the valley.

Later in the morning when a formation of six German fighters screamed out of the sun and scattered a squadron of patrolling Spitfires, he wondered if the pilots were cooler up there than he was, sweltering in the sweet soil smell of his dugout. As he sipped a little tepid water through the tube from his water bottle a small Storch spotter aircraft droned slowly along the Allied-held line of hills, and the guns stopped firing until it had passed. He knew that all eyes would be on the plane and his small movement would be unnoticed.

A lizard with an electric blue tail was about to step onto his net, but it paused with its foot raised. It cocked its head and peered at him through the close mesh, then turned away and scuttled into the grass. At ten o'clock the shells of the morning barrage screamed overhead and he heard the muffled crunch of explosions on the reverse slope of the hills where the Stormbergs were dug in.

A slight shift of sunlight revealed a small spot at the foot of a sheer drop on the facing cliffs, where the texture of the rock looked a little too smooth to be natural. There was a bush in the centre of the smooth patch but it cast no shadow, and he realised it had been painted there. He was satisfied that he had found the camouflaged observation post which directed the accurate artillery fire onto the Stormberg's positions.

If the Colonel let him have a go at destroying that position, he wondered who he could take with him apart from Taffy and Spud. They would need a fourth man to help carry the necessary explosives and there was nobody available with the right kind of training. Certainly no other unit would lend them a sniper. It was not a sniper's job and they wouldn't risk losing a key man on a task like that.

The sheepskin handgrip wrapped around the wooden guard of the rifle rested snugly in his right hand. Again and again he sighted carefully at a mark on a wooden post beside the trough. It was about the right size and the right height of a top tunic button. The rest for his right forearm was perfect. The foresight of the No 4 Mk1 rifle rested steady and dead black in the centre of the mark. When he breathed out slowly, the front sight rose vertically above the mark, and when he breathed in it slid down until he checked his breathing to steady it again. The rifle was perfectly balanced on the palm of his right hand.

In the afternoon, when the angled sun beat into the sheltered yard of the farmhouse, a man wearing only a towel around his waist sauntered out of the house. Peter's breath caught in his throat and he stared aghast at the German. He was as young as Peter himself and there was no tunic button to aim at. There was only white skin with a small tuft of dark hair between the nipples on his chest.

His hand began to tremble and he lowered the muzzle of his rifle. "No," he whispered to himself, "Go back! Put some clothes on! Get your rifle! Please, God, I can't shoot him like this. He's not even carrying a weapon! This is murder," he thought in a panic of indecision. Forcing himself to raise his rifle he tried to take aim. But the top of the foresight wavered in a circle over the boy's chest, and before he could steady it, he saw the German turn away from him to look at the ridge above. Although he knew he was in full view of anybody who might be watching from up there, he stuck his two fingers in the air in a defiant salute.

Peter's sights were jumping all over the place.

"W-wait you bloody f-fool!" Cimela's voice was urgent in his mind. "Calm down..! T-take your time, Isinkwe. Slow and s-steady."

The young man pulled the towel from his waist and draped it over the post. Peter stared at his thicket of dark pubic hairs. He tried to force the image of the projector screen back into his mind, with the picture of the stark horror on the face of the Jewish girl with the rifle thrust between her legs. He tried to think of the starved Jewish mother with her dead baby in her arms, and the boy with the bullet-shattered leg, and the soldier striding towards him with his bayonet poised and a sneer on his face. He tried to think back to the horror of the Jewish children crowded into cattle trucks and eating the poisoned chocolates their heartbroken parents had given them, but the thoughts refused to form in his mind.

Peter's eyes wouldn't accept the logic of his brain. The target he saw through the aperture of the sight was a fine-looking, stark-naked youth, splashing water over his body and gasping and prancing around because the water was cold. Somebody inside the farmhouse must have passed some remark because the youngster threw up his head and laughed while he soaped himself.

"Please God! .. Please God!"

The Jewish children with the poisoned chocolates!

Peter forced himself to steady his foresight on the side of the enemy's ribs.

"N-not yet, you prick!" Cimela's remembered voice ranted, "N-not while he's jumping like a cricket all over the f-fucking place! Wait till the b-bastard stands still! Trouble is, you're just not a k-killer! I told you your old Z-Zulu didn't name you Isinkwe for f-fuck all. Bush-babies aren't k-killers either!"

The German capered to and fro across the trembling foresight as he sluiced himself with water to wash away frothy patches of soap suds.

Then the smell of leather from the sheepskin covering of the handguard sobered Peter. It reminded him of Mashona. He exhaled a pent-up gust of breath and breathed deeply several times while his fit of nervous revulsion left him.

"Observe, little warriors of the King. He has grown careless and the reward of carelessness is death!" Mashona's sobering words came back to him from his childhood. He was with Indabushe and they were watching the spider lose its caution and scuttle across its web to ensnare the flies Mashona had offered it. He felt Mashona's steadying touch on his arm, calming him, and the fog of terror cleared from his mind.

Grass stems leaned slightly to the stroking hand of a breeze and Peter realised he would have to aim an inch to the right of the centreline of the man's chest, to compensate for a little wind deflection. The standard battle sight was fixed at 300 yards. He would have to aim low because the bullet would throw two inches high at this short range.

The man put down his mess tin dipper and towelled himself vigorously. He wrapped the towel around his waist and stood erect, facing full on to Peter. The top of the foresight rose smoothly and checked rock-steady, two inches below the centre of his chest and an inch to the right of the centre line of his breastbone. The German jerked his two fingers up again in the direction of the ridge as Peter's hand closed and the trigger paused momentarily on the brink of the final pressure required to fire it.

The conditioned reflexes of a well-trained rifleman superseded all Cimela's professional tuition. The tendons on the inside of Peter's wrist raised a line of whitened skin. He inhaled fractionally and the flat top of the blade sight sank to an inch below the black pinhead of the German's navel. The rifle bucked hard in his hands. The crash of the shot slammed against his eardrums but his eye remained on the alignment of the sights, to follow the flight of the bullet onto an imaginary belt buckle.

Cimela's accusing voice exploded in his brain. "You b-bloody fool! You b-bloody arsehole! You've f-fucked the whole show! OK! Now die, you m-miserable little shithouse. I hope they shoot the shit out of you! I hope they blow your bloody b-balls off so you won't be able to breed any more stupid p-pricks like yourself!"

Then it was Captain Van der Walt's voice. "The trouble is, Isinkwe, you're just not a killer! It's not in you!"

Then Cimela's voice again. "If the m-mortars don't get him the first time, Henty, they m-might blast a bit of sense into his f-fucking thick head."

He felt drained. He felt miserable and confused. What had gone wrong? Thou shalt not kill. No! Not in cold blood, like shooting an unarmed man while he's having a bath. Was it God who had changed his point of aim? Was it God showing him only He had the right to create life or to destroy it? Didn't He care about the sufferings of the Jews? Where was His mercy towards them?

The German folded over his navel as his legs crumpled. He dropped to his knees and fell onto his back, with his feet folded under his buttocks. His bare arms beat the ground and he tried to turn over, but only his upper body turned, while the lower part remained facing the sky. He pressed his hands against the ground and lifted up his head and chest with his hips pointing obscenely in the wrong direction. He opened his mouth and screamed the unbearable agony from tattered nerve ends in his shattered spine. His hooked fingers clawed at the ground to drag his broken body to safety, but the dead lower half held him back.

"God, please finish him off for me! Please God! Put the poor bugger out of his misery. Please God! I can't fire another shot.. Not now. God, have you left this mess we have made for us to sort out? Did you send Mashona and Cimela to train me to kill and now you've left me to get on with it? If this is what you want me to do then I'll do it. I won't ask you for anything. Next time I won't think! I will kill the way I was taught to kill, and when it's all over I'll come back to you, God. If I live through it."

A salvo of mortar bombs exploded among the rocks along the top of the ridge as two men ran crouching from the farmhouse, looking fearfully up the slope as they ran. They grasped the wounded man by his armpits and lugged him along between them at a shuffling run towards the farmhouse, with his legs trailing uselessly along the ground and his screams of agony tearing at Peter's tortured nerves.

The deafening explosions of mortar bombs along the ridge above Peter stopped for a moment, then a bomb exploded in the storm gully where it started, just below the ridge. One after another, bombs exploded at twenty-yard intervals down the length of the gully behind him. The gunners were out to get him. The bombing stopped again while the gunners changed their aim. The brief silence was more frightening than the blast of explosions and Peter wondered if they had guessed how close he was. Then shattering explosions erupted among the big boulders above his position and he realised that the wounded man must have told his friends that the shot had come from close by. Shrapnel and shards of blasted rock howled over his head and thudded onto the ground beyond him.

He lay as low in his trench as he could get, while his skin prickled with cold sweat and he pressed his face to the ground to avoid attracting the eyes searching for him through field-glasses. He knew that if anybody as much as thought he might be lying behind the small boulders they would blast them off the face of the earth and himself along with them. Every gut-knotting explosion that deafened Peter and covered him in dust and the suffocating fumes of cordite, burned Cimela's teachings deeper and deeper into his consciousness.

The bombing stopped and he peeped up to see two men wearing broad white bands with red crosses on their arms, hurry from the house, bowed under the weight of a blanket-wrapped form on a stretcher. He watched them stumble down a pathway deeper into the valley, but a glint of reflected light made him close his eyes and lower his head again. "Yes Colonel," he thought, "stretcher-bearers .. doctors .. ambulance transport .. hospital .. specialists .. nursing .. Rehabilitation .. drugs .. money .. a wheelchair for life .. damaged morale. Yes, Sir! But never again, Sir! From now on it's going to be like Cimela said."

Peter crouched in the darkness with his finger curled around the trigger. He felt, rather than saw, a presence in front of him.

"Will it be yourself there, Peter me bhoy?" Spud's voice spoke from behind a rock. "'Tis himself, Taffy." Spud stood up. A stone grated behind Peter. Taffy had let him walk past in the darkness so he could shoot him in the back if failed to identify himself when Spud spoke.

"Holy Mother of God, Peter, we were worried when they laid down that mortar stonk!"

"It was OK, Spud." Peter felt his face would crack if he smiled the relief he felt. "They blasted the hell out of the rocks near me but they didn't spot my position. What are you two doing here, anyway? I thought you agreed to stay behind, seeing there was nothing you could do to help. If you'd been on the ridge you would've been blown to pieces."

"No," Taffy said, "we waited until the bombing stopped before we came up here. We, er, we thought with all that mortaring going on, we'd better be somewhere handy in case you needed a bit of covering fire, or perhaps you might have needed Big Dries to drop a few smoke bombs to help you."

Peter felt more relaxed and his smile no longer threatened to split his face. "Let's get going, I could do with a mug of coffee." He felt he couldn't point out the obvious fact that he carried a walkie-talkie radio to call Big Dries for smoke if he needed it and the two of them were well aware of the fact. But they were his buddies and they just wanted to be nearby in case he had got injured, so they all kept their thoughts to themselves.

"The cook's got some special grub waiting for you, Peter," Taffy said, to change the subject.

Peter shook his head. "No thanks, Taff, I don't feel like anything to eat. All I want is a mug of coffee before I clean my rifle, then I'm going to sleep for twelve hours."

"Don't worry about your rifle, Peter. We'll clean it for you, and if anybody tries to wake you up we'll stick a bayonet up his arse."

In his sleep, Peter heard small sounds of movements from Taffy and Spud. They were comforting sounds and they did not disturb him. They had been watching for him to waken.

Spud had a mug of steaming coffee standing over the small wavering flame of their home-made lamp. When Peter opened his eyes and sat up, Spud reached for the mug. "Top o' the mornin' to you, Peter," he wiped black soot off the mug with one of Taffy's socks, before passing the mug to Peter. "Slept like a bloody babe, you did."

"Morning, Peter," Taffy said cheerfully, "I was washing my kit so I just washed yours too. There's clean shorts, shirts and socks for you at the end of your blankets. The kit I washed is still wet. I'll bring it in before the shelling starts at ten. And you, you bloody Irish bog-trotter," he glared at Spud, "the next time you use my socks to wipe anything, I'm going to use yours to wipe my arse."

"Sorry, Taffy," Spud lied with bland innocence, "I thought it was my sock, honest I did! The new medics have arrived," he said to Peter, "one of them's a corporal. Funny sort of a bugger. A coloured guy. He's been making a nuisance of himself since sparrow fart this morning. Some silly sod told him we've got a sniper called MacTavish, and he's been wafting around like a fart in a bottle, waiting for you to wake up. Bastard thinks he knows you."

Taffy laughed shortly, "Spud threatened to shoot him if he woke you up. He must be an educated tit. He speaks good English. Damned site better than this Irish potato thief. The bastard got in here this morning before we knew who he was. That was when Spud threatened to shoot him if he didn't fuck off quickly. Perhaps he's never seen a sniper before. He just stood and stared at you with his eyes sticking out like a dog's balls."

The gloom in the dugout deepened as a shadow obscured the daylight coming in through the gap at the end of the sandbagged shrapnel wall. "Hooray – Fuck!" Spud's voice was dangerously edged, "It's you again, is it? Tell me, Corporal darlint, and tell me quick, what it is you'll be after wantin' from Peter MacTavish? O'course if it's something as simple as a foight, just say the word and I'll oblige."

Spud stood up but Taffy stepped between him and the coloured Corporal. "Permit me, Spud!"

"No! Wait, please." With the light behind him the man was a silhouette without features. He held up his opened hand to stop Taffy. He removed his steel helmet politely. "I heard you talking and I guessed the sniper, MacTavish, was awake."

"Yes, Corporal, that's me. Did you want to see me?"

"There is a small dark cloud in the sky and I had to call you, no matter how fiercely the friends of my brother cover his back! 'Ndadawethu ke khona!' – By our sister," the Corporal broke into Zulu, "By our sister, Isinkwe, my brother, the cloud in the sky is an omen! It is the shield of Mashona, our grandfather. He holds it up in the sky in rejoicing at our meeting!"

"Indabushe!" Peter sprang to his feet and grabbed Indabushe in a bear hug. "I see you .. My brother, I see you!"

"You are breaking me, Isinkwe!" Indabushe gasped, "Put me down, my brother, before my bones crack. Your arms are made of steel."

Taffy and Spud looked on in amazement. Spud spoke first. He stuck out his hand. "Any friend of Peter MacTavish is a friend of Spud Mahoney. And that goes for Taffy Reese, too. Right, Taff?" They shook hands warmly with Indabushe. "What did I hear you call him? Something like, `Isinkwe?'"

By the time they had drunk their second mugs of coffee, the excitement of their unexpected meeting had calmed down. It was only then that Indabushe explained how he had obtained a mission bursary to study medicine at the University of the Witwatersrand. He told Peter how he had finally been unable to concentrate on his studies after the Jewish doctor who had taken him under his wing had informed him of what the Germans had done to his family in France.

"We were both reared to be warriors, my brother. I could no longer remain at University while brave men were dying, to make it possible for me to become a doctor. It was clear to me that if the Germans win this war there will be no career in medicine for me, or any other man of coloured blood."

Indabushe shook his head sadly. "When the war is over I will resume my studies. I left the University and now here I am, to hold the shield of our grandfather over the back of my brother, Isinkwe. I arrived here in Italy three weeks ago and the spirit of our grandfather guided my feet along the path to find you."

It was not until later, when they were alone together, that Indabushe laid a confiding hand on Peter's shoulder and probed his mind with searching eyes. "In the last two years of my medical studies I found my interests lay more in the problems of men's minds, rather than with the ailments of their bodies. Tell me, Isinkwe, what is it that clouds your eyes with trouble?"

"I'm a sniper," Peter's voice was harsh with self-condemnation. "I was trained by Mashona. I was trained by you. I was trained by an expert in the art of killing."

Indabushe nodded an invitation to him to keep on talking.

"Yesterday I was sent to kill a man and I cocked it up. At the instant of firing a bullet into his heart, I shot him in the guts instead."

"You mean you missed?"

"I wish to hell I could say so, but I didn't. I deliberately dropped my aim and shot the poor bastard in the guts. He wasn't wearing any clothes. They told me at the sniper's school I wasn't a killer. I thought they were wrong, but it was me who was wrong."

"Was it because the man was naked?"

"Yes .. No .. I suppose so. I don't know what to think. All I know is, I cocked it up just when I thought I was a professional at my job. Indabushe, at that sniping school there was an instructor who was as Zulu at heart as you and me. He told me Mashona named me `Isinkwe', because bush-babies aren't killers and he had divined my future lack of the killer instinct."

"No.." Indabushe started to speak but Peter interrupted him.

"In the job of sniping the basic rule is simple. Kill or get killed! I broke that rule yesterday and only sheer bloody luck allowed me to come out of it in one piece."

Indabushe's hand gripped his shoulder tighter. "Our grandfather named you Isinkwe for your powers of observance. He named you

Isinkwe, because your eyes will notice what others will never see."

"He named me Isinkwe, because bush-babies aren't killers!"

"They also kill, my Brother. They kill to eat. Locusts, lizards, nesting birds..."

"That doesn't make them killers! Lions also kill to eat. So do leopards, hyenas, hunting dogs, jackals. Every predator kills to eat. Man is the only animal I know of that kills for the sake of killing."

"Tell me of the others, my brother. Tell me of the creatures that don't kill their own kind."

"Eland, kudu, sable, impala, duikers and every other kind of buck you can think of. None of them are killers," Peter replied.

Indabushe shook his head. "Isinkwe, whenever any of these buck you have named see another buck of their own kind come into the territory they have claimed as their own, they will attack it with teeth, hooves and horns. They will fight the intruder to the death, in defence of what is their's. Try taking a chicken from a domestic hen and see what happens. Or a new-born calf from a cow! If a bush-baby enters the tree of another bush-baby to claim it, there will be a fight to the death. Only one of them will survive. The fight will be so fierce even the victor will be crippled or badly mauled.

"Think, my brother, Isinkwe. Professor Darwin tells us we are descended from animals and we, like every other animal, are conditioned by an inherited instinct to fight for survival. In the case of bush-babies, survival depends on the cluster of trees which provide food, shelter and a place to breed. With us it is the same." He shook Peter's arm and smiled. "We are facing a nation who want what is ours and we are fighting to deny him the right to possess our cluster of trees. Only, we are fortunate enough to have a gifted bush-baby hidden in our tree, who will kill the marauding bush-baby to save the rest of us.

"Old Mashona was not wrong, Isinkwe. Use your finely tuned senses to save us from attack by stealth and your gift of markmanship to fight fire with fire. As a Medic I am pledged to preserve life. But in a time of war I am prepared to kill, if that is what is necessary to preserve the trees which provide the means of survival for my family of bush-babies. You have been conditioned to kill. Don't worry about it .. just do it, so the rest of us can survive."

Peter and the Operations Officer knelt side by side studying the updated map of the valley. Colonel Hamman squatted beside them to have a look. "If you follow this red line," the Ops Officer said, "you won't come within a hundred yards of any enemy positions we know of. The gap through the first minefield has been marked with tape.

"There are two other minefields; one here," he jabbed the map with his finger, "and another one further along." He moved his finger to another position hatched with blue pencil. "Our patrols have not been able to clear paths through these two minefields yet, so you'll have to find your own way through them. Neither one of them is very wide. Seeing that you refuse to return by the same route, we've marked out an alternative route for you. This one." He moved his finger onto a zigzag line marked in green. "You understand, of course, that the success of this proposed raid of yours will depend almost entirely on accurate navigation on your part?"

Colonel Hamman cleared his throat. A worried frown creased his forehead. "We've discussed this project very carefully, MacTavish. For five nights we've witheld our patrols. We've patrolled only as far as the first minefield and this should help you a bit. The enemy has been given a break and hopefully become a little less watchful, but don't rely on it.

"They haven't found out yet who we are and they still think we are the Canadians, who were never too keen on night patrolling at the best of times. They believe the South African army to be moving up through Turkey to attack Europe from the south-east. They will torture all the information they want out of you if they capture you, so don't get caught.

"If you are in certain danger of capture and you have no chance of fighting on, you will use your last bullets to shoot whoever's left of your patrol. Then you'll pull the pin out of your spare grenade and you'll lie on it. It will be a far better and less painful end than you will get from German interrogation." He fixed Peter with a look that lacked any compromise.

"The observation post on the mountain won't be protected by either wire or a minefield. Both would be too obvious and we would have seen them long ago. I'm satisfied the spot you suspect is the right place. If so, it will be protected by camouflaged trip-wires, booby traps and of course, sentries. Those sentries will be in a position where they will be able to dive into the bombproof observation post at a second's warning of approaching shells.

"You will leave here at O-two-hundred hours. You will reach the first minefield at O-three-hundred hours. By that time, their forward troops will know from months of experience that all our patrols will be heading for home, to be out of the valley before sunrise. They will not be expecting any patrol going in at that hour of the morning."

The Colonel placed his finger on a red-marked X on the map. "At precisely O-four-thirty hours, two of our 5.5 medium artillery guns will drop a concentration of armour-piercing high explosive shells, exactly on this spot. Each gun will fire five shells. This spot is in the middle of an old ploughed field. The ground should be soft enough there to blast some quite deep craters. When you've counted the tenth shell, you will move into those craters without delay and get under your nets." He indicated a nearby bucket. "There's some subsoil from the valley in this bucket, for you to use to stain them the right colour."

He moved his finger a little to the left. "After five minutes, the 5.5s will drop two shells each, here and here and here. These are just to make the enemy wonder what the hell's going on and to mask the purpose of the first shells." He stood up and flexed his cramped knees and Peter and the Ops Officer also got to their feet. "When you reach the observation post," the Colonel continued, "you'll have to kill the sentry on duty, quietly. Your report from the sniping school stated you're a bit of an artist with a knife." He raised his eyebrows at Peter for confirmation. Peter nodded.

"Good! From twenty-three hours thirty, we'll lob odd shells against the mountain side. This will cover the noise of your blast when you blow the observation post. When we see either your explosion, or else your flare, in the mouth of the cave, the artillery will lay down a barrage along the crest above the cliff, to keep the enemy in their dugouts while you get away from the place.

"Time your attack for midnight. Germans are painstakingly thorough. They'll change their sentries as regularly as clockwork and I bet my bottom dollar, midnight will be one of the fixed times they change them. Jerries don't do anything without giving orders and you'll be able to rely on this to give away the exact position of the sentry in the dark."

The Doctor walked over to speak to Colonel Hamman and stood waiting for him to finish his business with Peter. The Colonel acknowledged the Doctor's arrival with a brief smile and carried on with what he was saying.

"MacTavish, when you've gained your objective, half the German army will be standing by to cut off your retreat. Follow your green route as fast as you can and play the rest by ear. Remember, you boys are good at night work and the Jerries hate it. As you know, where we operate in patrols of three to five men, they patrol in columns of fifty. They wear boots and carry full battle kit, so you should be able to hear them in plenty of time to hide.

"Do those new crepe rubber-soled brothel creepers fit your men's feet comfortably?" He paused and looked questioningly at Peter. They knew each other well and Colonel Hamman guessed his sniper had something up his sleeve. "Well that's about it, MacTavish! Have you any questions?"

"Colonel, I'm still a bit worried about the men you've given me. You say the Engineer Sergeant is a first class man and I must take his two Corporal assistants, instead of Spud Mahoney and Taffy Reese. Apart from the last five days Sir, I've never worked with these men before. I

91

feel if I'm carrying explosives, I will need an extra pair of eyes I can rely on.

"The man I have in mind is the new Medic Corporal, John Dunn." Peter shot a furtive glance at the Doctor. "Colonel, he is called Indabushe, the lynx, because he can find his way around in the dark. We grew up together, Sir, and we were trained since childhood to work as a team. Of course, Colonel," he added hurriedly, with another quick glance at the Doctor's disapproving frown, "I'd just like to take him along as a medic, in case one of us gets hurt."

"No!" There was no compromise in the Doctor's emphatic refusal. "MacTavish, you are fully aware medics are strictly non-combatant troops, recognised as such by the Geneva Convention. Any coloured man in the South African army is allowed to carry a rifle only for his own protection. If any one of you has the misfortune to get so badly hurt he is unable to walk, the kindest thing you can do for him would be for every man to inject him with the full contents of the tube of morphine each of you'll be carrying. He will then die painlessly."

Colonel Hamman nodded in agreement with the Doctor. "You heard what the Doctor said, MacTavish. In fact, I'm sending your coloured friend back to Echelon to fetch medical supplies and that should keep him well out of temptation's way."

"Thank you," the Doctor nodded to the Colonel and turned to answer a question from the Ops Officer.

The Colonel's eyes followed him as he leaned towards Peter. "That should satisfy the Doc," he whispered, "take your coloured lynx with you, but I know nothing about it. I'm sending your two buddies, Mahoney and Reese, to Aquafondata, to get rid of them until you get back, so I won't have to charge them with insubordination." The Colonel's eyes twinkled. "This morning those two hellions cursed me up hill and down dale for forbidding them to go with you, regardless of the consequences. Me, their Colonel! But the village of Aquafondata is full of pretty girls and that should keep their minds off the war for a day or two. Especially that wild Irishman. They're both good men and I'm sorry I can't let you have them, but I believe any more than five men would jeopardize the success of your patrol."

Three minutes from the start line, two black ghostlike forms emerged from a thicket of scrub oak at the edge of the valley. Peter sank to one knee with his German Schmeisser carbine covering them.

"Don't shoot! It's us!" Peter lowered his gun at the sound of the Irish voice. Spud and Taffy came closer. They were armed with Thompson sub-machine carbines. Both of them had four No 36 hand-grenades hooked by their levers onto their web belts. Each carried an almost empty backpack. "We came to lend a hand with the explosives," Spud whispered. "The Engineers'll travel easier if we pack half their loads into our bags, and we've got enough grub to keep us alive for a couple of days."

"We can't take a whole platoon along with us," Peter complained helplessly, even though he was delighted to have them. "We'll make too much noise for starters. And what about the Colonel? You two are supposed to be in Aquafondata."

"First things first, me bhoy," Spud answered, "how do two plus five make a whole platoon? And if anybody makes a noise, it'll be these sappers and not us. You taught us to go quietly and if we take some of the load off the sappers, it'll help them go quieter, too. As for the Colonel, God bless his cotton socks, and fuck him anyway."

"Go for it, Spud," Taffy chipped in, "I'll hold him for you."

Spud ignored Taffy's offer. "There's no charge in the book he can throw at any man for attacking the enemy in the front line, is there now? We're coming with you, me and Taffy, and if you want to argue, I'll stick the thin end of this Yankee fire stick up your arse and pull the trigger."

Indabushe's and the sappers' teeth showed in white grins in the darkness. They took off their packs and shared their loads with the newcomers. "Where did you get the tommy-guns, Spud?" Peter asked.

"Father Christmas put them in our stockings," Spud grinned back at him.

"We bloody nearly got caught swiping them from the drivers of the ammo trucks," Taffy laughed.

"Don't use them, for God's sake, unless you have to," Peter advised. "The flat bark of those tommy-guns'll be a dead give-away. The rest of us have got German Schmeissers. If we have to use them, it will sound like Jerries shooting."

"Why've you got a rifle, Indabushe?" Spud asked, "Wouldn't these miserable bastards give you a Schmeisser, too?"

"A bayonet's no good without a rifle for a handle, Spud. Until the days of our childhood, both Isinkwe and me, my people used stabbing spears to kill herdsmen in their raids for cattle and girls." His smile widened. "They also used them to wipe out entire villages, men, women, children, dogs, goats and even the fowls, of those who stole our cattle. My civilization's only skin deep, Spud. We Zulus are like you Irishmen! On a job like this, I'd rather have a stabbing spear in my hand, but a rifle and bayonet are the next best."

"Indabushe's bayonet'll come in handy," Peter added. "We have to prod our way through two minefields on the way there and the same coming back."

The stench of putrifying bodies scattered in the valley nauseated everybody in the patrol. Peter stepped carefully over the decomposing remains of a soldier wearing the shreds of a Canadian uniform. Behind him one of the engineers failed to notice the corpse and his rubber-soled boot sank into the rotting chest, releasing a swirl of ghastly stink. The man clamped his hand over his mouth and vomited into his sleeve as quietly as he could.

The German observation post was as Peter had expected it to be. The only booby trap they encountered was a trip-wire threaded through a stem of grass at the foot of the cave. The four-foot-high concrete wall enclosing it was covered by a grey camouflage net. They crawled between the net and the concrete to wait for midnight. At the top of the wall the concrete was pierced by two narrow slits through which the Jerries could observe with field-glasses. The sound of music came through the slits. At twenty-three hours thirty, odd shells tore through the night and exploded along the mountainside below them.

The Colonel's shrewd guess had been right. At midnight the sentries changed. An unseen guard commander posted the relieving sentry on the left side of the wall where he was protected by the wing of concrete that hid the entrance to the outpost.

Peter bent down to draw the sniper's knife from the sheath strapped to the side of his leg, but a hand grabbed his wrist and held it fast. He looked around and saw Indabushe grinning at him woolfishly. Indabushe held his fixed bayonet under Peter's nose and released his grip on Peter's wrist. He pointed at his rifle and tapped the point of his finger at his chest and eased Peter firmly aside. He slipped past as silently as a shadow, with Peter following him.

The sentry's grunt of shock as Indabushe's bayonet drove through his heart was drowned by a girl's sweet voice singing 'Lili Marlen' in German. Peter leaped forward and clamped his hand over the sagging sentry's mouth and nose. He pinched the man's nostrils closed between his thumb and forefinger. Indabushe helped him lower the dying man quietly onto the flat rock floor and gripped the jerking limbs until they were still.

Spud and Taffy stepped soundlessly past them into the entrance of the emplacement. The roof of the cave had been blasted away to allow plenty of headroom. There were two platforms with mattresses on them for observers to lie on during the day while they watched the line of hills across the valley. The cave had been deepened to provide sleeping quarters behind a second concrete wall, with a heavy curtain hung over the doorway to hide the light of the lamp. The music was loud inside the cave.

As the dying sentry quietened in Indabushe's confining arms, six muffled shots thudded inside the observation post. The double walls deadened their sound. The sappers moved into the entrance, unfastening the straps of their packs as they went.

Peter and Indabushe released the dead man. Taffy and Spud emerged from the entrance and crouched beside them. The four of them searched the night with straining eyes and ears. All they could hear was the voice of the girl still singing 'Lili Marlen'.

The sappers knew their job. They were quick and thorough. They emerged after a few minutes as unflustered as though emerging from the doorway of their own home. The sapper Sergeant waved them away and they hurried across the slope and flattened themselves against the base of the rock face, while one sapper followed, paying out wire from the reel in his hand.

The sapper crouched and flicked the key on his box and the rock jarred against Peter's back as the entire front wall of the lookout cave leaped outwards in a flash of light and noise. It crashed and tumbled down the mountainside in an avalanche of cascading rubble and dust.

Smoke swirled from the mouth of the cave as Peter scrambled back. He jerked the pin from a flare and shot a ball of blinding magnesium light into the blasted-out hollow the wall had once covered. Across the valley, muzzle flashes of field guns flickered from behind the hills. Indabushe grabbed Peter's hand and led him stumbling down the steep slope.

Despite his tightly closed eyes, the light of the flare had blinded him temporarily. Shells howled overhead and exploded along the ridge above them and on the reverse slope of the mountain.

By the time they reached the plain, Peter's eyes had fully recovered and he took the lead from Indabushe. He gave his knife, gun and grenades to one of the sapper corporals to carry. His navigation had to be exact and he couldn't allow his compass to be deflected by the magnetic attraction of metal. Nor could he afford to walk as carefully as the others, as he had to count his paces accurately on each leg of the zigzag course drawn on the map.

They picked their way gingerly through two minefields and had almost reached the river when they heard a German patrol approaching. The land was flat and there was no place to hide. They lay down and waited for the patrol to come towards them. Peter showed each man a hand-grenade and held up four fingers to indicate the four-second delay fuses in the grenades he wanted them to use. "Wait for me to throw first," he whispered, "then throw together."

The German patrol marched past them in columns of four and from force of habit, the men marched in step. Peter allowed the head of the column to pass the place where they lay in the grass. When the centre of the column came abreast of him, his arm swung over and his grenade arced into the middle of the marching men. Six other grenades landed close to the centre of the patrol.

German voices cursed and shouted and the column broke formation as some dived for cover and others simply stood or crouched. They did not know what had caused the confusion until the grenades exploded in quick succession, in a roar of thunder and a howl of shrapnel. Peter, Indabushe, the sappers, Taffy and Spud jumped up and stormed into the tangle of German confusion, with their automatic weapons blazing. The differing sounds of firing from 9mm Schmeissers and .45 tommy-guns in the centre of the seething column compounded the chaos.

Men shouted and screamed as Peter's patrol ran through them and disappeared into the darkness. Behind them bursts of automatic firing ripped through the night as those from the dispersed ends of the column fired at each other in panic. Somebody had the sense to fire a flare and Peter dived flat as it soared skyward. "Keep your eyes closed," he warned the others. "Turn your faces away from the light."

They were three hundred yards from the flare which hung suspended in the sky, illuminating the scattered patrol. Gun flashes flickered from the Allied-held hills. "Run!" Peter commanded and raced off across the valley as the first shell exploded a hundred yards in front of the slowly drifting brilliance of the flare. "They can't see us out here in the darkness. It's our own guns we've got to get away from."

A second shell dropped fifty yards behind the flare. "Bracketed, by God!" Spud panted. A salvo of shells screamed overhead and burst among the milling Germans. Peter slowed to a walk. The flare had burned itself out and he headed in the direction where he hoped the river to be. There had been no time to take a compass bearing, nor to count the number of paces they had run from their planned line of retreat.

A German Spandau machine-gun made a sound like canvas ripping, somewhere on their left. The flat tat-tat-tat-tat-tat-tat of a tommy-gun firing an answering burst warned him to move further away to his right. Some other patrol had made contact with a German machine-gun post.

They found the warning wire of the main minefield and the triple concertina barbed wire entanglement beyond it. It was getting late. They would have to hurry to cross the intervening ground and the river before daybreak. Peter heard a faint sound like somebody stumbling over something in the dark and they squatted and waited.

Dimly silhouetted against the false-dawn sky he saw the form of somebody approaching. He seemed to be enormous, outlined against the fading stars. He was alone and he was coming directly towards Peter. When he was close enough, Peter discerned the unmistakeable outline of a German helmet.

The soldier paused in mid-stride as though he had seen Peter, but

Spud's tommy-gun stuttered and the man staggered backwards on sagging legs and collapsed. Spud jumped up and ran towards the heap on the ground. "Holy Mother!" he whispered loudly, "and there's himself fetching a present for Isinkwe, and I ups and shoots him."

Indabushe walked past Spud to examine something he thought he had seen. "Hist! Isinkwe", he called quietly. Concertina wire was stretched across their path and a short length of it had been lifted a little from the ground. There was a well-worn groove under the wire, such as a crawling dog makes under a netting fence. A tape tied to a strand of the wire led into the darkness of the minefield.

Spud pushed a rifle into Peter's hands. The butt was fitted with a wooden cheek rest and a telescopic sight was mounted above the breech. "He was bringing you this, Isinkwe. Maybe he was tired of it!" The man Spud had shot was a sniper. He had been making his way to a cleared lane through the minefield to take up his position for the day, and the shooting behind him must have decided him to return. They followed the sniper's tape through the minefield and ran for the river, knowing there would be no Jerries operating in front of one of their own snipers.

"I hope the Colonel remembered to warn all the listening posts," Taffy said through chattering teeth as they pulled on the clothes they had taken off and held above the water to swim the river. "What's the password, Isinkwe?"

"Eleven," the sapper Sergeant answered.

"Sorry, Taff," Peter replied, "I should've told you before, but it slipped my mind. We all knew, except you and Spud. I should've told you in case we had to scatter and make our way back individually."

"Eleven, you say?"

"Yes. Eleven."

"We must hurry, Isinkwe, my brother. The horns of the cattle are in the sky." If the nearby bushes had been cattle, the silhouettes of their horns would have been visible in the sky against the growing light of dawn.

Peter chuckled. "Indabushe, I haven't heard that expression of old Mashona's, since we were kids."

They walked on in single file with Peter in the lead. Spud brought up the rear. Peter's skin prickled. He felt he was being watched and he dropped to a crouch. They had reached the bottom of the forward slope of the hill sheltering the Stormberg's positions.

"Seven!" A quiet voice behind Peter challenged from behind a rock to the left of Taffy.

"Five!"

"No! No! No!" A chorus of desperate shouts drowned out Taffy's reply, as everybody in the patrol, except Taffy, threw themselves flat on their faces. "Four! Four! Four," frantic voices corrected Taffy's "five".

"Four!" Peter called again, to make doubly certain the sentries had heard correctly.

"Six!" the unseen sentry challenged again.

"Five!" Peter answered him and got up slowly from the ground.

A second unseen sentry on the other side of the patrol spoke to Taffy in a voice edged with fury, "You, you stupid tit! You'd better go back to school to learn some arithmetic! Seven and four makes eleven .. not seven and five! If I'd challenged you with nine, I suppose you'd have said three, instead of two!"

Four men stood up. Two on either side of the patrol. The man who had challenged Taffy still held his tommy-gun at the ready, covering Peter in the lead. He stalked cautiously forward and looked closely into Peter's face. "Peter MacTavish! OK boys," he spoke over his shoulder to the other three sentries, "it's them alright. Say, Peter, you'd better tell this dumb bugger," indicating a subdued Taffy with a waving thumb, "to leave the answering to somebody who can count."

"I bloody nearly opened up on you guys," one of the other sentries said tersely, "You're fucking lucky! We were told to expect five of you, not seven! Anyway, you guys did a bloody good job! We watched from the top of the hill. The Colonel danced around like a madman when we saw the flash. What the hell happened on the other side of the river? Looked like you started a private war or something.

"Kom, Gert," he called over his shoulder without waiting for Peter's reply. "It's getting light and we'd better get a move on. Are you there, Gert?"

"Ja, Corporal," another man said quietly, approaching them from behind. "There's nobody following them, Corporal."

"OK, Gert. Cover us for five minutes and then follow us to the crest. Stop there on the crest and watch our back spoor until the sun comes up. We'll have some grub waiting for you."

The Corporal crouched and spoke briefly into the radio in the side pack at his feet. He stood again and grinned at Peter. "That's your pal, Big Dries Maritz. He hasn't moved an inch away from that mortar of his since you left, in case you needed a bit of support. When you started your private war in the valley he nearly crapped himself. He wanted to plaster the whole bloody place with bombs, but he was afraid of hitting you boys."

By the end of April the hot Mediterranean sun had sucked up the moisture from the deep alluvial soil of the flats of the Liri valley. The surface was sufficiently dry to support the weight of the "armada" of British and American tanks, huddled, waiting in echelons of hundreds, in enclaves among the Allied-held hills. Piles of shells stood heaped beneath camouflage nets beside each of the thousands of field guns sited behind ridges, in clefts and on the sides of rocky hills – it was amazing that men were capable of hauling them up there. Long-barrelled 17-pounder anti-tank guns stood hitched to lines of parked trucks. Countless new trucks stood empty, with their tailgates down, waiting for their sections of assault infantrymen.

Immediately after the sketchy morning shelling, Colonel Hamman addressed the Stormberg men who were sitting or squatting among the shattered rocks along the hillside.

"Today is the eleventh of May," he shouted so everybody could hear him. "Tonight at twenty-three hundred hours every gun in the British 8th and the American 5th Armies is going to subject Monastery Hill, Monte Cairo and Monte Cifalco to the most saturated shelling ever employed in the history of warfare." He smacked his fist into the palm of one hand with excitement as he paused to get his breath.

"Batteries of guns will concentrate their fire onto every listening post, every machine-gun post, and every mortar and gun emplacement your patrols, and the patrols of every other unit in the line, have pin-pointed for the artillery. We're going to do a second El Alamein on the enemy tonight, but on an unprecedented scale. Under an umbrella of our own bombers and fighters we're going to launch a tidal assault on their Gustave line." The listening men shuffled with anticipation.

"Our waves of attack will swamp the enemy," he shouted louder, "and we'll surge on to their next line of defence at the Adolf Hitler line. We're going to burst through that line like a dose of salts and race up the Liri Valley for Rome. There we'll join up with the Yanks who've broken out of their beachhead at Anzio."

The RSM raised his arms and held his palms out towards the assembled men to quieten their excited clamour. "Give the Colonel a chance, boys! Quiet! Let the Colonel finish first!"

"The Yanks have supplied us with new trucks," the Colonel continued, when the noise had subsided. "Immediately the Gustave and the Adolf Hitler lines have crumbled, this Stormberg Regiment is going to spearhead the 6th South African Armoured Division's advance. And we're going to spearhead the advance of both the British 8th and the American 5th Armies.

"We'll be supported by tanks from the Prince Alfred's Guards and the Special Service Battalion. We'll go into battle in our new trucks. There'll be a truck for each 10-man Section. We'll chase the retreating enemy in those trucks, until we're shot out of them!" He paused to get his breath and wait while a salvo of shells howled overhead.

"If any truck is shot up, the others'll bypass it. There'll be no stopping for survivors. Our task will be to maintain maximum pressure on the enemy withdrawal, until such time as we can go no further." He clenched his fists and shook them beside his ears.

"Our intention is to force their retreat into a rout, and to chase them right up the length of Italy and out the top. If we do this, the war'll be over and we'll all be home for Christmas."

The men jumped to their feet and cheered until the RSM fired a short burst with his tommy-gun over their heads to restore order.

"Enemy forces opposing us," the Colonel shouted, "will be the German 10th Army under the command of General Von Vietinghoff. Our main adversary is Gruppe Hauck, comprised of One," he held one finger in the air, "305 Infantry Division. Two," a second finger shot up, "334 Infantry Division. Three," another finger, "114 Jaeger Mountain Division, and the L1 Mountain Corps, including the 5th Mountain Division, the 44th Infantry Division, and the 1st Parachute Division."

"Holy Mother o' God!" Spud shouted. "And will it be the whole fucking German army ye'll be after having us foight, will it Colonel darlint?"

By way of answering Spud's outburst the Colonel's teeth showed white in a grim smile. "It could well be, Spud, and all these units are tough, seasoned fighting divisions and they are going to contest every yard of our advance. Are there any questions?"

Spud's hand shot up. He heaved himself slowly to his feet and waved his arm to and fro for everybody to see his wrist. "Colonel darlint, I'll just be after askin if anybody wants to buy a watch I'll no longer be needin?"

At twenty-three hundred hours the night sky suddenly lit up with the flickering lightening of gunflashes and the air trembled with their thunder. The sweating bodies of straining gunners bent and straightened rhythmically as they fed shells into the breeches of their guns. Flashes of gunfire flared for as far along the hills as Peter could see. Enemy guns returned their fire in a howl of shells and blast and screaming shrapnel, but there was no thought of sleep or of danger. Helmeted heads stuck up from the rims of dugouts for the wondering men to watch the holocaust.

One by one the German guns fell silent as the crews who served them fell in flurries of shrapnel. Or the guns themselves, along with their gunners, disintegrated in the blast of a direct hit, and pieces of gun and pieces of men erupted in the air.

Throughout the following day, convoys of trucks ground their gears along torturous tracks to retrieve the bodies of hundreds upon hundreds of Polish Infantrymen who had fallen under the shuddering muzzles of Spandau machine-guns on the slopes of Monastery hill.

On the 20th of May, the Stormbergs marched out through the wreckage of Hove's Dump, to climb the one-in-five gradient of

"Inferno Road". Their marching feet slipped and tripped on the shell-holed mesh wire, spread over the framework of steel rods covering the pitted surface, which had been laid to offer a grip to the wheels of supply jeeps.

In places the track wound between sheer walls of rock, and in other places it traversed ledges on the rock face in full view of the few remaining enemy guns, which shelled them defiantly, until they reached the safety of sunken sections covered over with camouflage netting.

The heavily burdened men marched through Aquafondata and Vellerrotunda, shouting ribald invitations to the pretty Italian girls to wait for them to come back. And the wildly cheering girls crowded around the marching men plying them with bouquets of flowers, bottles of vino and tempting kisses brimming with promise. But the marching columns plodded on down the few remaining miles to St Elia on the plain of the Rapido river and forged on the Frosnelli, where the exhausted men sank thankfully to the ground at one o'clock in the morning, falling asleep with their packs still on their backs.

In the morning the Division regrouped at Limatola and the Stormbergs embussed in the darkness onto their new Dodge trucks.

The urgent notes of a bugle call pierced the chill dawn air, sounding the "Charge!"

Gears grated; truck engines snarled; and the race for Rome was on!

Excited men, their loaded weapons at the ready, lurched past growling bulldozers, gouging trenches for the burial of the corpses of American infantrymen that littered the approaches to the enemy defences. The Stormberg's trucks bumped over the pitted tracks behind Scorpion tanks fitted with front-mounted rotating drums of flailing chains, which detonated buried mines and shredded barbed wire entanglements. One after the other, leading Scorpions burst into flames from direct hits by 75mm guns on Mk IV Special Tanks sited hull-down in pits, with only their guns showing above the ground.

As each Scorpion blew up in smoke and flames, others roared past the burning crews writhing in the agony of incineration, to take their places and flail lanes free from mines and wire for the Stormbergs to follow. Hedge-hopping Spitfires, Hurricanes, Mustangs and Tornadoes – engines screaming and guns blazing – blasted the German tanks with streams of cannon fire and raked the motorised columns of their routed infantry.

Behind the Stormbergs, a pall of dust from the flailing chains of the Scorpions and the mines they had exploded hung like brown fog under billowing black clouds of smoke from burning vehicles. Anxious drivers grated gears and trod accelerators to the floorboards. The Stormbergs were through and the pall of dust ahead of them was raised by the churning wheels of the desperately retreating German rearguard.

In the deserted village of Cassino the shell-holed walls of roofless houses leaned drunkenly along the sides of the street as the trucks sped past. Spud looked at them and opened his eyes wide in amazement. "Peter, me bhoy," he said in an awed voice, "the mice must be bad in this place. Will ye just be after lookin at what they've done to the houses!"

Chapter 6

Peter put down the old tennis ball he had been squeezing to exercise the muscles of his left hand and forearm to maintain his perfect trigger squeeze. His flexing hand had worn the fluff off the ball. He picked up his German 7,92 mm sniper's rifle and tested its balance for the hundredth time.

He preferred it to his .303. The 4x magnification telescopic sight was superb. The cross-hairs and graduation marks for elevation and deflection were finely etched and did not obscure the target like the clumsy aiming post in the British 'scope. Nor did the German model tend to kick out of zero when it was fired or accidentally bumped. And although it was graduated in metres, there was no need to make any allowance for conversion into yards because the bullet was much faster. This gave its flight a flatter trajectory than the slower bullet of the .303.

The Mauser action operated smoothly and the rimless bullets fed cleanly into the breech without the possibility of jamming if they were not correctly placed in the magazine. Meticulous German machining ensured perfect trigger action and release of the sear at the instant of firing. Yet, with all these refinements, the rifle remained a rugged weapon, capable of withstanding the inevitable knocks on the back of a hard-sprung truck.

Most of the men were using German weapons. Because of the speed of the advance and frequent encounters with the enemy, ammunition stocks had run dangerously low and replenishment had been impossible, whereas captured weapons and abandoned ammunition were readily available in the wake of a stampeding enemy.

Rome was 38 miles and twenty burning villages and hamlets behind them when the Stormbergs were ordered to halt their headlong assault on the German retreat. Their supporting tanks and gun-towing trucks had run out of fuel and lagged far behind. General HQ had underestimated the ferocity of the Stormberg's attacks and the tenacity of their pursuit. Their pleas to press forward to maintain the momentum of the rout until their trucks ran out of petrol fell on unsympathetic ears.

They had punched such a deep enclave into the German retreat that they had bypassed fully equipped enemy armoured and infantry columns which now threatened their flanks. They were also in danger of being cut off by enemy forces closing in behind their unprotected rear. A furious Colonel Hamman was ordered to prepare his regiment for all-round defence until such time as other forward support units could catch up and consolidate his position.

The Germans took full advantage of the temporary halt. Formidably armed retreating columns turned back to do battle. Whereas the Allied advance had protracted supply lines of men and equipment, the German withdrawal had the effect of a concentration of resources. In terms of infantry, armour, artillery and supplies of every kind, their fighting strength was dangerously superior to that of the isolated Stormbergs. The Germans desperately needed a victory, however localised, to boost the disintegrating morale of their panicking troops. The weather was on their side. A ceiling of low cloud grounded the Air Forces of the Allies.

Section corporals hurriedly marked the spots where they wanted their men to dig slit trenches to repulse the massing German counter-attack. While the men stripped off their shirts to start digging, the Section Leaders searched for sticks to push into the ground in front of each man to limit his arc of fire so there was no danger of those behind shooting into the backs of those in front during a night attack. Lance corporals in charge of Bren gun crews sighted their arcs of fire to overlap the arcs of fire of the guns on either side of them. Within an hour the men were dug in and ready for action and every man knew the limits within which he could add his contribution to the Battalion's fire plan.

Peter heard the drone of enemy tanks crawling like a noisy swarm of beetles across the farmlands behind a low ridge as they were deployed in preparation for attack. Gun-towing trucks added their growl to the background rumble and anti-aircraft guns elevated their slender bar-rels to engage the anticipated arrival of bombers and fighters of the Allied Air Forces as soon as the sky cleared.

While they waited, the Stormbergs deepened their trenches and dug towards one another to form an interlinking network of trenches to facilitate movement of casualties and ammunition without exposing themselves to enemy fire. They excavated narrow slits in the walls of their trenches where they could shelter from air bursting shells and from the rain when they slept.

During the heavy afternoon shelling, Peter crouched in the Battalion aid post watching Indabushe and the Doctor attending to the blood-soaked casualties as they were carried in. He was waiting for darkness to fall. Colonel Hamman had asked him to get close enough to the enemy positions to gauge their strength and to watch what they were doing during the day. The Colonel guessed that the Jerries would not counter-attack immediately as they probably imagined the Stormberg's strength to be far greater than it actually was. The Germans would not admit, even to themselves, that they had been routed by such a small force.

Peter lay still in the darkness and listened to the Germans working. They made no attempt at silence. They considered themselves safe from immediate attack because they had not seen any tanks arrive to support their adversaries. Sounds of digging came from everywhere in front of him. Gangs of men erected wire entanglements and behind the wire others were laying mines.

A burned-out German tank skulked blacker than the night darkness twenty yards on Peter's left. Five yards to his right a road angled across the German front. The drainage ditch beside the road was deep enough to afford cover for a crouching man to run to safety. There were two burnt-out tanks a hundred yards behind him. He had passed them on his way. The metal sides of those tanks were still too hot to touch and he had seen the charred remains of a man hanging out of the turret of one of them. Both tanks stank of burnt flesh and bone and oil.

Firing from advancing Allied guns grew heavier as the night passed and a few of their shells exploded behind Peter's position. Their shelling was dangerously inaccurate. They had come up from the rear after dark and started firing without having had the chance to sight in properly.

He dug a narrow slit trench and dumped the lighter coloured sub-soil into the road drain. He saved the carefully removed sods of root-ed grass to camouflage the low embankment he formed to provide bulletproof cover for his head and shoulders. The remainder of his body was hidden just below ground level.

Lying under his net, he wondered whether he had come too close to the Jerries, but reassured himself with the thought that the working parties would withdraw before morning. It worried him that he was so close to the burnt-out tank on his left. If he had to fire a shot, the enemy would immediately suspect the tank as his hiding-place. Some keen-eyed observer might accidentally discover his real position near-by. Perhaps the ditch on his right would provide him with a safe line of retreat. The Germans would immediately suspect that any sudden shot had come from that ditch which they would promptly rake with machine-gun and mortar fire. When their firing ceased and they turned it onto other suspect areas, he could use it as a line of escape. He doubted whether they would start firing at a point as close as where he was lying.

The memory of Indabushe's parting words warmed him. "The spirit of our grandfather goes with you, my brother. Remember he swore that you would walk all your days in the shadow of his shield." The fact that his words had been spoken in Zulu was strangely reassuring.

Somehow they had a deeper meaning in the language in which Mashona himself had pronounced them so long ago.

He smiled spontaneously. The guarding presence of the spirit of Mashona was unquestionably real to Indabushe. For all his sophisticated learning, the ingrained beliefs of his forefathers, both Zulu and Scottish, were just below the surface of his brown skin. There was no distinctive line which completely separated the living from the spirits of those who had already passed on into the land of shadow. There were many places in Indabushe's beliefs where the two overlapped.

The day passed reasonably quickly despite his raging thirst – a fragment of flying shrapnel had punctured his water bottle. Fortunately, the day was cool and full of movement and favourable shellfire – the supporting guns had got their range and delayed the enemy counterattack. Peter lay watching and thinking of Mashona and the thirst-quenching numbela fruit the old man had always given him when he was thirsty.

Another burnt-out tank which he had not seen in the darkness was of particular interest to him. It crouched, fire-blackened and stark, a hundred and fifty yards in front of him. It was resting on its side on a broken track, with its gun pointing desolately at the ground. The Germans had dug a trench around it and thrown up an embankment of fresh red earth. It was a little higher than his position, so people could come and go to and from it without being seen. Several times during the day he saw the top half of the bodies of groups of men beside the tank searching the approaches to the Stormberg's trenches with their field-glasses.

In the late afternoon the heads and chests of three German officers appeared above the bank surrounding the tank. The setting sun broke through a gap in the cloud bank behind him and beamed onto them as he watched them with mounting excitement, forgetting about his thirst. The officers on either side of the central figure pointed this way and that. They seemed to be explaining the situation to the officer who stood between them. Peter decided he must be a senior staff officer. His guess was confirmed by a fourth officer who appeared suddenly and bobbed his head stiffly to the central figure. The officer on the right also nodded in a curt bow to the senior and departed together with the newcomer.

The cross-hairs of Peter's rifle rested steadily below the centre of the senior officer's chest. He dare not shoot while both of them were looking in his direction and he watched in peeps to avoid attracting their searching eyes. And while he watched, he thought of Cimela.

"Ta-take your time, Isinkwe! Wait for the right m-moment. When it c-comes, steady your sight and squeeze the t-trigger very gently. The instant of firing must come as a s-surprise to you. Then f- follow through. If you lower the muzzle to see where you've sh-shot, your bullet will strike low. Somehow it pulls the fucking bullet d-down. Don't ask me how, but it d-does."

The senior officer lowered his field-glasses. He said something to the officer beside him, who also lowered his glasses. He nodded politely in response to the senior officer's words. Peter exhaled a little breath through parted lips and the cross-hairs rose to the centre of the senior officer's chest. His finger drew the trigger smoothly back to the end of the first pressure.

Both officers turned to step down into the trench behind the wall. Peter made a small adjustment to his point of aim. The rifle bucked in his hands and for an instant he saw the centre point of the bisecting hairs in the telescopic sight were still resting in the precise centre of the top half of the officer's back. Then the officer hurtled forward and dropped out of sight.

Whoever it was he had shot was somebody important. Heads bobbed up and down behind the earth bank. Germans with more guts than sense stood up and swept their field-glasses to and fro searching for him, and he noticed that every one of them was an officer.

A stream of machine-gun bullets tore the ground two yards from his right shoulder. For an instant he went cold with the certainty that he had been discovered. He couldn't see the machine-gun, which was hidden by the end of the track of the burnt-out tank. The gunner corrected his aim and a long stuttering burst of fire ripped the ground along the lip of the drainage ditch. Thankfully, Peter let his breath out and lowered his gaze. If the end of the tank track blocked his view of the machine-gun, it obviously blocked the gunner's view of him.

Flame streaked from the muzzles of turret guns on several of the tanks and slammed into the hulk of the burnt-out tank on his left, exploding inside. The heavy hatch cover was torn from its hinges and thudded onto the ground close to where he lay. A well-aimed fragmentation shell exploded under the belly of the tank. Any sniper hiding in or under that tank would have been blown to pieces. He heard the metallic clunk of mortar bombs being dropped into their tubes and several moments later they detonated in thunder claps and screaming shrapnel a hundred yards behind him.

He smiled grimly to himself. The Germans were hopping mad. They mortared and shelled and machine-gunned every probable and improbable place where a sniper may have hidden himself. They concentrated salvos of shells onto the hulks of the two burnt-out tanks he had passed in the darkness, and they laid down a creeping curtain of fire until it sounded about a thousand yards behind him.

A barrage of howling shells arrived from the guns supporting the Stormbergs. Colonel Hamman would have guessed what had happened and alerted the Artillery. The South African fire was accurate. Shrapnel snarled through the air and forced the enemy gunners to take cover, while the sun set and darkness closed in, making it possible for Peter to escape.

For the Stormbergs, the war settled down to a deadly slogging match. The enemy clung desperately to each defensive position until they had prepared a suitable position further back to which they could retreat under cover of heavy fire. Frontal attack followed frontal attack against prepared defensive positions. The orderly retreat of the 10th German Army dictated the speed of the advance of the British 8th and the American 5th Armies, and the 6th South African Armoured Division continued to spearhead the Allied thrust. They fought their way through defended villages and rivers and over ridges where the sweet-ly putrid stench of bloated bodies of dead horses, dead soldiers, dead partisans and communities of dead civilians hung in the air – all had been shot in reprisal for disobedience to some German dictate.

Casualties mounted. Sweating men buried their dead whenever they got the chance. Staggering stretcher-bearers carried wounded men from Battalion aid posts to casualty clearing stations, leaving behind them crimson trails of fresh blood on the chocolate-coloured alluvial soil. Ambulances loaded with blast-dazed, groaning men bumped along shell-pitted roads to overworked base hospitals.

Exhausted regiments rotated and rested every three days whenever it was possible, to give the men a chance to sleep, eat cooked food, wash their clothes and their stinking bodies, and to absorb replace-ments for the men they had lost.

A trickle of Allied prisoners of war made desperate escapes through the German lines and told horrific tales of German brutality – of forced marches through slush and snow, of prisoners who were sick and starved and often barefooted, and of how German guards shot those who could go no further. They reported that the Germans had commandeered the food resources of the entire country to the north, leaving the civilian populations to starve.

They told of people being shot merely on suspicion of aiding parti-sans or escaped prisoners of war, or for hoarding a few potatoes, or for referring to the approaching Allies as liberators. They said entire com-munities, including the aged and infirm, were forced at gunpoint to dig tank traps. They murdered and plundered and raped. They lined people up indiscriminately and shot them in the streets for killing some depraved or sadistic German soldier.

In the front yard of the ruin of a farmhouse, Peter, Spud and Taffy found the corpses of six young men dressed in peasant working clothes. Their hands were tied behind them with wire and they lay in a line on their backs. Their dead eyes bulged from the impact of the pistol bullet fired into each man's forehead – they had been executed. Marks in the sand showed signs of scuffles, indicating that the men had been pinioned and shot one at a time.

Further away, the body of an attractive girl of about seventeen lay sprawled in the dust. The ends of her fingers were raw and blood caked and covered in flies. Her fingernails had been torn out before she died. They were scattered in fly-encrusted blobs on the ground around her. Her face was bruised and swollen and her staring eyes were bloodshot. The front of her simple dress was ripped open from neck to hem to expose her thin body. Her scalp was bloody in patches where clumps of hair had been pulled out.

Taffy's black eyes smouldered. "I suppose they were partisans," he said through stiff lips. He looked at the body of the girl. "She's about the same age as my kid sister," he whispered. "Did they force you to betray them?" he asked the dead girl.

Spud took his arm. "What's done is done, Taff. All you can do is to pray for her soul."

"And remember her the next time we get hold of a bloody German." Taffy's voice was hard with hatred.

Inside the ruined farmhouse an old woman crouched in a corner. Her rheumy eyes were vacant and puffy from weeping. One side of her face was swollen and purple. She trembled and tried to cower further into the corner when Peter crossed the room towards her. She would neither speak nor accept the piece of emergency chocolate he offered her. When he took her arm and tried to help her to her feet, she shrank away, whimpering.

The mouth-watering aroma of sizzling fat, dripping from grilling meat onto hot embers, mingled with the smoke from Spud's fire. The sheep they had managed to "liberate" from a German foraging party had probably been intended for the table of some senior German officer.

Spud, Peter and Taffy had been out all night on reconnaissance, so they were not part of the assault force getting ready to move forward. Spud had timed it perfectly. The rest of the men would be gone before the meat was cooked. Not that they would have wanted any, anyway. Men going into battle have little appetite, especially when they have been under heavy bombardment for six days and nights. The threat of a sudden counter-attack had kept the Stormbergs in the front line and they had missed their turn of rotation for their three days of rest.

In the tussle that resulted from the sheep's spirited resistance to being "liberated", Taffy's elbow had accidentally collided with Spud's left eye – it was swollen, closed and turning purple. The point of Spud's knife had inadvertently gouged a deepish wound in Taffy's forearm which had bled profusely for a short while. The handkerchief he had bound around it was sufficiently saturated with blood to make the wound appear far more serious than it was.

"Fuck it!" Big Dries grumbled, looking up at the five trucks squealing to a halt nearby to disgorge their cargoes of fresh, clean-shaven replacements. He grabbed Spud's knife and cut off two juicy, half-cooked ribs from the sizzling rib cage. "They're not getting any of my share; bugger them! Not after a week of iron rations." He licked his fingers appreciatively and stood up. "Look at their bloody eyes," he said. "They've seen the meat already. Man, this tastes good! Thanks, Spud. Thanks, Taff. I'm on stand-by so I must get back to my mortar. Keep another piece for me and don't let these new guys get it." He clamped the two ribs between his teeth and used both hands to gather up his equipment.

The hungry newcomers sniffed the sweetly scented smoke wafting towards them and stared at the mutton fat dribbling into the six-day stubble on Big Dries' chin.

Taffy cocked his head to the distant howling of approaching shells. None of them moved. Their experienced ears told them the shells would pass harmlessly overhead. "Those are for the cooks," Taffy said, jerking his thumb in the direction of Brigade HQ, far in the rear. Leaning over the fire, he screwed up his eyes against the sting of the smoke and raked the embers under the grill with his bayonet.

A few of the newcomers threw themselves flat on the ground. Others crouched, fearfully scanning the sky with anxious eyes. Seeing the three by the fire ignore the shells that whined overhead, they stood up a little shamefaced.

"Fucking Army's got no heart," Spud complained, glancing in the direction of the assault force men, shrugging themselves into the straps of their webbing equipment as they moved towards their start line. "Poor buggers have got to rush a minefield at full gallop. Bloody Army knows they're going to lose eight per cent casualties but you'd think HQ would have the decency to wait till they're out of sight before they send up the eight per cent replacements."

"Gives me the shits, too," Taffy added. "When we've got to attack a mountain and I see twenty-five per cent replacements arriving before the attack starts, it makes me hate the poor bastards worse than I hate the enemy. Especially when I wonder which one of them's standing there waiting for me to drop in a bloody heap so he can jump into my place."

"Will ye just be lookin' at this little bastard following his nose towards our meat." Spud glanced briefly at the well filled-out boy of eighteen or so wearing a clean uniform, approaching cautiously with a hungry pack of others following him. "Just be looking at him, will ye now.

Young fuckpig's still fat from his mommy's milk and he's after scrounging our hard-earned sheep. Bugger it, no! He's getting fuck all o' this. Not after Taffy half blinding me, trying to get a grip on the woolly bastard."

"Stuff your eye, Spud," a grin tugged at the corner of Taffy's lips. He held his blood-soaked bandaged arm under Spud's nose. "Next time you try to grab a sheep, Spud, don't try to grab it with the point of your knife."

Spud was too intent on slicing between sizzling ribs to reply. The reserves edged closer, sucking their lips hopefully. They stared uneasily at the three filthy figures squatting on their heels around the small fire. They had not had the opportunity to wash, shave or comb their shaggy hair for six days and their eyes were bloodshot with fatigue.

The front of Spud's shirt was streaked with filth from his scuffle with the sheep. A flap of torn material hung like a spaniel's ear from the triangular rent slashed by a flailing hoof, exposing a patch of blood-flecked and bruised flesh on his stomach. The awed eyes of the new men flickered from the gory handkerchief on Taffy's arm to Spud's torn shirt and bunged-up eye. They stared fearfully at the telescope-mounted rifle cradled across Peter's lap. Polished boots shuffled back when Peter slid the gleaming blade of his knuckleduster-handled sniper's knife from its leg sheath to slice off an almost cooked strip of succulent meat.

Spud ignored the new men. He cut off a morsel and impaled it with the point of his knife, blowing on it to cool it a little, then licking it with rapt appreciation. "Bejayzus but this is good, Isinkwe! Tender and juicy as a baby's arse. 'Tis a damned site better than that stringy, tough bastard of an unter-offizier you shot for us last week." He looked up and fixed the tubby newcomer with a one-eyed stare from an eye that looked like a sapphire in a patch of corn stubble.

"Fat Boy, this one couldn't be better if it was you. He was about sixteen/seventeen years old at the most. He was on his way for a shit. Isinkwe here, waited until the kid had finished his crap, to get the taste of it out of his system. Then he plugged him through the head so's not to damage any of the meat. Here!" Spud picked up a fat-dripping rib with dirty fingers and poked it at the new replacement's nauseated face. "Try a piece. There's nothing to compare with roasted German. As long as they're young," he added as an afterthought.

The new soldier recoiled, ashen and desperate eyed. He clamped his hand over his mouth and turned away, squirting jets of vomit through his fingers.

"Attention!" Spud yelled at the top of his voice at the retreating backs of the new replacements. Colonel Hamman and his 2IC were approaching to welcome them. "In this regiment, when you see the

Colonel you brace up to attention!" Spud yelled at them.

The newcomers, including a young Sergeant and a sprinkling of Corporals, stood ramrod straight with their rifles at their sides. They stared blank-eyed at the two unkempt and exhausted looking officers who wore no insignia of rank.

Colonel Hamman stopped beside the fire and loomed hugely over his still squatting sniping team. Strands of cotton dangled from his armpits where he had ripped the over-tight sleeves from his shirt which had been made for a man with normal-sized arms. He grinned down at Spud. "Thanks for the leg you sent over," he said. "My driver's roasting a chunk of it right now in a Jerry helmet. The smell of it makes me drool."

Spud cut off two ribs and handed one to each of the officers. Colonel Hamman licked at a dribble of juice and tugged a sliver of meat off with his teeth. He chewed briefly and swallowed. "Hmmm! Thanks. This is the tastiest piece of meat I've had for a long time."

The tubby newcomer dropped his rifle and staggered away towards the trucks with his hand clamped over his mouth.

"Carsickness," Spud said to the Colonel by way of explanation, "its hell in the back of those closed trucks."

"I'm Colonel Hamman. Who's the senior man here?"

"I am, Sir," the young-looking sergeant spoke up, "Sergeant Hulley, Sir."

"Stand your men at ease, Sergeant."

"Standat .. ease."

"Stand easy, men." Colonel Hamman and Major Jonker walked among the men shaking hands and welcoming them to the regiment. He came back to stand beside the three still squatting around the fire. "Sergeant," he called, "form your men up into three ranks facing me."

The men formed up.

"At the slope. Sergeant."

"Attention," the Sergeant shouted. "Slope .. ARMS!"

"One, two, three .. One, two, three .. One." A corporal called out the time as he had been taught to do in training camp.

"Men," Colonel Hamman said, "we're all too buggered to make speeches or to stand on pomp or ceremony. After we've had a bit of sleep I'll see you again and my 2IC here, Major Jonker, will allocate you to your platoons. I have a very pleasant task to perform and you men can act as guard of honour until this can be done properly." He grinned at Peter. "Come on, you three. Get on your feet. This is your parade.

"At the Present, please, Sergeant!"

"Pree-sent .. arms!"

"One, two, three .. One, two, three .. One."

"Up!" Spud called, and the three of them stood to attention, wondering what it was all about.

"Peter MacTavish," Colonel Hamman said, "General Poole has instructed me to award you the Distinguished Conduct Medal for gallantry in the field, in the execution of your daring raid to neutralise the enemy observation post at Cassino. Major!"

Major Jonker drew a four-inch length of medal ribbon from his shirt pocket and handed it to the Colonel, who stepped forward and pinned it on the right side of the faded ribbons of the Africa Star and the General Service Medal on Peter's shirt. "Peter," he said, as they shook hands, "or should I call you Isinkwe, now? I've waited so long for this to come through I thought they'd forgotten it. Congratulations! No man in this regiment has deserved a medal for distinguished conduct more than you have. I'm proud to have you in the Stormbergs. If we ever get a chance to get ourselves clean again, General Poole himself will present you with your medal.

"John Patrick Mahoney and Dennis Alfred Reese, for your illicit part in the same action, the General has seen fit to award you both with the emblem for honourable mention in dispatches." He shook hands warmly with them too.

"OK, guys," Spud relented when the brief parade was over, "you can come and get a piece of meat now." The replacements smiled uncertainly, but the thought of eating the meat no longer appealed to any of them.

"Excuse me, Sir."

Spud looked up at the young Sergeant standing to attention in front of him.

"Are you also an officer?"

Spud's one incredulous eyebrow shot up to his unkempt hairline. He chewed hurriedly and gulped down a mouthful of meat. "Holy Mother, Sergeant darlint, and what is it ye'll be after calling me next? Me, an officer? Hooray fuck!"

Colonel Hamman's eyes were etched with worry as he watched Peter's retreating back. He had lost six of the Regiment's snipers in quick succession. The school of sniping was training men as fast as they could, but the men who qualified lacked the grounding the earlier trainees had. Able Company's Jan Botma and his replacement, Frikkie Nel, and his replacement, Josh Tyler, had been blown to bits by German mortars. Baker Company's Jack Murray had been torn to a bloody pulp by machine-gun fire. Charley Company's Marnie Minnie had been caught in an unexpected counter-attack. He had been bayoneted seventeen times.

Colonel Hamman sighed deeply. He had just finished writing a letter to the parents of Dog Company's Herman van der Poel, to offer his condolences on the heroic death of their brave son. He couldn't tell them that Peter had found their son's body in a farmhouse. He had been taken alive. The Germans had crucified him with bayonets to a tabletop and stood it on its end against a wall. He had been castrated and his naked body mutilated with burns and knife wounds.

On the other side of the hog's back confronting them, the new replacement for Dog Company had reported an enemy tank hidden somewhere in the two acres of trees growing in a wide band along the reverse slope. He reported he had seen the tracks of a tank leading into those trees. Colonel Hamman didn't trust the new man's report. He had to know for certain what else, in addition to that single tank, the Jerries had hidden in those trees, waiting to shatter the Stormberg's advance. The only man he could trust to reconnoitre effectively was his over-worked and exhausted sniper, Peter MacTavish. An ominous silence hung like a cloud over the sector of the front line he had to attack.

Spud and Taffy lay waiting for Peter, a little below the crest on the reverse slope of the hog's back that obscured the Regiment's view of the suspect wood. Static crackled faintly in their ears as they waited tensely for a signal from Peter. Behind the Stormberg's dug-in perimeter, Big Dries sat in his mortar pit with one hand pressing the earphone of his radio to his ear and open cases of fragmentation and smoke bombs ready beside him. He drew through the stem of his pipe and puffed out clouds of acrid smoke. The rank tobacco he had "liberated" from captured supplies, stung his tongue.

After a surprisingly short wait, Taffy jerked with shock when he felt a tap on the side of his boot. He was searching the skyline so intently through his field-glasses he had not seen Peter creeping through the grass towards him. Peter signalled him silently to remove the larynx microphones strapped around his throat.

"We can't use radio signals, Taff," Peter said in a hushed voice, "they've got a radio direction-finder tied to the top of a tree, aimed this way. That new Dog Company's sniper's got his eyes up his arse. The track of the tank he reported to the Colonel is so wide and deep I'd guess about twenty tanks used it to follow each other into the trees. I saw three pairs of birds fluttering nervously above scattered trees where they've probably got their nests. The tanks have most likely deployed under cover of the trees and are waiting for our attack.

"I want you to go back to the Colonel and tell him what I've seen. Tell him I can't see a bloody thing through the leaves. I want him to send me an artillery officer and to get the 5.5s ready. Tell him when I'm ready, I'll signal one word, `fire'. I want a quick stonk of high explosive from every mortar we've got, to blast the leaves off the trees and expose the tanks." He watched Taffy slither down the slope and then crawled to where Spud was hiding to tell him what had happened.

Lying like a pair of rabbits on the top of the hog's back, Peter and the Artillery Captain had a grandstand view of the devastation. A hailstorm of mortar bombs exploded among the trees on the right hand side of the wood and crept thundering towards the left side, blasting off leaves and small branches. The Captain spoke urgently into his microphone. He had seen the first of the lurking tanks. It was one of the latest enormous Tiger Mk VI tanks, armed with an 88 mm gun.

Heavy shells from the 5.5s howled low overhead and flying earth and smoke obscured the tank. An orange flash like a bolt of lightning glowed in the heart of the pall of dust and smoke. "Direct hit, No 1!" the Captain called excitedly into his microphone. "Left 3 .. up 50," he directed, as he spotted another tank.

Peter's earphones came to life. It was Spud's voice calling Big Dries on their frequency. He had also climbed to the hog's back on their left to watch the bombardment. He'd realised the danger of German direction-finders locating the Artillery Officer's voice as he directed the fire of his guns. "Dries, darlint, I'll be after singing you a song," his voice announced in Peter's ears.

"Hi, Hi Cathusalem, Cathusalem, Cathusalem, Cathusalem,"

Screaming shells, thuds of explosions and a strong German voice using the same radio frequency, interrupted Spud's fine baritone for a second. "Will ye just be getting off my fuckin' air now!" Spud's voice ranted at the German, "I was after singing a song to my. friend, Dries, back there!

"Hi, Hi, Cathusalem," he started up again,

"The harlot of Jerusalem.

"First there came a man of might,

"An Israelite, a dirty shite,

"He fuc..!"

The shattering explosion of an 88 mm shell blasted Spud's voice off the air. At the risk of his own life he had succeeded in diverting the German direction-finder to his own position.

After a few minutes his panting voice crackled back, mixed with static. "Bejayzus, that was close," the voice croaked. "I had to take off like a whore's drawers."

Taffy's voice came in crowing with laughter.

"Fokking Irishman's mad," Big Dries' Afrikaans-accented voice interposed.

During the early days of June, enemy resistance intensified. Interrogated prisoners revealed that the 6th South African Armoured Division's advance was being contested by the 10th and 11th Parachute

Regiments of the 4th Parachute Division, and the 356th Infantry Division, which formed part of Army Group Von Zangen. These forces were reinforced by units of the 362nd Infantry Division, which included the 3rd Panzer Grenadiers and one brigade of the Herman Goering Division.

Following the fall of Bagnio Reggio, the enemy fought ferociously to cover their withdrawal along densely wooded, rugged high ground, West of Allerona. In the forested hills where their tanks were unable to support them, the Stormbergs fought their way forward through devastating sniper and machine-gun fire, amid the blast of hand-grenades and the clanging of bayonets. They drove the enemy from their natural fortresses and finally broke through into a valley of farmlands where they met up with their sister tank regiments.

Taffy and Spud sat on the edge of Spud's slit trench talking earnestly in the early morning sunrise over mugs of steaming coffee cradled in cupped hands. Peter was asleep in his slit trench beside them. Taffy's forehead was creased with lines of worry. Nothing could shake his conviction that the Germans had got to know Peter and they were deliberately out to get him. During the past few weeks they had intensified their use of snipers and the Stormbergs had lost ten men to their bullets in three days.

"I tell you, Spud," Taffy said, "they've got to know Isinkwe now and they'd rather nail him than the whole bloody Regiment. I'm talking about their real snipers. Not the silly tits who shoot from tree tops and other stupid places. Sure, they're dangerous enough, but they're sitting ducks for a guy with the kind of eyes Isinkwe's got. I'm beginning to believe what Indabushe says about his old grandfather always telling Isinkwe where the bastards are waiting for him.

"Nobody's told those German pricks yet that trees aren't bulletproof. Either he puts a bullet through the tree and gets them himself, or he calls Big Dries to blow them to hell with his mortar. It's the other fuckpigs that make my arsehole shiver. They're professional snipers that don't shoot at people like you and me. They're good! Bloody good! And the reason why they're so good is because," he jerked his head at Peter's blanket-wrapped form, "he's shot or got Big Dries to blow up every one of them that's not first class. The ones who are left are not only expert, but they're getting better every day, because they're learning from Isinkwe."

Colonel Hamman's driver came walking towards them blowing into his coffee, with his tommy-gun clamped under his armpit. Spud shook his head at him warningly. "No you don't, Dolf," he said. "Every time I see you, you're after telling Isinkwe the Colonel wants him. Now you just fuck off quietly and tell the Colonel our boy's been out all night and if he goes out again half asleep, the Jerries'll nail him."

"Bugger it, Dolf," Taffy added, "Isinkwe's only had two hours sleep in the last two days."

Dolf smiled a wry smile. "He's bloody lucky," he said, "the Colonel hasn't slept at all."

The sound of Dolf's voice wakened Peter. Like an animal, he slept with his senses alert. Without a second of transition from exhausted sleep he was instantly wide awake.

Colonel Hamman's mug of coffee stood unheeded beside the four overlapping aerial photographs lying on the bonnet of his jeep. "These've just arrived," he greeted Peter perfunctorily. "I've had two conflicting reports about these farmhouses." He jabbed the tip of his forefinger on the line of minute doll's houses on the photograph. "The new sniper from Charlie Company .. What's his name?"

"McKinnon, Sir."

The Colonel nodded absently. "Yes, that's right. He reported there's no sign of life at all in those houses. Now the Ops Officer tells me you reported all ten houses occupied?"

"Yes, Sir," Peter nodded. "They've got sentries hidden under vines and bushes so I couldn't get as close as I wanted to. I didn't see anything but I worked my way along downwind and I smelt cigarette smoke from every house."

"What are you grinning at?" Colonel Hamman asked suspiciously.

"I also smelt shit, Sir. It smelt like a dog or something had fallen into one of their shit holes and crawled away in the direction of the stream." He pointed at the thread of a stream meandering around the western end of the high ground. "It was getting late, Sir, and I didn't have time to follow it up."

"So those houses are occupied, you say?"

Peter nodded.

Colonel Hamman shook the sleep from his tired brain. "Yes," he muttered half aloud. "I couldn't accept that they would pull out and leave the gateway into the valley farmlands wide open for our tanks to cruise through."

The morning was suspiciously quiet. Peter looked along the line of high ground hiding the valley farmlands from their view. He moved closer and studied the photographs.

"Perfect terrain for our tanks," the Colonel spoke beside him "Just too perfect to be left wide open. The General has ordered a massive tank attack by the combined Natal Mounted Rifles and the Special Service Battalion. We're to give them close support."

Peter glanced at the lines of Sherman tanks jockeying for position behind the spur of high ground along their front. He lowered his eyes and studied the photographs again. "The only obstacle I can see, Sir, is the row of houses I had a look at last night." He ran his finger along the straight line of the ten farmhouses. The photograph showed clearly that one was roofless and the others had shattered windows and shell holes through their roofs.

"They look innocent enough, Sir. If there were minefields anywhere, all these vehicle tracks would converge at various points where they had to pass through cleared lanes. You say, Sir, the spotter plane saw no sign of dug-in anti-tank guns behind the houses?"

"Not a sign. But I tell you, Peter, there's something fishy somewhere. I don't believe for one second the Jerries are going to let us sweep up the valley all the way to these hills where they're digging in, waiting for us."

"There's only one way to find out, Sir."

"What've you got in mind?"

"I'll go and have a look, Sir."

"You must be bloody mad, Peter. In broad daylight?" He pointed to the trees lining the high ridge a thousand yards away on their right. "Look, young Peter MacTavish, we know there are no guns up there. If there were, they'd have opened up on us long ago. But that ridge hasn't been cleared yet and I'm damned sure they've got machine-gun nests there watching us. Hell man! If a mouse tried to crawl up this slope they'd rip it to pieces with their Spandaus."

"I wasn't thinking of a mouse Sir. I was thinking of a tadpole." Peter put his finger on the map and traced the stream flowing around the end of the spur. "If you can call one of the support tanks to drive along next to that stream, I'll walk beside it where the Jerries on the ridge can't see me. When I find a good spot I'll slip into the water. The tank can carry on a short way as though looking for a place to dig in. Then it can change its mind and come back to where I left it and wait to give me cover when I come back."

The water was cool, but not cold. Peter crawled along the fern-lined stream bed with the water washing over his submerged body. He kept himself pressed against the right side bank so nobody on the high ground could see him. Opposite the end of the spur, something on the shoulder of the hump attracted his attention. He parted some rushes very carefully and searched the hump yard by yard until he made out the dull gleam of sunlight reflecting from the enamelled strip of a radio antenna. "Bastard," he whispered to himself. "Artillery spotter." There was nothing he could do about the man for the time being. Except for his knife, he was unarmed. When he got back he would point him out to his cover tank and the gunner could blast him to pieces.

He crawled on until ahead of him he saw a pool at the foot of a natural sluice, where the .water gushed between clusters of papyrus and

broad-leafed arum lilies. From the top of the sluice he knew he would
have a clear view of the farmhouses. He was about to move a cluster of
lilies aside when he suddenly smelt human excrement. Almost hidden
in the stream bank vegetation he saw the fingers of a human hand. His
skin prickled as he eased his knife from its sheath on his leg. He slid
his fingers through the gunmetal loops of the knuckleduster handle
and eased towards the hidden man, breathing silently through parted
lips.

When he was close enough he made out the form of a body hidden
in the vegetation. The fugitive stank of excrement and appeared to be
asleep. His starved-looking body was dressed in tattered clothes and
his feet were bare. Peter avoided looking at him until he was within
reach. Clamping his hand over the stinking scarecrow's mouth, he
jerked him into the water, where he pinned him to the bank with his
leg and held the point of his knife touching the skin under his ear
lobe.

The man's eyes flew open and stared at Peter in abject terror. He
made a few feeble attempts to free himself, then slumped helplessly.
He was certainly no German soldier, nor did he have any weapon, so
Peter relaxed his grip over the man's mouth and nostrils to allow him
to breathe. "Tedesci?" Peter demanded in a whisper, asking him if he
was German. He kept the point of his knife pricking the skin of the
man's neck.

"Nein! Nein!" His voice croaked with terror.

"Italiano?"

Peter's captive shook his head fearfully away from the point of the
knife.

Stuck for words and keyed to kill, Peter grabbed a handful of the
scarecrow's hair and hissed through clenched teeth, "Then who the
fuckin' hell are you?"

The starved man's face crumpled and the terror faded from his eyes.
His shaking hands crept hesitantly up Peter's arms and his body trembled with waves of shivering. "Tha-thank Christ! Oh, thank Christ!" he
whispered through violently trembling lips. "Thank God .. Thank God
.. Thank God." His hands fastened like claws around Peter's arms. "Are
you English?" He was shaking so badly he could hardly speak.

"South African," Peter whispered back. He released his hold as the
man began to cry brokenly, and he gathered the stinking scarecrow
into his arms protectively.

"Transvaal Scottish," the man in his arms sobbed against his chest ..
"Tobruk .. We escaped .. four of us .. We tried to get through to you ..
I was at the back .. I ran for it .. It was dark .. They caught my buddies
.. I jumped into their shit hole .. They searched for me .. They gave
up .. I heard my buddies screaming, screaming, screaming .. Then

nothing .. No shots .. Nothing.

"They must have used their bayonets." The escaped prisoner seemed a little more coherent. "One of them came from the house and crapped on me. I crawled away in the night. I fell into the pool and tried to wash myself, but I was finished. I hid in the rushes when it was getting light and must have fallen asleep. Then you found me." He broke down again and sobbed.

"What house?" Peter asked him.

"There's a line of houses near here. It was one of them," he said.

"Wait here for a few minutes," Peter told him. "I'll come back for you after I've had a look at those houses."

"No!" The prisoner's eyes dilated with terror. "They've broken out the back walls of all of those houses and driven Tiger Six Tanks into them. They'll blow you to pieces. Those tanks are waiting to shoot through the windows and blow your tanks to bits."

"Thanks for telling me, Buddy. That's all I need to know. We'll get out of here and tell the Colonel. He'll call the Artillery to blow those houses off the face of the earth. Hold tight onto the back of my belt, keep low in the water and I'll get you safely home."

Taffy's worrying about the growing professionalism of the German snipers was infectious. The Regiment had lost two more of their sniping school replacements the previous day. He had spoken to Indabushe about it and together they had gone to talk to Peter. They hadn't seen much of each other over the previous four weeks. Indabushe had been too busy with the wounded to take time off to talk, while Peter had been either out scouting or snatching a few hours sleep. They found Peter and Spud sitting on the edges of their slit trenches and Big Dries sitting on the edge of Taffy's trench with his elbows on his knees and his head resting in his hands, staring at nothing.

"Are you feeling sick, Dries?" Indabushe asked.

"I'm fokking dying," Dries replied.

"Hang on, Indabushe," Spud held up a staying hand. "I always wanted to be a Quack. Let me diagnose this case."

They all smiled to dispel the cloud of tension that hung over them.

"Dries, me bhoy," Spud regarded his new patient with a professional eye, "your bones are aching?"

Dries grunted his affirmation.

"And your skin's too sore to touch?"

Dries nodded.

"Your eyes are burning and your throat feels like you're breathing fire?"

Dries gave a disinterested nod of agreement.

"Your nose is running? .. Your chest feels full of barbed wire? .. Your mouth tastes like you've been chewing on a turd?"

"Oh, fok off, Spud," Dries sighed, "I'm sick enough without your bullshit to make it worse."

"Ah Ha! Spud clicked his fingers and smiled brightly at Indabushe. I've got it, Doc! I know what's wrong with this bloody Dutchman. His underpants are too tight!"

"Seriously, Dries," Indabushe said after the burst of laughter following Spud's diagnosis, "come to the aid post and I'll give you some muti to make you feel a bit easier. But I warn you it will make you drowsy and slow your reflexes, so I suggest you hand over your mortar to your Number 2 until the effects of the drugs wear off."

"Thanks, but you can stick your drugs," Dries growled. "Taffy's given all of us the shits about Jerry snipers waiting out there for Isinkwe, tomorrow. No, fok it! I'm not taking any bloody muti to fok my reflexes while Isinkwe's out there." He jerked his thumb in the direction of the Germans on the other side of the hill. "I'd rather die next to my mortar with a smoke bomb in my hand, ready to give my buddy a smokescreen if he needs it."

He lumbered to his feet and, towering over Peter, put a huge hand on his shoulder. "Don't let these buggers spook you, Isinkwe," he growled hoarsely, "your friend Dries Maritz will be ready to support you, sick or not sick. I'm going to sleep off this bloody 'flu now so I'll be OK for tomorrow."

"Hold on, Dries," Peter also stood up, "there are a couple of features on the map I'd like you to have a look at. Don't go to sleep for the next five minutes while I get it from Ops.

Taffy, Spud and Indabushe sat in silence for a few minutes, watching Big Dries and Peter walk away towards the Ops dugout. "Tell me, Spud," Indabushe asked, "are you also worried about Isinkwe going out tomorrow?"

"Tonight," Spud corrected. He bent down and lifted a heavy back-pack from his slit trench and opened it for Indabushe to see the two-inch mortar bombs he had packed into it.

"What are they for, Spud?" Indabushe asked.

"Smoke!" There was no trace of the natural laughter in his eyes. "Now he's out of the way, I can tell you I'm so shit scared about tomorrow I'm not even taking a rifle with me."

"Nor am I," Taffy chipped in.

"He never needs one at the best of times," Spud said to Indabushe with the hint of a glint in his eyes. "I don't know why the army ever gave him one. This bloody Welshman couldn't hit a cow in the cunt with a handful of rice at five yards, let alone try to shoot a German at 50. Perhaps they thought he looks more ferocious with something in his hands and that's why they gave him a rifle."

"Piss off." Taffy was about to say more but he saw the glint of laughter leave Spud's eyes as he turned back to Indabushe.

"I'm taking a two-inch mortar and this pack of smoke bombs," Spud continued. "I've got a feeling in my water something's going to happen. If it does, I'm going to stoke this little mortar so fast, the bombs will be passing each other in the air. Vesuvius has fuck-all on the smoke I'm going to lay down if the Krauts spot Isinkwe. I'm going to make this part of Italy look like it's on fire."

There was no trace of Irish accent in Spud's voice and it worried Indabushe. He had never heard Spud speak so tersely before. His own psychic interests made him acutely aware of Spud's inner tension. Not only that of Spud. He glanced at Taffy and read the disquiet reflected in his eyes, too. Even their stoic friend, Big Dries, had admitted he was worried.

"It must be that bloody grandfather of yours," Spud said with a weak attempt at humour. "The old bugger's warning us he's taking a day off to go fishing or something, and he's leaving us on our own."

"No, Spud," Indabushe shook his head in vehement disavowal of any such notion. When he spoke there was unswerving conviction in his voice. "When Isinkwe and I were children, old Mashona would let us play with fire until we burnt our fingers. He did this to teach us to respect fire and thereby avoid getting ourselves seriously burnt in the future. Rest assured, my friend, the day Mashona lifts his shield and allows Isinkwe to get hurt, he will only do so to protect him from some major calamity."

Spud shook the ghosts off his shoulders. "You bloody witch-doctors give me the screaming shits," he said.

"It's like this, Indabushe," Taffy answered. "We know Peter well enough now to sense he's spooked."

"That's what's got us crapping our nappies," Spud agreed. "You see, things have changed in the last couple of weeks."

"Yes," Taffy interrupted. Indabushe's head swung from one to the other as they spoke. "Our old plan worked like a bomb. Isinkwe had them taped. He would get so close to them they wouldn't believe he was right under their noses. Spud and a couple of dummies would lie further back."

Spud leaned towards Indabushe. "When he fired, I fired. This got their tits in a tangle. For a few minutes they didn't know whether to scratch it or wipe it. Eventually they would find one or other of the dummies and blow it to hell. When they saw the dummy's rifle fly into the air, they thought they'd got Isinkwe."

"Then I called Big Dries," Taffy took over again, "and directed his mortar fire onto any target Isinkwe indicated. I was further back than

Spud and I was able to speak to Big Dries in reasonable safety."

"Mostly, Isinkwe didn't have to shoot at all," Spud said. "Those telescope eyes of his picked out the targets. He couldn't say much, or the direction-finders would pinpoint him. He'd tap his microphone to warn me to stand by. Then he'd give me the enemy position in degrees from where he was lying. Then the distance. Once I had picked out the target I would call Taff and he'd get Big Dries on the job with his mortar."

"We've nailed so many of them," Taffy added, "the pick of what's left have got wise to us."

"You see," Spud took over again, "every time we push them back, Isinkwe examines every inch of the ground they were holding." He shook his head admiringly. "He's the most thorough bugger on God's earth. You see him pacing up and down and you think he's flipped his lid. But what he's really doing is measuring distances to every machine-gun, mortar, rifle pit and observation post. But most of all he examines the positions of their snipers.

"He doesn't miss a thing. When he's finished searching, he sits there with a far-away look in his eyes like a dog having a shit in the moon-light. He's reconstructing the whole shooting match in his mind, through the eyes of a German sniper. And every time we've blown up a sniper it's been because he knew exactly what to look for and more or less where to look. He checks the sights on their rifles and not one of them has ever been set at less than 300 metres. Sometimes as far as 500."

Indabushe turned to Taffy as he took up the tale of what was worry-ing them. "Isinkwe won't shoot at more than 250 yards," Taffy said, "where he's certain of a heart shot. He never chooses a place the Jerries could identify as a good aiming mark for their mortars. Or any place that'd be easy for anybody to direct fire onto if they spotted him. And he always makes sure of a handy escape route he can duck away into. Most important of all, he never leaves his hiding-place without covering up every trace of his ever having been there."

Indabushe noticed Spud's agitation in the way he stood up and flexed his knees restlessly. "Now our whole plan's fucked," Spud said. "Somewhere along the line we've slipped up. Two weeks ago we were pushed back and Isinkwe had to move out like a squirt of gippo guts, under cover of smoke. The Krauts must have noticed something that's made them change their tactics.

"They must have noticed how close to their positions our smoke screen started, and they must have guessed why. Five days ago Isinkwe spotted one of their fuckpigs waiting for him and he got one hell of a fright. The bastard was using one of Isinkwe's own copyright tactics. Instead of using a mountain for cover, about half a mile away, like they normally do, this guy hid himself behind a small rock right out in the open. And he was only two hundred yards away. Big Dries nailed the bastard, then our tanks roared in and drove the whole fucking circus back over the hill. When they were gone, Isinkwe picked up that sniper's rifle. We were with him." Taffy nodded his verification. "The sights on that rifle were set at only two hundred metres.

"I tell you, Indabushe, Isinkwe got another hell of a shock. He stared at that sight setting for five minutes without moving. He looked like he'd seen his own arsehole without looking over his shoulder and he couldn't figure out how.

"That fuckpig of a Kraut had the range spot on. He knew how far Isinkwe would be from him."

"That Jerry made one fuck-up," Taffy said, "and Isinkwe spotted it as soon as it got light. Instead of circling to his position like Isinkwe always does, that tit of a Jerry had walked straight there. His feet had knocked the dew off the grass and his spoor looked like a black pencil line on a white page, pointing to where he was lying.

"If it hadn't been for that, he might have nailed Isinkwe. And I'll tell you another thing too. After Dries nailed him, the Jerry mortars ignored our dummies. They kept their searching fire closer to their own front than they've ever done before. It was sheer bloody luck they didn't get Isinkwe.

"The bastards know our boy now and they'll do anything to get him. I bet the man who can give them Isinkwe's head on a plate has been promised an Iron cross, Knight's Order, with a fistful of diamonds on it. And I bet Hitler himself will pin it on him with his own lily-white hands."

They sat with their thoughts for a few moments, then Taffy spoke again. "He hasn't said anything, but they've got him spooked alright. He knows they're not pricks and he knows they're after him. When he chose our positions for tomorrow, he did something he's never done before. He gave Spud and me a grass blade by grass blade area to search, behind where he is going to hide!"

"And I'll show you something else as well," Spud added. He stepped into Peter's slit trench and opened the wooden case in which he kept his rifle. Without disturbing the rifle, Spud lifted the case for them to see the telescopic sight. "He's never done this before, either," he said. The sights were set at 350 metres instead of 250. Spud looked across the rifle into Indabushe's eyes. "Our boy's had a bit of a shock, hasn't he? He's never ever considered firing from so far back!"

Intensely aware of their sense of foreboding, Indabushe's eyes moved anxiously from Spud to Taffy. "Does he have to go out tomorrow?" he asked them both. "Can't they send somebody else for a change?"

"We tried that," Spud shook his head. "We went to see the Colonel, both of us. But we had no luck. He's got to know what's in front of us before we attack and Isinkwe's the only one left he can send. The other two he would have sent out were the two poor buggers that copped it yesterday."

Peter had no sooner rejoined the group and taken his seat on the side of his slit trench than they saw Dolf Hanekom striding towards them with his tommy-gun tucked under his arm as usual. Dolf smiled a greeting and jerked his head over his shoulder in the direction of Battalion HQ. "Boss wants to see you, Peter," he announced.

Peter squatted on his heels, Zulu fashion, beside the Ops Officer. He didn't bother to look at the map spread on the ground in front of them. The map in his head was far more detailed. It even showed the lengths of the shadows of every feature at every hour of the day; it showed the movement he could expect from the plant cover when the wind blew at varying strengths; it showed the depth of every depression in the ground and the height of every tussock of grass and every rock.

The Ops Officer stopped speaking. There was nothing more he could point out that Peter hadn't already considered in the minutest detail. "Radio procedure as usual, Peter," he added unnecessarily. "Indicate targets from your position, again, as usual. We can work them out from there." He fell silent. There was nothing more that needed to be said.

"Ahummm!" Colonel Hamman cleared his throat. Peter looked up and saw the strain on his face. "That wild Irishman of yours and Taffy Reese came to see me this morning while you were sleeping. If they'd had their way I wouldn't send you out tonight without a full armoured regiment to support you. In fact I wouldn't be sending you out at all, because they demanded you be sent home on six months' leave." He smiled as he remembered Spud's insubordinate approach. He had taken no offence as he knew them by now and appreciated their concern for their overworked buddy. "Those two hellions demanded support from every mortar we've got in the Regiment. They want them on stand-by with enough smoke bombs to black out half of Italy. They're really worried about you this time. They don't give a damn about themselves. Anyway, I made them a promise."

He leaned towards Peter, tapping his fist into the palm of his hand, and spoke earnestly. "You'd better listen carefully, Peter MacTavish, because this is a direct order I'm giving you. You will not fire a single shot tomorrow. If General Kesselring himself stands up in front of you in full view, you will not shoot!

"However, if it happens to be Adolf Hitler, instead of General Kesselring, I'll allow you to give him a quick shot, with the compliments of General Smuts. Aim high up between his legs and give Eva Braun something to cry about at the same time." His smile was warm and friendly. "Good luck, Peter." He reached out to shake hands. "Remember, all I want to know is what's in front of us, nothing more!"

"Good luck, Peter," the Ops Officer held out his hand. His quick smile did not hide the permanently anxious look in his eyes.

"Let's eat," Peter said to Taffy and Spud. "We're going out as soon as it gets dark. I don't know why, but I've got a feeling I'd like to get my position ready as early as possible."

Behind his back Taffy's and Spud's eyes met and for a second they looked at one another tight-lipped. This had never happened before either. Nor had Peter ever chosen a position so far back.

The fragrance of freshly dug soil always reminded Peter of his childhood days in his mother's garden. It was a smell he loved, deep in his soul. But he gave the smell of the earth scant thought as he soundlessly prepared his hide and settled himself under his net. The night was chilly and his clothes were wet from the dew. He had crawled through the grass on his stomach for the last hundred yards, keeping his head low so he would be able to see anybody standing silhouetted against the faint luminosity of the night sky. His skin was goose-pimpled with cold beneath his thin cotton shirt and trousers. He could see from the night sky that the day would be hot. If he had put on a jersey or a battledress blouse, there was nowhere to hide them when he took them off at dawn. Or if he kept them on, he would swelter in his airless hollow under the net and they would hamper him if he had to get out quickly.

Peter adjusted the larynx microphones resting against the sides of his throat. His neck would swell when he got hot and the strap would get too tight. Then he lay still and closed his eyes so his mind could concentrate on every detail of his surroundings and his escape route. Five yards to his right, a knee-high line of stones had been cleared from the nearby patch of potato plants. Allowing for the initial stiffness of his body, he would be able to stand, bound three paces and dive over the line of stones. That would take him two seconds. There would also be the extra tenth of a second enemy reaction time; and he would have half a second's grace before anybody could align his sights and shoot at him.

The potatoes were planted in rows at right angles across the German positions. The rows were a yard apart and about a foot high. If he dived flat between them they would give him cover from shrapnel and small-arms fire. If he leaped and dived over five rows at a time, he could do so quicker than the Jerries could register, aim and fire with any likelihood of hitting him.

He had carefully paced out the field; it was fifty yards wide. He would be able to cover most of the distance in short dashes between the rows, on elbows and splayed knees. At the end of the field the waist-high stone wall was an obvious escape route and the Germans would have sighted mortars to bomb the uphill side of it. By the time he got there, the smoke should be thick enough to allow him to double back through the potatoes and leave the Germans to bomb up and down the wall, while he escaped in the smoke. Reasonably satisfied, he concentrated on relaxing his body limb by limb until he lay in a state of half sleep, to wait out the night.

At first light, a sudden awareness of danger released Peter from torpidity. He felt his skin crawl and he remembered Cimela straddling him with his knife pressed to his throat and his accusing voice saying, "I let you sweat to teach you to trust that f-feeling you get. M-move immediately! Don't just lie there with your f- finger up your arse waiting to get shot."

His eyes searched the darkness but he could see nothing and he looked down at the ground remembering what Cimela had said about the attraction of searching eyes. His nostrils flared and twitched but all he could smell was freshly exposed grass roots. He pressed his hands flat on the ground but could detect no vibration of movement. He held his ear to the damp earth but there was no tremor warning of footsteps.

Whoever was out there had stopped moving. Then the faintest clink of metal on metal reassured him that the danger was directly in front of him and not behind him. He moved his head slowly from side to side, keeping his eyes lowered, and the sensation of danger was strongest straight ahead.

A childhood recollection appeared vividly in his mind. He and Indabushe were squatting side by side listening wide-eyed to Mashona "If that enemy had had just one scout, we would not have been able to destroy them. Victory goes to the one who can surprise the other." Peter remembered the stuffed greatcoat `scout' concealed behind the wheelbarrow.

He shivered at the memory of the fright he had got that day. "You, Isinkwe, would not listen! Three times while I spoke of the battle, I saw your eyes drawn to this wheelbarrow. The spirits were warning you but you would not listen. Though the voice of the spirits is but a whisper, it will be there to warn you all your life, so you must be listening for it at all times."

With the stealthy approach of day, the night shrank back. Peter's body was tense with anticipation. The tip of the rising sun would show him most of what he needed to see. Flat rays of sunlight would probe across the land and peep under bushes and banks for a moment. Then it would illuminate secret places beneath ledges of rock and sparkle on lenses of field-glasses and telescopic sights. The rays of sunlight would light up dew-wet domes of steel helmets and glint on the barrels of rifles, machine-guns and mortars; show the dark line where a man had crawled through grass and bushes and shaken the dew from their leaves; splash black shadows across hollows and the indentations of footprints which had trodden on grass in the night; and cast shadows like accusing fingers pointing at every stone and bush and tussock of grass.

He waited for that moment with his eyes half closed, watching with the furtive glances of a drowsing leopard. With the German sniper somewhere in front of him, he was afraid to use his field-glasses with their large circular lenses. He would leave the assessment of the enemy positions to Spud and Taffy. They would know what to look for to report to the Colonel.

A scarlet finger-nail-paring of rising sun crept up onto the high ground, sending shadows sneaking across the ground in front of him. His breath caught in his throat. He closed his eyes and opened them again. Twenty yards in front of him and a little to his left, a long oval shadow stretched across the cropped grass. He looked down between his arms to consider what he had seen. There was only one explanation for that isolated patch of shadow. If it wasn't for the wind-tattered shrubs on either side of him, his own humped net would be casting an identical shadow.

There was something not quite right with the shadow in front of him. He took another brief look. The German sniper was facing away from him! "Bastard," he whispered. "Thank you, Baba Mashona, for warning me not to get too close." It could only have been his guardian spirit's warning in his subconscious that had told him not to get as close to the German positions as he usually did.

He realised with a chill of apprehension that Taffy had been right. The Germans had finally got him figured out. If he'd taken up a position at his usual distance of 250 yards from the enemy, that sniper would have been seventy yards behind him, facing his back! That sniper also knew his enemy would have chosen a safe line of retreat but he'd guessed the wrong one. He'd guessed it would be the stone wall. He had not thought anybody would use the banked ridges in an open potato field as a line of escape.

Considerations crowded his mind. The German sniper knew too much about his tactics, so he would have to get rid of him. It would be easy enough to put a bullet into the back of his head, but far too dangerous from such an exposed position. If the German had learned so much, he'd probably also learned the advantage of having his own back-up team like Taffy and Spud.

The long shadow cast by the German would only last for another few minutes. When it shortened he would never be able to indicate the target to Spud or Taffy. If Taffy couldn't see him and he called down mortar fire onto the German, the first bracketing sighter shots could also wipe him out, they were so close to one another. One glance at the map and Big Dries would understand the situation perfectly clearly, so he'd leave it up to him. If he was going to do anything about the sniper, he'd have to do it immediately. He moved his hand slowly and tapped his microphone once with his fingernail.

"Standing by!" Spud's voice answered clearly, to deliberately distract enemy direction-finders away from Peter. Spud snuggled lower into his slit trench, half expecting the first searching German mortar bomb. He felt reasonably safe as he focused his field-glasses on where he knew Peter was lying. He lay still and tense, listening for Peter's indication.

"34 zero." Peter's voice told him the target was 20 degrees left of his position.

Big Dries' face was taut with concentration as he listened to the exchange between Peter and Spud. A frown of worry creased his forehead. Was there something he had forgotten? His bloodshot eyes wandered over the other two stand-by mortars in their nearby pits. The wish that Taffy and Spud had not asked for them niggled in his mind. He could see their gunners' heads above the rims of their pits, pressing their earphones to their ears.

"Two-ah zero." Peter's voice crackled faintly.

"Hooray fuck!" "Fok!" "Hell!" the startled voices of Spud, Big Dries and Taffy ejaculated simultaneously in the headphones. The target was only 20 yards in front of Peter. An involuntary shudder shook Big Dries' shoulders. "Zero two," Spud's voice came in quickly. "Visual!" He had identified the target. "Legs Eleven!" The target was eleven degrees from his Zero.

Big Dries made a pencil dot opposite the eleventh graduation on his protractor and pencilled a line which intersected Peter's indicated line. He bent and made a small adjustment to the mortar sight, then stood up a little unsteadily with a fragmentation bomb in his hand, hovering over the open mouth of his mortar.

Taffy was some time in coming through. Through his field-glasses he searched the ground in front of Peter but could detect nothing that might be an enemy.

The shadow was shortening and Peter realised Taffy didn't know what to look for. He'd have to take a chance with the enemy radio direction-finders and give him a positive indication. He tapped his microphone twice and waited for Taffy's acknowledgement that he was standing by.

Instead of Taffy's voice, Spud's baritone sang loudly in his ears:
"The good ship's name was Venus,
By Gad you should have seen us,
The figure head was a woman in bed
And a man with a standing penis."
"Shadow Taff!" Peter said quickly, taking immediate advantage of the distraction Spud had caused the direction-finders.

"Zero three," Taffy's voice calling Big Dries, was excited. "Visual! Visual!" He sighted carefully through his compass. "Zero three, fiva, fiva!" he called.

Big Dries tried to shake the muzziness from his head. He blinked to clear his vision and drew a line at 355 degrees from Taffy's position to meet the intersecting point of the lines from the other two positions, but he was a fraction slower than the other mortars.

He heard the metallic clunk, clunk of the bombs dropped down the tubes of the two support mortars, followed by the explosions of their propellant charges. Dropping his own bomb down the tube, he crouched as it banged and flew into the air. Then he realised what it was that had been worrying him. The support mortars would follow the usual bracketing procedure and Peter was too close to the target. He lurched to his feet to shout to them to wait, but lost his balance and fell against the side of his mortar pit. Before he could right himself he heard the clunk, clunk of their bracketing bombs hitting the firing pins and their exploding charges drowned his shout of warning.

Two bombs erupted ahead of Peter's target and blasted away the morning silence. Peter ducked his head in his shallow trench. Suddenly another two shattering explosions detonated right in front of him and a flying clod of earth stripped away his covering net and showered him with earth.

"Holy Mother." Spud's shocked shout of surprise died as Peter ripped away the wires of his headphones. He bounded out of his nest and dived across the line of stones piled along the edge of the potato patch. Machine-gun bullets stuttered along the ground and sang off the rocks behind him. He leapt up and dived into the ridged field. A host of rifles joined the machine-gun, and bullets cracked sharply through the air above his head. Crawling, leaping and dodging, he dived deeper into the field.

Spud was quick and accurate. Smoke shells burst and plumed in a line between Peter and the enemy. Peter did not see the bomb from Big Dries' mortar cartwheeling the dismembered body of the enemy sniper into the air.

A pattern of heavy bombs thudded into the field and exploded in billowing smoke. As he reached the wall, the first of the barrage of German bombs burst behind it. A fusillade of small-arms fire ripped randomly through the spreading blanket of smoke and raked the field.

As Peter doubled back, a mortar bomb exploded on top of the wall and shards of shrapnel screamed around him. Simultaneous blows like hard swung cricket bats smashed against his shoulder and the side of his face, propelling him off his feet into the furrow, between two rows of potatoes.

A sound like an air raid siren screamed inside his head and he writhed on the ground from a flare of pain. Pain stabbed into his brain. It felt as though two bayonets were being stuck into his head through his eye and his ear. He dragged himself uphill over the ridges through a red haze of pain, while thickly swirling smoke burned his lungs. The screaming in his ears changed to a roaring sound and each time he tried to take his weight on his right arm, he fell onto the damaged side of his face. Tears of pain blinded him and he could hardly see where he was going.

Shells, like express trains with their sirens wailing, screamed by overhead, but Peter crawled along the plough furrow doggedly, weak with shock. He didn't notice that the enemy fire had petered out. In the thick fog of smoke he heard Spud's voice calling him, "Isinkwe! .. Isinkwe!"

"Isinkwe! .. Isinkwe!"

He tried to answer. "Spud, here. Here Spud." His own voice sounded like a croak.

"Holy Mother of God!" Spud was beside him. "It's OK now," Spud was saying. "The shells are ours. They've silenced the bastards." He was on his knees beside Peter.

He didn't know where to grip Peter to help him up, as he was drenched with blood. Blood oozed from his right ear and from the corner of his bunged-up right eye. Spud looked around anxiously, hoping the smoke would cover them long enough to get out of the field and over the rise.

"Spud! Spud! Isinkwe!" Taffy's voice was shouting for them in the smoke.

Spud called him over and between them they hoisted Peter to his feet and half dragged, half carried him up the slope. Every yard of the way Spud's grunting voice promised what he was going to do to the stand-by mortars when he found them, if Big Dries hadn't already done it for him.

At the edge of the curtain of smoke Indabushe waited for them to emerge. He had a rolled-up stretcher over his shoulder and a medical pack slung at his side. His feeling of impending disaster had been so acute he had come forward at daylight, to be close if needed.

"Put him down .. Put him down," he called to Spud and Taffy when they staggered out of the smoke. He examined Peter's wounds, then strapped two field dressings over the bleeding pulp on his shoulder and the back of his upper arm. He slipped a needle into his other arm and depressed the plunger.

"You're going to be OK, Isinkwe," he said thankfully. "These wounds will heal, but I can't tell how much damage has been done to your ear or your eye. There's only one thing I'm sure of, and that is you'll never snipe again."

Taffy tried gently to prise Peter's fingers loose from his rifle. "Let go, you silly bugger," he coaxed, "let go. You're not going to need this thing again in a hurry."

Chapter 7

Peter's bones ached from the unaccustomed softness of the mattress. He longed for a piece of flat ground to lie on. He longed to turn over onto his back and stretch himself.

His right arm was folded across his chest and strapped tightly to his body. He lay still on his left side, knowing that if he moved, pain would blaze in his right shoulder as if coals from a hot fire were being pressed against his flesh. When he lay still, the pain subsided to a bearable burning pull of tight stitches drawing together the raw edges of the wounds in his shoulder and at the back of his upper arm. Under the dressing covering his right eye his eyeball felt full of grit and too big for its socket. There was a dull roaring in his padded ear like the distant sound of the ocean.

But the pain in his bladder was worse than the pain of his wounds. This was what had wakened him from the drowsy aftermath of the anaesthetic. Little by little the ache in his bladder nagged his doped mind back from a world of painless blackness, through moments of awareness and lapses of doziness, into full pain-filled consciousness.

The hazy grey blob filling his first muzzy awareness gradually defined its outline into the softly rounded curve of a nurse's bottom, two feet in front of his face. She stood with her back to him as though she had been there forever and would remain there, unmoving, through all eternity. His straining bladder ached for relief. He lay still while his awakening brain grappled with the problem. He could not suffer the indignity of asking a lady where the lavatory was. And the lady herself was deeply engrossed with the man in the bed next to his own. He closed his left eye while he considered his dilemma. Like the cutworms he had watched as a child in his mother's garden, he sought escape in immobility, from death, or worse still in his own predicament, from indignity.

He heard faint sounds of movement; a light crepe-rubber tread on the planks of the duckboard floor of the ward tent and the whisper of starched material. He opened his eye a little to see what was happening. The nurse had turned and her hip was towards him. Her veil hid the side of her face. She was slender and he sensed she was young.

A full-bosomed Sister with grey-streaked hair had taken the girl's hand and elbow. There was something purposeful in the Sister's grip. The grey skirt in front of his face moved and the two Sisters went quietly from his field of vision around the end of his bed.

His left eye opened wide and he strained to listen to the receding footsteps but the droning in his ear muffled the sound of their feet. He knew if he could see their footprints on soft ground, one set would be crisp and the other set would be blurred at the tips of the toe and heel showing the tiredness of the one who had made them.

A furnace of pain flared in his shoulder when he turned his body and sat up slowly. He shook his head carefully from side to side and blinked his eye to dispel a wave of dizziness.

"Are you alright?" a voice with a Cockney accent demanded from the bed on his right, which he couldn't see because of the dressing over his eye. "Lie down, you bloody fool! I'll call the Sister for you."

Peter turned his head slowly until he could see the person who had spoken. He moved his lips and tongue and chewed his teeth to restore saliva to his parched mouth. When the poles of the tent stopped gyrating he relaxed his frantic grip on the side of the bed. "I'm fine," he mumbled. "It's just my shoulder and my arm .. only flesh wounds." He chewed the saliva in his mouth and ran his tongue around his lips. "I'm busting for a leak. Where's the piss-house?" His voice came out much stronger.

Across the aisle, a patient sitting up on the side of his bed grinned and indicated with his head. "It's down at the end of the tent on the left," he said.

Peter eased his legs over the side of the bed. His top was bare except for the white bandages, which contrasted with the deep tan of his skin. Somebody had dressed him in a pair of blue and white candystriped flannelette pyjama trousers. He wondered where they'd put his blood-stained shirt and trousers, what had happened to Mashona and why his old guardian spirit had let him get wounded, but his need to relieve his bladder crowded Mashona's treacherous neglect out of his mind. He stood up carefully and braced a knee against the bed and waited while the wave of dizziness passed.

"Lie down, you bloody fool. I'll get somebody who can walk to call the Sister."

He ignored the querulous Cockney voice.

"I told you to lie down!" the voice insisted. "That's an order! I'm a Sergeant, and I'm ordering you to lie down."

Straddling his wobbling legs to maintain his balance and hunching his bandaged right shoulder to his ear to ease the burning, Peter leant forward slightly to relieve his bursting bladder and walked erratically down the aisle between the beds.

Waves of well-being surged through him as his bladder streamed water into the trough in the toilet. The relief was overwhelming. The roaring in his ear deadened the sound of the quick steps of the Sister, until she bustled into the cubicle and steadied his swaying body with a grip on his left shoulder and a firm arm around his waist. The stream had ceased. His bladder was empty and his face flamed as he fumbled frantically to make himself decent.

"If you get out of your bed again without permission, I'm going to have you tied down." The Sister's tone was severe. He glanced at her and saw the kindness in her eyes and the lines of weariness on her face. Her jaw was set and determined. "When your bladder is full, you must ask for a bottle," she ordered.

"I'm alright, Ma'am. I didn't want to trouble anybody. I'm just a bit weak." He wondered vaguely what she meant by a bottle.

"Are you alright?" she spoke sharply, still holding him with her arm around his waist and turning him around to go back to his bed.

He nodded his head. "Yes, Ma'am," he said. His voice was weak. Clearing his throat, he tried again. "Yes, thank you, Ma'am," he repeated in a stronger voice.

"You're a South African?" It was more a statement than a question. Her arm tightened for an instant as he stumbled and tottered forward. The kindness in her eyes belied her stern bearing.

"Thank you, Ma'am," he murmured. "How do you know I'm a South African?"

"It's the way you South Africans say `yeeees'. You drag the word out. We British say a crisp `yes'. And you are to address me as `Sister' and not as `Ma'am', although it does sound very nice in your slow South African way of speaking."

They had arrived at Peter's bed. He lay down gratefully and the Sister covered him with the sheet and a coarse grey blanket. He felt drowsy and relaxed and the relief of an empty bladder stole over him like submersion into the oblivion of anaesthesia. Far in the distance he heard the Sergeant's voice complaining to the Sister in his strong Cockney accent.

"Anovver one of them Saarf Africans, Sister. Seems them's all the sayme. Insubordinate and insolent. When the orspital Sergeant-Major makes 'is rounds, I'm charging Saarf Africa 'ere wiv failing to obey a lawful command. And cor lummy, Sister, if 'e don't speak to you like you was 'is favverite aunt! And you a Captain an all."

As Peter drifted off to sleep he heard the Sister say, "Let him be, Sergeant. He is still half doped from the anaesthetic. These boys are not career soldiers like our British men and their ways are not our ways..."

He heard no more as he floated into a world of warm darkness where there was neither pain nor discomfort nor the nerve-shredding blasts of explosives.

The day was far advanced when he woke again. Once more it was the fullness of his bladder that wakened him. He felt rested and clear headed. He had slept deeply for most of the day.

For a while he lay motionless. Only his open eye, an inch above the pillow, showed he no longer slept. Carefully, limb by limb, he tested the muscles in his body. Except for the burning pain in his shoulder when he moved it, he decided he was not much the worse for being wounded. He saw bottles clamped to wooden stands at the side of the bed next to him. Rubber tubes, fitted with small clamps, led downwards from the bottles. Their ends were hidden under crepe bandages around the arm of the person in the bed next to him, strapping it to a piece of plank at his side.

He raised his head a fraction from his pillow to see better. He could not hear the man breathing above the background noises of the ward – there was a subdued hubbub of male voices and a distant clatter of crockery – but he noticed from the faint rising and falling of the blanket covering the patient beside him that his breathing was faint and shallow. His head was swathed in bandages except for the crown, where a tuft of red hair stuck up like the comb of a cockerel.

Peter sat up slowly and swung his legs over the side of the bed. He was no longer dizzy. Provided he made no quick movements, the pain in his shoulder remained bearable. He stood up to try his legs.

"Get back into your bed, Saarf Africa! Hey you! I said get back into your bed."

For all the notice Peter took, the Cockney Sergeant might as well not have spoken. Peter walked soundlessly across the floorboards to the toilet. He relieved himself and returned slowly to his bed with a growing awareness of the fact that he was hungry. He ignored the spluttering threats of the Sergeant. For a while he stood looking with his unblinking left eye at the soldier in the bed beside him. The smell of death hung around the bed but the man was still breathing, albeit almost imperceptibly. Peter bent over the bandaged head with his mouth close to where the ear should be.

"Can I help you?" he asked quietly. He saw through the slit in the bandages that the soldier had a piece of lint between his lips. "Is there anything I can do for you?" he asked again. He saw lips tremble in the slit in the bandages and they seemed to form the word `water'."

"I told you to stay in your bed, young man," he heard the Sister's exasperated voice before she reached the end of his bed. "Now get back in immediately. And stay there."

He lay down obediently while the middle-aged Sister stood by threateningly, with her clenched fists resting on her hips. She leaned forward so her face was close to his and pressed the tips of her fingers to her stomach. "The boy has been badly wounded," she whispered, poking her abdomen to indicate multiple stomach wounds. "On no account must he be given any water. As for you, don't you dare move

136

from your bed." She turned her back and busied herself with her badly wounded patient. She moistened the piece of lint, and squeezed it and replaced it between his parched lips. Peter saw his head jerk convulsively a few times as he bit desperately on the lint, trying to extract a little moisture to ease his torment.

"They ain't got no discipline, Sister, them Saarf Africans," the officious Sergeant addressed her when she straightened up, "but while they're in this 'ere British orspital they comes under British Army discipline. King's regulations. Dumb insolence. That's wot it is. This 'ere Saarf African don't answer me when I speaks to 'im. Just does as 'e ruddy well pleases. I'll have 'im on OC's orders just as soon as Sar' Major makes 'is rounds. The ovver five Saarf Africans are already on report. I ain't seen nuffink like it in all me twenty-five years of service."

The Sister turned and look down at Peter. He felt pity at the lines of tiredness on her face and the strain in her eyes. "Your name is MacTavish, is it not?"

"Yes Sister."

"Very well. Don't go off to sleep now, MacTavish. Tea will be along directly and you're to eat it all to make you strong again."

Behind her mask of authority he sensed her compassion. Never in his life had he been addressed by a woman as `MacTavish'. He felt a little offended and wondered vaguely whether he should tell her his name was Peter, or even Isinkwe. He felt at a loss. He had never encountered a lady in uniform and the fact that this lady wore a Captain's pips on her shoulders made him feel even more at a loss.

The bulky dressing on his right eye conveniently obscured his view of the Cockney Sergeant. Nor could he see him when he sat up to have his `tea'. The `tea' itself was another surprise. He had expected a mug of tea and a rusk or two and he was quite unprepared for the meal of meat and roast potatoes and boiled vegetables an orderly placed on the locker beside him. Everything had been cut up so he could manage with one hand. He looked towards the end of the tent and saw through the open flap that the sun was still shining. He wondered why supper was served so early and why the Sister had called it `tea'.

He slept and woke again after daylight had gone. Once again he saw the back view of the young Sister standing looking down at the guy in the bed beside him. He couldn't say how he knew she was young. Perhaps it was the curve of her hip against the fabric of the drab grey uniform, or the texture of the tendril of brown hair escaping from the side of her veil. There was certainly nothing youthful in the way she stood. Her enveloping uniform could not hide the droop of her shoulders nor her slouch of weariness.

From the end of the ward he heard the raised voice of the middle-aged Sister. The young Sister had heard it too. Her back straightened a little and she turned abruptly and walked away, but Peter could not see her face.

"Supper time."

Peter opened his eye and sat up. He was given a tray with a mug of strong stewed tea, a wedge of sponge cake and a small bowl of toe-curling sour, stewed plums.

A soldier on crutches hobbled to his bedside as he finished eating. He rested on his crutches and held out his hand to take Peter's left hand in an awkward but friendly handshake. "Van Vuuren," he announced his name. "Hannes van Vuuren." His smile was warm and his face seemed vaguely familiar. He spoke in Afrikaans. "We didn't get to know you boys in the rifle companies," he said. "I'm in Support – 17 pounder anti-tank guns. I got a lump of shrapnel in my leg. Nothing too serious. I'm a friend of Big Dries Maritz and he's told me a hell of a lot about you. You're Isinkwe the sniper, aren't you? Dries never stops talking about you and he tells some wonderful stories about the things you've done. I don't think there's anybody in the Stormbergs who doesn't know about you.

"I heard the ward orderly say there was another South African in the ward and I found out it was you. You came in last night while I was asleep, and all of today it's been you who were asleep," he laughed. "The old Sister says you're not too badly hurt, and me and the other guys are happy to hear it. Counting you, there are now six South Africans in this hospital and this bloody old Sergeant next to you has already got about ten charges against each one of us. We all have to go on orders as soon as we're better. Fuck him anyway! He'll have a lot more charges against us before we're finished with this place. Then he'll have to catch us, because we'll all be back with our regiments."

Hannes threw back his head and laughed loudly. He stopped suddenly and covered his mouth guiltily with his hand. His eyes swung to the bandaged head in the bed beside Peter. "Sorry," he murmured. "Poor bugger. He got caught under an air burst.

"It's been three days now," he whispered, coming closer, "and every day we expect to find him dead in the morning. When he does go, that pretty little Sister on night duty will fall to pieces. She watches all the time, waiting for him to give up. Perhaps he is her brother or something." He shrugged his shoulders, "I don't know. All I know is she comes to him in the night like a bloody ghost and stands dead still beside him until the older Sister takes her away. Eight men have died in this ward in the last week or so and the little Sister was with each one of them when they went. It's enough to give a man the shivers. I don't think she sees the rest of us, but when she stops next to my bed I nearly shit myself. She makes me wonder if I'm going to be the next one to be carried out feet first." He jerked his thumb at the bed beside Peter and still spoke in a whisper.

"This poor bugger keeps on living and crying quietly for water. I don't know why they don't give it to him, he's fucked anyway. God only knows what keeps him going. For a week we've been expecting the little Sister to break down. I won five hundred lire from Dirkie Uys, you know him too, from Charlie Company. He bet me she would fall down yesterday."

Peter felt an unaccountable flush of anger at Hannes' and Dirkie's apparent callous disregard for the Sister's sensitivities, but he could see Hannes meant no harm.

"Swarms of casualties have been pushed in here lately and I don't think the Sisters have had a chance to close their eyes for the past ten days or nights. Now I hear another hospital's been opened nearer the line, so perhaps they'll get a chance for a bit of a break. This place keeps only the ones who are too badly buggered to be moved further back and are going to snuff it anyway. And guys like us who will get better soon and go back to their units. The more seriously wounded go to base hospitals near Naples where they can get patched up enough to be sent home.

"They tell me as soon as we are discharged we get sent to a rest camp for three weeks and charged with all our crimes. But they can stick their rest camp up their arse. As soon as we are fit enough, me and the others are going to fuck off back to our units. How about you, Isinkwe?"

"No, Hannes," Peter smiled, "when you and Dirkie get back to the Stormbergs you'll find me there waiting for you."

"There's not much time to talk now," Hannes had seen the night duty orderlies come into the ward, "they'll put the lights out in a few minutes. Then we're supposed to shut our eyes and go to sleep by numbers. No!" he laughed again, "I forgot. First they bring the bloody bottles and we have to lie and piss in them by numbers. These Englishmen are something else! They've got times for us to have a piss and times when we mustn't feel like a piss even if we're bursting. We're supposed to eat by numbers and shit by numbers in this place. I tell you, I've never seen so much bullshit in my life.

"We are even supposed to lie to attention when a Sister speaks to us. They've got me for insubordination for trying to chaff the little Sister. These silly buggers think girls were made for saluting. The hospital Sergeant Major's a miserable old bastard, too. If he was on fire I wouldn't walk across the road to piss on him to put it out."

"Lights out!"

Hannes fumbled in his dressing-gown pocket. He placed three ripe plums on the bed beside Peter's hand. "One of our Lieutenants is in here with a neck wound. He steals plums and brings them to us when he gets a chance. There's an orchard right next to the hospital. There are sheep there too, so we're planning to have a braai, but I'll tell you about it tomorrow." He gave Peter a friendly wave as the lights snapped out.

Peter couldn't sleep. He couldn't adapt to a darkness that didn't flicker and rumble with gunfire. His mind was wide awake. He thought about Hannes van Vuuren and all he had said. The aspect of the discipline of the hospital didn't worry him. He would only stay until his wounds had healed sufficiently for him to get back to the Regiment where Indabushe could take the stitches out for him. He was left-handed anyway, so whatever was wrong with his right eye didn't matter much.

The other patients in the ward drifted off into the restless, dream-ridden sleep of men whose nerves have been strained to snapping point from daily danger, shattering explosions and the terrifying possibility of being overrun by attacking tanks. He lay listening to their sleeping torment. Some tossed and groaned as their restlessness hurt their wounds; somebody whimpered in the darkness; somebody in the row of beds opposite him sobbed in his sleep. He started violently and wrenched the stitches in his shoulder when the Cockney Sergeant shouted out in his sleep, "Look out! Take cover! Oh my Christ! Oh my Christ! It's all over now, lads. Look lively now! Cover them up! Put that arm in wiv wot's left of them. Don't just lie there! Pick up that bloody arm!"

He could visualise the scenes causing the men to cry out and utter snatches of sentences. The middle-aged Sister was still up. She walked slowly down the aisle between the rows of beds, murmuring soothing words to the restless sleepers. Here and there she covered men who had kicked off their blankets and she patted their twitching bodies. And under the touch of her compassionate hand they sighed in their sleep and settled down to rest.

The dim light from the torch which she pressed against her thigh seemed to Peter like the spirit of motherly love flitting among the beds to bring peace to the tormented sleepers. For an instant the light stole over his bed and she saw his open eye. "Settle down, MacTavish," her hushed voice commanded. "Don't be a difficult patient. God knows we can't cope with more than we have already. Close your eyes and try to sleep." She turned her back and busied herself with the badly wounded patient in the next bed. Peter heard her sigh of utter helplessness.

"Sister," he whispered, "I'm not tired. You go and get some sleep and I'll sit up and watch over him. I'll call you if he needs you."

The Sister turned around. "Go to sleep like I told you." Her voice was hoarse with exasperation. "There's nothing you can do for him. Just go to sleep and give us one less patient to worry about."

Peter woke, instantly aware of his surroundings and that something was wrong. Behind him the Sergeant was breathing heavily, almost snoring. He could hear him clearly through the dull roaring in his blasted ear. He lifted his head a little from the pillow. At the end of the ward the black moon shadow had shifted across the entrance and he realised he had slept for four hours. He listened carefully with his good ear and watched the badly wounded soldier, but he saw no sign of movement or of breathing.

Suddenly the rasping sound of death rattled through the mouth slit in the bandaged head and the soldier's chest deflated. The end of his suffering had come at last. There would be no more pain in that shattered body.

If Taffy were here, Peter knew he would bless himself with the sign of the cross. And Spud too. They were both Catholics. Accustomed as he was to death, the sound of its coming chilled him. He gripped the leather cover of his watch with his teeth to open it and looked at the luminous dial – 02-55 hours. Five minutes to three, his lips formed the words, "the hour of death". He raised his head until he felt the stitches in his shoulder begin to pull and wondered whether he should get up and call the Sister, or cross the man's arms on his chest. Looking dubiously at the arm strapped to the plank and the tubes leading from the bottles, decided he had better leave well alone. But he couldn't simply go back to sleep with a corpse lying neglected in the bed beside him, and he wondered whether he should pull the dead soldier's blanket over his face.

As he was about to get up to call the Sister, he heard the soft tread of crepe rubber and the faint drag as each foot was lifted tiredly after the other. He lowered his head until his ear touched his pillow. The young Sister appeared. She carried no light but the faint glow of moonlight through the canvas roof of the tent was sufficient to show her her way. She knew where she wanted to go and it seemed she had come there walking in her sleep. Peter breathed carefully through parted lips as he watched her turn around the foot of his bed and stop in front of his face with her back towards him. Very carefully he eased his left elbow under his ribs to enable him to rise easily if he were needed.

The Sister bent over the patient. She drew a sharp breath and her body jerked as though from an electric shock. Tearing the blankets back she lifted the dead arm and held its wrist. It seemed as if she had forgotten to breathe as she stood with her fingertips feather light on the dead pulse.

Peter raised his body soundlessly, moved his blankets aside and swung his legs over the side of the bed. "Breathe," he whispered soundlessly to the swaying girl. "For God's sake, Sister, breathe."

The girl uttered one wrenching sob, shockingly loud in the silence. She turned away suddenly from the dead man and covered her face with her hands, pressing her fingertips hard against her forehead. Peter got up and stood uncertainly beside her. She still held her breath and slowly bent over. His arm encircled her waist without quite touching her, ready to catch her if she fell. She gulped a shuddering breath and exhaled it in smothered sobs. When she leaned further over and appeared to be about to fall, he caught her firmly around her waist with his open hand between her breasts, supporting her chest.

For a moment she leaned heavily against his hand, then straightened and, turning towards him, clung to him, sobbing hoarsely. Pain seared his shoulder from her grip. Her eyes were tightly closed but he could see no gleam of tears. Her dry hiccupping sobs jarred his body as he held her. Her head dropped onto his shoulder and she buried her face against his neck. Then her fingers relaxed their hold and her knees gave way under her.

Peter dropped his hand to her stomach and grasped a handful of her uniform to steady her against his out-thrust hip. He turned and pulled her around so that she fell face down onto his bed. For a moment her body shook violently – her hands covering her face pressed into his pillow. He rested his hand on her shoulder in sympathy and felt her tension-knotted muscles and tendons. A nerve twitched at the base of her neck.

He began to massage the muscles and ligaments of her neck to relax them. His fingers and the ball of his thumb kneaded her shoulders and neck. From the looseness of the skin under the material of her uniform and the protruding bones of her shoulder blades, he guessed she had lost weight recently; her skin had not yet shrunk to fit her newly thin body. He manipulated the muscles on the sides of her neck from her shoulders to her ears. His movements grew stronger and more sensitive and he wished he had both hands to work with. With his sensitive left hand he felt out the hardest knots and kneaded them, while she shivered and shook with sobs.

After a while he felt the tempo of her sobbing change and he realised she was crying. She had given up the fight against her emotions and her surrender was being rewarded by a flood of healing tears. He carried on working methodically along the columns of muscles on either side of her spine, wishing he could massage her bare skin with rubbing oil. It would do her more good. Little by little he felt the beginning of relaxation softening the hardened muscles.

He removed her hands from her face, spreading her elbows with her cheek resting on the back of her folded hands and massaged her back while her flood of tears quietened to gentle weeping. He realised with surprise that an hour had passed since the girl had collapsed on his bed. Her weeping had stopped and she sniffed in her sleep.

He stopped massaging to ease her shoes from her feet and to pull the blankets up to her waist, then resumed his firm and gentle kneading of her shoulders and her neck with a hand that ached from exertion. He thought of Taffy and Spud and Indabushe and Big Dries, and smiled as he wondered what they would say if they could see him massaging the back of a sleeping nurse at four o'clock in the morning. He wondered what his mother, Uvemvane, would think, and if she would approve. He wondered what the girl looked like and leaned over her but could not make out her features in the darkness under her veil. Hannes van Vuuren had called her "the pretty nurse." He wondered what colour eyes she had. For another fifteen minutes he watched her veil rippling from the movements of his hand beneath it.

The beam of the ward Sister's torch flashed as she came hurrying along the aisle between the beds of sleeping patients. For an instant it shone into Peter's eye and flickered over his bed and the Sister almost ran towards him. She was wrapped in a shapeless dressing-gown and her dishevelled hair hung to her shoulders.

"What's happening?" She was almost incoherent with agitation. "What's going on?" her hoarse whisper sounded threatening and hollow with fear. "Why are you up? Dear God! Is that Sister Marsden in your bed? Oh my God! What have you done to her?"

Peter stopped kneading, with his hand still hidden under the young Sister's veil. "She's asleep, Sister. She broke down when she found him dead." His chin jutted towards the adjacent bed.

The Sister was at a loss for a moment while she struggled to regain her composure. "Take your hand off her, at once." Her ingrained professionalism overcame her fear. She stepped to the dead man's side and her fingers touched the side of his neck to confirm what she knew instinctively. Then she prised open the bandages on his head and beamed her light into the dead eyes. She checked the level of the liquid in the drip bottles. With a swift jerk, she covered his face with the blankets.

Turning, she brushed Peter aside angrily, grasped the sleeping girl's shoulder and shook her roughly. "Get up! Get up at once," she hissed. She shook the girl again but her body seemed boneless and flopped from side to side without awakening. "What did you do to her? Oh my God! What did you do?"

"I massaged her, Sister."

"You what?"

"I massaged her. Her tendons were as taut as a tangle of wire." He leaned over and rested his hand protectively on the sleeping girl's shoulder, but the Sister grabbed his wrist and flung his hand aside.

The old Sergeant mumbled in his sleep, disturbed by the noise of the Sister shaking the sleep-drugged girl. He turned over onto his side, farted loudly, mumbled something and sank deeper into sleep.

"She cried herself to sleep, Sister," Peter tried to explain. "She broke down when she found the guy dead." Peter stood up and pulled the blankets gently off the girl and slid his hand under her chest to lift her. "I'll help you, Sister. Take her legs off the bed and steady her shoulders while I lift her." They hoisted her into a sitting position on the edge of the bed but Peter could see she was only half awake.

"I'll manage now," the older Sister said brusquely. "Mind out of my way."

The girl might have fallen, had Peter not steadied her against his thigh. He had to help the ward Sister lift the limp body onto her feet. It was growing faintly light in the tent and there were sounds of restless movement as sleeping patients made signs of wakening. The Sister looked around distractedly as she began to lose her composure.

Peter said nothing. He took a firm grip around the girl's waist while the Sister pulled one of her arms around her neck. Between them they got her onto her feet and hurried the staggering, dazed girl between the rows of beds, past the duty room and into a partition of the tent where there were two rumpled beds and uniforms and underclothes draped over chairs. They lowered the girl onto one of the beds and Peter turned and left silently. In a few minutes he was back with the girl's shoes in his hand. He smiled at the ward Sister's stern, lined face. "It wouldn't look too good if the Sergeant found these under my bed," he said as he put the shoes down.

"Now go back to your bed at once," the Sister snapped, "and thank you. You'll catch cold without your top on." She opened her mouth to say something more but saw his smiling look of understanding and closed her mouth again. She divined that what had happened would remain between them. Peter saw the cautious gratitude in her worried eyes as he turned and hurried back to his bed.

Only the men who woke early saw the orderlies carry the dead soldier out on a stretcher. And in their beds they braced themselves to attention as best they could, to pay their last respects to the blanket-shrouded form of another comrade.

After a few minutes the orderlies returned, accompanied by the ward Sister and two other Sisters whom Peter had not seen before. Their drab grey uniforms robbed them of every shred of individual personality. The lights snapped on and the regimented routine of the day began without preamble. Sleeping patients were wakened by the orderlies, and a Sister who followed them pushed a thermometer into each sleepy mouth. The second Sister followed. She withdrew each thermometer, noted the reading and marked its position on the graph clipped to a board at the foot of each bed. She then rinsed the thermometer, flicked it vigorously and popped it into the next waiting mouth.

Peter watched with surprise. It had not occurred to him that a hospital ward could run with the precision of a trained artillery team serving a field gun in action. The only difference he could detect was the absence of shouted commands. He watched as the orderlies marched from the ward and returned in minutes with clattering trolleys laden with stainless steel bottles for the men to urinate into. Each man took a bottle, pulled it beneath his blankets and turned on his side to relieve his night-full bladder. Sisters moved purposefully from bed to bed to help the men who were unable to help themselves. There was a bit of a rumpus from the group of South African patients, demanding bottles with wider mouths, protesting loudly that they were no longer little boys.

Peter's unused bottle remained standing on the small locker beside his bed. He had already emptied his bladder in the toilet while the others slept. A Sister noticed and came to him with a purposeful tread. She took the empty bottle and glared at him. "You've been out of your bed again," she said accusingly. She lifted the clipboard from the foot of his bed and glanced at the temperature chart. "Your temperature is above normal. You .. are .. to remain .. in .. your .. bed! Do you understand?" She whirled around to face the Sergeant. "Sergeant, MacTavish is not to leave his bed. If he does, send one of the up-patients to call me."

The Sergeant braced to attention under his blankets. "Very good, Sister. Beggin' your pardon, Sister. These 'ere Saarf Africans don't know wot orders is. Gawd only knows how thems manages to fight regular soldiers like them Jerries." He turned and glared at Peter. "You will do as the Sister 'ere orders, do you 'ear? Or must I get down onto me bended and beg you bastards, beggin' your pardon Sister, to obey Sister's orders?"

Peter looked at him for a minute from one eye. "Try it Sergeant," he suggested, "it might help."

The Sister turned abruptly on her heel and walked away, with the ghost of a smile tugging at the corners of her tightly compressed lips.

The bottles were no sooner cleared away when the orderlies reappeared with two steaming urns on one trolley, and a second laden with metal mugs. They poured bitter, dark, stewed tea into the mugs and distributed them to the patients. The orderly snorted through his nose when Peter asked him if he could have a mug of coffee instead.

"This ain't no bleeding 'otel, mate," the orderly scoffed. "Only orficers gets cawfee." He grinned at the Sergeant. "Sergeant, Saarf Africa 'ere finks 'ee's in a bleedin' 'otel. King's Arms it is."

They cleared away the tea mugs and replaced them with basins and jugs of warm water. A Sister came to Peter's bed. "Ward Sister told me to give you a bed bath," she said. "Off with your trousers now."

Despite Peter's protestations and struggles, the Sister stripped him and washed him with the professional ease and thoroughness of years of practice. He noticed that most of the patients had been allowed to wash themselves and he felt he was being victimised. The Sister retied his pyjama cord and pressed him down onto his back on the bed. Despite the pain in his shoulder from her rough handling, he lay still, but smouldered with fury. He decided they could do what they damned well liked to him until he was sufficiently recovered to escape and return to the Stormbergs – although he felt he could never tell Taffy, Spud or the others that a Sister had held him down and washed his private parts.

The Sister stood back and examined him with a critical eye. His hair was combed. He lay rigid in his bed. The bedclothes had been pulled tight and tucked in. She leaned over and tugged one small remaining crease in the folded back sheet. The few items on his locker stood at attention like a depleted section of Infantry. "There now," she said, "that looks better." Then she turned away and marched down the ward.

The first rays of the rising sun lit up the side of the tent behind Peter's head. "It's time to change the guard, Sergeant," Hannes van Vuuren's English was strongly accented. "Don't keep them waiting, Sergeant. Dismiss the night guard and march in the day shift." The Sergeant mumbled something about "'bleedin' Saarf Africans".

Two new orderlies, accompanied by a Sister, brought in plates of thick oatmeal porridge, fried eggs and slices of fried bread. Peter ate quickly and asked for more. He would eat and sleep and eat and sleep until he was strong enough to get up and out of the place. When he was finished he turned onto his side to sleep away the sleeplessness of the disturbed night, but he had no sooner fallen asleep than he was wakened again by a Sister and an orderly progressing from bed to bed administering medicines. The Sister paused at the foot of his bed and consulted the clipboard.

She handed him four large M & B tablets and stood by while he swallowed them with gulps of water. When she gave him a graduated vial of dark liquid, he looked at it dubiously. "What is it, Sister?" he asked.

"Cascara," she replied briskly. "Drink it down now. It's for your bowels."

Peter smiled at her and shook his head and held out the vial for her to take back. "No thank you, Sister," he said, "my bowels are quite alright. I don't need anything at all, thank you."

"Gawd's truuf!" the Sergeant spluttered in the next bed. "Refusin' medication he is, so's he can stay 'ere longer. Drink it!" he thundered.

"You will drink it while I stand here and watch," the Sister's voice was uncompromising.

"Drink it, Isinkwe," Hannes called across to him in Afrikaans. "It will only make you shit. I also refused to drink mine when I first arrived, so the buggers held me down and pumped a gallon of soapy water up my arse through a pipe. Then you know what it's like to shit. You squirt crap like a starving cow on green grass after a long drought."

Peter grimaced and shuddered and handed the empty vial back as though it were too hot to hold. There was no expression on the Sister's face as she took it and moved on to the next patient. He lay down again determined to sleep, to hurry his recovery. He was almost asleep when he heard somebody stop at his bedside. He kept his eye closed until he felt a hand touch his shoulder. "Come on, South Africa, wake up. It's time to be rubbed."

"I don't need any rubbing, thank you, Sister." He wondered what they wanted to do to him. He sat up wide awake and mistrustful.

"Why are you South Africans so difficult?" she sounded exasperated.

"I'm sorry, Sister, I don't mean to be difficult. Here, just give me that bottle," he suggested helpfully, and tell me what to do and I'll do it to myself."

"Lie down and turn over onto your side," she ordered. Her hand slid down his body and loosened his pyjama cord. He smelt methylated spirits and felt its chill on his behind. The Sister rubbed his skin briskly. Then he felt the chill on his hip and the shoulder he had slept on. He was thankful to see the Sister leave, only to see another coming towards him purposefully. She turned him onto his back, regardless of his grimace of pain, and worried and tugged and patted and smoothed his pillow and the coverings of his bed. "Don't you move," she admonished him. "Don't go to sleep now. You must lie still and wait until the MO has done his rounds."

Peter watched the procession make its way slowly towards his bed. A Major led the little group, with an elderly, stern-faced woman beside him. The tired-looking ward Sister followed half a pace behind the Major's right shoulder. A Captain slow marched behind the Sister. Two paces behind the Captain, two Sisters walked slowly side by side. Their veils stood out stiffly to their shoulders. A pair of bored orderlies brought up the rear. One wore the solitary stripe of a Lance Corporal. The procession paused for a moment at the foot of each bed. The Major glanced at the clipboard with no expression on his face. Occasionally he muttered a few unintelligible words to the ward Sister, who wrote hurriedly on the board she carried. Each man in the bed lay stiffly to attention until the procession had moved on to the next bed.

The Major glanced briefly at the clipboard at the end of Peter's bed. He looked over the rims of his glasses at the ward Sister and smiled faintly at her. "I see you have another of our South African Allies to keep you busy, Sister," he remarked. He nodded curtly at Peter. "Are you comfortable?" he enquired briskly.

Peter smiled back politely and heaved himself up onto his left elbow so he could see the Major clearly. "How long will it be, Doctor, before I can get back to my Regiment?" he asked.

The Sergeant jerked around in his bed as though he had been kicked in the ribs by the recoil of an anti-tank gun. "Gawd's bleedin' trewf," he bellowed, "It's Sir, when you speak to an orficer."

"I'm sorry, Major," Peter amended hurriedly, "I thought you were the Doctor."

Splashes of colour flamed on the Sister's cheeks. "In their army they address their officers by their rank, Sir. They do not say, `Sir', as we do."

"Major, er, I'm sorry, Sir, can I get up now, I don't feel at all sick? If I lie in bed my muscles will get soft, and a soft man doesn't live long in my job."

The Sergeant groaned and clamped his jaw tightly shut. The cords of his neck stood out as though he was being garrotted.

"The Sister will tell you when you're to get up," the Major said. He turned to the Sister. "Sister, see this man is moved in with the other South Africans. I don't want him to cause a perfectly good Sergeant of the British Army to die of a heart attack."

Peter was dropping asleep when an orderly came to his bed. "The ward Sister wants to see you in the duty room," he announced. "Do you need any help?"

"No thanks, Corporal, I'll manage fine," Peter replied. He sat up and swung his legs over the side of the bed and stood still for a moment to make sure he was quite steady on his legs. When he reached the end of his bed the Sergeant's roar stopped him in his tracks. The Sergeant informed him in blasphemous Cockney that patients did not visit the duty room wearing only a pair of pyjama trousers. Peter draped a pyjama top and a blue dressing-gown over his shoulders and tied the cord of the gown clumsily at his waist.

The Sister did not hear his soundless tread on the floorboards. She sat waiting for him with her elbows resting on her table and her temples cradled on the heels of her hands. She looked unutterably weary. Peter came closer and watched her for a few moments with a steady, one-eyed gaze. "You need a good rest, Sister," he said quietly. "Why don't you take off your uniform and get right into bed and have a proper sleep?" His voice was gentle.

Her arms flopped helplessly onto the tabletop. She looked up at him and blinked her eyes to focus them.

"We won't get any worse while you have a sleep, Sister," he assured her. "If you don't get some rest, I'll have to hurt myself again catching you when your knees give way." He waited for a moment while she gathered her thoughts. "How is she, Sister?" he asked to give her time. "The little Sister, I mean. Has she had a good sleep? I'm worried about her. I could feel her skin is so loose it's about a size too big for her. She must have lost a lot of weight, very quickly."

The ward Sister sighed deeply and her shoulders slumped. She shook her head slowly from side to side as though she was hearing something she simply did not believe.

"I want you to know, MacTavish, I have been nursing soldiers for twenty-one years and never, never, never have I encountered anything like you South Africans. They break established rules with utter impunity. They sit half naked on Van Vuuren's bed in their corner of the ward and play poker all day long, quite unashamedly. It's open gambling, but they don't care if they are seen. There are small heaps of money all over the bed." She shook her head and seemed at a loss as how to continue. Then she took a deep breath and carried on. "Yesterday they had the temerity to invite me to have a game with them. They treat Sister's orders as though they were merely sugges-tions. I'm afraid they're going to be the death of the hospital Sar'nt Major. The poor man is in quite a state about them. He has had more backchat and insolence from five men in the last week or so than he's had in all the many, many years of faithful service he has given his country."

It was only the Sister's obvious sincerity that suppressed Peter's urge to smile. He hadn't seen the hospital Sergeant Major yet, but thought if he was anything like the old Sergeant in the ward he deserved all he got.

"They invite my Sisters," she said, "to sit on their beds and have a chat with them, and yet they don't seem to mean any harm. They joke with the Sisters and display utter disregard for their senior rank. To them the Sisters are simply girls, irrespective of the fact that some of the Sisters are almost old enough to be their mothers." She sighed heavily again and sat for a while looking at her hands resting palm down on the top of her table. She looked up slowly at the sympathetic and wondering look on the face in front of her. Peter could see noth-ing wrong with anything the men had done to cause her distress.

"But now I've heard it all," she said quietly as though to herself. "A young South African soldier, younger even than my own son, with the rank of Private.."

"Er, Rifleman, Sister," Peter corrected her gently, but she ignored the interruption.

"A young rifleman creeps soundlessly into my duty room and tells me to take off my clothes and go to bed! And then he tells me, without batting an eyelid, that he has actually felt the skin of one of my Sisters, and decided from the feel of her, that she has got thin suddenly. Tell me, MacTavish, exactly how much of the Sister's skin did you feel?"

Peter's jaw hardened dangerously and it pleased him to see her sudden fear. "The poor kid collapsed," he said in a tight voice.

The ward Sister looked up to Heaven and slapped her lined forehead with her open hand. "The `poor kid', he says! Please, MacTavish, spare me. We are not talking about any `poor kid'. We are talking about a trained nursing Sister with the rank of full Lieutenant. Her name is Sister Marsden. If you simply refer to her as Sister, it will do."

"Anyway, she collapsed." Peter's voice was truculent. "I couldn't carry her with one arm, so I put her on my bed. She was strung like a banjo, so I massaged her neck and shoulders and her back, until the tightness eased. Then the tears came and she cried herself to sleep."

The Sister rang the little bell standing on the table beside her. An orderly appeared and stood to attention.

"Please bring two cups of cocoa," the Ward Sister said to him. For several moments she sat in silence and looked at Peter. She saw the challenge in his eye and he thought about her grey hair and the lines of worry and kindness etched into her face, and he relented. Her eyes were bloodshot and tired, and they did not look like particularly fierce eyes to him.

"I only wanted to help the girl, Sister," he murmured disarmingly. "She was so upset, I thought perhaps the man who died was her boyfriend or perhaps her brother." The ward Sister made no reply. Her searching look could detect nothing threatening in the demeanour of the young man facing her. The orderly brought a cloth-covered tray with cups of cocoa on saucers. He put the tray down carefully at the Sister's elbow and stiffened to attention, about-turned smartly and marched from the tent.

"Please sit down, MacTavish," she indicated a canvas camp chair, "and have a cup of cocoa with me. We might as well break all the rules while we are about it," she smiled fleetingly.

"Yesterday when I first saw you, I decided you were just another nice young soldier who had been wounded in our fight to free Europe from German tyranny. Then an excited delegation of South African patients accosted me in the ward. You were asleep at the time. They told me about your exploits as though you were some sort of sinister killer with a rifle or a knife." She shuddered at the thought of anybody using a knife to kill with. "According to them, you are some sort of a prodigy. They told me you are the most lethal and dangerous man in your

South African Army. I was informed that you hunt Germans as a fox hunts pheasants – mostly on your own, in the dark, or right out in no man's land, under the very noses of the Germans. I must admit, I was surprised. You seemed to me to be far too young to have acquired such a deadly reputation."

Peter shook his head. "Sister, I'm a sniper," he told her simply, "I only do what I was trained to do."

"They also told me," she interrupted, "that you are the recipient of the Distinguished Conduct Medal for gallantry in the field, for your heroic deed in destroying an enemy position that was inflicting casualties among your men at Cassino."

Peter looked away. He felt embarrassed. "It wasn't only me, Sister. Indabushe silenced the sentry. The Sappers blew up the observation post. Spud shot their sniper, and I got the medal."

"You don't have to be so modest about a brave act, MacTavish." She leaned towards him with her eyes narrowed. "The point is, with the kind of reputation you've earned for yourself, you must understand the shock I got when I discovered Sister Marsden, apparently unconscious, in your bed. After what the men had told me about you, I must admit, I feared the worst. I was beside myself. I didn't know what to do. I wanted you dragged out and shot against the nearest wall. But.." She looked intently into his brown eye, "from what I'd seen of you, I decided to give you the benefit of the doubt." She omitted to say she had run her hand over Sister Marsden's hip and felt the elastic of her panties was still in place. "I decided to wait until Sister Marsden could tell me herself exactly what you had done to her. You see she, er, Sister Marsden, er, well I feel sort of responsible for her. I knew her parents very well."

She could see Peter was appalled at her insinuation, so she added hurriedly, "I waited for her to wake up and tell me what happened, before I sent for you. The poor g.. Sister Marsden drifted off to sleep again while she was telling me. But she did say that you were wonderfully kind and gentle with her. She also said you were understanding without saying anything, whatever that means." The ward Sister smiled warmly at him. "Sister Marsden insists you have `the touch of healing' in those reputedly deadly hands of yours, and I wonder what she meant by that? She doesn't know, of course, that you had only one hand with which to soothe her."

Peter looked down at his hand wonderingly. He waggled his fingers experimentally and flexed his hand.

"I don't know, Sister. Perhaps it's because I have to do special exercises with my hands. I work them on a rubber ball to keep them supple. It develops a steady squeeze on the trigger of my rifle so I won't jerk it and bungle my shot. That could be fatal!" He looked up at her and smiled a little uncertainly.

"Oh yes," she smiled back, remembering something, "the South African Lieutenant who's here recovering from a neck wound told me that snipers in your army undergo very specialised training, besides possessing natural skills. So the gentle hand which soothed Sister Marsden's agony is also a gifted instrument of killing? I must say, I find that very strange."

Peter shrugged his shoulders. "I suppose so, Sister. I hadn't thought about it before," he said offhandedly.

"I don't know that I should tell you this, MacTavish, but perhaps you have deserved it for the interest you displayed in Sister Marsden's well-being. The man who died was neither her, er, boyfriend, as you so delicately put it, nor her brother. She's just that kind of caring gir.., er, Sister. She had the misfortune of coming straight from a sheltered schoolroom into the shocking casualty wards of the first victims of the bombings. The transition was too sudden. Too brutal altogether. Sister Marsden was one of those who were thrown in at the deep end, but she survived where many others didn't. Sister Marsden has been one of those unfortunate nurses who has only seen death and mutilation since her first day of nursing. She has never been afforded the opportunity of seeing any of her patients nursed back to full recovery. This is a nurse's greatest reward. Circumstances have denied her that pleasure."

Peter listened attentively, with the growing hope of meeting the girl for whom he experienced such a protective feeling.

"She has faced the death of her patients almost every day of her nursing career," the ward Sister continued. "She is a sensitive person and very courageous. A less resolute person couldn't have endured the strain as long as she has. But it seems she is nearing the end of her tether, and only now, for the first time, have we been able to relieve her of her duties for a while. She has been granted ten days leave to rest and recuperate, but what she needs is some interest totally removed from nursing for a while."

Peter felt cheated. He was hoping to be able to see her. Within ten days he would be back with the Stormbergs and the opportunity would be gone. Something in his attitude made the Sister raise her eyebrows in dismay at her own outpouring.

"I don't know why I'm telling you all this. I've never done such an unethical thing in all my life. Perhaps it's because you South Africans have upset all our conservative notions." She laughed shortly at the thought. "But it's such a relief to let off a little steam now and again, believing, as I do, and I can't say for the life of me why, that not a word of this will be repeated."

Peter nodded his head reassuringly, hoping she would finish her story of Sister Marsden; he wondered where she would go for her leave, and what she would do. He felt a sort of proprietary interest in her.

"Anyway," the ward Sister continued, "Sister Marsden qualified and was posted with me into the slaughterhouses of the first landings and the great battle at Cassino. Since then, every day has been a day of blood and death for her. And you are quite right. She has recently lost weight very rapidly. I wanted you to know she is grateful for your gentleness. When she comes back on duty, be kind to her, and please see to it the others are too."

Peter did not mention the fact that he had no intention of staying in the hospital for as long as ten days, but the ward Sister's sudden peal of laughter startled him.

"Oh, you South Africans are priceless. Each and every one of the six of you, and the Lieutenant too, has asked, with the blood hardly dry on your wounds, how soon we will let you get back to your regiment in the front line. Do you men enjoy fighting and killing and dying? But I'll tell you now, MacTavish, you're going to be here for some time with that eye of yours. It'll be needing attention long after your other wounds are healed."

Her last words disturbed him. He'd hardly thought about any damage to his eye. He stood up hurriedly to hide his disappointment, but the Sister noticed it. "And don't forget, young man," she added, "there'll be a three week recuperation period in a rest camp, for outpatient therapy, after you leave here."

Peter thanked the ward Sister politely for the cocoa and left her staring after him thoughtfully, wondering how she could ever have mistrusted his intentions with Rosemary Marsden. She did not guess the rebellious thoughts turmoiling in his mind.

"Hey, Isinkwe," Hannes van Vuuren called, "come over here, we've got a bed fixed up for you in the corner with us. The Lieutenant here wants to meet you so he can shit on you along with the rest of us."

"Pleased to meet you," Lieutenant Joubert held out his hand. He was several years older than the others who faced each other across a bed. Peter twisted his left arm around, shook hands and sat down. The Lieutenant's handshake was warm and firm.

"Shit on you blokes?" the Lieutenant queried. "I like that! It's you blokes who got me so shat on by the Matron and the ward Sister that I'm still wiping the shit out of my eyes.

"I don't know what you buggers have been up to, but you've certainly upset the Pommies," he grinned. He spoke in Afrikaans so the British patients wouldn't understand. "The old girl in charge of this ward sent for me and gave me a hell of a talking to. She's had the

Matron on her neck about your behaviour in her ward. And the old Sergeant with the leg wounds has scared her fartless with reports of your disregard for ward discipline. The poor old girl can't make up her mind whether you bunch are on the point of open mutiny, or whether you are going to rape a couple of her Sisters, just for the hell of it."

"Oh Lord," Hannes raised his eyes up to Heaven. "I wouldn't rape any of them if they gave me home leave for it," he breathed reverently. Then he added as an afterthought, "I wonder what happened to that pretty little Sister. She wasn't here this morning when we woke up. I wouldn't mind a little nibble of that even if she does walk around like a Zombie."

"I wouldn't mind a little bit of friendly copulation in that direction, either," the Lieutenant said with a lecherous wink.

Dirkie Uys grasped his penis through the material of his pyjama trousers and lifted it up. "I've got something here," he grinned, "that would lift her off her feet and make her forget all about whatever's worrying her."

"Cut it out, boys!" There was a warning edge to Peter's voice. "For a hell of a long time that kid has had nothing but dying men to work with. We blokes have got a couple of holes in us from bullets or shrapnel, but she's had to take a bit more than she can handle."

For a moment there was dead silence. Dirkie Uys took his hand away from his penis and the grin faded from his face. The men exchanged uneasy glances.

"You seem to know a lot about her," the Lieutenant looked at Peter with a puzzled expression, "and you've only just got here?"

Peter jerked his head in the direction of the part of the ward where his bed had been. "Last night when that redheaded guy died, she collapsed. I helped the ward Sister with her." He turned from the Lieutenant and gave Dirkie Uys a one-eyed stare. "So you can just forget you've got a prick, Dirkie. And that goes for the rest of you, too." Peter hitched up his pants. "Deal me a hand in the next round," he said, "I'm going for a piss."

"I want to talk to you guys," Lieutenant Joubert said, "including you, Isinkwe, but we'll wait 'till you get back, and so will the next hand of cards."

Peter walked away, not because his bladder needed relief, but to hide the spontaneous surge of protective emotion he had felt for the girl. He knew the boys were only joking, but the subject they had chosen to joke about incensed him.

The group around the bed maintained an uneasy silence until Peter had left the tent. "Boys!" Hannes nodded his head solemnly, "that bloody Zulu wasn't joking," he warned. "You must hear the stories about him in the Regiment. Even the prisoners we capture know all about him. Dirkie, if Isinkwe MacTavish looked at me like he looked at you, the drawstring of my arsehole would snap and I'd shit myself. Don't even look at that little nurse, because I warn you now, that guy can be murder."

Peter came back and sat on the bed. The Lieutenant smiled at him. "We meant no harm, Isinkwe. I assure you, we all admire the Sisters as much as you do."

"Ja," Hannes added quickly, "we chaps are organising a braai and we've even asked the Lieutenant here to invite them, too."

"Wait," Lieutenant Joubert held up his hand like a policeman stopping traffic. Before we talk about a braai, we'll talk about hospital discipline first. Otherwise there won't be any braai. You five, and now Isinkwe and myself, are the only South Africans in this hospital. You buggers have got yourselves deep into the shit and now you've got me into it, too. If we want to have any braai, the first thing we've got to do is try to make a good name for ourselves."

Hannes interrupted, "No, wait, Lieutenant. We're going to have our braai and bugger the Pommies and their bullshit ideas of discipline."

"Hang on, Hannes," Lieutenant Joubert gave him a sly wink. "I learned long ago that bullshit baffles brains, and that's the method we're going to adopt. The old Sergeant hates your guts. Don't look now, but he's watching us and he's wondering what the hell we're up to. In all his life he's never seen an officer mixing with privates."

"Maybe their privates aren't polite like us," Dirkie suggested helpfully. "Maybe they're choosy about who they mix with."

Lieutenant Joubert ignored the interruption.

"The Sergeant's an old soldier," he continued, "and the only way he understands discipline is the British way. The old British way.

"Their army is run by their NCOs and they expect ours to be the same. Seniority among their NCOs is something holy – when a British NCO talks to a private, he expects that private to jump six feet in the air. He is the senior NCO in the ward, therefore he feels he is responsible for the discipline in the ward, and the only way we're going to get around this problem is to have an NCO of our own, who is senior to him. Hannes, I told the ward Sister this morning that you are our senior man. In fact, I told her you are a Staff Sergeant, or Colour-Sergeant, as they call them. This means you outrank him.

"I explained to the Sister that you didn't say anything about your rank because nobody asked you, and in any case you knew you wouldn't be here for very long. And you couldn't prove your rank because you didn't have your shirt or your pay book on you when you arrived. So from this minute on you're a Staff Sergeant, and that should keep the old Sergeant off your necks for a while.

"Now, to make it look like you are proper soldiers, we are going to hold an order group. Three of you sit on opposite beds facing me and you, Staff Hannes, sit on the right." They arranged themselves as the Lieutenant directed. "Hannes, you will call the men to attention, loudly, and in English. I'll give the headings in English, so the Sergeant will understand what's going on, but today we will conduct our business in Afrikaans. OK Staff Van, do your stuff."

Hannes stood stiffly at attention on the right of the front rank. "Move out into the aisle, Lieutenant," he spoke out of the corner of his mouth. "Come in on the other side of the bed. There's no bloody room to move here.

"Order group: A .. ten .. shun!"

A man who'd been dozing peacefully in the opposite row of beds across the aisle nearly jumped out of his bed. The entire ward braced up to attention. Hannes took a pace forward and made as smart an about-turn as his crutches would allow.

"Order group present and correct, Lieutenant!" he reported briskly in English. The men sat up straight-backed and rigid on the edges of the two beds. Peter's one arm was ramrod stiff at his side. He tucked in his chin and braced his shoulders as best he could.

"Thank you, Staff." The Lieutenant's voice was loud and clear. "At ease!" he barked. The men slumped comfortably and Hannes resumed his seat. Lieutenant Joubert stood facing the ward across an empty bed, so he had a clear view. The ward Sister and the two duty Sisters bustled from the duty room and stared down the ward with puzzled frowns. Behind them, two orderlies craned their necks to see what was going on.

The Lieutenant addressed the other patients. "This is a disciplinary order group for South African personnel only," he told them. "The rest of you, as you were!" The Sisters hesitated for a moment then turned and disappeared. The ward Sister's face wore a disbelieving look and she left shaking her head. She had a premonition her South African patients were up to some mischief again, but she could not guess what it might be.

The Lieutenant addressed his men in Afrikaans. "Don't any of you turn around, but the old Sergeant's jerked up in his bed as though somebody's stuck a hot bayonet up his arse. Orders!" he gave the command in English and the Sergeant braced up at sitting attention.

"Intention."

"One: It is the intention of this order group," he spoke in Afrikaans, "to bullshit the Poms we have this matter of discipline firmly under control, so we can proceed with the preparations for our braai.

"Two: We also intend to get out of this bloody place as soon as possible, and in order to do this we've got to keep ourselves as fit as we can.

"Three: We also intend to enjoy ourselves as much as we can while we're here, and the only way we're going to get that right, is to gain ourselves sufficient credibility as disciplined soldiers, before these buggers decide to nail our balls to the floor.

"Information." He called the heading in English and switched immediately back into Afrikaans.

"One:

A. We don't like their regimented crap.

B. We don't like their idea of getting better by numbers, and

C. We don't like their stewed plums and we're still going to get ours fresh.

"Two: You bastards have got us so deep in the shit we're going to have to battle like hell to get out of it again. Hold it, boys, something's happening. Our shares must be going up with the old Sergeant. He's sent an orderly running out of the ward as though his arse hairs are on fire. I bet he's sent him to call the Sergeant Major.

"Three: We're going to make peace with the Sergeant Major by our good example and a bit of well-directed arse creeping."

"You can creep up his arse, Lieutenant," Dirkie mumbled, "I was never in the Navy."

"Quiet, you!" The Lieutenant barked in English. You can ask questions afterwards. Don't be a tit, Dirkie," he turned his head so the Sergeant wouldn't see his lips moving, "the old bugger's watching us like a hawk. Give me a chance, man."

"Four: Gambling. In future you'll play for matches. No money is to be displayed. You can settle your debts or winnings privately, when nobody's looking.

"Five: The entire area surrounding the hospital is out of bounds to other ranks, but I've got a plan of how to get to the orchard.

"Six: We'll carry on with our arrangements for the braai and we'll still invite the Sisters. You never know your luck!

"Method:

"One: To keep you gainfully occupied," the Lieutenant looked a little sheepish, "I've volunteered you buggers to work in the kitchen."

"No! Wait, Lieutenant! No! Fuck that for a joke." Hannes half stood up in agitation. "Now you're getting carried away."

"No, bugger it," Dirkie chipped in. "Fuck their kitchen!"

"A .. ten .. shun!" the Lieutenant called the group back to order. "Wait boys! How the hell d'you think we're going to get our hands on all the things we need for the braai, if we can't wangle free run of the kitchen? Listen, none of us are in a fit state to steal sheep, pigs, charcoal or anything else we need. We can't buy them either, because money's no bloody use to the Italians or to anybody else.

"But for tinned meat, sugar, butter, coffee or tea, they'll sell us their

157

favourite grandmothers. The only place to get this sort of stuff is the kitchen. And the only way we're going to get into the kitchen is to offer our willing assistance there, until the Poms get used to seeing us buggering around all over the place."

Peter's opinion of the Lieutenant's leadership rose several notches. Hannes was not fully convinced. He stared at the Lieutenant dubiously. "Lieutenant," he said, "if you think I'm going to spend every day grafting my arse off in the kitchen, you've got another thought coming to you."

"No, hell, Hannes," Lieutenant Joubert replied, "If ever any of you buggers does enough work to make you feel tired, you can go back to your beds immediately. That's part of the plan. I want you to be able to get into and out of the kitchen as often as you can. Especially you other three with your arms in slings. Your job will be to get the stuff out, after the legless buggers have stolen it.

"Anyway, you're not supposed to ask any questions until the order group's ended.

"Administration.

"One: Hullo! The Sergeant Major's just come into the ward. He's standing listening to the Sergeant. The look on his face tells me he doesn't believe a bloody word he's hearing.

"Two: We'll hold daily order groups which will be conducted in an exemplary manner to:

A. Impress our British friends – that's every other day, when we hold the order group in English and,

B. To coordinate our thieving activities, when the order groups are held in Afrikaans.

"Communications.

"One: Isinkwe MacTavish will be platoon runner. There's nothing wrong with his legs and I've obtained permission for him to break bounds for the purpose of finding me at frequent intervals, to pull you buggers back into line when you look like you're about to cause shit. That, and the sling on his arm, will enable him to smuggle in all the fruit you blokes are going to need to keep you fit.

"Are there any questions?"

Hannes van Vuuren stood up and balanced on one leg. "Yes, Lieutenant. Doesn't the Lieutenant think it will be a good idea if he came and helped us work our arses off in the kitchen? It will also save Isinkwe the trouble of going to look for the Lieutenant, because there won't be any trouble if the Lieutenant is with his troops."

Peter laughed at Hannes' obtuseness. He'd missed the point completely. "Lieutenant," he smiled, "you made a bloody good choice when you picked Hannes for Staff Sergeant. He's almost dumb enough to be a real one."

"Oh-oh!" Lieutenant Joubert exclaimed. "The Sergeant Major's about to decide whether to come and speak to us or not. He's got that cautious, pained look on his face, like a cow about to give birth to a roll of barbed wire. He's reached a decision. Here he comes! Staff van Vuuren, dismiss the order group."

"Order group! Dis .. miss!"

"'Day, Sir!" The Sergeant Major saluted. His hand quivered for a moment before it steadied at the side of the pulled down peak of his cap. "Sergeant Aitcheson tells me you've held a right proper order group and you've read the riot act to this shower, Sir."

The Lieutenant braced to attention and almost saluted before he realised he was hatless. "Please be at ease, RSM." His manner was friendly, but the look on his face was the most serious he could manage. "I understand from Matron, RSM, that you've had ample cause to lay several charges against these men. Matron has appointed me responsible for the discipline of any South African personnel while they are in this hospital.

"In view of Matron's request I was about to visit you, to assure you that the conduct of any South African personnel is subject at all times to the South African Military Disciplinary Code – very much in line with your own King's Regulations. However, there are a few minor differences, and in view of this, I believe it only fitting for each of these men to be brought on orders before his respective Commanding Officer, to answer the charges you will bring against him."

"One question, Sir." Mistrust was etched in every line of the Sergeant Major's face.

"By all means, RSM."

"Why, Sir, did you give the headings of the order group procedure in English, which the whole ward can understand, and then change to some gibberish for the rest of it?"

Lieutenant Joubert shook his head disarmingly. "I'm afraid, RSM, you have either been misinformed or you're uninformed. The `gibberish' you refer to is my own mother tongue, and it is one of the two official languages of our Country. South Africa is a bilingual country, RSM. Three of these men speak English in their homes and Afrikaans as a second language. The other three speak Afrikaans in their homes with English as a second language. The use of both languages is mandatory in the Union Defence Force. During the order group today, I gave the headings in English and the orders in Afrikaans. Tomorrow I'll give the headings in Afrikaans and the orders in English. This, to my way of thinking, is a fair arrangement. Then I'm prepared to translate for anybody who fails to understand."

The Sergeant Major nodded and his look of mistrust faded a little. But only a little.

"Do you mind telling me, RSM, the nature of the charges you've laid, so I'll know where I stand in my dealings with these men?"

"Certainly Sir. For each and every man:

One: Contravening Hospital Standing Orders.

Two: Absence Without Leave, alternatively, Non-attendance Where Required, in that they are never in their beds where they have been ordered to remain."

The Lieutenant's lips drew disapprovingly together. He nodded thoughtfully. "That contravenes Section 4B of the MDC," he muttered to himself.

"Quite so, Sir." The Sergeant Major nodded his approval.

"Three: Disobeying Lawful Commands or Orders."

"Yes, yes!" Lieutenant Joubert nodded. "Contravenes Section 9(2) of the MDC."

The Sergeant Major watched him with narrowed eyes and dawning respect.

"Four: Using Threatening, Insubordinate or Insulting Language."

"Ah, yes," the Lieutenant nodded again in agreement with his thoughts, "that contravenes Section 17."

The Lieutenant's evident knowledge of Military Law impressed the Sergeant Major. It was an aspect of leadership which he considered suspect in all lieutenants, most captains and many majors. It delighted him to find one junior officer, and a foreign one at that, who had taken the trouble to go as far as reading the regulations.

"Five," he continued stonily: "Conduct Contrary to the Prejudice of Military Discipline and Good Order."

"There's no dodging that one, is there RSM?" Lieutenant Joubert smiled mirthlessly. "Contravenes Section 46 of the Code."

"Quite so, Sir!"

"Before we go any further, RSM, there's a point I don't think anybody has brought to your attention, and I feel it is one which you would understand if you knew about it. The situation in the British Army is very different from that in the South African Army. To start with, not one of these men is a soldier."

"You didn't have to tell me that, Sir," the Sergeant Major smiled mirthlessly. "I figured that one out for myself. The insubordinate conduct of your men speaks for itself."

"Lieutenant," Hannes said in Afrikaans, with a disarming smile, "please tell the miserable old bugger to go fuck himself."

"What's that man say, Sir?" the Sergeant Major asked suspiciously.

"Yes, certainly," Lieutenant Joubert nodded consent to Hannes. "He has had cascara, RSM, and he asked permission to go to the toilet." Hannes hurried away looking as if he was about to explode.

"What I was trying to say, RSM, is that every man in our army is a volunteer. Like myself, not one of them is a career soldier. The last thing any one of them wants to be is a soldier. They are here of their own free will, to help Great Britain defeat the Germans, who are not even threatening our land." He pointed to the men on the beds, staring defiantly at the Sergeant Major. "Not one of these men knows what a barrack-room looks like, because they've never seen one. Few if any of them have ever been on a proper parade ground. They are just not soldiers. But when it comes to fighting, they're as good as the best in the world. In fact, this man wears the DCM."

The Sergeant Major looked at Peter with raised eyebrows. "Well done, lad," he said. "DCMs don't come in glory bags."

"He's the man I asked Matron if I could use to find me whenever I'm needed. This might entail entering restricted areas from time to time."

"Sounds like Matron's trying to take over my job, Sir," the Sergeant Major actually smiled. "Next thing she'll be wanting me to do the nursing in her place." He turned to Peter. "Any man wearing the DCM has free run of my hospital, excluding the Sister's quarters," he smiled properly for the first time.

"RSM," Lieutenant Joubert continued, "there's another thing I'd like you to know. Not one of these men, myself included, will wait to be discharged from this hospital. When we consider ourselves fit enough, we'll desert. And I'll tell you where to send the Provost to arrest us. They'll find each one of us back with our regiments in the front line of the battle.

"Now, RSM, if you will be good enough to prepare your charge sheets I'll be most obliged if you will let me have them for forwarding to the men's respective OCs. I will also require affidavits, signed by witnesses, for each contravention of Military Law."

"Sir," the Sergeant Major asked suspiciously, "are you a lawyer, or something?"

"Barrister," the lieutenant lied, with a nod of confirmation.

"And you're an Infantry Officer, Sir?"

"We've all sorts in our army, RSM. Professional men serve side by side with scholars and clergymen, in the ranks. This man," he pointed to Koen Taljaardt, "owns a farm half the size of an English county, but he is serving as a Private."

The Sergeant Major cleared his throat and stared at Lieutenant Joubert. "Sir, are you telling me that none of these men had to be here if they didn't want to? Are you telling me each one of these men just left whatever he was doing, and came to give us a hand to win this war? Lord love a duck!"

He took off his cap and scratched his wiry head. An incredulous grin appeared on his lined face. "Sir, if you'll pardon the familiarity, I'd like to shake their bleeding hands. And as for charges, Sir, I don't know of any charges against these men!"

When they'd shaken hands, Dirkie moved over on the bed. "Would you like to have a game of cards with us, Sergeant Major?" he asked.

The Sergeant Major looked uncertain for a moment. Then he clamped his cap back on his head and tugged the peak down over his nose. He stamped to attention and saluted Lieutenant Joubert. "Beneath the dignity of a Warrant Officer of His Majesty's Armed Forces to play cards with the men, Sir. Good day, Sir!" He marched smartly down the ward past the disbelieving eyes of the old Sergeant.

Chapter 8

Peter lifted the padded pink celluloid eye-shield from his right eye to help him see better, but the bright morning sunlight hurt and he lowered the shield again. A small worried frown drew his eyebrows together. Something was wrong. His injured eye was unable to help him discern what he had seen. In his brain a red warning light of danger flashed with compelling urgency. He stood still in deep shadow beside the trunk of an apricot tree on the outer edge of the orchard where nobody would see him, unable to decide whether he had seen some minute movement out of place with its surroundings, or whether he had been alerted by his sixth sense.

The hayfield in front of him was a pale sun-bleached yellow of stubble and neatly packed haystacks standing in parallel lines, like rows of country cottages. Behind the paling in a paddock beyond the hayfield, a flock of sheep wandered aimlessly with their heads down to nibble here and there at a blade of grass or a wisp of fallen hay. They seemed peaceful enough, nothing was disturbing them. Without conscious effort, his mind divided the hayfield into three equal strips along its length and labelled each strip: immediate foreground, middle ground and far ground. Then he divided the ground again at right angles into left, centre and right.

With his good eye he searched methodically across the centre block of the immediate foreground. His meticulously trained mind nagged him to complete the search of the left and right foreground, but instinct, stronger even than his exacting training, drew him to search the centre middle ground and the centre far ground.

On the far edge of the field one end of a cottage-shaped haystack was almost obscured by the end of a stack in the centre of the field. He moved his head slowly to the left, so the gap between the stacks widened slightly and he saw a barely noticeable haze of white vapour waft across it. Discarding his dressing-gown and slippers, he sprinted across the field towards the far end of the haystack, which was up-wind from where he had noticed the wafting white haze. He did not want to charge around the left-hand corner into searing smoke or a wall of fire. The jerking of his arm inside the confining sling hurt his shoulder as he ran.

He ran around the haystack and stopped dead, staring in wonder at the startled girl who sat there. Her body jerked away from the hay against which she had been leaning and her hand flew to her heart as she gaped at him with frightened eyes. Wisps of yellow hay stuck to her shoulder-length, light-brown hair which Peter noticed was streaked with pale, unequal bands, the same colour as bleached hay. He looked from her startled eyes to the cigarette between her fingers from which a trickle of smoke wafted towards the edge of the haystack.

The girl was seated on a mound of hay and beside her a long-handled pitchfork rested against the spiky stack, not yet slicked down by rain. Peter smiled self-consciously, not sure of what words to use, or how to pronounce them. "I'm sorry I frightened you, Signorina." He stopped helplessly, lost for words. Moving closer and pointing to the trickle of smoke from the end of her cigarette, he made elaborately descriptive signs with his left hand. "Smoke," he said, "Fire. Fiyume!" He lifted his arm and waved it in the direction of the top of the haystack.

He was still breathing hard from running. "Hell," he said, shaking his head and laughing, "I thought the whole ruddy hayfield was about to catch fire."

The girl stared at him silently. He didn't know if she understood him or not. She glanced down at her bare white thighs and tugged her floral cotton skirt to cover them, and it seemed strange to Peter that her legs should be so white in such a sunny climate. He thought that perhaps she had been sick in bed for some time. She certainly looked as if she had been. Her face was drawn and there were tear marks on her cheeks, and he decided she looked as though she needed feeding.

"Shame," he said. "You've been crying. What bastard made a sick girl like you pack this ruddy great stack of hay? Are you hungry? Mangaria? Angari?" He tried a mixture of what he thought was Arabic and Italian. He patted his stomach and pointed to his mouth. He saw her eyes dawn with interest and light up with a smile barely touching her lips. At least she understood what he was getting at.

"Wait here a moment. Uno momento." He held up his hand to show her to wait where she was. "I've got some plums. I'll get them for you. Pruima." He searched his mind for the few Italian words he knew, or similar-sounding equivalents in English or Afrikaans. He turned away and ran back across the field for his dressing-gown, with its pockets bulging with ripe plums.

Although the Germans had taken all the food when they retreated, he could not see how anybody could starve where there was ripe fruit, sheep and the cockerels he had heard crowing at the dawn of each day. He decided that after he had taken the plums to the girl, he would swipe some of the tinned food from the kitchen and smuggle it to her as soon as he could.

He found her sitting as he had left her. She had stubbed out her half-smoked cigarette. He squatted in front of her and polished a plum on his dressing-gown and held it out for her to eat. Her eyes never left his face while she took the plum from him and bit into it. Her eyes looked thoughtful. It appeared to him that behind their thoughtful look there lurked a smile. Her eyes were a little too big for her face, under the sweeping curve of her widely spaced eyebrows.

"If you put on a little weight, you'll be lovely," his voice was gentle and soothing. It didn't matter if the girl couldn't understand a word he said. "Your eyes are the colour of amber." He took another plum from his pocket and polished it for her, without moving his one-eyed gaze from her face. He smiled at her again. "There are flecks in your eyes. When you look at the stubble in the field, the flecks are greeny-gold, but when I first saw you looking at the trees where the sheep are, the flecks looked green."

The girl held the stone of the plum between finger and thumb and picked off the remaining flesh delicately with strong, white teeth. She put the stone down beside her and took the second plum he offered, but did not lift it to her mouth. She wiped her fingers, wet from the plum juice, on the thin fabric of her loose-fitting blouse.

Leaning slightly towards him and looking earnestly into his one eye, she asked quietly "Are you Sir Galahad, rushing in the nick of time to rescue a maiden in distress, perhaps to save her from the ignominy of collapsing in a heap on the floor of the ward; or from being burned to death in a raging hayfield; or from starving to death?" Her voice dropped to a whisper "Or are you the good genie from some Oriental lamp, who appears magically when a girl is in the greatest need of help? Or are you Peter, alias Isinkwe, MacTavish DCM, scourge of the armies of the German Third Reich; sniper 'par excellence' and possessor of the most gentle hand in the whole world? A hand for easing the torment of that most despicable of all creatures – a nurse who crumples when she should be ministering to the men who need her help most; the brave men who have done the fighting and faced the dangers and the hell of battle?"

Tears welled up in her eyes. She raised her hand and rubbed the back of her neck slowly, rolling her head around on her shoulders. "My neck aches," she said with a wan smile. "The pain creeps up into the back of my head and begins to throb right through to the back of my eyes."

"I'm sorry," Peter mumbled, feeling embarrassed "I should have known you weren't an Italian girl by the whiteness of your legs, and by the cigarette you were smoking. I'm sorry about your pain, too. It's quite common among the men also, especially when they're waiting to go into a big attack. Or when they're in a place where there's no cover and they hear enemy tanks coming. It's strain and tension that causes it."

"Does it happen to you, too, Isinkwe MacTavish? Does your neck also

get stiff and sore before a battle?" She watched his face while she waited for him to answer.

"No," he laughed shortly. "I've taught myself to concentrate my
thoughts on bees collecting nectar from flowers or gathering pollen
and packing it in the hairs on their legs, to take back to their hive. Or
I think of an old Zulu warrior I knew as a kid. He promised he would
cover my back with his shield and hold it over me all the days of my
life, and I sort of believe he'll bring me through this lot somehow or
other." He dropped to his knees beside the girl. "Let me try and help
loosen up your neck like I did the other night, then your headache will
disappear." She dropped her arms to her lap and Peter gripped her
lightly around the back of her neck. "How do you know so much
about me?" he asked. His hand rested on the back of her neck without
moving, while he waited for her reply.

She lifted a little against his hand as though his touch had already
eased some of her pain. "Every girl wants to know about her own Sir
Galahad," she said simply. "I asked Sister Anderson and she asked your
very nice Lieutenant Joubert. Lieutenant Joubert asked your friendly
Colour Sergeant, van Vuuren, and he seems to know lots and lots
about you."

"Which one is Sister Anderson?" Peter asked.

"Sister Anderson's the ward Sister you South Africans have nearly
driven to drink. But I've a feeling she's beginning to get a soft spot for
all of you. She's been like a mother to me all my life. She brought me
up as her own daughter when my mother died while I was still a baby.
She bullied the MO into giving me ten days excused duty to have a
complete rest, even though she, poor dear, has been under a great
deal more strain than I have. However, I start again in a few days on
day duty and I'll try to get her to rest for a while." He felt her shudder
under his hand. "For a long time it's been hell," she said with no
expression in her voice. "There've been Poles, Americans, British, and
now you South Africans. An endless procession of dead and broken
bodies being carried out of the wards day after day." She buried her
face in her hands and her shoulders began shaking.

Peter felt uncomfortable. "Why are you crying?" he asked in a con-
cerned voice. The girl looked so vulnerable and he felt a surge of sympathy for her. He pressed her shoulder reassuringly and felt the tension in her muscles. "What's wrong?" He sensed she needed to unburden herself of whatever was causing her heartbreak, and he remembered Sister Anderson asking him to be gentle with her. "Won't you tell
me what's troubling you?"

As she responded to his light squeeze, he kept his hand on her
shoulder and rolled the taut muscles smoothly. The girl dropped her
hands back into her lap and looked at him with imploring eyes and a

pathetic smile. "This is no time to talk of death," she said sadly, "not out here in the sunshine."

"Tell me," Peter coaxed. "You'll feel better when you've got it all off your chest."

She searched his face with pleading eyes and rolled her shoulder under his gentling hand. "Yes," her voice was barely audible. "I don't know why, but there's something inside that makes me want to tell you what's happened to me." She shook her head as though she didn't quite know what she wanted to say. She spoke in the bemused voice of a lost child. "If I tell you, you'll understand, won't you? Something tells me I can talk to you."

"Yes," Peter whispered, "just tell me what's got you so tied up in knots." He felt her shiver. He peered into her eyes and her innocent, unfocused gaze troubled him. She no longer seemed aware of his presence. She was a thousand miles away, lost and alone, and he watched her with pity.

For a few minutes she sat in silence moving her shoulder under his kneading hand as though the feel of it gave her courage to unburden herself. He released her shoulder and took her unresisting fingers in his hand, willing her to talk, and when she spoke it was as if she were telling herself her troubles in a small, unemotional voice.

"There were only men, and I've never loved a man before," she whispered in a monotone. "I went straight from school into nursing men who were shattered, burnt, blasted and broken by the bombings of the docks. Whenever I was off duty I flopped onto my bed exhausted. Some men tried to take me out but I could feel nothing for them at all. Instead of getting better, it got worse. There were airmen with their eyelids and ears and noses and lips burnt off, and others shattered by shell fire. It was the same with sailors when the warships docked, but they weren't quite as bad because most of the worst cases had died before the ships came in."

She stopped talking and Peter prompted her quietly. "Tell me," he whispered. "Don't keep it bottled up inside you."

"I was with the first landings, here in Italy," she continued. "If it had been hell before, this was worse. Bombs, gunfire and sleeplessness, and patients blasted from their beds. Before you came there was only death and heartbreak. I'd had too much of it. Too much of pulling blankets over bloodless faces and straightening arms and legs curled in terminal agony. I began to wonder with every death, who it was who would be left heartbroken. I became obsessed with the dying. I wanted to be with them in their lonely last minutes and give myself to them, body and soul, to comfort them as they died. I fancied myself in love with each of them."

Peter squeezed the girl's hand in sympathy.

"Most of them were all a girl dreams of," she said. "Young men who were brave and fine and who were dying far from their loved ones. They had done their duty and they were dying alone, for all of us. They were dying for proud fathers, doting mothers and worshipping children. They were dying for loving wives, dazed with longing, and for broken-hearted girls who cried over past misunderstandings and mourned for having refused their boys the rights of a lover. They died for me."

Peter sat holding her hand, hardly breathing, for fear of breaking the spell of her unburdening.

"Oh God, if only those men could live and go back to the girls who loved them, they would find them ready to throw off their inhibitions along with their clothes and lie under their heroes and give them all a girl can give the man she loves – her body and her heart. And she would receive a gift that would germinate into a new life and a new love in her body, in place of fear and death."

Peter looked closely at the distraught girl but she appeared to be mesmerised and totally unaware of his presence. He had to lean towards her to hear her softly spoken words.

"All I saw was the broken and dying remains of a thousand loves which never had the chance to blossom. And I thought of the babies – those wonderful new lives that will never be lived. I was haunted by the ghosts of shattered families and the ghosts of the unborn children of those dying men. Their spirits haunted the wards at night. When I tried to sleep, the cries of those children wanting to be born tore at my heart."

Peter felt helpless. There was nothing he could think of saying to help her in her agony.

"Now I'm beginning to realise that life struggles on to conquer death. But I've only thought of it like this since you came. The moment the shock effect of being wounded is past, the urge to perpetuate life exerts itself. In the early mornings when I turn on the ward lights, I see that life is winning.

"The lust that is in the men's eyes on my body as I work in the ward is also a pure urge to perpetuate life. At first I only knew about death, but now I realise what love and life are all about. I know now that love must be expressed without fear and without reserve. You came with your gentle hand and plucked me from the whirlpool that was sucking me into insanity, and gave me back my belief in life. Even men like you, with flesh-wounds, were only a hair's breadth away from death, yet you are vibrant and alive."

Peter felt a sense of shock at the girl's unconscious revelations, especially about what she had said concerning her feelings regarding him.

She was about to say more but she stopped talking suddenly and looked at him as if she didn't know, for a moment, where she was. She stared at him, thoroughly alarmed, and withdrew her hand from his.

"I saw your eye looking right into my soul," she breathed, "and I knew I had to tell you everything in my heart. Are you a hypnotist?" she asked fearfully. "What did I tell you?"

"You told me about your feelings for the men you've seen die," Peter replied. "If I'm a hypnotist, it's the first time I've heard about it." He smiled at her. He felt it prudent not to mention what she had said about love and about him.

The girl watched him for a minute and he saw that the fear had cleared from her eyes. "I don't know what's happened to me," she said bewilderedly, "but I really feel as though a crushing weight has been lifted off me. I feel strangely at peace with myself." She blushed slightly at some fleeting thought. "I don't really know exactly what I told you but I hope I didn't tell you too much," she smiled self-consciously. "I find you very strange," she murmured. "The men say you're a killer, but if you are, you must be the most gentle, kind and understanding killer in the whole world. I suppose the needs of our times call for men like you, to save us all; and for women like me, to look after you when you're hurt."

Peter felt at a complete loss for words and to cover his embarrassment he emptied the plums out of his pockets and spread his dressing-gown for her to lie on. "Lie on this," he patted the gown. "It'll be more comfortable for you and easier for me to massage you, if you still want me to." The girl nodded and lay down obediently. "Lie on your tummy with your arms at your sides." He made a pillow for her cheek with a handful of hay pushed under the gown. "Is there oil in that little bottle?" he asked.

She nodded her head. "It's coconut oil. I rubbed a little on my legs before you found me. I was sunning them; trying to get a bit of a tan."

The oil made Peter's massaging easier. He leaned over her and pulled the collar of her loose blouse down a little with his teeth, to avoid soiling it with oil. As soon as he started kneading gently he felt her relax under his moving hand.

"I expected you to be black, or at least a lot darker than you are," she said with her eyes closed.

"Why?" Peter asked.

"Well, I thought all South Africans were black. Anyway, according to your Colour Sergeant, van Vuuren, you are half Zulu, and they are black people, aren't they?"

Peter grunted with amusement. "I was more or less brought up by a Zulu, that's what he means. I'm as white as you are, except for the parts that are brown from the sun."

"Why were you brought up by a Zulu? Were you orphaned?"

"No. My mother and my father are still very much alive. It's just that old Mashona, he's the Zulu, sort of adopted me at my naming and brought me up to be a warrior."

"Naming?" she queried, "You mean your Christening? Is he your Godfather? I wondered why you had such a strange-sounding name. Is Isinkwe a Zulu name?"

Peter wondered how to explain it to her. "Well, yes .. sort of. You see, when a child is `named', the name it is given will be immediately understood by the people of the land. It will describe that person's dominant characteristic. It's like a label for easy identification." He could see half of her face and noticed her brow wrinkle in puzzlement. "By the time a child cuts its first teeth," he explained, "the Zulu's have studied that child's characteristics and decided on a name which will describe the child perfectly. Every child throughout the land is given a name, irrespective of the name he was christened by."

"Do you mean each child's name has a meaning?"

"Yes, that's right."

"Then what does Isinkwe mean?"

Peter smiled at her curiosity. "There's a little fluffy animal that lives in the trees," he told her, "called isinkwe. In English it's a galago, but better known as a bush-baby. It's a wonderfully alert little creature that appears to be all eyes and ears and it's so aware of everything around it, you can never take it by surprise. Even when it's asleep, it seems to be aware of what's going on nearby."

The girl pushed herself up suddenly so she was kneeling beside him, staring at him as though she had not seen him properly before. "How marvellous," she whispered the words as though something wonderful had been revealed to her. She nodded her head in complete agreement with her thoughts. "How wonderful! The name fits you like a glove. You must be the only Isinkwe in the whole world and I'm quite sure there's nobody, anywhere, who is as aware as you are."

She placed her open hands on her thighs and leaned towards him until her face was almost touching his and gazed into his eye as though she were trying to see through it into his mind. Her lips barely moved as she whispered, "You were wounded and should have been sleeping after your operation, yet you were aware of death coming to the man in the bed beside you! When I came to him, you were aware of the exhausted state of both my body and mind and you were ready to catch me when I collapsed. You were simply aware of the tension about to destroy me with a complete nervous collapse. In the darkness of the night, without a word being said, and without even seeing my face, you were aware of my immediate need for gentleness and sympathy.

"You were aware of the danger of a fire from a tiny haze of smoke, from the far side of a field of hay, which nobody else in this world would have noticed. And you were aware of a poor Italian girl's plight and need for food." She sat back on her heels, closed her eyes and shook her head, then opened her eyes again and smiled at him. "How utterly uncanny. Sister Anderson has also remarked on your sensitivity and awareness. She also says she has never yet come to your bed in the darkness and found you asleep. I suppose a bush-baby hunts at night and sleeps by day?" She stared into his eye again and noticed for the first time how large the pupil was.

"I think I can see in the dark better than most people," Peter said self-consciously. Her intense interest in him embarrassed him. "Lie down again," he said to cover his confusion, "I haven't finished loosening those neck muscles yet."

The girl turned her head left and right from shoulder to shoulder. "I don't know when last I could do that, without it hurting. My neck feels lovely and loose." Then she frowned as though suddenly perplexed. "My headache's gone completely, as well. There must be some Zulu magic in your hand." She lay down and closed her eyes. "If only you could massage me like this every day with your magic hand, I'd be a new person again within a week."

"Of course I'll massage you again. Whenever you want me to, I'll meet you out here." He stopped kneading the muscle on the top of her left shoulder. "Please put a few more drops of oil on my hand or the rubbing will chafe your skin."

"I don't see how we can meet here," she said, "don't you know this place is out of bounds? What were you doing here today? By now your Colour Sergeant, Van Vuuren, will have noticed you missing and you'll be in serious trouble."

Peter smiled to himself. "There's nothing to worry about," he told her. "Er, er, I can't call you Sister, not out here in the sunshine, but I don't know what to call you."

"My name is Marsden. Sister Marsden."

"I know that. But I can't call you Sister, or Miss Marsden, either. Not here, anyway. Not while I'm massaging your back. What's your Christian name?"

"Rosemary. But please, for heaven's sake, don't call me Rosemary in the ward or in front of anybody else. Now answer my question, Sir. What were you doing here in the first place?"

"Stealing fruit for the boys in the ward," Peter said as though stealing fruit was the most natural thing in the world. Then he added as an afterthought, "I have permission to go almost anywhere, to look for Lieutenant Joubert if he is needed, so I wander around and enjoy the fresh air and the sunshine."

"That's all very well," she protested, "but what about Lieutenant Joubert and your Colour Sergeant?"

"It was all the Lieutenant's bright idea in the first place," Peter laughed. "He couldn't care less what we do as long as we don't cause any serious trouble. In fact, he invented Hannes' rank of Colour Sergeant, except in our army we call it Staff Sergeant. Hannes is really a Rifleman, but the Lieutenant gave him a bogus promotion just to keep old Sergeant Aitcheson off our necks."

"But your men listen to him," Rosemary objected, "and carry out his orders very smartly. In fact I've heard recently that the South Africans' behaviour is exemplary and they are being tremendously helpful."

Peter laughed aloud. "It's all a sham, Rosemary," he felt a small thrill of intimacy at the use of her name. "In army terms, we are creating a diversion to mislead the enemy! What is actually happening is that we are stealing food from the kitchen – luxuries such as the Italians can't get, like butter, cocoa, coffee, tea and sugar – and we're trading them with the Italians for the things we need for our braai. We've included a few bottles of good vermouth and cognac, for bribing the cooks in the off-duty Sister's kitchen, to supply what we can't steal."

The notion of the South African's thieving activities both shocked and amused Rosemary. She had never heard such blatant levity in her life. "Aren't you ashamed of yourselves?" she asked.

"Not in the slightest," Peter replied. "It's all for a good cause. You're being invited to the braai too, and you'll see when you get there what it's all about."

"Yes, I've heard about your braai. Sister Anderson found out from Lieutenant Joubert that a braai is the same thing as a barbecue. He told her it's the South Africans' traditional way of thanking us Sisters for nursing you. I can't imagine how he's talked Matron around into letting you hold it, but I believe she's even agreed to attend. She's decided, unless more critically wounded patients are admitted, the Sisters can be relieved by the orderlies for a few hours, to go along as well."

"Rosemary, the idea of our braai is to break the ice and make friends with the Sisters. It's really got nothing to do with tradition at all. We thought if we're going to be here for a while we might as well make this hospital a happier place to be in. We can't understand why you British treat people, including yourselves, as numbers and not as people. Even you Sisters call each other, Sister Smith or Sister Jones or Sister Anderson, instead of Mary or Sally or Rosemary, or whatever your names happen to be. You call us by our surnames and we don't like it. Hell, Rosemary, even our senior officers call us by our Christian names, because we're individual people and very important to one another. So we decided to have a friendly braai and all end up calling each other by our names."

He felt her shoulders shake with silent laughter. "Now I understand why Sister Anderson despairs of you South Africans. You're the most accomplished band of charming liars I've ever heard of. Is it safe for me to believe anything I hear from a South African?" she smiled as she asked."

"Yes, of course! We only lie when we want to wangle ourselves out of being pushed around. Now lie down, I haven't even started on your back yet and the muscles of your shoulders are still tied in knots." She lay down again and closed her eyes. "Do you mind if I pull up your blouse? I don't want to make it oily."

She lifted up her arms and pulled her blouse up to her neck. Her skin was very white. Peter dripped a few drops of oil onto her skin and spread it carefully above and below the strap of her brassiere. He looked dubiously at the catch of the strap in the centre of her back, wondering how he would massage her properly without loosening it. As though reading his thoughts, she pressed her cheek to the straw pillow and brought her arms up behind her and unclipped the catch.

Peter cleared his throat quietly. He felt as though he were choking. "Thank you. I was too shy to ask you to loosen it."

She lay with her eyes closed. "I know about men who haven't seen a woman for months or even years," she said softly, "but I know I can trust you."

Peter felt a little disappointed. Perhaps it would be better if she were afraid to trust him, he thought, then it would relieve him of the responsibility of self-restraint. On either side of her rib-cage he saw the beginning of the swell of her neat breasts and he bit his bottom lip. He imagined how soft and exciting the feel of those breasts would be in his hands and began to experience an exquisite sensation of sexual arousement. He shook his head to clear his thoughts, then leaned over her to work the muscles of her back with strong rippling movements.

"Please tell me about the old Zulu who brought you up." Her words restored him to his senses.

"Don't talk now," he said softly, "relax as completely as you can. Relax your mind too. Think of whatever it is that calms you most. Like your favourite music, or whatever it might be."

She sighed languorously and her hips wriggled with a small sensuous movement. "The most wonderfully soothing experience I've ever known in my whole life, is the feeling of your healing hand on my back." Her words were barely audible. "It takes away all my pain and tension and sorrow. But please talk to me; I'm bursting with curiosity to know all about your childhood with your old Zulu. The sound of your voice soothes me as much as the gentleness of your magic hand, and I'm beginning to wonder if it was my guardian angel who sent you to help me. But I'm a woman, and therefore curious, and there are all sorts of questions I need you to answer. I promise I'll lie quietly and listen, but you must start at the very beginning of your life and please don't leave anything out."

As his hand touched her skin, half-forgotten memories of Mashona crowded his thoughts. He was a child again, squatting in Mashona's hut. It was the night they had said their last farewells. He remembered the narrow grey 'imphepo' leaves curling and charring on the embers of Mashona's small fire, and the aroma of camphor in the twist of smoke rising from them and stinging his eyes. He looked at Rosemary's white skin and the old man's words hovered soundlessly on his lips:

"Side by side we drank the waters of many streams and we were refreshed. In the steep places among the rocks when the sun was hot and we were weary, we found numbela trees heavy with fruit and we ate our fill of their white flesh, and it revived our spirits."

He noticed her eyes were wide with wonder. "You're using coconut oil to rub me with," her voice sounded perplexed, "yet for a moment I had the strangest notion I smelt camphor. You're not using camphorated oil, are you?" She closed her eyes again. "The smell's gone now. I think I must be going mad, or something."

Peter sat for a few seconds with his eye closed. He wondered if Mashona had really come to them to bless their meeting. He shook the phantoms from his mind and continued massaging her back and began to tell her about his childhood. Several times he thought she had fallen asleep, her breathing was so faint and slow. But each time he stopped talking, her lips curved in a small smile and her voice prompted softly, "Don't stop. You were telling me how Mashona taught you to be cautious and patient, by watching the spider get greedy." She surprised him with her quick grasp of the correct pronunciation of Zulu names and words.

She relaxed into a dream world, avidly absorbing his tales of the enchanted childhood of a happy boy, growing up in the shadow of an old warrior's shield. When Peter spoke of his parting from Mashona to go to boarding school, her sympathy was spontaneous. She groped for his hand and squeezed it to convey her understanding of the hurt that far-off calamity had caused him. His bewilderment and heartbreak at Mashona's death struck a responsive chord in her heart, and she cried like a bereaved child. She sat up slowly and turned towards him, oblivious of her dangling brassiere. At at the sight of her breasts, his breath caught in his throat. Her hands stole behind his head and she pulled him gently towards her and pressed her tear-moistened lips softly against his.

She released him and as unconsciously as though she were alone, settled her breasts in the cups of her brassiere and reached up behind her back to fasten the catch. She was a simple Swazi maiden in a beatific vision, in a far-away land where clear streams meandered among ferns and lilies. As innocently as a child, she smoothed down her blouse and lifted her eyes to his. "What a wonderful, beautiful story." She sighed deeply, then waggled her shoulder-blades and swung her head in slow circles on her neck. "I feel absolutely marvellous, inside and out. No tension, no headache, no pain, and my heartache has eased. And now I'm hungry." She raised her brows as though surprised at her own statement. "That's strange," she smiled, "I can't remember having felt hungry for months. In fact, I'm ravenous! It must be close to dinner time. What time is it?"

"A little after twelve," he answered absently.

Rosemary smiled at him. "Look at your watch, silly. How can you say it's a little after twelve, without even glancing at your watch?"

Peter pointed at the stubble beside them. "Ten past, near enough," he said, "look at the shadows."

Rosemary took his arm and unclipped the leather dial cover of his watch. "Twelve minutes past," she smiled. She dropped her hands into her lap and cocked her head to one side. "Yes, Mr Isinkwe, the bush-baby, your old Mashona was quite right, wasn't he? You are totally and completely aware of your surroundings at all times. That one eye of yours misses nothing, does it? You don't have to look to see the time is twelve minutes past twelve. Without any conscious effort, you are simply aware of the angle of the tiny shadows of small stalks of straw, not even four inches high. Now tell me honestly, what else have you noticed? Have you noticed my hair's got blond streaks in it?"

"Yes," he said without looking at her hair. "I thought it strange, what happened?"

"Wonderful," she clapped her hands, "full marks. Nothing happened. It took me a long time to brush in the peroxide to get those streaks just right."

Peter laughed at her. "Don't lie to me, Rosemary. Those streaks weren't made with peroxide. Every individual hair is blond right to its roots, and every streak starts in a tiny scar."

"Nobody else would have noticed those scars," she smiled. "You see, you're not the only one who's been wounded. We were bombed during the blitz and I got peppered with fragments of concrete in my scalp. That's what caused the white strips. You must go back and have your dinner before they start suspecting something. We'll meet here tomorrow?"

"No, not here." he shook his head and smiled at her. "It's against my instincts to start any pattern of behaviour. Mashona wouldn't approve. Sooner or later some observant person will notice that pattern.

"In four days there'll be a discernable line of footprints leading to this place and in any case, although this spot is sheltered from the hospital, it's in full view of anybody visiting the farmhouse. We'll meet down there," he pointed, "behind the third stack from the right, in the second row."

She laid her hand lightly on his uninjured shoulder. "Thanks, Isinkwe, for what you've done for me." She pressed her body briefly against his and kissed him fleetingly on his cheek, then jumped away to avoid his reaching arm. "Go now!" She pushed him around. "Go gently, Isinkwe. I'll wait here until you've had time to get back to your ward."

"Stay gently, Princess." Peter turned and ran across the stubble with his dressing-gown in his hand.

Rosemary had been waiting for some time before Peter appeared soundlessly at the end of the haystack. He was breathing silently through parted lips and she was not aware of his presence nor of the surprised look on his face. She lay on her stomach on a bed of hay in the bright sunlight, her face turned to catch the sun and one cheek resting on the back of her folded hands. She had taken off her blouse and pulled her skirt up to her bottom, to expose as much oil-smeared skin to the sun as she could, and still remain decent. Her brassiere strap was still fastened in the centre of her back and her hair, gathered into a pony tail, was tied with an unbecoming piece of bandage.

The sudden coolness of his shadow and the feel of his lips on her cheek startled her out of her doze. She pushed his face away gently and opened her eyes. "You are late, Sir!" she said accusingly. "Don't South African gentlemen know it's unforgivable to keep a lady waiting? So start your massaging this instant, Sir. It must be almost time for you to go to dinner."

"It's just on eleven and I'm sorry I'm late, Rosemary. It was impossible to get away sooner. This morning's order group went on for hours. Thank God it was an Afrikaans day. There were lots of loose ends to be tied up and we had the Sergeant Major breathing fire down our necks, and demanding translation of almost every word anybody said. There was a matter of heavy wire mesh grills missing from the radiators of three ambulances, and one mysteriously very drunk driver. You see, we need those grills to cook the meat on. The damned driver said it was one of us, or he thought it was one of us, who'd given him a bottle of good cognac to get him drunk enough to pass out. Then there was the matter of two bags of charcoal missing unaccountably from the boiler-room."

Rosemary listened with her eyes closed and a smile flickering at the corners of her lips.

"I simply can't tell you all the things he wanted to know about," Peter continued. "Tumblers have been disappearing from various messes.

We can't expect our guests to drink good booze out of tin mugs, can we? Sugar is missing and tea and teacups and butter and cocoa and heaven knows what else! Nobody's noticed the coffee missing yet. Then there were questions about paper serviettes that disappeared right out of Matron's office. We don't mind wiping our greasy fingers with toilet paper but damn it all, we can't offer rolls of toilet paper to our guests."

Rosemary laughed merrily, but Peter interrupted her amusement.

"Quite serious things have been happening too, and all because of that fool, Gunnar Olsen! He got a bit carried away with the booze side of the braai he was elected to organise. He's rounded up enough drink to entertain a whole regiment and he's far too heavy-handed with his bribes. It seems the Sergeant Major's coming across drunk bodies around almost every corner: drunk clerks who supplied the white invitation cards from the MO's office; a drunk Second Lieutenant who's a calligrapher and a bit of an artist, and has agreed to prepare the invitations; the Transport Corporal who's collecting the sheep, suckling pig, trifle and other goodies from the Italian farmers round about; and even Matron's orderly, who borrowed her coloured inks.

"You see, Rosemary, the trouble is, the braai is tomorrow, and we're only one short jump ahead of the Sergeant Major, and there are still stacks of things to be organised. There's the cutlery and crockery from the Officer's Mess, and the wine goblets; vases for the flowers and finger-bowls from the Sisters' Mess; folding tables from the wards and a few other odds and ends. The problem is, most of it has to arrive at the last minute, so that the whole braai will be a surprise."

Rosemary sat up, shocked at what Peter had told her. She reached quickly for her blouse and held it bunched to her chest to cover her brassiere. "From what you've told me, your preparations sound far more like the organisation required for a grand ball, rather than a barbecue. Braai, sorry. I had no idea you South African pirates were preparing on such an elaborate scale."

"Nor did the Sergeant Major," Peter laughed. "At the moment he's our main worry. He's no fool, and knows damned well we're behind the recent wave of crime, by simple virtue of the fact that nothing like this ever happened before we got here. He would have jumped us already, but for the fact he's guessed we're operating as a syndicate, and when he throws his net, he wants to catch the whole lot of us together, including Lieutenant Joubert. I can just see his face when he arrives at the braai and finds everything that's gone missing, and a few more besides, spread out right under his nose."

"He's not coming to the braai, surely?" Rosemary's face was horrified.

"Of course he is." Peter sounded surprised. "It wouldn't be a braai

177

without him. In any case, we've invited him as Matron's partner so the two of them can hit it off together."

"Oh! The impudence of it! You South Africans are nothing but a crowd of conniving criminals!" Then the corners of her eyes crinkled at the thought of the Sergeant Major and Matron `hitting it off'. She covered her lips with the tips of her fingers and giggled.

Peter laughed at her outraged giggle. "When he gets to the braai and finds all the evidence he so dearly wants spread out under his nose, and all the culprits there too, he's either going to blow his top or else his British sense of humour's going to make him collapse laughing. It's going to be one or the other," he said. "When the party's over, we'll clean up and return everything to its rightful place. Now I want a little help from you. I want the names of three more girls to invite, so there'll be nine men and nine ladies. We'll deliver the invitations to them first thing tomorrow morning." He drew a white card from his sling and gravely presented it to her. "Madam," he said, "your invitation."

"Oh it's beautiful," Rosemary breathed as she read the exquisitely illuminated request for the pleasure of her company at a 'braaivleis', to be held as a token of esteem to honour the courageous ladies who had ministered to wounded South African Soldiers. The card bore an Indian ink drawing of a naked black warrior squatting over a small fire, cooking a piece of meat on a stick. Opposite him, across the fire, a uniformed Sister squatted, eating a morsel of meat in her fingers. Rosemary pressed the card to the bunched-up blouse on her bosom. She leaned forward and touched her lips to Peter's. "I'll treasure this card forever," she murmured.

"Lie down for your treatment, Sister, there's not much time left," he said with the air of an overworked Doctor. "And kindly unfasten that strap."

Rosemary turned her head and rested her cheek on the back of her folded hands. "I've been thinking about all the things you've told me," she said, "and I've got a hundred questions to ask you." She spoke with her eyes closed as he started massaging her shoulders. He noticed as soon as his hand slid down across her skin that her muscles were smooth and relaxed.

"Did you sleep well last night?" he asked.

"I slept like a baby. For the first time in weeks I didn't need anything to help me go to sleep. I simply closed my eyes and dropped off into a dreamless sleep, until the sunshine woke me this morning. And I was hungry too. I ate a good breakfast for the first time in ages. I've been lying here thinking about people having such lovely Zulu names. Now I also want a name, so I've decided to give myself one. What is the Zulu word for a shield?"

"'IsiHlangu'. Why?"

"Because you see, I've decided I'm going to be the one who covers your back, so I'll have to be a shield, won't I? I'll cover your back while you're here in hospital and when you go back to your Regiment to fight again," her body shuddered at the thought, "I'll cover your back with my prayers."

"Thank you," his tone was serious. "Nobody could do anything nicer for me. I need something better to cover me than Mashona's old moth-eaten shield. I'm cross with that old man," Peter laughed, "he's supposed to look after me, but he must have gone to sleep or something, because he let me get wounded."

Rosemary lifted her arm and silenced him with her fingers across his lips. "I know you're only joking, but please don't talk like that. If Mashona hadn't let you get wounded I'd never have met you, and then what would have become of me?"

She was silent for a few moments before she spoke again. "Don't you think, Isinkwe," Her use of his Zulu name sounded excitingly intimate to him. "Don't you think perhaps he let you get wounded to keep you out of the way of something far worse that he could foresee? Can they, the 'Amadl' .. what did you call the Zulu ancestral spirits?"

"Amadlozi," he prompted.

"Yes, the Amadlozi." Her pronunciation of the foreign word was perfect. "Can they see into the future?"

"They can see into the future all right, and it's strange you should say he might have wanted to save me from something worse, because that's exactly what Indabushe said to Taffy and Spud. They're my buddies; them and Big Dries Maritz."

"Anyway, I thought if I'm going to cover your back, I'll be a shield, so my name will be 'isiHlangu'. Don't you think that's a lovely name for me to have?"

Peter massaged in silence for a while. He kneaded the scapula muscle beneath her arm and pressed his fingertips sensuously into the soft flesh where her breast commenced to swell out from her ribs.

"Don't you think 'isiHlangu' would be the right name for me?" she asked again, disappointed at his lack of response.

"No, not really, Rosemary. 'isiHlangu' is the great war shield that covers a warrior from his mouth to his feet. But there's another shield. It's a small shield used in certain dances and ceremonies. It's far more dainty and feminine than a great war shield. They call it, 'iHawu'. But people don't just go around picking any old name that takes their fancy. You see, the given name has to fulfil two functions. It must describe some personal attribute, and it must also describe the essence of the person's character. Then of course, it must be a masculine name which will fit a man, or a feminine name which will fit a woman."

He stopped kneading for a moment and gently squeezed the soft flesh of the side of her breast and leaned lower to kiss her neck. "I've got a name for you. A proper name, that fits you body and soul, and belongs to you and only to you. Old Mashona told me what to call you."

Rosemary opened her eyes and pressed her hands against the ground to lift herself so she could see him. Her loosened brassiere hung from her shoulders and Peter slid his hand under her ribs and cradled her velvet breast in the cup of his hand. He kissed her lips with a soft, lingering kiss. "What is it? What did Mashona tell you to call me?" she asked with her lips almost touching his.

"'Numbela'." The name sounded like a caress.

"'Numbela'?" She drew away and turned to watch the movement of his lips as he pronounced the name. Her brassiere dangled free from the breast he caressed with his hand. "'Numbela'." Her pronunciation was perfect. "What does numbela mean?"

He turned her gently onto her back, slid the straps of her brassiere away from her shoulders and arms and laid the small garment on top of her blouse. He gathered her breast in his hand and leaned over her to kiss her other breast and mouth its nipple between his lips until he felt it harden against his moving tongue.

"What are you doing?" she breathed. She took his face between her hands and lifted it so she could look at him. Her lips were parted and gently smiling.

"In the steep places among the rocks," he repeated Mashona's words, "we found numbela trees and we ate our fill of the white fruit and it revived our spirits. I'm tasting the fruit which revives the weary traveller and sustains him and strengthens him so, having eaten his fill, he places his feet strongly on the path once more and continues his journey, refreshed."

The brown of her eyes was soft and misted as he leaned and kissed each nipple in turn. Her hands pulled his face towards her and their lips touched and locked in a hard kiss expressing their need of one another and brimming with promises that quickened their breathing.

She pushed him away and laughed unsteadily. "What does Numbela really mean?" she asked.

"There is a footpath," he told her quietly, "leading from the coast of Zululand into the distant upland country, which is the heart of Africa. It was trodden into the veld by burdened traders carrying beads from foreign ships to distant tribes, and returning with gold and ivory. It seems an endless path to a man who's burdened."

Rosemary listened without stirring. She did not wish to disturb the magic of the moment even with the soft sound of her breathing. Peter looked into her misty eyes and continued in a whisper.

"That path winds endlessly up the face of the Dragon Mountains to the rocks along its crest, where the traveller may rest for a while in the shade of the trees of salvation. There he picks the fruit of those trees and peels off the red husks, to eat the sweet, white fruit which will revive him and restore his strength."

Rosemary pulled his head towards her and kissed his lips. She placed her hand over the hand cupping her breast and held it to her. "It's a lovely story," she whispered, "but I asked you the meaning of Numbela."

He caressed her lips with the tip of his tongue. "Numbela is the name of that fruit," he whispered.

He sighed deeply and sat up. "It's twelve o'clock," he said. "I must go. We don't want anything to go wrong at the last moment, or the Sergeant Major will drop on us like a ton of bricks. If I stay longer they'll miss me." He kissed the nipples of her breasts and her lips and stood up to leave.

Rosemary held out her hands to be pulled to her feet. She smiled at him, with her brassiere and her blouse in her hand. "In the short space of two weeks, you South Africans have turned our world upside down." She looked down at her bare, white breasts. "If anybody had told me I would ever in my life stand in front of a man half-naked and quite unashamed, I would have said that person was stark staring mad. And me a nursing Sister and the man my patient! Kiss me again before you go." She clung to him and moved her lips hungrily against his and then pushed herself free.

"Hambe kahle – Go gently," her voice trembled.

"Sala kahle, Numbela – Stay gently, Numbela," Peter replied. He ran dodging among the haystacks to keep out of sight of the hospital, impatient to get the braai over and done with and have his Numbela to himself again.

Chapter 9

1

Peter stopped stirring the enormous blob of butter into the steam-ing maize meal 'pap' in the three-legged pot he had borrowed from the Italians. He crouched a little lower and hoped the Sergeant Major wouldn't see him through the cloud of rising steam. From the corner of his eye he noticed that the others had also stopped whatever they were doing and stood unmoving over their various tasks. Jan Booysen and Gunnar Olsen applied themselves to the meat, grilling on the radiator screens above beds of glowing embers. Through the smoke Peter saw the glint of their averted eyes.

The Sergeant Major stood dead still for a moment, then saluted Lieutenant Joubert and removed his cap. His chest was resplendent with colourful medal ribbons of an earlier war, and campaigns fought desperately and soon forgotten, in remote corners of an ungrateful Empire.

Only Hannes van Vuuren appeared oblivious to the tension of the moment. He was no longer on crutches. He limped across and halted in front of the Sergeant Major, holding out a glass half-filled with deep amber liquid. "Welcome to our braai, Sir," he said. "Would you care for a little refreshment? It's prree-warr cognac, Sirr, the best we could get." His strong Afrikaans accent rolled the r's at the end of `sir' and `pre-war'.

Without a word, the Sergeant Major took the glass from Hannes' hand and sniffed the liquor suspiciously. He sipped a little and thoughtfully rolled it around on his tongue. Then he tipped the glass up, swallowed its contents and exhaled a blast of gratified breath. "Very good," he said curtly to Hannes. "Thank you, Colour, I'll have another."

Lieutenant Joubert, coughing discreetly behind his raised hand at the Sergeant Major's elbow, said politely "Excuse me, RSM, we were wondering, er, if you would, er, do us the honour of acting on our behalf this evening, as our, er, Master of Ceremonies. It occurred to us, er, RSM, that you know a great deal more about military protocol and etiquette than we do – you being a professional soldier while we're only amateurs."

Hannes hurried back with a refilled glass. The Sergeant Major indi-cated towards him with a jerk of his eyebrows. "Why don't you ask Colour, here, to act as MC, Sir? He seems to have excellent manners and quick attention to the needs of his guests." He turned to Hannes. "Your name is van Vuuren, is it not?" His face was grim and forbidding.

"Yessirrr!"

"What do you know about military protocol and etiquette?"

"Fuck all, Sirrr!" There was no expression on Hannes' face.

A bellow of laughter escaped from the Sergeant Major. Accepting the refilled glass, he turned to the Lieutenant. "With due respect, Sir, you are as big a bastard as this thieving shower that serves under you, but I like an officer who stands by his men." The Sergeant Major laughed heartily and gave Lieutenant Joubert a friendly slap on the shoulder. "One word of warning!" His voice hardened. "See that your men insist on a receipt for every item they return tomorrow, or that item will be stolen by somebody else and sold to the Italians, and I will hold you personally responsible for its loss."

The sound of feminine voices came through the darkening foliage of the orchard. The Sergeant Major moved to an uncluttered corner of the table and put down his cap and his drink. He smoothed his short hair and his clipped grey moustache with the flat of his hand. Standing ramrod straight, he tugged an imaginary crease from the front of his immaculate battledress tunic. A smile of welcome beamed on his face and he walked briskly, with his hand outstretched, to receive Matron.

"Good evening, Matron. Good evening, Sisters, and to you, Sir," he included the young Second Lieutenant who was hanging back nervously. "Our gallant South African allies have done me the honour of asking me to welcome you on their behalf, to this magnificently organised braai. As you may be aware, they have prepared it as a token of their gratitude to you, Matron, and to you Sisters, who have nursed them back to health.

"They have asked me to invite you to eat and drink and enjoy yourselves. They have wine and vermouth and cognac available and various meats they are busy grilling, which will be ready shortly. As you will see," he smiled at Matron, "they have gone to endless trouble to procure their needs from .. ahum .. various sources, for the enjoyment and pleasure of their guests."

Matron's eyes crinkled as she chose a serviette from the carton Peter offered her. She smiled brightly at him. "Your invitation cards were beautifully done." She dropped her voice to a whisper and raised her hand to hide her mouth. "Please return my bottle of black Indian ink if there's any left, it's so difficult to come by these days. I can do without the paper serviettes," she added with a twinkle.

At first the Sisters were uneasy guests. The presence of Matron and the middle-aged Sister Anderson made them feel embarrassed and inhibited them. Being a little reluctant to eat grilled meat with their fingers and blobs of maize meal pap dipped into a sauce of tomato and onions, they were abstemious and hardly allowed themselves more than an occasional sip of their drinks. They were ill at ease mixing socially with their dressing-gowned patients who cooked their food and waited on them attentively.

The four duty Sisters were dressed in their uniforms. The three who were off duty, wore dresses. Rosemary wore a simple dress of plain unadorned red and her hair hung loose to her shoulders. She chatted brightly with the other Sisters and charmed her hosts with her friendly attitude and her obvious enjoyment of the food they offered her. She could not have made herself more enchanting if the braai had been her own doing and she the hostess. She didn't notice Sister Anderson watching her with thoughtful eyes.

The Sergeant Major enjoyed the food enormously and repeatedly plied Matron with wine and choice pieces of meat. He joked and teased the Sisters and told stories which soon had everybody doubled over with laughter. Little by little the atmosphere of the braai lost its stiffness and the Sisters began to enjoy what they ate. Soon they were licking their fingers and holding up their empty glasses to be replenished, chatting brightly among themselves and to their hosts with less reserve. They got up from their seats to be shown how to roast pieces of meat and to try doing it for themselves. While they listened to explanations and watched demonstrations in a cloud of aromatic smoke, they bit into succulent morsels and picked at bones with their teeth, licking their fingers and asking for more.

Peter felt a tug at his sleeve. Turning, he looked into Sister Anderson's eyes. "Now, you just come along with me," she ordered, "and squat beside me on your heels like the young savage you are, and tell me where you have been these last few days. I've hardly seen you. You're never in the ward."

Rosemary saw them together and came from the smoke of the fire to sit in an empty chair beside Sister Anderson. She smiled at Peter. "Good evening, Isinkwe," she greeted him. "I heard Sister Anderson's question, so would you please answer her as I'd also like to know where you've been hiding yourself."

"Oh!" Sister Anderson raised her brows, "it's 'Isinkwe', is it?"

Rosemary smiled guilelessly. "It's the only name he answers to, Sister. Isinkwe's companions say he's more than half-Zulu and completely savage."

Sister Anderson held up an admonishing finger in front of Rosemary's nose. "You just keep out of this, child," she said, "I'll come back to you later. Young man, where have you been hiding yourself?"

"I've been busy, Sister, helping with preparations for the braai. I've been begging, borrowing, and stealing whatever I couldn't get hold of by honest means," he said with a disarming smile.

"I can well believe the stealing part, from what I hear. I wonder why you even bothered to try the other methods of getting what you needed. I've been hearing the strangest tales about you and your outlandish customs. Whenever I ask your whereabouts, I'm informed you've gone to get cleansed. Or you've gone to get medicine from the witch-doctor for your `purification'. Whatever that means!"

Peter squirmed with embarrassment. He had been caught completely off guard. He promised himself he'd break Hannes' neck as soon as he could escape from Sister Anderson's riveting gaze. A deep blush reddened his face, which was fully exposed to the glaring light of a pressure lamp hissing in a nearby tree.

"Ha! Guilt! Look, Sister Marsden! It's written all over his face." She noticed the sudden flush on Rosemary's face, too, but she turned back to Peter. "Now for the truth," she demanded. "The full truth, Sir!"

"They're just teasing me, Sister," Peter looked around desperately for an excuse to escape but Sister Anderson leaned over in her chair and grasped his wrist with a firm, strong hand.

"No, my young Zulu," she smiled, "you will not run away. You will tell us all about this gruesome `purification' business. If we're to stay here all night, we will not let you go until you have told us everything!"

"I'm also waiting to hear," Rosemary added with a mischievous look.

"I wonder if you're old enough to hear what this young man has to tell?" For a full minute Sister Anderson regarded Rosemary with speculative eyes and saw her blush as red as the dress she was wearing. "Yes, I suppose you are," she mused aloud, "just the right age, in fact. Now talk!" she commanded Peter.

"Sister, in the old days when Zulu warriors returned from battle, they had to be purified. The witch-doctors had to cleanse them of the malevolent spirits of the enemies they had killed, and they had to purify them before they could go back and kill again. They call it 'ukungcwelisa', it's a kind of spiritual cleansing." Peter paused for a while to plan his words.

"Yes, go on. Keep talking," Sister Anderson prompted.

"Well, Sister, there is first the ceremonial bathing, to cleanse the outside of his body. Then each warrior has to take medicine to cleanse the inside. A purgative. Then .. then .. then .. "

"Don't sit there like an idiot saying then, then, then! Then what?"

"Then each warrior has to find a .. a girl who isn't of his totem and .. and .. and he has to lie with her," he ended defiantly.

There were a few moments of silence.

"Was that the end of the purification?"

"Not quite, Sister. The warrior had to drink some vile stuff to make him vomit out the evil spirits so they couldn't harm him."

Sister Anderson was still holding his wrist. She had turned in her chair so she could watch his face while he talked. After a few minutes of thoughtful silence, she released his wrist and pointed her finger at his nose, warningly. "Young man, I did not know you were half-Zulu when you first came here, even if your Zulu half was only in your upbringing."

For a few moments she sat still with her eyes boring into his. "And it was lucky for you I didn't know. However, for your cheek I ordered you well bathed and rubbed with spirits in your bed. That made sure you were cleansed outside! Then, because of the fright you gave me over Rose .. , Sister Marsden here, I had you dosed with cascara. In fact you were given a slight overdose. That certainly cleansed you inside.

"According to what you've just told us, you have been halfway purified already. Now my young warrior, seeing you are only half-Zulu, you require only half the purification! The remainder of the purification is therefore not necessary, nor will it occur in this hospital! Do I make myself quite clear on that point?"

Peter didn't know where to look. The thrust was far to close to home for his liking.

"Naturally," she continued, "should you feel a little cheated, I won't mind arranging the vomiting part, to round off your purification, if it will rid you of the evil spirits of those enemies who have fallen to your deadly rifle. But nothing more!"

She turned quickly in her chair to take Rosemary by surprise. "And as for you, young lady, I have never in all my life seen anybody make such a quick and thorough recovery from the very brink of a complete nervous breakdown. And that from only one massage from an expert hand!"

Rosemary blushed scarlet.

"Now just you make quite sure that you have nothing to do with any Zulus or half-Zulus and their shocking customs." She looked closely at Rosemary's confusion and spoke to her in a gentle tone. "It's wonderful to see your appetite returned and your new and very charming gaiety of manner. Go along both of you, and roast yourselves some more of that delicious meat. And do a piece for me too, slightly underdone, with salt, but no pepper."

As they chose pieces of raw meat from the basin on the table, Peter saw Rosemary was still blushing and biting her bottom lip. He was still wondering what to say to her, when the Sergeant Major's voice distracted him.

"Colour!" the Sergeant Major's imperious bark at Hannes' retreating back was not loud enough to attract the attention of the other guests. Peter excused himself to Rosemary and walked quickly around the fire. He saw Hannes coming back sheepishly from the darkness, carrying a plate heaped with food in one hand and a beermug filled to the brim with vermouth in the other.

"Where the hell are you off to with that?" The Sergeant Major's face was flushed with fury.

"Well, Sir," Hannes said apologetically, "seeing old Sergeant Aitcheson can't walk yet, Sir, I thought I'd take a little piece of braaied meat and a drop of vermouth to him in the ward."

The Sergeant Major deflated visibly. He stared at Hannes and smiled approvingly. "Good man, Colour! Fortunately I'm not a nurse and I know nothing about any vermouth going into any ward. A drop, you said?" he glanced at the brimming beer- mug. "I'm beginning to believe if I live long enough to get used to you bastards breaking every bloody rule in the book, I might start liking the way you men stick together and help people. Carry on, Colour!"

Peter thought his voice sounded unusually gruff.

There were no shadows in the bleached hayfield. A mottled midnight full moon smiled down on Rosemary as she peeped around the corner of the haystack, waiting to surprise Peter – blissfully unaware that he was standing right behind her.

"It's twelve o'clock," he whispered in her ear.

Rosemary gasped with shock. Her arms fell to her sides and she leaned against the hay, sagging with fright. "I was waiting for you," she whispered in gasps, "I was waiting to surprise you. Don't your feet touch the ground when you walk, like other people's do? What made you appear suddenly from that side?"

Just for an instant his eyes hardened, then softened again. As the gentle moonlight caused him no discomfort, Peter had removed his eye-shield. He gathered her to his chest. "I told you I never go any-where twice by the same route," he whispered with his lips against her hair. "People in my job live longer that way. We've only just finished making the place tidy after the braai. I'm sorry I kept you waiting."

She stood away from him and realised with a thrill of anticipation that his eyes were searching her body intently. It unnerved her that his first glance had detected the absence of a brassiere and the erectness of her nipples – pinched by the night coolness and the unaccustomed sensuous caressing of her dress. She watched his eyes pass fleetingly over her body and pause for an instant to search the curves of her hips as he took in the absence of any indentation of panties.

Peter stepped towards her and pulled her gently to his body. His lips were warm on hers but she knew his concentration was in the tips of his questing fingers. They touched lightly where her brassiere straps should have been and passed down her body, feeling for the waist elas-tic of the undergarments she had pushed hurriedly under her pillow before she left her tent. She tried to control her breathing as a pulsing sensation crawled across her stomach and prickled her nipples.

His hand slid intimately over the swells of her bottom as he drew her tighter against him and his kiss hardened on her lips. She lifted her arms and clasped them around his neck and her lips flattened against his.

Peter smelt the warm, milky smell of love in Rosemary's uneven breaths. His hand on her bottom drew her harder against him and he felt the curve of her hips thrust forward to challenge the rigidity of his own compelling need. Their lips parted and their tongues touched and moved against each other, tasting the intoxicating nectar of passion. Their breaths trembled and caught in the excitement of their mutual desire and the thrill of certainty of its fulfilment.

"Numbela, the fruit of salvation." His breathless voice whispered her name like a caress, into her open mouth.

She brought her hands down from behind his head and pushed him gently away. As she freed herself and stood back from him, he saw her chest labouring with uneven breaths. "So this is love," her shaky words caught in her throat, "oh – it's beautiful. Now I understand. It's a kind of magic. Even the moon is as bright as day and the world is all silver and black. Do you think there's magic in the moon?" she asked. "Does it stir your heart like it stirs mine?"

Peter smiled at her. "There's magic there, all right," he replied. "Strong magic that draws the tides of the oceans and makes jackals lift their muzzles and howl to the heavens. The moon makes lions grunt and roar and prowl restlessly through the night. Even the fish in the rivers feel its call and rise to sip its silver on the surface of the water."

"And what about bush-babies, can they feel it too?"

"Oh yes," Peter's smile widened. "On full moon nights you can hear them crying to the plovers, dipping and swooping among the clinking bats, and calling back to the bush-babies, `tlooo-tlui-tlui-too-ee-u'."

She pressed herself against him and rubbed her hips against his with an exciting, abandoned movement, rekindling the fire of his need. She took his face between her hands and slid her tongue across his lips. "Who am I?" she whispered against his lips.

"You're my Rosemary."

"No, my darling. I'm not your Rosemary. Not tonight!" She laughed breathlessly. "Tonight I'm the fruit of the tree of salvation. I'm your Numbela. I didn't wear this red dress for nothing. I'm the red-skinned fruit with the white flesh which refreshes and renews the tired spirit, so the weary traveller can rise up once more in all his strength and resume his journey." She kissed him again and pressed her body against his.

Once more he felt the thrust of her pelvis against him. He covered the swell of her breast with his hand and felt the hardness of her nipple against the centre of his palm and knew from her tenderness and the slight tremor that she had said all she wished to say. He sensed that the moment of her surrender had arrived and that she was ready to give herself to him, but that a new fear of the unknown had gripped her.

He knew her soul was crying out silently for his leadership and understanding. As he caressed her bare body under her dress, he drew her against him and locked her lips in a lingering kiss. He began to move against her until his own breathing quickened and the throbbing urgency of his desire would no longer be denied. Taking hold of the hem of her dress, he tried to peel it from her body. "Help me, Numbela! I can't peel the skin off the fruit with only one hand," he said breathlessly.

"Wait," she whispered in a shaky voice. With a brief hug and a thrust of her hips against him in a fleeting gesture of abandonment, she stepped away, took the hem of her dress and drew it upwards and over her head. She heard Peter's sudden intake of breath as she revealed the secrets of the nakedness of her body, shining silver in the moonlight. She bundled the dress and pressed it shyly to her groin to cover her dark triangle, and pressed her knees together, bending forward a little. But it was her last gesture of reserve.

Peter took the crumpled dress from her and dropped it onto the stubble beside him. He barely breathed as he shook the sleeve of his pyjama jacket impatiently from his arm. "Help me!" his voice was choked as he struggled clumsily with the knotted cord of his pyjamas. She helped him with trembling hands and he kicked his feet free from the fallen trousers frantically.

Rosemary saw his rigid need for her and came to him, clinging to him desperately with her face pressed into the hollow of his neck. Their bodies pressed sensuously against each other and she felt a thrill of abandonment and the urge for him to possess her. In a daze of confused emotion she responded to the guidance of his hand and lay down on his dressing-gown on a bed of straw, then reached up her arms to draw him into her embrace.

"Are you frightened?" Peter whispered with his lips touching hers.

"I'm only frightened because it's my first time." She breathed the words against his lips in an unsteady voice. He felt the quiver of her arms holding him to her and the touch of her nipples against his chest. To cover her nervousness, she tried to laugh but the sound that came out was almost inaudible. Her arms tightened around him and she hugged him onto her body.

Peter stroked and caressed her, stimulating her gently to bring her to full arousal. She was soon transported to a level of response when he could move more urgently against her until she yielded to his thrust.

"Yes .. Yes .. Oh! .. Yes!." Her words came in stifled gasps.

He felt an instant of resistance as he entered her to claim her virginity, then she yielded completely with a gasp, and her body tensed beneath him.

"Fill me! Fill me with life!" she breathed as the slight pain subsided. Peter shifted position so he could see her face. Her eyes were tightly closed and her lips pressed together. With all the discipline of his trained body, he stopped moving and stroked her gently, whispering words of endearment and reassuring her with kisses.

Her body began to move experimentally in response and lost some of its tenseness. A careful, slow rolling motion of her hips and a rhythmical upward thrust against him aroused the beginnings of a sensation she had never known. She felt his body begin to quiver and his muscles harden. As he thrust against her and lunged suddenly down on her she felt another slight twinge of pain. His body hardened in her arms and leaped against her with spasms of convulsions, driving her breath from her in gasps.

His spasms slowed to shuddering breaths as the tenseness of his body relaxed and he leaned heavily on her. Gently, she took his face between her hands and kissed him with parted lips. All the love and tenderness and compassion of grateful womanhood was in her kiss.

Rosemary's boldness grew. Her body glowed warmly its new awakening. She was aware of the spontaneous movement of her hips and her need was expressed in the hunger of her kiss. She whispered breathless, unintelligible words of love against his lips.

Peter heaved himself onto his elbow. "I'm too heavy for you, Numbela," he whispered.

"No! Don't go!" Rosemary's voice was urgent. She clung to him with her arms and with her legs wrapped around the back of his knees. "Don't go," she pleaded urgently. "Stay where you are and let me love you."

Peter rested on his forearm and looked down at her face. Her eyes were wide open, looking past his shoulder in wonder at the moon. Her eyes were untroubled yet dark with desire and love. In their expression there was no trace of her former reserve or fear. Peter moved to ease his weight on her and instantly the grip of her legs tightened and her eyes shaded with alarm.

"Don't go!" she pleaded. Her hands stroked his back and his sides and his hips, and her calves moved caressingly over the backs of his legs. "I wish every one of the warriors you've put into me could be born and grow to take the places of those who've been killed." She spoke without shyness "I feel warm and excited and happy. There is no more death for me. We've just destroyed it." For a while she was quiet, but her sensuous movements continued.

"I think I understand the essence of the custom of purification of your old Zulu warriors. They felt when they were purified they could go back into battle and face death fearlessly, because they knew their souls lived on in the bodies of the girls who had cleansed them." She looked questioningly from the moon into Peter's eyes. "Something wonderful's happening to me. There's something more my body wants and I can't keep it still. Kiss me again till I know what it is."

The movements of her hands and stroking legs and rhythmically undulating body became imperative, in response to the demand of his kisses. Peter felt a rekindling of his own passion and the growing feeling throbbed in his groin. He pressed against her and drew back and pressed again.

"Don't go. Don't go!" There was a breathless urgency in her plea and she pulled him hard to her with her legs.

"I wasn't thinking of going," he assured her and thrust against her once more.

"Mmmmmm, that's lovely." She opened her mouth over his and poked her tongue in and out between his lips. The movements of her body became hurried and sensuous, relieving him of all restraint and galvanising his own passion.

"Oh yes! Yes! Yes, my darling." The tempo of their thrusting bodies escalated to a frenzied climax of exquisite sensation. From somewhere deep down in Rosemary's throat, Peter heard a sound he had never heard from a human being. It reminded him of the purr and soft growl of a leopard, and the animal sound of it incited an animal response in him, stripping away the last shred of his restraint. In unison their bodies leaped together in an ecstatic moment of oblivion and they clung together heaving and shuddering. Their spasms lost their urgency and they subsided little by little to sighs and shudders. After a while they lay still.

"Dear heaven, what happened to me?" Rosemary sighed. "I'm so weak, my arms don't feel like they belong to me." Her voice was breathless and exhausted. Her arms slid from Peter's back and flopped loosely onto the hay at her sides. "All my strength's gone." She smiled a weak, tired smile and tried to lift one arm languorously, but her wrist hung loosely and her fingers refused to function. "Look," she sighed, "I haven't got the strength to close my hand." Her voice was breathless from his weight.

"I'm too heavy for you, Numbela." He touched his lips to hers and laboriously heaved himself up on his elbow. The darkness of passion had faded from her eyes. They were softly brown and misted with love.

"Stay with me a little longer," she whispered. With considerable effort she lifted one leg after the other and draped them over the back of his knees. "Just for a little while longer," she murmured.

They lay for a while until Peter's elbow could no longer support his weight. He rolled over onto his side and Rosemary turned and rolled with him. She had been on the brink of falling asleep. She sat up beside him and rolled him onto his back. "Rest, my darling. Close your eyes for a while and rest. I want to sit beside you and look at you and think about the wonderful thing that's happened to me."

It was Peter's turn to look up at the moon and at the naked girl sitting on her heels at his side. Her head was bowed over him and a curtain of hair hid the side of her face. For a while she sat perfectly still, then her bottom rose an inch from her heels as she leaned over him. Her hands began moving over his body, exploring, caressing and touching.

"Every night when I come off duty we'll make love like we did tonight. Again and again, until we're too weak to stand," she whispered with a gentle smile. "I never dreamed making love could be such a wonderful thing."

Day followed day, impatient for the night. Peter could not lie on his bed and sleep away the hours of waiting, it would look too suspicious. He busied himself absently with whatever tasks needed doing in the kitchen or in the ward, while Rosemary floated through her duties smiling to herself and to those who spoke to her. She was oblivious of the unpleasantness of some of the tasks she had to perform but she was happy in her thoughts of the warmth of her love and its nightly consummation. An aura of peace and contentment surrounded her, which endeared her to her patients and awed the Sisters who shared her hours of duty.

Peter made certain he had as little to do with Rosemary as he could possibly arrange, without appearing to avoid her. To further allay suspicion, he also made certain Sister Anderson saw him frequently during each day – carrying bottles to those who needed them and helping others who could not help themselves.

Once or twice when he noticed Sister Anderson's eyes following Rosemary, he thought he detected a knowing look in her level gaze and the tightening of her lips. These were times when he was almost certain that she suspected something of the consuming love between Rosemary and himself, and of that love's fulfilment.

Once she caught him watching her. She called him aside and surprised him with unexpected questions about his family and the job waiting for him when the war was won. It was obvious to Peter that Sister Anderson was interested in his well-being, but he was sure this was more because of her interest in Rosemary and the responsibility she felt towards her.

There were times when Peter was worried about Rosemary's casual acceptance that their secret could not be kept forever. When he spoke of it one night she merely shrugged her shoulders. "I suppose she knows," she said in a matter-of-fact voice, "but don't worry about it. One day she will definitely know, because if I'm not pregnant already," she smiled and touched his lips with her finger, "I'm certain I will be very soon, at the rate we're going!"

"And what about Frances Houghton who shares your tent," Peter asked with a worried frown, "Doesn't she suspect something when you're out just about all night, every night?"

"What's troubling you, my Isinkwe? Have you changed from being the finest of warriors into the biggest of worriers? Frances Houghton doesn't guess, she knows. And she knows because she's my friend and I told her. When she got married she was much younger than I am and she had to hide the fact she was married because she was still training. Her husband was in the Navy." Rosemary looked sad. "He was lost at sea. Frances won't tell anybody about us, because she knows what love is like in wartime."

Peter was still not satisfied. "We'll have to get married," he said, trying to make her think seriously.

"How can you talk of getting married?" Rosemary asked. "You want me to be serious and now I want you to be serious. Tell me the truth. How long does the army say snipers are supposed to last in the front line? Some of your men tell me it's six hours and others think it's four. None of them think it's longer than that. But I know you'll survive because you're that kind of man. I also believe the spirit of old Mashona is watching over you and will continue to watch over you. But if you start worrying about getting married, or about anything else, you'll lose the razor-edge of your concentration and not even Mashona will be able to help you."

Peter felt chilled at her words but he could see she was serious and he knew she was right, but the belief was deeply rooted in his mind that if a man fathered a girl's child he was morally bound to marry that girl. There was no other possible consideration for any man who had been decently brought up.

"No, my darling, Isinkwe," she kissed the frown on his brow, "you mustn't even think of getting married, as long as this war rages on. You're only twenty-two, and I can't for the life of me picture you as a husband coming home dutifully from the office each day, wearing a bowler hat and carrying your umbrella and your brief case. We are simply two lovers thrown together to cling to one another in the maelstrom of a savage war. You are a desperately frightened girl's dream of the perfect fighting man who will save her from death or slavery. You were born gifted by the spirits to conquer the enemy, yet you have the sensitivity of a poet. You also have the awareness of a wild animal and your natural gifts have been refined and channelled by expert tutors, into the deadly killer the war has made of you.

"Stop frowning at me like that and listen to me."

Peter started to reason with her but she kissed his lips closed and pressed her body against his for a moment.

"I love you, Peter, Isinkwe MacTavish, can't you understand? I'm the embodiment of all desperate womanhood. To you I have given my body, my soul and my love. I love you with all my heart. Isn't that enough? At the moment I am to you what the Numbela fruit is to the gasping traveller. Take what I give you with all my heart. Refresh your spirit and be glad to know your soul lives on in my body, and through me you can never die."

Peter caught her shoulder and held her away for a moment. "Forget about us for a second, Numbela. What about the child we might have? You can't have a child without a name!"

His voice sounded so trite, Rosemary laughed aloud in the darkness. "Oh my darling, Isinkwe. I'll be the happiest young mother of an illegitimate child this world has ever seen. Every fifth child in the world is conceived in love and out of wedlock. And most of the marriages that break down, do so because the couple married only to give a love-child a name. My own little Isinkwe will grow up free because of you and happy and loved because of me.

"You've got two hands now that your stitches are out," she held up her arms, "so take off my dress and refresh your troubled spirit with a feast of Numbela fruit and fill me again with the seeds of our love." She lay down on the dressing-gown and held up her arms for him to come into her embrace, but he knelt beside her instead.

"Wait a moment, my Numbela," he smiled, "I've loved you with every part of my body, but my right hand has been tucked away in a sling, and now I want that hand to feel all it's been missing. Turn onto your tummy and when I've finished feeling your back I want to feel your front." Softly and sensuously he combed her hair with the fingers of his right hand and then moved his hand lightly over her cheeks and around her neck and across her shoulders. He caressed the smooth skin of her back and her ribs and he felt it contract into a rash of goose-pimples.

Rosemary shivered as Peter's sensitive hand caressed over the hollow of her back, the swelling outline of her hips and the curves of her bottom and moved on to stroke the back of her legs and the insides of her satin thighs, and her breathing quickened into tiny gasps. Her hips began to move with a hurrying circular motion. She stretched out her hand and felt upwards along his thigh and she knew he was ready for her love.

Rosemary released him and pushed herself up quickly with her hands, onto her knees. The dark tinted skin of the aureoles of her upstanding nipples was wrinkled and tight, and the nipples themselves were pinched hard with exquisite anticipation. "Lie down," she whispered urgently, in a breathless, husky voice. She tugged Peter impatiently and pushed him onto his back on the dressing-gown. She threw her leg across him, straddled him and lay down on his chest to kiss him briefly, while her breath, like her movements, was quick and desperate.

Before Peter could embrace her she placed her hands flat on his chest and pushed herself upright and wriggled him into her moist warmth. She pressed down on him with all her maddeningly squirming weight. Her hands slid down his body from his chest to his hips and then behind her to his thighs, as her body straightened and arched backwards. Beneath her she felt him thrust upwards despite her pressing, jerking weight. An exquisite sensation seized her and froze the muscles of her backward bowed body, and she sat motionless and taut as a strung bow, growling softly in her throat.

For a moment she sat with her head thrown back and her upward thrust breasts silhouetted against the night sky like a pagan statue of ivory, paying homage to the moon goddess of love. She quivered for an instant then her body convulsed in galvanic spasms and she cried out aloud into the silence of the night. Gasps and ripples of shudders shook her body and she felt Peter thrust upward suddenly, hard against her. He gasped and jerked again and again until the convulsions of their fused bodies quietened and he sagged beneath her.

Rosemary leaned slowly forward with her head slumped limply so that her chin touched her chest. She supported herself with her arms still extended backwards and her hands pressing down on him. A wave of lassitude drained her last vestige of strength. Her arms could no longer support her limp body and she subsided onto his labouring chest and they lay warmly together until their breathing quietened.

Rosemary raised her head and touched her lips to his. "Roll over and lie on me," she whispered. As she felt him roll over she clasped him to her body with her remaining strength, and held him to her with her arms and her legs so as they rolled over he was held in her embrace of love. They lay for a while with their lips pressed softly together. The edge of the black moon-shadow of the haystack had inched slowly towards them, pushed back gently by the encroaching tide of faint moonlight creeping over the stubble. Rosemary began to croon quietly in Peter's arms.

"Sh!" Peter pressed his finger across her lips. "Quickly," he whispered into her ear, "somebody's coming." Rising without a sound, he picked up his gown and Rosemary's dress. He took her hand and pulled her behind him around the corner of the haystack where they waited unmoving, with the waning moonlight silvering their naked bodies.

Rosemary reached for her dress but Peter held up his hand to caution her to stand still. After a few minutes she grew restless and frightened, but he touched her again and signalled her to remain quite still. Peter stood like a statue, breathing through parted lips. His entire concentration was focused in his undamaged ear. Then Rosemary also heard the faint sound of footsteps. A beam of yellow torch light slashed suddenly through the black moon shadow at the base of the haystack where they had made love, and it rested there for a moment like a yellow blob on the pale stubble.

A click sounded sharply and the light snapped off and Peter listened to the whisper of soles brushing fainter and fainter through the dew softened stubble. He pulled on his gown hurriedly and held his pyjamas crumpled in his hand. "Go to the end of the hayfield," he whispered to Rosemary, "then run to the Sister's toilet. Don't run straight back to your bed."

Rosemary caught him by the shoulders of his dressing-gown. "How did you know?" she whispered. Her eyes were wide with consternation.

Peter smiled at her and kissed her quickly. "There was a pratincole singing, and it stopped suddenly. Then I heard its `piree-pre-cluck' alarm call, and knew something had disturbed it. I listened for a while and heard footsteps, then I waited to get their direction so I'd know which corner of the haystack to duck behind. It would have been a bit awkward if we'd run out naked into Sister Anderson's arms."

"Was it her? How do you know?"

Peter nodded. "I know the sound of her footsteps. Her left foot is a little heavier than her right. Hurry now. She'll look for both of us, but I think she'll look for me first."

Rosemary pulled his dressing-gown open and pressed herself against him. "If the spirits had given me half the sensitive awareness they gave you, I would have let out a scream and fainted with ecstasy, the first time we made love. If the sensation is so exquisite for me, I wonder how you survive what it must be like for you." She turned away and walked quickly and erratically along the outer line of haystacks, pulling the dress over her bare body as she walked.

"You've been in the toilet a long time," Sister Anderson said accusingly, as Peter came into the ward. "At least twenty minutes have passed since I came in last." Peter glanced at his bed. He thanked his lucky stars it was empty. Somebody had spirited away the sleeping dummy he had left in it. He caught Hannes' eye and saw his wink.

"Yes, I was a long time, Sister. I was a bit constipated," he said, as he took off his dressing-gown and sat in his pyjamas on the side of the bed, "but I'm all right now, thank you."

"I'll see you get a good dose of cascara, first thing in the morning, MacTavish."

"No thank you, Sister," Peter said hurriedly, "I don't need it now."

"If I say you'll have cascara, you will have cascara. Is that clear? In fact I'll give it to you myself, just in case you're thinking of talking Sister Marsden out of giving it to you. Refusing medication is a very serious offence and I'm quite certain the Sergeant Major will know which section of the King's Regulations it falls under."

She put her hands on her hips and glared at Peter. "There's something disturbing in the air tonight," she said. "I can't seem to settle down, and whatever it is, it has unsettled two others I know of. There's you spending half the night in the toilet suffering from constipation, and there's Sister Marsden chattering and giggling like a schoolgirl, and keeping Sister Houghton from her sleep. Tomorrow they'll be like a pair of zombies, the two of them. Now get right into your bed and go to sleep, or you'll get a dose of cascara every morning until you leave this hospital."

The whole atmosphere of the ward had changed. No more dying casualties had been brought in for some time. Alternative accommodation had been found for them nearer the front line, to spare them the additional trauma of an unnecessarily long journey.

Hannes van Vuuren, Dirkie Uys, Gunnar Olsen and Lieutenant Joubert had been sent to rest camp and they had all deserted and returned to their units. In a week or two it would be time for Koen Taljaardt and Jan Booysens and Peter to follow suit. All the beds in the ward were occupied by men with flesh wounds and most of the patients were South Africans. The 6th South African Armoured Division was still in the van of the Allied advance, steadily driving the Germans back towards Florence. The lightly wounded men looked after themselves and each other and there was little the Sisters had to do apart from dressings and medication. The daily order group disintegrated into a friendly leg-pulling gathering. There were mornings when the Sergeant Major took off his cap and sat on one of the beds joking with the men. It was noticeable that the bed he chose to sit on, was always the bed of a South African.

The ward orderlies were idle and the cooks had little to do. Sister Houghton relaxed her discipline and laughed merrily at the pranks of her free and easy patients. Even Sister Anderson allowed herself to be teased gently, although she set limits. If anybody ventured to became too familiar with her, he would have to spend most of the following day in the toilet.

Rosemary put on weight and became more desirable to a ward full of men who had fallen in love with her. But it was the men's respect for

197

Peter's reputation that prevented them from pursuing her too fervently.

Sister Anderson made no further attempts to find out whether Peter was in the ward at night or not. Nor did she enquire after Rosemary once the duties of the day had been handed over to the night staff. The moon had waxed again and waned once more to a sliver of silver and the nights were dark. Rosemary had to hold on to Peter's shoulder and follow his footsteps to each new place he had chosen for their late night loving. They did not discuss marriage again, nor did Rosemary tell him she had missed her period. As each night of passion passed she sensed his growing restlessness and listened with a numb ache in her heart to his frequent reminiscences of the things that had happened when he, Taffy, Spud, Indabushe and Big Dries Maritz had shared their lives and their dangers.

Rosemary slept restlessly through a night tormented with dreams of war. She whimpered and winced in her bed to the crack of bullets aimed at Peter. In the early light of dawn she got up and hurried to the bathroom to sponge away the marks of her tears, wondering if her dreams were some sort of an omen – perhaps they were a spiritual warning of disaster from Mashona.

Later in the morning she found Peter helping stretcher-bearers to unload five ambulances and bring the new batch of patients into the ward. Four small stretcher-bearers were struggling to lift a stretcher carrying an enormous man. Rosemary saw Peter grin at their sweating efforts and move towards them to help with his good hand. She also went towards the struggling group to make sure the patient was not hurt in the handling.

Rosemary saw the enormous man's eyes suddenly light up with pleasure. "Jesus! Isinkwe!" his bull voice bellowed a greeting.

"Dries!" Peter's voice rang with gladness. "Christ man, it's good to see you!"

Big Dries pulled a leg-sized arm from beneath the blankets and held out a huge hand to Peter. Suddenly his smile faded and the creases of laughter died on his face and he shook his head sadly. He pulled his other hand from the blankets and turned with a grimace of pain, to take both of Peter's hands between his own. "Hell, Isinkwe, man, I'm bloody sorry about Taffy and Spud." He shook his head sadly.

Rosemary's breath caught in her throat. She saw the smile freeze on Peter's face and the sudden narrowing of his eyes.

"What happened to them, Dries?" he asked in a toneless voice.

Big Dries shook his head again. "Fuck it," he groaned, oblivious of Rosemary's presence. "Christ, man! It happened four days ago. I thought you would have heard by now!"

"What happened, Dries?" Peter's voice was tight with suppressed emotion. "What happened to them?"

"It was the 88s. The bastards were waiting for us. They got us at close range, with high explosive. The Jerries had them hidden inside a row of pigsties. They hit us with shrapnel at a thousand yards. They caught us in the open with our fingers up our arses. Taffy and Spud were quite close to me. They dived for cover beside a tree. A bloody high explosive hit the tree plum centre and went off like an airburst. Taffy got most of it. Poor bugger. I don't think there was a whole bone left in his body."

"So it was quick?" Peter asked through clenched teeth.

Big Dries shook his head. "It was quick for Spud. He never knew what hit him. He was dead when we picked him up, after the shit stopped flying." He stopped speaking and gulped. "But it wasn't quick for Taffy. Indabushe told me he'd just died as we were going in to attack yesterday. Indabushe kept him at Battalion. He was too buggered to be moved back. I'm sorry, Isinkwe! Christ man, I'm sorry! If only you'd been there it wouldn't have happened. You'd have seen those bloody 88s from a mile away. But if you had been there you'd also have copped it. Indabushe said if I saw you, I was to tell you this was what your old Mashona saved you from when he let you get wounded."

Rosemary saw Peter close his eyes and squeeze them tightly for a moment. She saw the muscles working at the sides of his jaw and ran to him to hold him to her heart. "Oh I'm sorry" she said with a catch in her voice, "they meant so much to you."

Big Dries released Peter's hands when he saw the tears in the pretty Sister's eyes. The stretcher-bearers were staring at her, open mouthed. "Pick me up and take me into the hospital before I break your bloody necks!" he bellowed in a voice that shocked everybody into sudden movement.

"What about Indabushe, Dries, wasn't he there?" Peter asked urgently.

"Oh ja! He was there, but further back. The blokes say he reported seeing marks that looked like tracks of gun wheels, leading in the direction of the pigsties, but it was too far for him to see properly. You know how it is. Most of the men are new and they ignored Indabushe's warning. What's a Medic supposed to know about gun tracks, anyway?"

Sister Anderson sat behind her table with her arms folded across her breasts. A graduated glass vial containing straw-coloured liquid stood on the table beside her. The lines on her face were deeply etched and her level stare was fixed on Peter. As she watched him her mind filled with the picture of a caged tiger padding tirelessly backwards and forwards along the line of steel bars of its cage. Yet she could detect no outward signs of the restless impatience Rosemary had tearfully told her about.

"I sent for you, young man, because I believe you have decided to leave us shortly. In fact, tomorrow morning. Is this true?"

"Yes, Sister," he said. "I was coming to tell you later today, and to thank you for everything you've done for me. I wouldn't have gone without saying goodbye."

For a moment Sister Anderson remained silent. Her Adam's apple rose and fell as she swallowed, and she blinked rapidly to rid herself of some irritation. "You are due to be discharged from this hospital in ten day's time to go to a rest camp near Naples for three weeks recuperation leave. This has been decided by the Chief Medical Officer of this hospital. But it would seem, with typical South African disregard for anybody's decisions other than their own, that you are leaving tomorrow to find your Regiment and to resume your deadly duties. The fact that your eye is not nearly back to normal, or that the tissues of your shoulder are not sufficiently healed, seems of little importance to you. You have no intention of going to the rest camp, have you?"

"No, Sister."

"You have no intention of waiting until the Medical Officer decides you are well enough to go, have you?"

Peter shook his head. "Sister, my Regiment is advancing fast. My two buddies have been killed and if I'd been there they'd still be alive, because I would have seen those German guns. It's my job to scout the front before we advance, and if I lie around here any longer, others will die because I wasn't scouting ahead of them."

"From anybody else I would call that boasting, Peter, Isinkwe, MacTavish. But from what I've heard of you, you have just made a simple statement of fact." She blinked her eyes again rapidly. "Of course, you have attended to all the little details such as illegally getting your bloodstained uniform back from the locked locker room, and illicitly obtaining food from the kitchen for your journey?"

A smile touched Peter's lips. "I've done better than that, Sister," he said. "I've got hold of a brand-new uniform. The old one was full of holes and bloodstains, anyway. I've only taken condensed milk for rations. It doesn't take up much space and I can swop it along the road for anything I fancy."

"Yes," Sister Anderson said to herself thoughtfully. "I have come to realise you men have no difficulty in obtaining anything you want. Was all this difficult to organise?"

"No, Sister. You see, we had a few bottles of vermouth left over from the braai."

Sister Anderson nodded understandingly. Despite the severe look on her face, her eyes twinkled. "Yes, yes. I see only too clearly. And I suppose you've arranged with the sentries at the gate to swear blind they didn't see you go out, when you leave us, tomorrow morning?"

Peter's smile broadened. "I won't get them into trouble, Sister. The gate isn't the only way of getting out of this hospital."

"No, of course not," Sister Anderson clasped her hands in front of her bosom, "there's the orchard, and beyond it the hayfield. I'd forgotten about them and I've good reason to believe you know every inch of both."

Peter's smile looked a little sickly and his eyes slid away from hers. He experienced the same chilling feeling he always had when he suspected the Germans had become aware of his whereabouts, if not his exact position. He sat unmoving, waiting for the mortar bombs of her words to crash about his ears. But instead of her wrath, she blinked away what appeared fleetingly to be tears in her eyes. The knuckles of her clasped hands were white and strained.

"Your secrets are quite safe with me, young man," she said ambiguously and swallowed as though to keep her voice steady. "I admire your spirit and the spirit of all you South Africans. I understand why you feel you must get back to the fighting, and pit your deadly talents against the skill of the enemy. I also believe the enemy will never overcome spirits like yours. Defeat him on the ground just as soon as you can." The tears in her eyes were plain to see and it seemed she no longer cared if he saw them.

"End it for us all as quickly as you can. You see, my only son is a bomber pilot in the Air Force." Her voice dropped to a husky whisper. "War is hard on us women. His father was killed in the beginning, at Dunkirk." She swallowed repeatedly before she could carry on, then sat bolt upright in her chair and tried to blink back her tears, and smiled bravely at Peter.

"I'm sorry, Sister," he shook his head in sympathy. "I didn't know."

"No! No!," she said in a firmer voice, "you know what it's all about now, so just you go and do what you can to end it all, before it's too late for my son's sake. Now I have a little surprise ready for you. It will give you something to think about after you've gone." She picked up the medicine vial of straw-coloured liquid and held it towards him. "I want you to take this medicine. It tastes vile, so you simply have to gulp it down."

Peter pulled his hands back quickly against his chest and sat up ready to escape. "No thank you, Sister," he pleaded, "I don't need any more medicine. No thank you!" His upward extended fingers made little pushing away motions as though holding off some approaching horror.

Sister Anderson regarded him with her old stern look, resting her elbows on the tabletop, still holding the little glass of medicine towards him.

She spoke slowly and deliberately. "I prepared this draught especially for you the minute I heard you were leaving us, and you are to drink it – for your own good."

Peter still hesitated. His eyes were fixed on the vial of medicine and his head swung mistrustingly from side to side.

"Oh dear me! I'd quite forgotten!" Sister Anderson said. "You prefer cascara, don't you? Wait where you are, while I get you some."

Peter held up his hands in surrender and reached out slowly for the glass.

"Now do as I say," Sister Anderson said primly. "The taste is quite vile, so you must gulp it down."

"What is it, Sister?"

"Drink it down first like a good boy, and then I'll tell you what it is," she said coaxingly.

For a second Peter looked at her bland face dubiously. Then he took the glass from her hand and lifted it to his mouth. He tilted back his head and swallowed the contents in one enormous gulp. Then he banged the empty glass down on the table top and shook himself like a dog emerging from water. He wore a hideous grimace on his face. His teeth clenched and his eyes screwed tightly closed. After a few moments of death-like stillness he lurched to his feet and grabbed his stomach with one hand and his mouth with the other. His eyes flew open and he looked wildly around the duty room.

"Use the basin on the locker." Sister Anderson's tone of voice was mildly complacent.

Peter staggered to the locker and leaned over the basin. He hiccuped and gulped and saliva drooled from his lips. His shoulders heaved and he vomited violently.

Sister Anderson got up and went to him. She put her arm around his heaving shoulders and her hand supported his clammy forehead as he gagged agonisingly over the half-filled basin. "Yes, Isinkwe, my poor, dear, Zulu warrior." She pressed a brief, compassionate kiss onto the back of his head. "I was so afraid you'd go back into battle uncleansed, that I took it upon myself to act as your witch-doctor. Now you can go back completely purified. I was terrified you'd forgotten to vomit up the malevolent spirits of those you have killed in battle. But now you've completed every aspect of the purification rites, in accordance with your Zulu custom, and you can go and kill again with a tranquil heart.

"To answer your last question," her voice was matter-of-fact, "the medicine I gave you was tincture of ipecacuanha." She pulled his exhausted body against the softness of her ample bosom.

"Now let me see if I can get this part right: Go gently, my young warrior. We will both pray for you, and I will keep your Rosemary safe within the shelter of my armpit."

Chapter 10

Peter was shocked at the change he saw in Colonel Hamman. He appeared to have aged six years during the seven weeks Peter had been in hospital. He took Peter's outstretched hand between both of his and held it for a minute while his emotions settled. A new Major stood nearby, looking on disapprovingly.

"So you've come back to us, Peter, and just in time," Colonel Hamman greeted him. "I need those eyes of yours most desperately. God knows we've lost a lot of good men while you were away." He clapped his hand sympathetically on Peter's shoulder and squeezed it to emphasise his feelings.

"I can't tell you how sorry I am about your mates. Both Taffy and Spud were fine men, and the Regiment will remember them with pride. Men like those two are impossible to replace. We took a hell of a pounding in those hills guarding the approaches to Florence. That's where we lost a lot of our old hands, but even more of the new chaps. They're the ones who cop it worst every time we have to go in. They get killed before they've had a chance to learn whether a shell's going to fall short or if it's going to hit them, or go over.

"Very few of them have had any training and they're nowhere near ready to be thrown into a fight, especially against seasoned enemy troops. They're keen enough to get at the Jerrie's throats, but it burns me up inside when I have to order them into an attack. I only wish I could keep them in close reserve long enough for them to learn a few of the things you old blokes know.

"Anyway, thank God you're back, and at least I'll be getting reports I can rely on again. You're looking well, except for that eye of yours. It still looks as though you got too close to the back end of one of the pack mules and stopped a kick." They both laughed briefly at the thought. "But first of all," Colonel Hamman smiled, "what the hell am I supposed to do with you? You've been posted as a deserter by the British Military Police and I'm supposed to hand you over for court martial on a capital charge. `Desertion in the face of the enemy'. You're supposed to get shot for that!" He laughed at Peter's sheepish smile. "It's quite a problem. The Brits can't get used to the idea that you blokes desert from their hospitals and run away back to your regiments.

"There are Hannes van Vuuren and Dirkie Uys too. By the way, they told me you've teamed up with a pretty nurse, so I'm surprised to see you back so soon. Did she give you the push or something?

"There are a lot of others besides you three, so I think we'd better get the problem sorted out right now. Consider yourself severely reprimanded and taken back on strength."

"I know what to do with deserters, Colonel."

Peter turned to look at the Major who had spoken and noticed the bulge of his stomach not yet flattened by the hardships of battle. He took an instant dislike to the new Major and it appeared that his feelings were shared by the Colonel.

"Major," Colonel Hamman said with a dangerous edge to his voice, fixing him with a hard, level stare, "in this Regiment, it is the prerogative of the Sergeant Majors to maintain discipline, and I expect my officers to respect that initiative. That rule applies to all the men in the Regiment, except for one man, Major. This man," he pointed at Peter. "This man's name is MacTavish. Commonly known as Isinkwe. He is number one battalion sniper and he is answerable to me, and only me. I will give him his orders personally, and whenever I haven't given him a specific order he can do as he chooses, without question!"

He turned away from the red-faced Major and addressed Peter. "Go and find that Medic friend of yours, Corporal Dunn, he's got your rifle. When you've got it zeroed properly you can sort out a few senior enemy officers to let them know you're back in business. While you've been away the bastards haven't been shot at often enough and they are beginning to think we haven't got any snipers. Jerry has some bloody good officers for you to sort out – I don't want a single one of them anywhere near their frontline troops to tell them what to do in emergencies."

Peter walked away to find Indabushe, feeling pleased the Colonel had given him a free hand to go out sniping. He guessed the Colonel understood how he felt about Taffy and Spud and had given him the opportunity to even the score with the Germans for their deaths.

He would hunt alone. He remembered what Mashona had said the night before he had left for school. "Choose two good men to cover your back in the battles that lie ahead of you, and when they can no longer cover your back, my own spirit will hold a shield above you." He would leave it to Mashona. All he needed was a good mortar team to give him some backing, until Big Dries got back. His hurt was too deep to permit him to try to find replacements for his own two buddies and even if he could find another two to hunt with, there wouldn't be time enough to train them.

Peter and Indabushe shook hands wordlessly and gripped each other's arms. There was very little they could say to each other. Indabushe looked grey and haggard from the strain of tending to a seemingly never-ending line of casualties. The look in his eyes wrenched Peter's heart with the memory of the helpless look he had seen in Rosemary's eyes when he had first met her, and he realised Indabushe too was overwhelmed by all the death and suffering.

Indabushe released Peter's arm and turned away to remove a piece of canvas from some boxes in a corner of the aid post dugout. He lifted a narrow, green wooden box with rope handles at either end and brought it to Peter. "Taffy told me to keep this for you, until you came back."

Peter opened the lid and picked his rifle up from its padded rests. It had been thoroughly cleaned and oiled.

"They kept it for you and it was the first thing Taffy spoke of when he regained consciousness. He sent for it even though his pain was driving him mad. Isinkwe, my brother, Taffy knew he was dying and he said you would be needing your rifle to punish the Germans for not giving him time to fulfil his last wish." In spite of his heartbreak, Indabushe managed a faint smile at the memory of Taffy. "His sense of humour never deserted him, despite his agony. Do you remember him telling us he didn't want to die until he had one last crap in a shit house with a door that closed? That wish was never realised.

"He was full of courage, but most of the time he was incoherent. I nursed him for the last three days before he died. In the end he gave up struggling. He had fourteen wounds in his body, seven of them in his stomach. There was hardly one bone in his chest left intact." Indabushe shook his head as he remembered Taffy's suffering. "Towards the end, all he wanted was water, and I gave it to him to end his suffering."

They sat together in silence for a while, sipping their coffee. Peter replaced his rifle in its box and got up to go out. He needed fresh air to ease the pain in his chest as he remembered the red haired man in the hospital, whimpering for water and desperately sucking the piece of dampened lint for a little moisture. He was glad Indabushe had given Taffy water.

"I've got your bedding here, Isinkwe," Indabushe said. "You can share the dugout with me. I'll fix up a stretcher for you to use as a bed. You might as well make yourself comfortable whenever you get the chance for a bit of a sleep. There's a letter for you too." Indabushe opened his pack and handed Peter his letter. "It arrived yesterday. I was going to send it on to you in hospital. In fact, I was handing it to the Company clerk, when I got a strange feeling you'd be back with us soon." He shook his head wonderingly, "It was our grandfather, Mashona, telling me you were on your way."

Peter looked at the letter. The handwriting was strange. He turned the envelope over and his eyes widened with pleasure as he read the address of the sender:

176661818 Lt R.Marsden N.S.

No.105 British Field Hospital,
F.P.O. 223,
Italy.

He frowned thoughtfully, wondering how it could possibly have been waiting for him, and realised that Rosemary must have posted it to him while he was still with her in the hospital.

Indabushe saw his friend's face soften as he slipped the letter, unopened, into his shirt pocket.

Peter decided he would read it when he was alone. It would give him pleasure just knowing it was there and feeling it over his heart, in his pocket. He buttoned the flap and left the dugout.

A few men walked towards Peter and shook his hand, while others glanced at him, wondering who he was and why he appeared so popular with the scattering of older men still left in the regiment. The new men turned away and their thoughts went back to the disturbing sound of distant gunfire, which was more important to them than thoughts of the newcomer – or of the young men with old-looking faces who greeted him and then walked away as though, in some strange way, they were afraid of him.

Indabushe was out when Peter jumped into the aid post dugout. His kit had been neatly laid out at the head of a bed made up on a stretcher. His blankets had been washed and his webbing had been scrubbed. The green rifle case stood at the end of his bed. He sat down and drew Rosemary's letter slowly from his pocket and held it for a few moments, staring vacantly over it at the earth wall of the dugout. His eyes were soft with memories. Then he opened the letter carefully and held it to the light from the entrance to read the small neat script. She had written on both sides of the page:

"Isinkwe, my darling, I'm writing this letter in the hope you will find it waiting for you when you rejoin the Stormbergs. I'm writing because I can't sleep and the thought of losing you is tormenting me so.

"How is it possible for the heart of one small woman to contain so many conflicting emotions at the same time? I love you. This emotion overrides all the others and burns as steadily in my heart as the eternal flame on the altar in a church.

"In a few days you will be gone from me. I can see it in your eyes. I can see it in the restless way you look at a magazine without seeing it, or stop talking in the middle of a sentence and forget what you were talking about. And there is an alienation and desperation in the feel of your body when we make love.

"Your desire to be with me and your dedication to your duty tear you apart. But there is nothing I can say. I watch the struggle with a breaking heart and I know with a woman's intuition what the outcome will be. You will have to leave me and go. And you will leave me sooner than you need to go.

"You will do this because it is the right and manly thing to do. The world is burning and you know you have specialised skills which will help to extinguish the conflagration, and hasten the end of the suffering of millions of other people. You cannot stay here and love me while those others suffer. You are not that kind of man and it is this which makes me love you as I do.

"If only I had the courage, I would rush into the ward and leap onto the nearest bed and hold my arms out wide to embrace everybody. I would shout out in the RSM's voice: `Look at me! Look at me! I am Isinkwe's Numbela. I am the fruit of salvation. I have been loved and I have conceived from the spirit of that love. I am pregnant! Nations may perish, but I contain the spirit of eternal life which will pass from my womb through the generations yet to come.'

"Yes, my darling. I am pregnant and I'm exultant. My spirit rejoices, yet the tears roll down my cheeks here in the darkness, as I write these words. Such is the heart of a woman!

"I know you are the living embodiment of all warriors, past and present. You kill in order that your loved ones may live their lives without fear. For this reason you will fight on, and the tender, dedicated nurse's heart which loves you will scream like a siren: `Kill! Isinkwe. Kill, Kill, Kill, Kill for my sake, so the life which is within me may be spared'.

"I see myself as a mere creature created and entrusted by God, to perpetuate the human race. Yet I have the heart of a woman and I will yearn for my warrior lover when he's gone. Already I cry at night for the empty longing which is still to come. I cry because I am terrified for your safety. At least I have your spirit. A new life lives within my womb. A new soul has been breathed into life by the meeting and exquisite love of your spirit and mine.

"I didn't know I had a spirit until you stalked into my life with your soundless footfall. But I know now it was Mashona who led you to me and I know his spirit will be with you always. When you speak of him I can almost see him standing at your shoulder, holding his shield above your head.

"And now I know I carry the miracle of life within my body, I also know that because of it, I will have the strength to carry out my task as you carry out yours. I will be a better nurse. Already I no longer fear death and I can look him in the eye, because through you, I have conquered him. Now I will be able to whisper into the ear of a dying man that there is nothing for him to fear while I stand beside him, because I am the instrument of eternal creation. While I live, he too will live. It is only his body that he is leaving – his spirit will triumph. He will understand and I will see his understanding in his dying eyes.

"I know now it was the hand of an old black warrior who led you to me to be purified. And now that hand reaches out to lead you away again towards your destiny in the hell and glory of battle. On your path when you were exhausted and could go no further, it was that same spiritual hand that led you to the tree of salvation, from which you plucked the fruit that revived and refreshed you. You planted the seed of that fruit and it has taken root. In time it too will bear fruit to refresh those who follow.

"So, my darling, take that spirit hand and follow fearlessly.

"I had to stop writing here for a while because my thoughts saddened me so much I cried and cried and couldn't see to write. I long to find in our son the qualities of valour and chivalry and tenderness which you have. You who were born to destroy so much life and yet create something so wonderful.

"I have told Sister Anderson about my `condition' and instead of blasting me, she took me in her arms and cried. But her tears were tears of happiness for us both. She said it was inevitable and she loves you. Naturally I will have to leave before my belly bulges and presents a threat to the mythical image of chastity and sanctity of all nursing Sisters. But my going will not be missed because I am also a soldier and when I fall there will be another to step forward to take my place.

"So fight on, my Zulu warrior, and may God sustain you to do those courageous things which must be done. May He sharpen your vision in your undamaged eye. May He steady the trigger squeeze of that deadly and unutterably sensitive left hand of yours. May He preserve you to fight on and conquer the enemy for the sake of your spirit – which is to be reborn in our child – and for the preservation of what is left of the free world: for our child to live in.

"Go with good courage when you are ready to go. I know it will be soon. Don't look back to see my tears. Fulfil the destiny which was pre-ordained for you by Almighty God and for which He shaped you so carefully through His agent, old Mashona, and may the living spirit of that old warrior keep you safe within his armpit.

"My heart will be with you, always!

"Numbela."

Peter searched the spot where he had seen the quick flash of reflected light until he finally located the German observer. The position he had chosen for himself was perfect. He was cleverly concealed between two rocks. But what had made him so difficult for Peter to find, was the two-inch thick sheaf of grass he had planted directly in front of him between the two lenses of his field-glasses. The small sheaf of grass cast a shadow across one of the lenses and if the man hadn't moved slightly to scan the countryside, there would have been no tell-tale flash of sunlight from the one lens. The German had camouflaged the outline of his steel helmet with another tuft of grass standing a little higher than its surroundings.

Peter considered the situation in minutest detail. The man's expert use of natural cover warned Peter that he was potentially very dangerous. His position on high ground afforded him a commanding view of the Stormberg's positions and also those of their supporting guns and tanks, sited a little further back. Somehow the man had to be eliminated. If he wasn't, his expertise as an observer would enable the German Artillery to inflict considerable damage from well-directed fire.

Peter remembered Captain Van der Walt saying: "If you aren't certain of a kill, don't shoot. And never, under any circumstances, try for a head shot. The brain is a hell of a small and tricky target, particularly when it's partly protected by a steel helmet." But his memories of Taffy and Spud crowded out the echo of Captain Van der Walt's emphatic advice. This German's head was completely protected by his steel helmet. The gap between the brim of his steel helmet and his nose was also obstructed by the rugged pair of field-glasses which would partly or completely deflect a bullet. And the bound sheaf of grass could also deflect a bullet and make the shot uncertain.

Peter dismissed the possibility of calling down mortar fire to eliminate the man because, unless the first bomb fell right onto him, it would be a waste of an opportunity to get him. And if he wasn't killed immediately, he would escape after the barrage and reappear somewhere else to locate targets for the enemy guns. He knew if he called down mortar fire the gunner would have to bracket his target with two sighter bombs for direction and range, before he stood a chance of a direct hit. And the very first bomb explosion would warn the German observer he had been seen. He would slide back out of sight below the ridge and take shelter in the dugout he would have prepared for just such an emergency.

Peter watched for an hour, trying to decide what to do. If he used his rifle he would be shooting uphill and the angle would make a kill impossible. If he shot at the bridge of the enemy's field-glasses and if the tuft of grass didn't deflect his bullet, all he could hope to achieve was to smash the glasses back against the man's eyes, or, more likely, hit them upwards against the brim of the helmet and over his head. With a bit of luck he might blind the man, but the chances of killing him were very slim.

Sunlight lit the rock on the left of the man's head and crawled down to its base, to reveal a light-coloured patch of smooth lichen below and to the left of where the observer's chin would be. Peter felt a twinge of excitement. "Kill! Kill! Kill!," the words from Rosemary's letter whispered in his mind. The muscles on the sides of his jaw tightened with determination. To hell with what Captain Van der Walt had said. This man was too dangerous to be allowed to live. Peter's eyes narrowed with concentration. He felt as certain of a kill as he could be in the circumstances. He studied the patch of sunlit lichen and gauged the angles as carefully as a professional billiard player.

He remembered the diagram on the blackboard at school and the insistent voice of the geometry master drumming the words into the heads of his pupils "The angle of incidence equals the angle of reflection."

The patch of illuminated lichen made a perfect aiming mark. If he hit it, his bullet would bounce off it at exactly the same angle as it struck. It would ricochet upwards and to the right, strike the enemy's throat and kill him in seconds. If he allowed an error of two inches to the right or to the left, his bullet would rupture the main arteries to the man's brain and that would also kill him in seconds.

"KILL! Kill! Kill!" He thought of Rosemary.

He thought of Taffy and Spud. Then he noticed that the cross-hairs in the telescopic sight had steadied just below the patch of lichen, without any conscious movement on his part. For a moment he considered the flight of his bullet. When its tip touched the rock surface, its heavier tail end would cause it to flip over and travel heavy-end first. But before it could complete its tumble, it would strike the man's throat or arteries broadside on and plough its way through the flesh, travelling sideways, and almost tear his head from his shoulders.

Peter exhaled fractionally and the cross-hairs rose into the centre of the patch of lichen. The rifle leaped in his hands and the crash of the shot rang in his ears. The man's glasses dropped and his dislodged helmet fell forward and lay upside down beside the sunlit patch of lichen, below a haze of blond hair half-hidden in the grass.

Peter waited without moving, but there was no response from the enemy lines to the single shot. He sweated in the stifling heat under his net and tried to concentrate his thoughts on bees sipping nectar or gathering pollen, to keep his mind off the man he had killed. But it was thoughts of Rosemary and of Taffy and Spud that drew his restless eyes to search the ground ahead for other possible targets, while he waited throughout the endless hours for darkness to cover his retreat to the dugout he shared with Indabushe.

Peter crawled under his camouflage net and pulled down the flap he had crawled through, then pushed soil over the loose edge and pressed it down with his hand. There was no sign yet of approaching dawn. He wriggled and made small adjustments until he was comfortable. He loosened the tie straps and opened the bottom of the canvas cover of his telescopic sight to allow the instrument to cool to night temperature, so the lenses would not fog from any sudden change when the cover was removed. The first of the coming winter rains had begun and it was still drizzling. His greatcoat was wet and heavy and stank like a wet dog from being damp for a week, but he pulled the collar over his head and spread the coat over his body. He had not brought his rainproof slicker with him because it would reflect a sheen of wetness from its smooth surface and a watching enemy would see it reflecting through his net.

His lack of professionalism worried him and he was glad Sergeant Cimela Brown was not near to criticise him, but there had been no time to select his position in daylight. He was uncertain of his escape route, but in the dark it seemed there were enough big boulders to dodge among to give him cover until he could reach the miniature ravine two hundred yards behind him.

Colonel Hamman had put a stop to Peter's killing vendetta. He had reassessed Peter's value to the Regiment and had decided he needed accurate reports on enemy activities more than he needed dead enemy officers or observers. So Peter's lonely war had settled into a sleep-deprived routine of watching and thinking and reporting his observations to Colonel Hamman.

Big Dries had come back to the Regiment three weeks previously, with a letter from Rosemary. And because Big Dries had returned, the Colonel had ordered Peter to leave the killing to Dries and his mortar. He couldn't afford to lose Peter's powers of observation in the deadly close fighting in the foothills of the high German-held peaks of the Apennine Mountains overlooking the Stormbergs.

During his lonely days of watching, Peter's thoughts were often drawn to that sunny day among the haystacks with Rosemary. It was the day he first told her of Mashona and she had asked him if he was using camphorated oil because she had smelt it so distinctly. More and more often his loneliness made him think of Mashona and at times he imagined the old man lying beside him watching the activities of the enemy. There were occasions when he imagined he felt a tap on his shoulder to direct his attention to the tip of the old man's stabbing spear pointing out something he might otherwise not have noticed. And there were times when he wondered if he too, was getting near the point where Indabushe would have to take him by the hand and lead him away as he had seen him lead others away from the battle, slack-mouthed and vacant-eyed.

A faint cheep from the grass in front of him snapped his wandering thoughts back into focus. He listened intently, but all he could hear was the drip of water from his net onto his greatcoat, sounding like hammer blows in the deathly stillness. If it was a bird, he wondered what had disturbed it and he slipped his knife from its sheath in case he should need it in a hurry. He listened for a long time, breathing silently through his mouth, but the sound was not repeated.

Peter felt uneasy as the grey light of dawn filtered through the low cloud ceiling. He wondered if perhaps he had got too close to the enemy positions and hoped Mashona was with him to cover him with his shield. A breeze trembled the net over his slit trench and he shivered under his wet greatcoat. The light increased imperceptibly and the bird he thought he had heard in the darkness chirped loudly in front of him. Watching carefully, he was soon able to make out the open beaks of two fledglings above the rim of a cup-like nest, demanding to be fed. A little grass lark hen perched on the edge of the nest and fed the chicks food regurgitated from her crop, while the cock fluttered up and clapped his wings as he piped his `Treee, treee, tip-tip, tippy, tippy, tippy' hymn to the newly breaking day.

The domestic scene crowded his mind with thoughts of Rosemary and the growing infant in her womb, drawing nourishment from her body. He had left her letter in the dugout, as nobody was permitted to carry anything other than his pay book. If he was killed or captured, any private correspondence falling into enemy hands could be used for propaganda purposes by German Intelligence.

Rosemary had written, "It's the breeding that counts, my darling. A mastiff pup is born with the instinct of possessive aggression and a fox-hound with the instinct to hunt. And so it will be with our child. He will be a son, I know, and for his sake I'll have to emigrate to South Africa, where he will find the right environment to suit his inherited instincts. I don't want his soul to shrivel in the confining environment of a city. He must grow up with natural things, as his father did."

She told him of events at the hospital. Dries was leaving in the morning, with stitches all over his legs. He was consumed with impatience to return to the regiment to back his friend, Isinkwe, with his mortar. "After every battle," she had written, "new casualties arrive in droves, and my heart is in my mouth as I rush to see if you are one of them. My whole body trembles with terror until the last patient is carried out of the ambulances. Then I go among them asking if any of them are from the Stormbergs, and if they know you.

"Some of them must think I'm mad, but I don't care. Every man who does in fact come from the Stormbergs knows you or knows of you. `MacTavish?' they ask, `Sister, do you mean Isinkwe MacTavish? The Sniper?' I see their eyes light up with interest. `Do you know him Sister? They say he made fourteen kills in the first fourteen days he was back from hospital, and nearly all of them were senior German officers.'

"Then they laugh and say, That Isinkwe MacTavish walks circles around them and they'll never get him. They say he's got some old Zulu spirit that helps him and guards him'. Oh my darling, my heart wants to burst with fear-filled pride when I realise I'm carrying the child of such a famous warrior."

Peter blinked with sudden shock. He realised he had been day-dreaming. A wink of watery sunlight brought him back to earth. He glanced at the sky and saw the cloud ceiling had lifted a little and the rising sun had found a small window to peep through. With a jolt he saw that he was closer to the German positions than he had wanted to be. He judged the range to the barbed wire entanglement to be a little over two hundred yards. Behind the wire men were forming themselves into platoons and companies.

He noticed tapes had been laid through their minefield and where each tape met the entanglement, men were busy cutting openings. With a chill of apprehension he realised that the Germans were preparing to advance in a mass counter-attack and he was lying right in their path. He was in the position every sniper dreaded.

The Germans were hurrying, as they had also noticed that the clouds were thinning and as soon as they dispersed a little more, squadrons of bombers and fighters would arrive to harass them.

As far as Peter had been able to judge, over the broken country he had covered in the dark, he had taken up his position about 1300 yards from where the Stormbergs were dug in. He reckoned it would take the Germans fifty to sixty seconds to cover the intervening distance to his position, if they advanced at the double. On the slope to his right, men hurried forward with machine-guns and mortars to provide covering fire for their attack. Already they were in a position to cut him to ribbons if he stood up and tried to race back to the Stormbergs. "Baba Mashona, cover me," he whispered urgently. He pulled his only hand-grenade from the pocket of his greatcoat and placed it beside his head.

Peter estimated that he would have time to shoot six of the enemy when they bunched into the cleared lanes through their minefield. He guessed that he would be able to shoot another four before his ammunition ran out and their first line of men reached him. When they were abreast of the rock thirty yards in front of him, he would pull the pin from his grenade so it would explode and kill or wound another half a dozen, including himself, before they reached him with their bayonets. In a detached way he wondered whether he would hear the explosion of the grenade before it blasted his brains out.

The grass lark cock had seen his movement under the net. It raised its rufous crest in alarm and `shreeped' an urgent warning to its mate. Peter and the agitated lark watched each other for a second through the mesh of the net before the lark flew into the air `shreeping' its anger and fear. Both the cock and the hen dived at him repeatedly, `shreeping' stridently, for the entire German assault force to hear. Their repeated ascents and dives pointed like an accusing finger at his position. "Where's your shield now, Baba Mashona?" he whispered, "or has the time come to say, `go gently'?"

Behind the minefield, the Germans were formed up and ready to march. The gaps in the wire were open. Company Commanders stood at the head of each Company. The Battalion Commander saluted a man in the tunic, breeches and jackboots of an SS Officer. The newcomer returned the Commander's salute and raised a loudhailer to his mouth to address the troops. From the corner of his eye Peter saw a flash of movement as a hawk dived with its wings folded back. It struck the grass lark cock with a thud and a puff of feathers, then spread its wings to break its dive and skimmed low over the grass.

Peter felt a wave of exultation tingle through his body. "So you are with me, my Father," he grinned. "Right! Then let's fight!"

The hen had vanished into the thick foliage of a nearby bush, leaving the chicks in the nest humping their backs against the cold and chirping restlessly.

The cross-hairs of Peter's telescopic sight rested fleetingly on the SS Officer's back, twelve inches above his black leather belt. He was not conscious of squeezing the trigger until the rifle bucked and steadied. Watching through the sight, in his mind's eye he could see the bullet strike in the centre of the upper half of the Officer's back. It sent him staggering three sagging paces towards the troops he was addressing, before he pitched forward onto his face.

In answer to a shouted command, the German troops trotted four abreast towards the tapes through the minefield. The cross-hairs in the telescopic sight paused several times a fraction below belt buckles in the congested ranks, but Peter was unable to fire. Again and again his finger touched the trigger within a fraction of the pressure required to fire, but each time something delayed that final touch.

The advancing column emerged from the wire and spread out as they ran towards Peter's hiding place. In the nest the fledglings chirped dismally and it seemed to Peter they were screeching at him to shoot, or to get up and run. He willed his finger desperately to complete the squeeze on the trigger, as his sights moved from one man to another, but his finger felt paralysed. The whole scene lit suddenly with brilliant sunshine, pouring through a rent in the thinning clouds. Peter knew his death was seconds away. He eased the pin from his hand grenade, but his fingers refused to release the lever he held clamped in his hand. Voices yelled commands and the line broke into a run towards him.

Mortars crumped behind the Germans pounding towards him, looking up at the sky anxiously and glancing down occasionally to watch their footing. Mortar bombs thudded among the rocks behind Peter and erupted in billows of smoke. He heard the roar of aircraft as a mare's tail of smoke ripped past him on the wind. Above the drumming of approaching boots, he heard the chicks screech louder. Streamers of smoke raced to meet the German troops to provide them with cover from the aircraft which arrived with their engines screaming.

They were almost onto him when thickening smoke dimmed their advancing line. The man on the right of his front inclined direction slightly to avoid the rock hiding Peter. He pointed out the cheeping chicks to the man beside him and shouted to the others not to trample them. They ran between Peter and the nest through thickening smoke, but their eyes were on the chicks and they didn't see him behind the rock. Guns stuttered overhead as low-flying aircraft strafed them. Bombs exploded and Peter felt the ground leap and tremble.

He could still hear the crump of mortars but could no longer hear their falling bombs as they landed further and further behind him, to generate smoke along the Stormberg's front. The attack had passed him and Peter replaced the pin of the hand grenade. The smoke was so dense, nobody would see him unless they walked on him. He left his position and hurried away to find a place to hide where he would be safe from the enemy when they returned, which he knew they would, or at least those of them who were still alive. They would have to attack the Stormbergs up the forward slope of a hill and they would never be a match for the South Africans in any battle of rifle against rifle. This time it would be the Germans who were standing up attacking, while the Stormbergs would be firing at them from the shelter of their slit trenches, and presenting the Germans with very small targets.

"Isinkwe, do you think there could be any leopards in these mountains?" Indabushe asked with his brow wrinkled into a frown of worry which had become almost habitual.

"No, Indabushe," he replied, "the only leopards left in Europe are the ones in Zoos. Why do you ask a question like that?"

"I asked, because last night I dreamt for the second time about a leopard, or something that looked like a leopard, lying waiting for you when you were returning from watching the enemy. And whatever kind of leopard it was, it could see in the dark, because it's always after dark when you come back. I know they were only dreams but somehow I feel they were a warning from our grandfather."

Patrick O'Neill Slabbert listened in silence. He hadn't been sure whether there were leopards in the mountains or not and felt uncomfortable listening to these two old friends talking about spirits, as if they were tangible. Patrick was a newcomer to the Stormbergs but during the month he had been with the Regiment he had proved himself to be a first-class sniper. He had also been trained by Cimela Brown and he had arrived one day asking for a "'l-little bastard of a sniper called Isinkwe M-MacTavish. The best f-fucking sniper Cimela has ever t-trained." Cimela had told him the Jerries would never get Isinkwe because he had a Zulu spirit looking after him.

Colonel Hamman had detailed Patrick to take Spud's place and cover Peter while he was observing. He had done this because each time the Stormbergs had advanced in the past few weeks, Peter had found evidence of a German sniper who walked on the outside edges of his feet and seemed to have been assigned to hunt him down. In recent weeks, while Peter lay watching the Germans, he had experienced spine-chilling sensations that he was being searched for – those sensations were strongest from somewhere behind him. The German sniper's positions seldom faced towards the Stormberg's lines. He always waited in well-concealed places designed to enable him to shoot Peter from behind, when he was returning from watching the enemy. The German seemed to have plenty of courage and animal cunning.

Throughout most of the night Patrick helped Peter prepare three firing positions. Their work progressed slowly because every now and then Peter stopped scraping soil and listened intently for possible warning sounds. He was restless and wondered whether Mashona's spirit had really warned Indabushe of a phantom leopard lying in wait for him, or whether Indabushe was beginning to succumb to overstrain. And he fretted over the loss of hearing in his right ear. While they worked he was worried by an uneasy feeling of a presence somewhere behind him in the darkness.

Patrick left him before dawn to take up his own position. It was situated three hundred yards behind Peter on the forward slope of the high ground behind which the Stormbergs were dug in. Patrick paid out green fishing-line as he disappeared into the night. One end of the line was attached to the trigger of a loaded and cocked rifle, tied to stakes in a covered dummy slit trench, fifty yards to Peter's right. A second and more obvious position on Peter's left was intended to tempt any but the most experienced of snipers to fire at the dummy, and in doing so, to reveal his own position.

Peter lay looking uphill, two hundred yards in front of the spot he thought was the most likely place for the Germans to site a concealed and well-camouflaged observation post. As a double protection, Peter had banked up earth behind him, camouflaged it with grass and covered it with his net. Fine rain fell from heavy black clouds until mid-morning.

Peter watched in poor visibility. He lay in an inch of muddy water in the bottom of his slit trench, and his clothes were sodden. And all the time he watched, he experienced the creepy sensation that he was also being watched. It seemed to him somebody, somewhere behind him, was sweeping the countryside with field-glasses. At times the feeling was strong, then it would fade as though the field of view of the searcher had moved past where he lay. He hoped the cloud would hold because he feared that, if the sun broke through and shone directly down on him, a watcher from a higher position would detect the blob of discoloration caused by the shadow under his net. He had taken every precaution he could think of and had promised Colonel Hamman he would not fire no matter what tempting target presented itself.

A little before twelve a rift appeared in the thick cloud and for a while visibility was excellent. A peculiarity on the slope above him caught Peter's attention. A line of smallish stones, each a little bigger than his hand, lay more or less evenly spaced down the slope and ended for no apparent reason at a low hump in the grass.

Peter smiled with satisfaction. "Good old methodical Germans," he thought to himself, like Spud had said, "when they were told to do something they said `jawohl', and did it." He imagined some Signals Officer telling an NCO to press the telephone wires well down into the grass and to hold them down with stones, to make sure they couldn't be seen. The NCO had apparently carried out his orders with German precision, selecting stones of uniform size and placing each stone five paces apart, to hold the wire down, as he had been ordered to do.

Peter half-closed his eyes and studied the ground at the end of the stones. There was something unusual about the grass in that area. He trained his field-glasses onto the place and noticed that lines of grass stems, heavy with raindrops, led from different points on the slope, converging on the hump where the stones ended. There were other lines of bowed grass leading away from the hump. He decided the hump was a superbly camouflaged observation post and the lines in the grass were made by people coming and going by different routes under cover of darkness.

The pull of eyes crawled over Peter's skin. He looked down and waited and thought. There was no way he could indicate the target from where he was. He would have to indicate it directly to the Artillery Officer, or he would never be able to bring the guns to bear on it.

Thunder rumbled and the light dimmed. Peter waited and worried. He could do nothing until darkness fell and even after he got back he would have to wait for sunrise before he could indicate the target to the Artillery Officer from a high position somewhere along the Stormberg's ridge. Thunder crashed closer and a scattering of heavy rain-drops pelted the ground. Peter decided that if it rained hard enough to block visibility, he would take a chance and race across the three hundred yards of open ground to Patrick's position. From there he would find sufficient cover to crawl up the slope and report what he had seen.

Guns boomed behind the German-held ridge. Shells screamed past overhead and Peter heard their distant explosions right on the Stormberg's trenches.

As if in answer to the challenge of the German guns, lightning flared and an instantaneous clap of thunder made Peter's nerves jump. Rain pelted down and Peter leaped to his feet. As he started to run, a bolt of lightning struck somewhere between himself and Patrick's position and his ears rang from the clap of thunder accompanying the flash. As he ran past Patrick's position he beckoned Patrick to follow him and they scrambled up the remainder of the slope and dived for cover into the Stormberg's observation post.

Peter called Colonel Hamman on the field telephone and the Colonel told him to come to Battalion Head Quarters to report in full. He left Patrick to wait for the Artillery Officer the Colonel was sending to direct fire onto the German post, as soon as the rain cleared sufficiently for them to see it.

Peter wrapped himself in his two blankets and lay down on his stretcher. Autumn was well advanced and the mountain air was bitterly cold. He was dog-tired and filthy and the mug of hot, sweet coffee Indabushe had given him warmed his stomach. For the first time in many days he felt free from the nagging worry that somebody was watching him and he drifted into a dreamless sleep.

A single thundering report of a 5.5 wakened him with a start and he sat upright.

"It's stopped raining," Indabushe said. "The guns are ranging. Patrick must have pointed out the target to the Atry Officer." His words were cut off by the crash of a second shot.

"Bracketing," Peter remarked. "The next shot should be right on the nose." The air in the dugout jarred with the third shot. There was a brief pause, then four guns fired in quick succession and reloaded and fired again and again. Then the guns fell silent and Peter said to Indabushe: "Sixteen shells. They must have blown that Jerry post right off the face of the earth."

Indabushe looked outside and drew his head back in. "The guns must have called the rain," he remarked, "it's started again. There'll be some hot grub ready for you in about an hour, so lie down and get a bit more sleep."

"Isinkwe! Isinkwe!" Patrick's urgent call woke Peter. Throwing off his

219

blankets, he grabbed his rifle and stood up as Patrick and the Artillery Officer barged into the dugout. Patrick dropped the bundle he was carrying and grabbed Indabushe by his shoulders and shook him. "You were right, Indabushe! There was a leopard. There was one lying less than a hundred yards in front of me, waiting for Isinkwe." He turned to Peter. "If it hadn't been for the rain, the bastard would have had a perfect view of the spot where you were lying. If he hadn't seen you in daylight he would've nailed you in the dark when you came back." Patrick was visibly excited. "Hell," he said, "I didn't see the sod until I took the Captain a little forward from my position so he could get a better view of the Jerry post. I tell you, I didn't see Indabushe's leopard until I almost walked on him. He gave me such a fright, I nearly crapped myself."

"Slowly, Patrick! Slowly." Peter grasped Patrick's shoulder to slow him down. "Tell me what happened. Start at the beginning!"

Patrick took a deep breath. "It was still raining when the Captain here arrived at the O Pip. The rain hid us from the Jerries across the valley. I told the Captain I'd take him a bit closer so he could see better when the rain let up. We headed for that old dead oak tree we kept clear of because you said it was just the sort of place the Jerries would shoot at if they thought any of our snipers were around. The bloody Jerry was hidden there under the exposed roots, watching the valley. The bastard was only eighty yards from my position and if it hadn't been for the rain he would have got you easy when you came up out of the valley. I actually touched the bugger before I saw him, but lucky for me, he was already dead. Stone bloody dead! That flash of lightning we saw killed the bastard. It struck the dead tree above him."

"But what were you saying about a leopard?" Indabushe prompted.

Patrick bent and picked up the bundle he had brought and opened it. A pair of boots fell out. He held up a greenish-brown jacket blotched with irregular-sized black marks. It was the first camouflage suit any of them had ever seen.

"He had this on, and trousers and cap the same. He looked just like a bloody leopard! I nearly shat myself! He matched his background as if he had been painted there. And look here!" Patrick picked up the boots and held them for Peter to see the soles. They were worn on the outside edges. "Now I know why everybody says you've got a Zulu spirit looking after you," he said.

Indabushe nodded and stared into Patrick's eyes. "You say he was killed by lightning, Patrick, while Isinkwe was running towards him? Would he have killed Isinkwe if the lightning hadn't killed him first?"

Patrick looked scared. "Too fucking right he would," he breathed.

"Yes," Indabushe said with conviction. "This was the leopard Mashona warned us about. It was he who sent the lightning."

There was little space to move in the cramped dugout. The Artillery Captain eased Patrick aside. "What do you think of this?" he asked Peter, holding out a rifle for him to see. It was a 7.92 Mauser sniper's rifle. The barrel was warped and scaled as though it had been heated in a forge and the bed of the hand-guard was charred. But it was the cumbersome sight with the large heat-blistered lense that focused Peter's attention.

"Do you know what this is?" The Captain's forehead was creased in a frown.

Peter nodded as he looked at the sight. "Yes, Captain. The Intelligence Officer briefed us a week ago. He told us the Jerries were experimenting with a new infrared sight for night shooting."

"GeeZUS!" Patrick exclaimed. "That fuckpig could've picked you off as you came back in the dark!"

Chapter 11

Indabushe was furious when he saw Peter walk a little unsteadily towards Patrick. "Put that damned rifle away," he shouted, "and get back into your blankets. You're too sick to be walking around. Anyway, where the hell do you think you're going with that bloody thing?"

Peter shook his head to try to clear it of the humming sound that had started when Indabushe dosed him with quinine. His body felt hot, despite the freezing wind. He had been sick for two days. At times his body shivered no matter how many blankets Indabushe piled on him. Then he would suddenly want to vomit and he'd break into a sweat and fight Indabushe's attempts to keep him covered. His urine was dark and his joints ached when he moved, and they ached when he lay still. Indabushe took his arm and tried to turn him around to go back to his bed in the dugout, but Peter pushed his hands away.

"Leave me, Indabushe," he said determinedly, "I'm going out just this once more. I'll guide the Regiment to the track that's supposed to be the start line for the attack. The Colonel's worried he won't find it in the dark, and if he doesn't, our men will get shot to hell by our own guns. Then I'll turn round and come back. I promise. I'll be back before daylight, and I'll report sick and the quack can send me to hospital."

He smiled faintly at the prospect of being sent to hospital. He might see Rosemary for a few days before she was due to leave for England. She had written to say her hospital had moved to a new position at the foot of the mountains, near Florence. She was seventeen weeks pregnant and it was showing. She wrote in her last letter that Sister Anderson said she had begun to waddle when she walked. Twice in her last letters she had mentioned her yearning to feel the baby's first movements in her womb. It could be any time now.

"What are you two arguing about?" Colonel Hamman walked towards them with a forbidding look.

"He's sick, Colonel." Indabushe spoke first, pointing at Peter with his thumb. "He should be in hospital."

The Colonel examined Peter in silence.

"Yes," he nodded, "I can see he's sick. But sick or not, I need his night vision for just three hours. Can you make it, Peter? Can you guide us in the dark for just three hours? After that you can bloody well lie down and die, if it'll make your friend feel better about it."

"Colonel, this man is sick, Sir." There was a note of pleading in Indabushe's voice.

Colonel Hamman nodded his head. His face was grooved with lines of exhaustion. He held up his hand to silence Indabushe. "Yes! Yes, Sergeant Dunn, I know only too well he's sick. And yes, it's Sergeant Dunn now. Your well-deserved promotion has just come through. I'll pin that extra stripe on you myself, if there's any of us left after tomorrow's battle." he shook hands with Indabushe. Peter and Patrick also shook his hand.

Colonel Hamman spoke directly to Indabushe. "Sergeant, whether there will be any of us left after tomorrow will depend very largely on your friend, Isinkwe MacTavish. I can see how sick he is. He looks half-dead on his feet. But I can't hesitate when it comes to weighing the fate of my entire Regiment against the well-being of one man." He pointed to the rain-shrouded peak of the mountain, where unseen shells were bursting. "That peak is the top of the Apennine Mountains and we're going to capture it at dawn tomorrow. Monte Stanco's behind us now but it cost us 28 killed and 58 wounded to capture it, and it's going to cost us more before we take points 806, 734 and 826. From there on, all the way to Bologna, we'll be fighting downhill, and for a change we will have the advantage of high ground. This'll speed up both the end of the campaign in Italy and the end of the war itself."

The Colonel's words hardly registered in Peter's muzzy head. All he knew was that he had to find an obscure track somewhere below the mountain peak.

"We will attack at first light 200 yards behind a creeping barrage from our guns, designed to drop a shell into every square yard of the mountain face. The Italian maps show a track somewhere up there and we're to wait at that track for the Artillery to start dropping their shells 200 yards in front of us." He glared at Isinkwe and pounded his fist against his hand to emphasize the urgency of his predicament.

"If we don't go far enough in the dark, we'll be too far behind the barrage and the Germans will be waiting for us. If we miss the track and go too far, the Artillery will start the barrage behind us and we'll get slaughtered by our guns." He shook his head angrily. "I don't trust Italian maps, Sergeant. We've found them dangerously inaccurate in the past. And thanks to cloudy weather, we've been unable to get aerial photographs we can rely on to pinpoint the exact locality of that track.

"This leaves me with only one thing I can trust, and that is Peter's night vision, and his ability to smell danger."

Indabushe's shoulders slumped in a gesture of helplessness. He understood the Colonel's dilemma but his concern for Peter goaded him to try to make the Colonel understand what he was talking about. "Colonel," he said, with desperation in his voice, "the spirit of our grandfather walks with Isinkwe and covers him with his shield. This he swore to at Isinkwe's naming. And that spirit of old Mashona has made Isinkwe sick in order to keep him out of tomorrow's battle, because he has foreseen some disaster from which he will be unable to protect Isinkwe."

Colonel Hamman had heard enough. There were more pressing problems demanding his immediate attention than this talk of spirits. He held up his hand impatiently to stop Indabushe but he would not be silenced.

"This man," Indabushe pointed at Peter. "This man is the only man in the Regiment with a bad dose of malaria. And why, Colonel? It's the beginning of winter. This is not the time for malaria. Others are also sick; colds, flu, jaundice, but why must this man be the only one with malaria?" Indabushe saw Colonel Hamman was about to speak so he forestalled him "Wait, Colonel! There's just one more thing I have to say. If Isinkwe goes into battle tomorrow, he goes without his protecting spirit." Indabushe stood to attention and saluted with dignity. There was nothing more he could say.

"Hold it, Sergeant!" The bark of authority stopped Indabushe in the act of turning away. The Colonel stepped towards him and rested his hand on Indabushe's shoulder. "Sergeant," he said, "I understand and appreciate your concern for your friend. Let him make the decision. But I assure you, I won't allow him to go into battle tomorrow. In any case, he's too weak to fight his way out of a paper packet." The Colonel smiled reassuringly, "If he can just find that track for me in the dark he'll have done us a greater service than any fighting he could do.

"What do you say, Peter?"

"I'll guide you, Colonel."

"Then that's settled. Patrick Slabbert here will go with you. When you have located the track, you and Slabbert will return to Battalion and report to Sergeant Dunn. That's an order!

"Does that sound fair?" he asked Indabushe. "And one more thing, Sergeant. The next time you stand to attention and salute me here in the front line, I'll have you arrested." He smiled at Indabushe. "Do you want every watching German sniper to know I'm an officer, just to get me shot?"

It was the small but steep-sided gully that set Peter's skin crawling. It was not marked on the map. Peter wiped the sweat from his eyes. He turned and whispered to Patrick. "The bastard who drew that map probably drew it while he was sitting on his fat arse, drinking vino in some tavern in the valley. I bet the bugger never saw the top of this mountain."

Mist lay thick around them and the green luminous dial of the compass was difficult to read. They should have found the track three hundred yards behind them. They had retraced their steps twice and felt every yard of the ground with the palms of their hands. Peter and Patrick lowered themselves into the gully and climbed out on the other side. They made their way carefully up the steep slope ahead, over stone walls and through groves of olive trees growing on levelled terraces. Peter stopped and turned to signal Patrick to go back down the slope. He had smelt cigarette smoke.

Back in the gully, he lifted the leather cap from his watch and peered at the luminous dial. "Oh my God," he whispered through chattering teeth, "It's time for the Artillery to start their `stonk'. Quick, we must find an overhang in the bank to hide under."

His fit of sweating had passed and he was shaking with cold. They had left their greatcoats with the men of the Regiment, who were waiting far behind, for them to come back and tell them where the track was. They were soaked from crawling through the grass, searching for the non-existent track. Patrick tugged Peter's arm for him to follow. He had found a low overhang where storm water had gouged a hole in a bend in the gully. Peter held the small microphones to the sides of his throat with his left hand while he covered his mouth and his nose with his right hand to muffle his voice.

"One-a to S-sunray," he stuttered through chattering teeth.

"Reading you, One." Colonel Hamman's anxious voice sounded in his ears.

"T-teds on c-crest one-a zero-z-zero yards. B-bearing three hundred one-a fife-a d-degrees, your p-pos. T-track n-negative. Withdraw t-two hundred y-yards. R-repeat, withdraw t-two hundred y-yards immediate." Patrick's urgent tap on his arm warned him his voice was louder than he had intended it to be. "Out," he said, completing his message.

"Sunray to One. Message received. Withdrawing two hundred yards, immediate. Take cover. Action imminent."

Patrick was pressed against Peter with his ear hard against the outside of the earphone.

"My God One! Are you alright?" The unmilitary concern in Colonel Hamman's voice, came over loud and clear. Patrick took the microphones from Peter's shaking hand and held them to his throat. "Negative. Negative, Sunray. He's fucked!" he replied.

There was a moment of silence before Colonel Hamman's voice came crisply through the earphones. "Take cover! Good luck! Over and out!"

A light breeze had lifted the mist off the ground and Patrick noticed the faint luminosity of first light. He pushed Peter's shivering body hard up against the bank under the overhang and pressed his own body against him to offer what warmth he could. He put his arm around Peter's shoulders to hold their bodies close together. The mist flickered with orange light a few seconds before they heard the rumbling thunder of the guns. The wail of screaming shells shredded the pre-dawn silence. The earth convulsed as shells exploded down the side of the valley and Patrick pushed himself against Peter to protect him.

Shock waves of explosions crashed louder and louder as the wall of shells pounded towards them. Shrapnel and stones and clods of earth howled and thudded into the bed of the gully beside them. A tremendous explosion half buried them from the caving roof of the overhang and a second, more shocking explosion sucked the air from their lungs and bashed them against the bank.

Dazed and breathless, Peter realised the concussions had grown less and the howl of shrapnel and flying rocks was receding. The shells were exploding up the other side of the gulley among the olive trees on the terraces above them. His fit of shivering had stopped and Patrick had relaxed his fierce embrace. The shelling had passed over them and they were still alive. "It's passed us, Patrick! The stonk's has passed!" There was no longer any need to hush the excitement in his voice. A bedlam of yelling voices and pounding feet rolled over them as Section Leaders shouted to their men to keep their formations. Flares from German mortars, sited on the reverse slope of the mountain peak, burst into brilliant blobs of light and hung suspended on the cords of their parachutes. The glaring white light of the flares was diffused by the thinning mist and lit the mountainside with shadowless light.

Peter eased Patrick away. "Get up! We're OK," he said.

Patrick rolled away, sat up slowly and leaned back breathlessly against a projection of fallen bank. "I'm hit, Isinkwe," he gasped. "My side." He coughed weakly and Peter noticed his shirt was wet with blood. He saw two holes in Patrick's shirt over his ribs and drew his knife to slit the shirt so he could see the wounds. Patrick held his wrist weakly to stop him. "Give me a smoke," he wheezed, "tin's in my back pocket."

Peter fumbled with shaking hands to pull out the tin and open it. He found two cigarettes and a strip of flint torn from a match box, and six matches, in the small flat tin. Patrick had put them into a rubber condom to keep them dry.

Peter lit a cigarette and placed it between Patrick's lips. There was a dribble of blood from the corner of his mouth and down the side of his neck, into the open collar of his shirt. His face looked bloodless in the glaring light from the flares. He puffed three times, inhaling deeply, and Peter's eyes opened wide in shock. He saw the inhaled smoke from Patrick's cigarette stream out of the holes in the side of his shirt and through the open vee of the neck.

Patrick coughed a gout of frothing blood down the front of his shirt. He sat up, choking and struggling for breath, and Peter caught him as he fell sideways, with blood gushing from his open mouth.

For a minute Peter held the limp body in his arms while he stared after the troops swarming up the slope among the olive trees. His eyes were narrowed and hard. He eased Patrick's body gently to the ground and straightened his back. He waited on his knees for a few moments for a wave of dizziness to pass, then stood up and wiped Patrick's blood from his hands down the sides of his trouser legs. He picked up his Mauser rifle, clipped over the safety catch and climbed the broken bank of the gully. Steadying himself and picking his way among dead, dying and wounded soldiers, he walked up the hillside towards the sounds of machine-guns, rifles, exploding hand-grenades and the clash and clang of bayonets. He noticed the mist in the east was stained red with the blood of a new day.

Ahead of Peter the Germans had repulsed the Stormberg's charge on a terrace below the crest, where the ground was littered with bodies. Behind the shell of a ruined stone casa, bombs from the 4.2 inch mortars of the supporting Royal Durban Light Infantry exploded in salvos of thunder along the reverse slope of the ridge, to shatter the ranks of German troops swarming up the mountain to reinforce their hard-pressed front. The sharp crack of Mauser rifles and the tearing rattle of Spandau machine-guns answered the fire of the Stormbergs. The Germans were full of fight and courage. They were not prepared to surrender the strategically advantageous ridges of the Apennines.

Bullets zipped past Peter with sharp cracks like snapping sticks and in the jumble of confused fighting he saw the head and shoulders of a German in the act of firing at him. Peter tipped up his rifle and fired from the hip and saw the German throw his arms wide and fall backwards. A hand-grenade exploded near Peter and as he ducked, a bullet struck the pad of muscle on his left upper arm, like a kick from a mule, and knocked him off his feet. From the corner of his eye he saw a wave of yelling Germans charge through the Stormberg's right flank with thrusting bayonets. He tried to shoot at them but his fingers were too numb to work the bolt.

Spurts of earth jumped up around him from a burst of automatic fire as he threw his body around and changed hands, to fire from his right shoulder. The German breakthrough was thinning under a hail of Bren gun fire from across the gully, at the bottom of the slope.

A bullet cracked past Peter's ear as it missed his head and struck the outside of his thigh below his hip, ripping through flesh and bone, to lodge itself in the now shattered bones of his ankle. He writhed on the ground with his eyes screwed tightly shut. When he tried to rise, his leg buckled under him. He heaved himself onto his hands and knees and pitched forward face down in the dirt, as another bullet struck with the pain of a red-hot poker through the joint of his right hip. In a daze of agony Peter was dimly aware of running legs pounding past him up the mountainside. A Section Leader dropped dead beside him. The German fire on the right flank had stopped and he suddenly realised that he was in danger of bleeding to death.

He struggled into a sitting position, racked with pain. Resting his rifle on his shattered leg, he fumbled with the sling until he succeeded in unfastening the catches. He drew the loosened ends of the sling from the swivels and wrapped it loosely around a hand-grenade held to the pressure point in his groin. Then he leaned over, unclipped the dead man's bayonet from his rifle, slid the spike of the bayonet under the sling and twisted it into a tourniquet, before he fell onto his side unconscious.

He was vaguely aware of awakening from time to time to untwist the bayonet and loosen the tourniquet for a while. But each time he was weaker than the time before, and it seemed to him each time he wakened, there were more and more dead men lying around him.

The mist had lifted and the sun was shining when he felt hands turning him onto his back. He tried to lift his rifle to keep it out of the dirt.

"Take that bloody rifle away from him," Indabushe's voice sounded desperate. Peter hugged his rifle to his chest and opened his eyes, to see the terrified brown face of a coloured stretcher-bearer leaning over him as he tried to take his rifle. Men were shouting and running down the hill. "Damn you and your bloody rifle," Indabushe grated through his teeth, as he cut away Peter's trousers with jerking scissors. "Give the bloody thing to Alberts!"

"Take it carefully," Peter whispered, releasing his hold on the rifle. "Don't bump the `scope. Lean it against the terrace wall."

"To hell with your rifle," Indabushe shouted as he rummaged in the open haversack, marked with a big red cross on a white background.

Peter was aware of a chemical smell and felt a needle prick his arm.

"Stretcher!" Indabushe called sharply. "Stretcher!"

"Oh my God!"

Peter looked around and saw the stretcher-bearer slumped against the terrace wall, with the sniper's rifle lying across his legs. Blood was oozing through the fingers clutching his belly.

"Run! Run!" Men shouted at them as they raced past down the hill.

Indabushe took no notice. Battle was no concern of his. It was only the injured men who mattered. Especially his childhood friend, Isinkwe. "Alberts was the last stretcher-bearer, Isinkwe," Indabushe told Peter through clenched teeth. "There's not one left alive to help us. Lie still! I'll have to make a better job of patching you. You might be here for hours before you're picked up. If there's any blood left in your body, I'm going to have to try to stop it leaking out."

"Herr Oberst! Herr Oberst! Look at this!" A German soldier shouted wildly to an SS Major, pointing at the wounded stretcher-bearer with Peter's rifle across his legs. "Look at this Schweinehund of a South African sniper, with a red cross band on his arm!"

"'Das dreckige Schwein!'" the Major's voice bellowed. Suddenly he froze and pointed a shaking finger in utter disbelief at Peter's German Mauser. "'Jetzt haben wir ihn!' Now we've got him!" The German Major's voice was shrill with exultation. "This is the one we've been looking for! At last we've got the fucking bastard! 'Das ist das Schwein!' .. Das ist er!"

At last they had got the sniper who used a 7.92 Mauser, with such devastating effect, on the Senior Officers of the Army of the Third Reich! The Major bared his teeth. He levelled his Luger pistol and squeezed the trigger repeatedly until there were no more bullets in the magazine. Albert's body jerked as the first shot struck him in the groin. The second shot slammed through his bladder, and his body continued to jerk as each successive shot hit him a little higher than the previous one. He slumped nervelessly and fell sideways as a black hole appeared in the centre of his forehead from the last shot.

"You and you!" the Major pointed at two men. "Take this body, and his rifle, back to battalion. The Colonel must see this. And the General!" The Major turned on his heel and pointed at Indabushe's bent back, as he bound a second field dressing around Peter's hip.

"Kill him!" He ordered.

A soldier ran up behind Indabushe. He lifted his bayoneted rifle above his head and jerked it downwards with all his strength. The loose ends of the field-dressing fell from Indabushe's nerveless fingers. His face grimaced as a German boot stamped him down onto Peter's unconscious body and held him there, while the soldier jerked his bayonet from Indabushe's back.

The sun had moved. It was in the wrong side of the sky. Peter's doped eyes drooped closed while his exhausted mind struggled with the problem. Perhaps he had slept through the day and it was now afternoon. Something heavy was lying on him and he was too weak to move it.

The sound of concentrated small-arms fire brought his mind back from the brink of sleep. Men were running past him towards the crest of the mountain. There seemed to be hundreds of them. They were firing over him, shooting from the hip as they ran. A pair of brown boots pounded past his face, and he knew that only South Africans wore brown boots. They must have driven the Jerries back.

He felt the weight being lifted off him and the sound of a man's voice swearing. He half-opened his eyes again and saw Big Dries' face looming over him.

He felt Dries lift him up and hold him against his chest and heard him shouting, "Medics! Medics! Here! Quick! It's Isinkwe MacTavish, and he's still alive!"

Then Peter's eyes closed and he went back to sleep.

"Sister! Sister!" The man's voice called urgently from the adjacent bed.

Rosemary's eyes flew wide open. She was standing, swaying with exhaustion, beside Peter's bed. He had been unconscious for three days.

"The tubes, Sister!" The man called again.

Peter had reached out his wounded left arm from its sling across his body and pulled the tubes of the drips from his right arm. His eyes were half-opened and his lips fluttered as he tried to speak.

He wanted to tell Mashona it was all right now. He wanted to tell Mashona to let go his arm. It seemed he had been holding it for ages. He was alright. Mashona had brought him here. He was hurt. Thoughts marshalled themselves slowly into some sort of order in his muzzy mind. Mashona's hand holding his arm had given him strength.

Somebody was fumbling with his right arm. His eyes opened slowly but he couldn't see clearly through the mist. It looked like Sister Anderson's face floating above him. But where had Mashona gone?

"He's coming round, Doctor."

Peter smelt the tang of surgical spirits. He must be in hospital. Yes! Mashona had carried him in. He had been hurt and Mashona had held his arm until he was better. A little cold water trickled into his mouth. A wet cloth mopped the dribble from the corner of his mouth and wiped his forehead and his eyes and face.

"Thank God! Thank God! Thank God!" It was a girl's voice. He knew that voice. He opened his eyes again slowly. Something had changed. It was not Sister Anderson's face floating above him. The mist had lifted and he could see better. It was Rosemary.

"Numbela." His lips formed her name. Why was she crying? Why was her mouth slack like that? There was somebody on the other side of his bed. His eyes moved drowsily across. It was Sister Anderson. Why was she also crying? Peter swallowed. His throat was parched. He chewed his teeth together and moved his tongue around in his mouth, licking his lips. "What happened to Mashona?" he tried to ask.

His eyes wandered back to Rosemary. Turning his head a little to see her better, he worked his hand free from his sling to feel for her hand with groping fingers. She grasped his hand. "Numbela," he tried again. His eyes implored her to understand his confusion. "Numbela, where's Mashona? Where's Mashona gone?" His voice croaked but his words were clear.

Sister Anderson wondered fleetingly at the sudden perplexed interest on the Doctor's face.

"Numbela," Peter asked again, "where's he gone?"

Rosemary's face drew closer to his as she sank to her knees at the side of the bed. "Thank God! Oh thank God! Oh my darling, was he with you?"

Peter's eyes looked worried. "Yes. Yes, he was here all the time."

Rosemary looked up across the bed at Sister Anderson and her eyes filled with wonder and a kind of rapture. She had felt the first flutter of the new life in her womb. She held her hand to her belly and a ripple of movement squirmed against her palm.

Peter saw Sister Anderson come around the bed past the Doctor and help Rosemary to her feet. "Come, my love," she said. "Say goodbye now. That poor man in the Jeep has been waiting since yesterday with your bags packed and ready. We can't keep him waiting any longer. Your Isinkwe will be alright now. I'll see to that! Kiss him now, and I'll see you to your Jeep." She put her arm around Rosemary's shoulders. "Your Zulu will be safe with me. I'll keep him within my armpit, for you."

Sister Anderson was writing in the ward register when the Doctor appeared and stood in the entrance to the duty room. "May I come in, Sister?" he asked.

Sister Anderson removed her glasses and pushed the register aside. For a few moments she looked steadily at the Doctor's worried face. "Have you found something wrong, Doctor? You're looking worried. MacTavish is back from the theatre, he's sleeping peacefully. Has any decision been made yet about his leg?"

The Doctor placed a large buff envelope on the table top. "Sister, may I please have a cup of tea?" He did not really feel like more tea, but somehow it might help him clear up the matter which had worried him over the past three days. He was beginning to wonder if he was losing his mind.

"Here's your tea, Doctor. I'm sorry, I thought you had tea in the Doctor's Mess after theatre. You've looked so worried the past few days, you've got me worried too."

The Doctor tapped the large envelope with his forefinger. "I've brought the X-rays to show you," he said. "First of all, the wound in the left upper arm. It's practically healed. There was no need to cauterize. Whoever patched him up on the battlefield did a magnificent job. He not only saved MacTavish's life, but also his limbs. The bullet through the hip is not too serious. It punched a neat hole through the trochanter. The joint is cracked but it should heal nicely. It might trouble him when he grows older. The muscles below his right buttock are extensively traumatised where the bullet exited and will most likely cause occasional cramps, but nothing really serious.

"With the left leg, only time will tell. I was unable to amputate! The fibula is splintered from knee to ankle. It will take months to clear away the bone fragments driven into the flesh. The sciatic nerve has been almost completely severed, with only a few threads still holding. The knee is not too badly broken, but the ankle joint is shattered and will ultimately require stabilization."

The Doctor noticed Sister Anderson's tension.

"He was such an active boy," she said sadly.

"Oh, he'll be reasonably active again, I don't doubt," the Doctor reassured her. He lapsed into frowning silence while Sister Anderson watched him.

"What is it, Doctor? Is there something you are reluctant to tell me?"

"No! No, Sister." His lips twisted in an uncertain smile. "I don't want to tell you anything. I want to ask you something, but I don't know how to go about it." The Doctor folded his arms on the table and leaned towards Sister Anderson confidentially.

"First of all, Sister, let me explain. As you know, I'm a South African. I come from a little place called Lusikisiki. It's in the land of a people who call themselves Pondos. They are closely related to the Zulus, in that they have similar customs and speak basically the same language. I grew up among them. When I was a child, their men were armed for war at all times." The doctor looked at a loss as to how to continue.

"Sister, I've heard you refer to MacTavish as a Zulu. That was when Sister Marsden left. You also spoke of `Isinkwe'. The word means a bush-baby. It .. "

"I know what it means, Doctor." Sister Anderson nodded her head.

"Sister, I heard you ask Sister Marsden about somebody called Mashona."

Again Sister Anderson nodded. "In this case, Doctor," she said comfortably, "Mashona is the spirit of a long since dead Zulu warrior, who protects Isinkwe MacTavish. I know all about him. He swore Isinkwe MacTavish would walk all his days in the shadow of his shield."

The Doctor looked astounded, but Sister Anderson smiled at him.

"Doctor, you can hear all about that guardian spirit from every man from the Stormberg Regiment. Isinkwe MacTavish and the spirit of Mashona are a legend among them. I've heard it so often I believe it myself. Certainly there are no other explanations for some of his escapes from death."

The Doctor blinked his eyes rapidly as though to clear his head of the thoughts which had made him fear he was losing his reason. "Sister, I must tell you something I want you to keep to yourself.

"The first examination of MacTavish's leg indicated such extensive trauma that immediate amputation was imperative. There were three surgeons present in consultation and there was no need for any discussion. The decision to amputate was unanimous. I was operating."

Again the Doctor paused and frowned, with his bottom lip held between his teeth. "I was about to commence the amputation when I felt I was unable to move my hand. Sister, I grew up in my father's trading stores in the strong odour of naked oiled bodies and leather aprons and leather shields. It's a smell I shall never forget. I smelt it again, right there in the theatre, over the smell of ether, as I bent over MacTavish, with the scalpel in a hand that was unable to move. My assisting surgeons watched me over their masks as if I had gone mad. When I did move, my scalpel, not I, sliced that leg open from mid-thigh to ankle to expose the damage. It was a perfect incision, Sister. But I felt a hand guiding mine, as I drew the scalpel downwards. A hand which would not let me amputate."

The Doctor sipped a little tea while he regarded Sister Anderson speculatively over the rim of the raised cup. His thick eyebrows were raised in query.

"Yes, Doctor!" Sister Anderson's voice was complacent. "There is no doubt in my mind. The hand which prevented you from amputating, was the spirit hand of old Mashona. It was the same hand which guided your scalpel to make the perfect cut to reveal what could be done, to save our young man's leg."

They both sat in silence for a while.

"Doctor," Sister Anderson spoke first. She had a faint smile on her lips. "There is something I want to tell you."

The Doctor's eyebrows arched upwards in an invitation to her to tell him what was on her mind.

"Doctor, Rosemary Marsden is like a daughter to me. Her mother died and I reared her."

The Doctor's eyes watched Sister Anderson's careworn face intently. He saw compassion in every line, and her tiredness, and marks of deep sorrow. But the glint of challenge in her eyes and the determined set of her chin took him by surprise.

"Doctor," her tone was direct and matter-of-fact. "You will know all about the customs of those fine Zulu people." It was not a question, and the Doctor merely nodded in response. "The child Rosemary Marsden carries was conceived through the agency of old Mashona, in the traditional purification of a warrior returned from killing in battle."

The Doctor's eyes flickered in acceptance of the circumstances she outlined so briefly. His expression gave no hint of his astonishment that an English nursing sister should have any knowledge of such things as the ceremonial `Wiping Of The Axe' to purify a warrior.

"Doctor, you will also know about a ceremony which the Zulu people carry out – the laying to rest of the troubled spirit of some deceased relative?" The question in Sister Anderson's eyes was a request for the Doctor to confirm this.

"Yes, Sister. They call it 'ihlambo'. It is a ceremonial sacrifice made to pacify or to finally bury a restless spirit."

"Yes, yes," she interrupted as though he had finished talking. "That is what Rosemary Marsden has gone to do. That dear girl believes emphatically that the spirit of old Mashona has fully carried out the task of protecting her Isinkwe. She believes it is now her duty to lay the old spirit to rest, because she now carries the unborn spirit of a new warrior in her womb."

"How will she manage that, Sister? By now," the Doctor glanced unconsciously at his watch, "by now she'll be aboard her ship bound for England."

Sister Anderson smiled knowingly. "If my Rosemary has any intention of going to England I'll be most surprised," she remarked. "The ship she's sailing on is the Hospital Ship, the 'Amra'. And I happen to know, Doctor, that the ship will be putting in at Durban, to discharge many wounded South African soldiers."

Chapter 12

There were very few patients in the wards. The opposing armies had dug themselves in for the winter and no more pitched battles were being fought. The few patients who were admitted had been wounded during patrol activities, probing for weaknesses in the enemy defences which the Allies would exploit in the spring.

Sister Anderson had turned her chair away from her table and she sat staring vacantly through the window at the falling snow. Her hands were extended to the warmth of the paraffin heater burning silently in front of her in the duty room. The orderly had to knock twice before she heard him and called for him to enter.

He saluted and handed her three flimsy airmail letters. As soon as the orderly left, she opened one of the letters with shaking hands. It was from her son John. The muscle of his eye, damaged by blast from an exploding anti-aircraft shell, was improving, but the specialist doubted whether he would be allowed to fly again for at least a year. He complained about the dismal prospect of spending the remainder of the war sitting behind a desk. Sister Anderson removed her glasses to wipe away her tears of relief and looked up at the ceiling to offer a prayer that the war would be over before he would be allowed to fly again.

The second letter, bearing a strange Swaziland stamp, was from Rosemary.

"Dearest Aunty Megan," she read, "How lovely to be able to call you Aunty again, instead of Sister. I jumped ship in Durban and I'm now with Isinkwe's parents in Mbabane, a little village which is the capital of Swaziland. It is beautiful beyond words and his parents are absolute darlings. There is no sign of the war here and the lights are on at night with the windows open. My baby is as lively as a cricket and judging by his kicking I think he will be a soccer player.

"I can't tell you how happy I am to be here. The colonials are more English than we are, and very pukka! Everybody in the village has called to meet me and their welcomes have been quite overwhelming. Not an eyebrow has been raised at my `condition' and I'm not really surprised.

"Although everybody is more than friendly, they are all very `proper', which I find strange, because the Swazi people they live among are Nature's own. Perhaps this is why they accept me in the condition I'm in. Even the Swazi King, Sobuza, has sixty wives and heaven alone knows how many children. Swazi girls, and not such young ones at that, walk around almost naked. All they wear is a pair of little aprons in front and behind, about the size of a Scotsman's sporran. Most of the married women are pregnant and wear nothing from the waist up and their fat little brown babies are too adorable for words. They carry their beautiful babies tied to their backs and they suckle them openly wherever they happen to be, without any reserve whatsoever. The men are strapping-looking specimens. They wear their hair long and for clothing they wear only a blue or red sarong hanging to their knees.

"The Europeans all speak the Swazi language fluently and Isinkwe's mum and dad understand all their customs. Isinkwe's mum understands exactly why I want to lay Mashona's spirit to rest, as though that was the most natural thing in the world for me to want to do. She's got Isinkwe's dad to arrange everything.

"He's been an absolute gem in getting me all fixed up in connection with jumping ship. He took me to meet the Resident Commissioner and explained everything, and the RC, as he's called here, couldn't have been kinder if I were his own daughter. He's even got me a nursing job to save me from a charge of desertion, which is something I hadn't thought of.

"I'm running a little clinic for whoever needs my assistance. Because of my bulge I don't have to wear a uniform and Isinkwe's mum has made me some lovely light maternity dresses. It's summer here and the days are hot. I've never been so happy!

"Isinkwe's dad has been like a dog with two tails ever since the news arrived about Isinkwe's award of a bar to his DCM. Isinkwe is everybody's hero and the local Swazi men were so delighted to hear that `the King had hung a second oxtail around the neck of their 'Nkhosaan' (young chief) Isinkwe', as they put it. They have brought me presents of fowls and pumpkins and groundnuts because I'm their hero's 'Inkhosikhasi' (chieftainess). Swazi women bring me gifts and feel the little chief in my tummy in front of Isinkwe's dad. They chatter away to me and laugh happily for my sake, as though they've known me all their lives.

"There's no more space to write but I'll write to you every week. News of my darling Isinkwe is wonderful. Oh, how I long for him and also for you. Give him a hug and a kiss from me.

"Your ever loving

"Rosemary.

PS Give my love to Frances Houghton and the others."

Sister Anderson glanced at the signature on the bottom of the other letter. It was signed Marion MacTavish.

"Dearest Sister Anderson, or may I call you Megan? Rosemary talks of you so often we feel you are part of the family. We can't tell you the joy she has brought into our lives since her arrival. I had never guessed my husband's secret longing for a daughter until she came to us, and I wish he had shown me half the doting consideration and affection he lavishes on her. He fusses around her like a hen with only one chicken and already he is making all sorts of wild and wonderful plans for the new baby and for the wedding, as soon as Peter is well enough to get back.

"I'm really surprised at Hamish (my husband). He's always been a little Victorian in his conventional outlook and I was terrified he would look at Rosemary over the top of his glasses as he does whenever his sensibilities have been offended. But where I feared he would be outraged by Rosemary's obvious pregnancy, he went completely overboard and took her straight to his heart. And Oh, the relief I felt! She's a delightful girl and a great credit to your upbringing. We'll be so proud to have her as our daughter-in-law.

"God bless you for all you have done for Peter. Nobody can appreciate your kindness more than a mother. In his letters he lauds you to the heavens. He says he hopes to be home for Christmas and, being the determined sort of boy he is, I'm sure he will be.

"I'm old-fashioned enough to want to see the two of them married before the baby is born in February. Doctor Hope, our local MO, has examined Rosemary and says her pregnancy is advancing beautifully. He has taken her under his wing and I suspect, like everybody else in Mbabane, he has also fallen a little in love with her. He has placed her in charge of the clinic and I've never seen it so well attended before.

"Rosemary has told us all about your son John in the RAF and we pray for his safety. At last it seems this dreadful war is nearing its end and scattered families so tragically separated will soon be re-united. We know you will want to hurry home to your John in England just as soon as you can, but possibly you might consider breaking your homeward journey to visit us.

"My husband joins me in sending you our gratitude and our love.

"Yours affectionately,

"Marion MacTavish."

Sister Anderson put the letters away carefully and got up to tell Peter the news she had received. She found him sleeping peacefully, with a ghost of a smile on his lips. She saw that he had also received letters. They were on the locker beside him. He had fallen asleep with a third letter lying open next to his hand, on top of the bedclothes, where she could not help seeing the bold, scrawled writing.

"Isinkwe, you bastard," the letter started, "What the hell's going on? Snipers are supposed to get themselves killed, not wounded. Was it that old Zulu of yours who arranged it this way? As you can see, I don't stutter when I write!

"I saw your name in the seriously wounded column of the casualty list. Has that old bugger, Mashona, got holes in his shield that let a few bullets through, or what?"

Sister Anderson raised her eyebrows and looked around the almost empty ward to see if anybody was watching. The few men who were left were all asleep. She felt a little guilty as she leaned over the bed to read the rest of the letter:

"What the hell's this DCM business after your name? Perhaps I'd better get me one too.

"I've trained a few good snipers but the wankers they're sending to me these days are so piss poor I've applied for a transfer to your Stormberg Regiment to take your place. I can't stand working with these other bloody poachers a minute longer. They give me the screaming shits.

"When the war's over, I look forward to meeting them in the bush and I'll wring their fucking necks for them. Especially that bastard, Attie Oelofse. He's first. Bokkie van As and Shorty Charnaud will have to wait their turn.

"Anyway, while I'm killing time to get my hands on those three turds I'll go and even the score a bit with the Jerries for buggering you up and killing Patrick Slabbert. I'm going whether they give me a transfer or not. If the Jerries get me and I go the way of all good snipers, I'll look for your old Mashona and kick his arse for letting you get hurt.

"Get well soon.

"Yours,

"Cimela Brown."

Sister Anderson clucked her tongue disapprovingly and walked silently from the ward.

GLOSSARY

Amadlozi	ancestral spirits of the Zulus
biltong	strips of hard, sun-dried meat (Afrikaans)
black mamba	deadly venomous snake
braai	open fire for cooking (barbecue) (Afrikaans)
bush-baby	small African tree-climbing lemur (Galago)
casa	Italian mansion
dassie	rock-rabbit (Procavia capensis)
fundi	expert
kraals	African hut villages
meercats	small, ground living animal (Suricata suricatta)
muti	medicine (Zulu)
'stonk'	concentrated artillery and/or mortar bombardment
wadi	Sahara valley or depression
wildebeest	antelope native to southern Africa (Connochaetes)
witch-doctor	tribal magician